take it or leaf it

KIRBY FALLS
BOOK 1

LANEY HATCHER

This book is a work of fiction. Any resemblance to actual persons, living or dead or undead, events, locales is entirely coincidental.

Copyright © 2024 by Laney Hatcher; All rights reserved.

No part of this book may be reproduced, scanned, photographed, or distributed in any printed or electronic form without explicit written permission from the author.

Any use of this publication to "train" generative artificial intelligence (AI) technologies to generate text is expressly prohibited.

Made in the United States of America

Developmental Edits: Nicole McCurdy, Emerald Edits
Editing: Jenny Sims, Editing4Indies
Proofreading: Judy's Proofreading
Cover Design: Blythe Russo

For Dot,

You would have loved Will

Clark Family Tree

WILLIAM CLARK
GERALDINE OWENS

WILLIAM CLARK JR.
NOLA BURKE

WILLIAM CLARK III — **ROBERT CLARK** — **JAMES CLARK**
MAGGIE JENKINS — PATTY EMERSON

WILLIAM CLARK IV — **BONNIE CLARK** — **MACKENZIE CLARK**
DANNY JENSEN

WILL

There was a woman in my oak tree.

Well, technically it was the farm's southern live oak, but seeing as we were on my family's one hundred and ten acres and I'd been climbing that particular tree since I was a kid, it might as well be *my* oak tree.

Squinting beneath the bill of my ball cap, I peered up between the branches and tried to figure out what the woman was doing. She was draped across a thick branch about twenty feet up. All I could really see was her ass in a pair of dark-wash jeans.

With my hands on my hips, I moved around the base of the tree, trying to get a better look at her through the mess of green leaves. Despite the mild September day, this was one of the trees on the property that didn't display the beautiful fall colors which caused tourists to seek our small North Carolina town in droves. This tree stayed green most of the year. Maybe that was why I'd always liked it so much. It didn't try to impress anyone. It was just there, standing tall and out of the way. You could take it or leave it, but it wasn't going to change for you.

Speaking of out of the way, what was this woman even doing back here? We were on the far edge of the cornfield, not even close to the maze we made available to customers every autumn.

I finally found a break in the branches and got a better visual. She lay across the thick limb on her stomach. One hand was braced on the rough bark of another branch out in front of her face while the other hand clutched her phone in a frantic grip, and she muttered under her breath. She was too high up for me to hear what she mumbled, but her lips were moving a mile a minute.

Now that I'd gotten a good look at the woman, I recognized her. She was a *tourist*. One of the thousands of visitors who made their way through the front gates of Grandpappy's Farm to buy apples and pumpkins and cider doughnuts, to shoot the apple cannon and go on a hayride, or to find their way through the corn maze and pose with the Blue Ridge Mountains in the distance. She was one of the many who ventured south to enjoy our views and fall foliage. She was part of the double-edged spectacle that infected our small town and contributed to our livelihood.

The woman stuck in my tree was a *leafer*.

She'd hung around the Bake Shop at Grandpappy's for the past few weeks, I recalled. Usually on a laptop working at a picnic table out front with a mug of something warm and a slice of pumpkin bread. My dog, Carl, liked to work his way beneath her table. She was probably sneaking him table food.

I'd seen her when I stopped in for a coffee in the morning or when I was on my way to and from the office located on the back side of the bakery, usually to deal with any number of issues that arose during a day on my family's farm.

Most tourists came and went once or twice in a season. Not frequent enough to be memorable. Unless they were locals, it was rare to have the same visitor stop in every day for weeks. So, to see someone in front of the Orchard Bake Shop typing away like a romance novelist at a Starbucks was a bit more notable.

Now, though, her blond hair was a little disheveled. There was a leaf stuck in one side. And she wasn't focused on whatever work occupied her from midmorning to midafternoon. She clutched her cell phone like it could magically transport her to the ground.

"Are you alright up there?" I called, figuring I should just go ahead and deal with this problem, too.

My rough voice startled her, and she jolted. I stepped closer on instinct as her abrupt movement jostled her positioning.

Shit.

She emitted a panicked squeak as she tried to correct her balance. Her face went forward, and her ass tilted up even higher in the air. Releasing her phone, she clutched at a nearby branch to steady herself. She finally settled as quiet descended, and we both watched as her phone ping-ponged through the branches before landing with a thud on the grass near the trunk of the tree.

"Shoot," she exclaimed, sounding like a kindergarten teacher.

"I'm sorry. I didn't mean to scare you. You okay?" My voice was still coarse, so I cleared my throat. It was after two o'clock, and I realized I hadn't spoken to anyone yet today.

Finally, her eyes found mine before going wide.

I shifted a little uneasily. "I'm Will. I work here. Do you need help?"

Her cheeks were flushed pink, but she finally found her voice. "Yeah, I recognize you. If you could help me get down from here, I would really appreciate it. Really, really."

"Okay," I said, flipping my hat around to face backward. "Hang on. I'll come up and walk you through getting down."

"Thank you!" Her voice was high and overly bright. I imagined a perky cat getting stuck in a tree while trying to put on a brave face but couldn't get the image to stick.

Moving to the low branches that made this particular tree ideal for climbing, I tried to remember the last time I'd done this. Probably high school.

When my cousins, Bonnie and Mac, and I had been kids, we'd climbed this tree all the time. The branches were wide and sturdy. It had been fun to play out here. Later, in middle school, I'd come out with Jordan. We'd done stupid shit like racing each other up and down the tree, swinging from branch to branch, and one memorable time, trying to tree surf like Tarzan in the animated film and ending up with a wrist sprain for my best friend.

I tried to recall the handholds and foot placements I'd used in my youth as I quickly made my way up to where the woman was stranded. My shoulder was a little tight from my old injury. I felt the strain as I reached over my head for a branch, but I was all right.

"I'm Becca," she called down. "Sorry, I should have said that when you introduced yourself. I remember seeing you around the farm. I've been here for the past couple of weeks. Mostly at the Orchard Bake Shop. Chloe makes the best pumpkin bread, and Ms. Maggie is just the sweetest."

Ms. Maggie was my mom, and Chloe was the Bake Shop's newest hire. Mom decided to bring her on after Chloe left her asshole husband—and my former high school teammate—back in the spring.

The woman—Becca, apparently—kept up a steady stream of chatter as I moved. Maybe it helped her feel less nervous or calmed her worries. Hell, she'd been talking to herself when I first noticed her dangling thirty feet in the air. It could be that talking was her thing.

God, I hoped not.

"You're probably wondering how I ended up stuck here."

Not really.

Okay, a little.

I was curious why she couldn't handle something any eight-year-old could probably manage.

I hoped we weren't doing that thing that cooking blogs did where you had to wade through years of trauma or helpful life lessons to get to the recipe at the bottom. I hated that shit. I was a "jump to recipe" person every time.

Enthusiastic Becca seemed like someone who liked to take the long way around.

"You see, I've never climbed a tree before."

That had me pausing as I reached for the next branch. Who had never climbed a tree before? She looked like she was in her late twenties, or around my age, so thirty at most.

"I'm from Detroit," she offered helpfully.

"They don't have trees in Detroit?" I grumbled as I fit my boot against the bark and pushed myself higher. I was getting closer. Her legs were probably five feet above me.

Becca chuckled. "Well, they do. But not really where I grew up. And the occasion just never really presented itself."

"Until today," I said, moving to circle the trunk.

She laughed again, the sound surprisingly genuine despite her current circumstances. "Until today. I like to take a little break from my work and go for a walk on the property. I caught sight of this amazing tree." I could hear her patting the bark. "And I thought, why the heck not? Then I started climbing, and with all the leaves, I didn't really notice how high I was. Once I realized the ground was really far away, I got scared. And then I got stuck. I tried to turn around to start back down and lost my balance. That's how I ended up like this."

I assumed "like this" meant awkwardly ass up over a tree limb.

Her jean-clad legs dangled off to one side, and I wondered if she'd been here long enough to lose feeling in her feet. I didn't want her tumbling down to the ground, Plinko-style, the way her phone had. Her cell had a brightly colored hard-shell case on it and was probably fine. I didn't think Becca would make it back to the earth similarly unscathed. If we didn't do this right, she probably had a concussion and a couple of broken bones in her future.

I identified a few sturdy branches that curved around closer to her face and climbed out. I felt like a weird creeper talking to her backside.

"Coming around," I called, not wanting to startle her again.

She turned her head to meet my gaze from this new position, and her features lit, instantly warm and welcoming—like she'd known me her whole life, and we hadn't just met as a result of this whole hostage situation. "You made it! Gosh, that was fast. Thanks for helping me. I really appreciate it. I wasn't sure what I was going to do."

"You had your phone. Were you planning on calling for help?"

She grinned, full pink lips framing even white teeth. Her blue eyes crinkled, and I was shocked again at how friendly this girl was. I was a stranger. Why was she acting like we were friends?

True, I was very out of practice. Sociable was not something I'd ever been. But she was something else. Handing smiles out like she had a Santa sack full of them. Like she wasn't trapped in a tree. Her sheer positivity overwhelmed the worry and fear she had to be experiencing.

"Well, it seems silly now that I'm saying it out loud." Her grin turned sheepish, and pink flooded her cheeks again as she regarded me. "I was googling how to get down out of a tree."

I felt my lips twitch beneath my beard, but I figured I shouldn't laugh at her. I still had to get her out of said tree.

She chuckled a little to herself—at herself—before admitting, "And then I figured if worse came to worst, I could call the fire department. But I really didn't want to cause so much trouble. Seemed even more silly than a cat getting stuck in a tree. A full-grown woman with zero rural life skills." Another bright smile like we were in on a joke together.

My eyes narrowed as I took her in. Was she really this person? Here she was, in the middle of a fairly stressful situation, I'd imagine, and she was acting like a guest on a talk show. Could someone be this guileless and unbothered? Friendly and open?

Or was I just a suspicious bastard? Probably that one.

Her smile slowly wilted on her face the longer I watched her, so I should probably stop fucking staring like a weirdo. What was wrong with me?

Was I so unused to interacting with people that I couldn't manage this situation? I had Jordan, my best friend, who was an extrovert and had forcibly adopted me in elementary school. And now Chloe, since she and Jordan had gotten together over the summer. I occasionally went out and grabbed a beer with Jeremiah, our friend from high school, when he wasn't too busy with his baby and fatherhood. My hometown was fairly small and I knew business owners, local farmers, and just about everybody. And then there was my family. I saw them, like, every day at work.

Clearly, that was not enough human interaction to prepare me for Becca's unexpected warmth and smiles.

I cleared my throat. "I'm going to go back around. Just hold tight for a second. Then I'll guide your feet toward the branch below."

Carefully moving around to the other side of the tree, I positioned myself slightly below her, with an arm braced on each side, so if she fell, she'd fall into me, and I could . . . break her fall, I guess. Shit, I'd never done this treetop-rescue thing before. Maybe I should have called the men and women at the Kirby Falls Fire Department. Honestly, I didn't think they could get a ladder truck this far onto the property. Either way, I felt better about having me between her and the ground. We'd do it this way so I could guide her lower and lower until we made it safely back to the earth.

"Just shift your weight slowly," I said to the back of her denim-covered thighs, trying to ignore her admittedly nice ass that was *right there*. "Your legs might have lost feeling depending on how long you've been dangling up here."

"About two hours," she called easily.

My eyes widened, but there wasn't time to question how long she would have stayed stuck before calling for help. She was shifting back as I directed her leg down.

Shit, she was definitely going to be numb.

As soon as her feet touched the bark below, her legs buckled, and her ass pressed against the side of my face.

"Oh no! I'm so sorry!"

I could feel her frantic scrambling, clutching the branch she'd been draped across and trying to get her feet under her to remedy this new predicament, but she would only end up throwing herself out of the tree in her hurry.

Shifting my grip, I wrapped one arm around her thighs and held tight. "It's okay. Just rest here a minute until you can feel your feet again."

"But I'm—"

"You're not hurting me," I interrupted, rolling my eyes. Having a stranger's ass pressed against the side of my face was awkward as hell, but I was trying to be a gentleman here. My momma would kick my ass if she caught me ogling and enjoying this for even a minute.

Her—God help me—bright white sneakers were wiggling on the branch below us. Every shift of her weight had her backside rubbing against the side of my beard, so I closed my eyes and started thinking about baseball batting averages.

"Okay, I think I'm good. My toes are tingling, but they are definitely still there."

Opening my eyes, I tentatively leaned away. She was supporting herself, and now her ass was just directly in front of my face instead of resting on it.

Fantastic.

"I'm going to move down. Just stay put until you feel me reach for you."

I lowered myself, then placed my hand lightly on her calf to guide her to the next closest branch. Once I had her foot in position, I repeated the step.

We worked carefully and steadily over the next twenty minutes while I ignored Becca's repeated sounds—bright "thank-yous," positive affirmations on our progress, and perky "whoopsies" when her ass made contact with some part of my body.

Finally—*fucking finally*—my boots touched down on North Carolina soil, and I was able to release the rough bark of the tree and guide her by the waist to the ground below.

Becca turned in my arms. I had a moment to register her incandescent smile before she wrapped her arms around my shoulders and hugged me hard.

Alarmed, I left my own arms out like I was getting mugged as her tiny frame clung to me. She mumbled into the pale blue plaid of the flannel covering my chest, "Thank you so much. You saved my life. I don't know how I can ever repay you."

"You would have been fine." I patted her back stiffly to indicate that the hug should end soon.

She finally released me and stepped back. The pink was back in her cheeks, and she hurriedly reached up and tucked her hair behind her ears with nervous, bark-scratched hands. The leaf stuck in her blond waves dislodged and floated to the ground. She watched it and let out a nervous little chuckle. "Sorry. I got overwhelmed."

I watched her warily. "It's okay. I'm glad you're not hurt."

Becca smiled. "Right? That would have been a horrible headline. *City Girl Sightseer Plummets to Her Death at Local Apple Farm.* Probably be really bad for business." Another awkward chuckle.

God, she was so—and I hated to admit this—cute. She was just so fucking adorable. This girl with her ready smile, her warm demeanor, ridiculous "whoopsies," blushing awkwardness, and that memorable ass.

One corner of my mouth kicked up. "It's September in the mountains. I don't think one untimely death would discourage all those tourists."

Her grin turned triumphant that I'd played along. Something that I kept wound up tight in my chest loosened the smallest fraction at the sight. And I felt all the more uneasy as a result.

"I probably would have taken out every branch on my way down and killed that poor tree," she said, gazing back lovingly at the thing that had held her captive for the past several hours.

I shook my head and allowed my grin to stretch wide while her attention was elsewhere.

Becca turned to face me, and I thought she might have caught the tail end of my amusement because her blue eyes got impossibly brighter.

Reaching up, I spun my hat back around so the bill rested low over my forehead. "That tree has been there for a hundred years. It probably would have survived. You, on the other hand . . ."

Making her pretty eyes go wide, she filled in the blank with a handclap. "Splat."

I could feel my lips twitching at the corners.

"Seriously, thank you for your help, Will."

I nodded and took a step back. I couldn't even remember what I'd been on my way to do. Something up at the barn. Right, getting the forklift to move the pallets of apples tonight after closing.

"I'll let you get back to work," she said. "I know how to get back to the Bake Shop." She threw a thumb over her shoulder in the direction of the Pisgah National Forest and absolutely nothing else.

Squinting, I pointed my finger in the actual direction of the Bake Shop.

"Right." She laughed and repositioned her thumb.

I nodded again, like an idiot. "I'll see you around."

"Yeah." She grinned, rushing to add, "But not in any trees."

"Good," I said, nodding one more time to ensure I was inducted into the moron bobblehead hall of fame. Then I turned and strode off in the direction of the barn, away from friendly blond women and whatever the hell that had been.

BECCA

"Becca! Here's your pumpkin bread."

I set my cinnamon bun latte on the wooden picnic table and stood to retrieve my breakfast from the order window. Three weeks of regular treats from the Orchard Bake Shop hadn't dulled the serotonin hit that accompanied them. Not one bit.

Chloe waited near the half door with a smile. "I'm mixing up some chicken salad for lunch if you're hanging around."

I grinned at the woman around my age. I'd gotten to know a handful of the farm's employees in the weeks I'd been visiting, and Chloe was one of my favorites. She was sweet and friendly, and her cute boyfriend joined her for lunch after her shift almost every day. They were adorable. Was it weird to be so invested in someone else's relationship? Maybe. But they both seemed like great people, and I was really happy for them.

"Oh, I'm hanging around for that," I confirmed. I loved this place. The coffee was fantastic. The pastries were amazing. The pies were fresh. And the cinnamon rolls were the size of my face. I'd probably return to Detroit fifteen pounds heavier, but that was a problem for future Becca. Current Becca was living her best life in Kirby Falls, North Carolina, taking in the sites, getting to know the town, and eating all the things.

So, it wasn't a stretch at all to promise to stay throughout the lunch hour. When the weather was nice, I usually spent my workday here on the farm anyway. Early September in the southern part of the United States meant that I could sit under a covered porch with a hoodie in the morning and need to strip down to a tee shirt by lunchtime. It was amazing, and I still marveled over how much I loved being outdoors when the outdoors looked like this.

The bed-and-breakfast I was staying at had a weird vibe. The room was great and the place was gorgeous, but the owner was a little off-putting. So I preferred to spend my awake hours away from the B&B's nosy proprietor.

When I'd discovered Grandpappy's Farm during one of my first touristy outings, I knew I'd be returning. And the ladies at the Orchard Bake Shop had been so welcoming. They'd told me to bring my laptop, connect to the employee Wi-Fi, and come work on their front porch whenever I wanted. After the first four days of back-to-back visits, they'd even reserved my table—the one closest to an electrical outlet—with a cute little sign. *Becca's Table, Reserved Indefinitely.* I might have gotten a lump in my throat when I saw it.

"Good," Chloe replied. "I'll put it on that sunflower bread you like."

"Thanks, Chloe. You're the best."

Fiddling with the belt loop on my jeans, I waited for a moment at the window, expecting her to bring up what happened yesterday with the oak tree.

But when she just stared and asked, "Did you need something else?" I shook my head quickly and started backing away in the direction of my table. "No! Just daydreaming about that sunflower bread."

Chloe laughed. "See you later, girl."

Returning to my seat, I placed the pumpkin bread beside my latte and opened my laptop. Maybe Chloe didn't know about the tree incident with Will. That was good. Definitely better than everyone knowing how pathetic I was for getting stuck in a tree of all things.

I'd video called my best friends Pippa and Cece last night. They'd commiserated with me, and then we'd laughed about it. They'd also demanded a dramatic retelling of the event where I played the parts and did the voices. My friends had been very interested in Will and what he looked like. I'd played it cool, but I thought they might be onto me, judging from the shared video conference eyebrow wiggles.

A moment later, Maggie passed by with a box in her hands. "Good morning, sugar. How are you today?"

"I'm great, Ms. Maggie."

The older woman's eyes twinkled. "Got your pumpkin bread, I see."

"I sure do. You have a good day."

"Thanks, Becca honey. You too."

And then she bustled off without a single remark about tourists getting stuck in trees and needing to be rescued by her big strapping son.

I thought about that some more as I took a sip of my coffee. Will did seem like the strong, silent type. I couldn't really imagine him gossiping around the watercooler or sharing farm mishaps with his family at the dinner table. Maybe the Clarks didn't even have dinner together. In my head, they did. They seemed like the perfect family.

Maggie ran the Bake Shop. William, her husband and Will's father, spent most days at Grandpappy's working on the farming side of the operation. Patty and Robert were Will's aunt and uncle, and they ran the General Store up near the main entrance. And several of the Clark cousins worked on the property as well. I'd met Laramie and MacKenzie and liked them a lot.

When I imagined a family who worked together and created the magic that was Grandpappy's Farm, I was pretty sure they had dinner every night around a big oak table—scarred and scuffed from years of use—in a gorgeous dining room that overlooked the Blue Ridge Mountains. They probably used cloth napkins but put elbows on the table and all talked at the same time after they said grace.

I spent a lot of time imagining what healthy families looked like. Probably because I'd never had one of my own. Fantasies were great, but it would be nice to know what really went on between people who were connected by birth and loved and respected one another.

Anywho.

I guess it made sense that Will hadn't shared my mishap in the oak tree yesterday. He undoubtedly thought I was crazy or just a clueless city girl—which was probably worse in the eyes of a capable country boy.

I felt my cheeks heat in remembered embarrassment. I'd smacked him in the face with my butt. It would have been better if he'd laughed. Maybe. I didn't know. I couldn't decide. I'd already been so mortified to have this stoic, gorgeous man see me in such a vulnerable, incompetent light. And then I'd hugged him awkwardly when it had all been over.

Gosh. If I could just wake up with amnesia like a romance novel heroine, that would be great. Then I might be able to survive my next Will sighting.

I usually saw him once or twice a day while working in front of the Bake Shop. Always in passing and sometimes so quick, I might miss him if I was really focused on the design I was working on.

I didn't know how to feel about spotting him after he'd rescued me from the tree. Maybe he'd walk by like nothing ever happened—ignore me and my existence, just like all the tourists swarming the property this time of year.

I'd nearly finished my pumpkin bread by the time I felt a warm doggie body press against my calf beneath the table. My heart picked up as I looked down to see the friendly dog who had a thing for me rest his head on my thigh.

"Hey, you," I cooed to the dog with dark fur and a sleek, medium-sized body. There was some gray around his eyes and muzzle, so I got the feeling he was getting on in years. But I didn't know a whole lot about this dog. Not his name or breed or anything really. Just that Will Clark was his owner.

Practically every day, the dog would slink over to me for a hello and a few pats before Will would give a sharp whistle and call him back to his side. The duo made their way past the front porch of the Bake Shop at random times throughout the day, so I never really knew when to expect them.

That was probably why I'd been so on edge this morning, waiting to see if Will would show up and what would happen when he noticed me—if he noticed me. If he cared. Which he probably didn't. That was fine. Better really.

The dog's thin tail wagged happily, whacking me on the ankle.

A shrill whistle cut through the morning air, and I knew who it was. So did the dog. He looked at me with a mournful expression. "It's okay," I murmured. "I'll see you next time, bud."

He squirmed out from beneath the table and lumbered off in the direction of the main path. And I finally got up the nerve to glance that way too.

And there was Will, in dark-wash denim and a gray flannel, striding purposely across the wooden planks of the Orchard Bake Shop's front porch. He usually wore a ball cap on his head, but his dark hair was longish, like he didn't get to the barber's chair very often, and it peeked out from beneath the hat. Today, it was flipped backward, and I could see his strong profile as he passed by. With that bone structure, he should have been on a twenty-dollar bill.

The dog reached his side and then Will did something that he'd never done before. He glanced up from his determined stride and met my eyes over his shoulder.

Nerves and surprise and, if I was being honest, the beginnings of a schoolgirl crush had me grinning and raising a hand to chin height and waving like a dork.

He didn't wave back, for he was much too cool. But he did that guy thing where he nodded at me, and it felt like an acknowledgment from decades gone by. A cowboy saying hello to a serving girl in a saloon. A viscount giving an admiring chin lift to a well-bred debutante on the dance floor. A . . . guy nodding to the poor sucker he had to help out of a tree the day before so she didn't maim herself and end up suing his family's farm.

Definitely that last one.

Will strode off and went about his business, dealing with whatever farm thing he had to do next. And I shook my head at how ridiculous I was being and went back to work.

Around midmorning, the UPS delivery driver came through to drop something off behind the Bake Shop. His name was Garrett, and he liked to stop and flirt. It was fine. I didn't mind the attention, and he seemed harmless. About my age, maybe a little older, with tanned white skin and dark hair, it was hard to miss how nice his calves looked in those little shorts.

Just like every day we crossed paths, he came over and propped a leg on the bench across from me, and I made my eyes stay firmly on his face. "There she is."

"Hi, Garrett. How is your day going so far?"

Cue his standard response. "Better now."

I smiled, as expected.

We talked for a few minutes about the weather, the upcoming Orchard Festival, and his mother's heartfelt desire that he find true love someday. That last part was standard and always made me laugh. I could not imagine this ladies' man settling down in any capacity.

Eventually, Garrett had to get back out on the road, and with a wink, he took off toward the parking lot where his big brown chariot awaited.

I shook my head and tried not to be too affected by his flattery. Sometimes it was nice to have someone's attention on you.

Reflexively, my mind drifted to Will's nod from this morning. His quiet acknowledgment seemed infinitely more genuine than Garrett's over-the-top flirting. But neither actually meant anything, so I needed to cool my jets.

Several hours later, a plate holding a delicious-looking chicken salad sandwich landed in front of me with two glasses of sweet tea with lemon.

Maggie lowered herself onto the picnic table bench and gave me a smile. She wore an apron that said "Pie is always a berry good idea." Since I'd first met Maggie Clark, I'd decided she was basically the ideal mothering type. She was warm and welcoming—a nurturer. And she had enough meddling-momma vibes to knock a sitcom mother off her throne. Her lovely grin was giving big meddler on this sunny September afternoon.

"Hi, Ms. Maggie."

"Hi, honey," she said oh-so innocently. *Uh-oh.* "Chloe mentioned you were looking forward to her chicken salad, so I thought I'd bring over your lunch. And the sweet tea I know you love."

I did love it. Sweet tea was the best invention. And not to sound dramatic, but when I went back to Detroit, I would die without it.

"You didn't need to go to any trouble. But I do thank you."

She reached over casually and patted my hand that rested on the worn wooden tabletop. "It was no trouble."

I wasn't used to casual affection, but Maggie was a hugger. She thought nothing of squeezing my hand or patting my cheeks. One morning, she hugged me, and I thought I was going to burst into tears.

My life wasn't inundated with affection and certainly not from my own mother. I couldn't really remember the last time someone hugged me. It was probably a little over three years ago.

Briefly, my mind flitted to the embarrassing moment when I'd thrown my arms around Will in overwhelming gratitude. His body had been rigid and unyielding. Maybe I'd just caught him by surprise, but part of me wondered if crabby, stand-offish Will might be as unused to touch as I was.

"Tell me something," Maggie said casually. "Where is it you're staying?"

Reaching for the glass, I replied, "Over at the Sterling House."

The older woman nodded, her dark updo threaded with a striking silver stripe didn't move an inch. "That's what Chloe thought she heard you say."

I frowned. Was she about to tell me the place was haunted? I was already uncomfortable with the owner. At the beginning of my stay, I'd tried to do my design work on the large back porch. It was lovely, with ceiling fans overhead and bird feeders drawing in a variety of critters to watch. But Vera Sterling was a very curious sort of woman. She'd parked herself beside me and shared all sorts of gossip about people I didn't even know, and she had no problem asking me invasive questions. I didn't consider myself a private person, per se. But I didn't get the impression that Ms. Sterling's inquiries and observations were entirely innocent or benign. She seemed like a busybody with malicious intent, and talking to her made me feel icky.

As a result, I avoided Sterling House unless I was sleeping.

Maggie cleared her throat just as I took my first sip of sweet tea. *Ah, glorious.*

"Well, I wanted to let you know that you are more than welcome to stay here at the farm. I know you're sticking around for the next little bit, enjoying the autumn months in our fine town. And I thought you might be interested in staying at our tiny house on the property. Indefinitely."

"Tiny house?"

She nodded more vigorously. Her hair still didn't move. The marvels of Southern matriarchs and their hair products. "It used to be a rental property. It's on a real pretty stretch of land. Big glass windows make up the back wall looking out over the mountains in the distance." I sat up straighter at that. I loved the views here. Couldn't believe I'd gone my whole twenty-nine years without layers of hazy blue mountains right outside my window. "Chloe lived there until very recently, but now she's moving in with Jordan, just down the road. With Chloe out of the tiny house, it'll just be sitting there empty. I thought you might like to move in for the time being."

"Gosh, Ms. Maggie. That sounds amazing."

The woman grinned in such a way that I felt like I'd given the right answer on a test for good-hearted dummies. "Well, that's settled, then!" And she placed down two keys twined through the ring of an apple-shaped key chain.

She started to rise while I stared in shock. Eventually, I recovered enough to blurt, "But wait! We haven't talked about long-term rates or, well, anything really."

Maggie waved me away good-naturedly. "Oh, don't worry about that. How about you cover utilities at the end of the month, and we'll call it good."

"Maggie, I can't do that. It wouldn't be fair."

She smiled sweetly at me as if I was precious. "It's more than fair. We love having you here, and you'll be closer for your daily commute." She winked, amused at her own joke.

"But . . . but . . ."

"Becca honey, don't worry about it. I know good people when I meet them." Her hand patted mine once more. "And you are good people. Good people do not deserve to be trapped in Vera Sterling's mausoleum." I wondered what that was about but wisely kept my mouth shut. "We'll figure out the payment hullabaloo later. The house is being cleaned today, but it's yours after seven."

Still frozen in disbelief at this woman's well-meaning generosity and ability to completely steamroll me, I asked, "Where is the tiny house?"

I'd walked all over this property when I'd needed to stretch my back and take breaks throughout the day. I'd seen the pond and the apple cannon, the big red barn and the huge trees surrounding it, the corn maze, the event space near the gazebo, the pumpkin patch, the General Store, the sunflower field, and all the paths in between. I found it hard to believe I hadn't run across a rental property.

"It's down behind the big barn. There's a path that leads to a gravel lane off the main highway so you can reach it with your car."

"Oh," I murmured, still surprised by the day's events and Maggie's offer.

"Do you need any help bringing your things over? I can have Will—"

"No," I barked instantly, self-preservation kicking in where he was concerned. Maggie's dark brows rose on her forehead. I worked to gentle my voice, embarrassment making my cheeks grow hot at the idea that Will's mother would force him to ride to my rescue . . . again. "I just mean, I don't have a lot. Just a suitcase. It won't take much to get moved in."

Was I really doing this? I hadn't even seen the place. I supposed I could always just bring the keys back if something was off about the tiny house when I got there.

Maggie's expression cleared—for the most part. She still eyed me a little suspiciously, but she smiled and said agreeably, "Alright then. You're going to love it back there, Becca. I know you will. I'll see you tomorrow."

"Bye, Maggie! Thank you so much. I'm so grateful." I ran my finger over the smooth metal of the apple keychain.

"You're welcome, sugar. Now eat your sandwich."

I grinned and reached for the plate. Was this what it was like to have a bossy Southern momma? I had to admit that after a lifetime of neglect and indifference, I didn't mind so much.

When I decided to leave Detroit three weeks ago, I hadn't really known what I was doing. And when I'd read an online article featuring the best small towns to visit in autumn a week before that, I definitely hadn't known what I was getting into. I'd just felt like I needed to get away.

I'd been grieving the death of a loved one for three years, dealing with my own complicated family dynamics, and feeling lonelier than I thought possible.

All my friends were online, and while video calls and texts were so wonderful, my day-to-day human interaction was limited, to say the least. I wasn't close with any of my neighbors and even the Chinese place I ordered takeout from twice a week never even remembered me when I came in to pick up and pay.

I had been feeling uneasy for a while—like I lived and breathed in a bodysuit that was too tight. I needed space. I ached to fill my lungs with fresh mountain air. I wanted a break from my life in the city. The monotony. The anonymity. The isolation.

Working from home didn't really lend itself to meeting new people. I'd tried joining a book club at my local library, but they were pretty snooty about romance, which was my chosen genre. I didn't begrudge them their bestselling horror novels or their award-winning page-turners. But I was tired of reading books written by mediocre middle-aged white men and praising their obvious privilege.

So, I'd been researching a new hobby—the short list included pottery, wine tasting, and quilting—when I'd run across the article. Kirby Falls had ranked number 3 on the list of best small towns to experience the wonders of autumn. Numbers one and two had their high points, but there was something so charming about the pictures and attractions connected to Kirby Falls. I'd thrown caution to the wind and booked my stay at the Sterling House Bed-and-Breakfast for the following week.

I was a freelance graphic designer and could work from anywhere. I just needed my laptop. There were no pets to arrange service for or plants to water. I'd never been so glad for minimal responsibilities.

My friends Cece and Pippa—both authors I'd met through book cover designing projects—were ridiculously supportive of my extended stay in North Carolina. They'd both offered to host me in their respective cities, and while very tempting, I'd needed to do something just for me.

I'd tossed—okay, meticulously packed—clothes in my suitcase, locked my Detroit apartment, and emailed my building super that I'd be away for a while. Then I'd made the ten-hour drive in one day with frequent stops for snacks along the way.

Kirby Falls wasn't what I'd expected. Sure, the gorgeous photos from the article lived up to the hype. The mountain views were breathtaking. The water tower really was shaped like an apple. But the article failed to mention the amazing staff at Grandpappy's Farm. It couldn't have predicted the ridiculous clock tower on Main Street that was insanely loud. Or Jerry, the guy who played the trumpet on the street corners downtown. Kirby Falls also had this adorable fountain in the center of town shaped like an overflowing apple basket, and I'd never seen it turned on once. On weekends, a group of people—all ages and walks of life—met up for Pokemon Go community days.

I'd visited fantastic breweries, coffee shops, and restaurants. I'd even made the short drive to Asheville to do a bit of sightseeing. The Biltmore gardens and wine tasting had been top-notch.

But nothing could have really prepared me for how it felt to immerse myself in Kirby Falls. How calm I'd become when walking the tractor path next to the cornfield with a coffee in one hand and my anxieties evaporating in the other. I never imagined falling in love with a town and its people in such a short time.

Magdaline down at Apollo's on Main Street already knew what toppings I liked on my pizza and talked to me like I was someone she'd gone to high school with —like a friend. She gossiped and chatted every time I came in. Nelson, the septuagenarian from the bird-watching group that met in Tanner Park every Thursday and Saturday, gave me a book to help me identify local avian classifications and showed me an app to help me learn their calls. Now, Maggie Clark offered me a place to stay, as if I weren't a stranger who worked on her front porch and pilfered her Wi-Fi five days a week.

Kirby Falls was this wild and wonderful place full of characters and rich history. I was already falling in love with it, one apple cider doughnut at a time.

So when I unlocked the front door to the tiny house tucked behind the trees in the rear of the big red barn on the Clarks' land, what was left of my unoccupied heart sort of fell out of my chest and onto the floor in a pitiful offering.

The trees along the front and sides of the home allotted for privacy and were the reason I'd never noticed its presence behind the barn. But when I walked across the open-concept living room to the back wall made of glass, I released an involuntary little "oh."

The tiny house sat on the edge of a flat clearing. In the immediate vicinity was an endless meadow with waist-high wildflowers. Just these dots of pink and orange and purple and wisps of white. Farther afield was another cornfield. And beyond that wide swath of green were the gently rolling hills of the Pisgah Forest. Those long-range mountain views were right outside my back door. The leaves were starting their colorful autumn journey. Most were still green, but I could pick out patches of yellow in the higher elevations.

Without realizing it, my breath fogged the pane and obstructed my vision. I laughed a little at myself and slid open the glass door, stepping out onto the back porch. The sun was making its way toward the horizon, and the light reflected off the low-hanging clouds in shades of pinks and purples, making it difficult to look away.

A small wrought-iron café table and two chairs were on the wooden deck. If I wanted to, I could drink a glass of wine out here every night and watch the sun set.

I stayed until the layered mountains turned a deep navy blue as the daylight waned. And then the fireflies winked into existence among the wildflowers, and I stayed a little longer. Eventually, the bite in the evening air had me rubbing the skin of my bare arms and I went back into the house, reminding myself I could do this all over again tomorrow, and the next day, and the next.

I'd ignored the house and the amenities in favor of the scenery, but after I flipped on a few lamps, I took in the gorgeous space. It was on the cozy side, maybe four hundred square feet total. There was a real wood-burning fireplace that made me giddy to try out. The living room, with one small sofa and oversized chair, flowed effortlessly into the compact kitchen. The fridge and stove were small, but the fancy coffee machine looked expensive. A peek in the cabinets and drawers showed it was fully stocked for eating and cooking with dishes and cutlery. A microwave and toaster rounded out the rest of the appliances. And while there was no kitchen table, two tall stools beneath the countertop kissed the edge of the living room.

I continued my tour and took in the comfortable-looking furniture, the narrow desk tucked beneath the front window, the modern bathroom with a rainfall showerhead, and a bedroom hidden behind a sliding barn door with another wide window that looked out over the amazing mountain view. There was a closet in the hallway as well as another small nook that housed a stacked washer and dryer unit. This tiny home had everything I could possibly want. A place to work, a place to sleep, a place to just . . . be.

It was beautiful, and all the decorative touches felt perfect for the space. I spied a fluffy dog bed in the corner of the living room and smiled, thinking how nice it would be to share this house with a furry friend.

I sent a quick text to our group chat to see if Pippa and Cece were up for a video call to tour my new digs in a few minutes. Then I held my phone to my chest and turned in a slow circle, taking it all in.

Near the front door, I unrolled the welcome mat I'd purchased at a gift shop in town this afternoon. I'd seen it and had to have it despite this not being *my* house. It could be mine for a little while. And then I could roll up my welcome mat and take it with me when I left.

I ignored the pang I felt at the thought of abandoning Kirby Falls in a few months when November rolled around.

Without much effort at all, my feet took me back to the wall of windows. The sunlight had faded, and just a glow of orange highlighted the silhouette of the dark mountains in the distance.

With my fingertips pressed against the cool glass, I thought wistfully, *I could be happy here.*

WILL

Seth Rockford was the real deal.

The kid was seventeen years old and just starting his senior year at Kirby Falls High School. He could stand to put a little weight on his tall beanpole frame, but he had an arm—one you didn't see very often at the high school level.

I'd known him since he was born. Seth was the surprise baby brother of my best friend, Jordan, and the Rockford boys had been in my life for a long time. Jordan and I had played catch with Seth when he was growing up, not to mention all the T-ball and Little League games we'd watched from the stands. Seth didn't call me Uncle Will that much anymore since he was a too cool teenager. But my role in his life was one of the few things I was proud of.

Seth and I had bonded over our shared love of baseball. The kid still looked up to me despite my well-known status as a has-been and a pro athlete never-was.

But Seth had a real chance. And despite my complicated relationship status with the sport nowadays, I wanted Seth to achieve his major league dreams.

I watched another fastball go right over the middle of the plate. The teenage catcher pulled off his mitt and shook out his hand.

"How fast do you think that was?" Jordan asked from his place beside me on the uncomfortable metal bleachers.

I thought about the sound the ball had made against the leather at impact. Then memories intruded on that remembered knowledge. The sharp, bright smell of grass. The tackiness of a rosin bag in my sweaty hand. The heat of the sun beating down on the back of my neck during a summer day long since gone.

I cleared my throat and estimated, "It probably hit eighty-five."

Jordan gave a low whistle. "Damn."

An assistant coach—some asshat who didn't know a pitcher's mound from a hole in the ground—approached Seth and showed him the way he gripped the baseball in his hand. Seth was a good kid, so he nodded along to whatever Coach Asshat was saying. Then he threw another strike that blew right by the batter, and the idiot coach nodded like he'd revolutionized the sport with his stellar advice.

"I can hear you grinding your teeth. You should just volunteer to coach him yourself."

"I am not grinding my teeth," I argued, sure as shit not acknowledging the coaching part of his comment. If you gave Jordan an inch, he'd take you down the street to the Winn-Dixie and back.

But I did loosen my jaw a little and heard a traitorous crack.

From beneath a Kirby Falls Bobcats ball cap, Jordan said affably, "I heard that." While I considered the benefits of ending our decades-long friendship, he said, "And they say if you're grinding your teeth during the daylight hours, you're probably grinding them while you're asleep too."

I slid him a look. "Are you a dentist now?"

"It would actually be a sleep medicine specialist."

I rolled my eyes.

Jordan's bright white smile widened. "What? I heard it in a podcast. Chloe is very into them. Usually, the murdery ones, but every now and then, she finds one on history or stuff you should know. Like healthy sleep habits."

Chloe was our former high school classmate and Jordan's *one who got away* until she got divorced earlier in the year from her cheating asshole of a husband, and Jordan managed to hold on to her this time. They were newly cohabitating, which apparently made Jordan the expert on everything, including my teeth.

Unbothered by my lack of response, most likely because he'd known me my whole life and was used to my moods, Jordan continued, "You know, I would say you could just ask your bedtime partner about whether or not you're grinding your teeth at night, but I'm guessing the only one sharing your bed is Carl." Jordan paired this snipe with an exaggerated sad face. The laugh lines on his permanently cheerful face revolted, and he looked fucking ridiculous.

"You know, it's not like *you* had a string of one-night stands before Chloe came along. I'm not sure why you're giving me shit for not looking for an easy hookup," I accused with a narrowed gaze.

The thought of going to Magnolia bar and picking up a tourist for a quick lay sounded exhausting. It was honestly more trouble than it was worth. Maybe I was getting old. But my hand worked just fine, and I wouldn't have to deal with the *leafer* hotspot.

Jordan dropped the puppy-dog face. "That was never my thing. And I'm not saying it should be yours either. There are other options. You could ask someone out. You know, go on a date."

I sighed. I lived in the town I was born in. The women I knew, I went to grade school with.

Case in point, Jordan murmured quietly so he wouldn't be overheard by the few parents hanging around baseball practice on their phones, "I heard Janna Lewis broke up with the guy she was seeing long-distance."

Turning to glare, I hissed, "I went to prom with her my junior year. Why in the hell would I want to date her now? We're thirty years old, for Christ's sake."

Jordan looked affronted. "Well, you liked her then. Maybe you'll like her now."

I resisted the urge to sigh again. Like it wasn't bad enough that I was back in Kirby Falls—hell, *still* in Kirby Falls—after my career-ending injury a decade ago, working on my family's farm. My best friend really thought I needed to be dating someone I'd already dated back in high school, too? I hoped I wasn't that much of a damn cliché.

"Or," Jordan kept right on going with zero encouragement, "you could try online dating."

The beleaguered sigh did escape at that. "What are you doing? Trying to marry me off? Just because you and Chloe are happy and in love and all that shit does not mean that we need to have couples night and double-date down at the drive-in."

"Man, I wish the drive-in was still open."

"Oh my God," I muttered, lifting my hat in frustration and tugging it back down even lower as if I could block out the world and the idiot next to me.

He whacked me on the shoulder. "That is not what I'm doing, okay? I want you to be happy. I'm your best friend."

Jordan and Chloe *were* happy. I was honestly thrilled for them. Chloe got out of a horrible situation with her terrible ex-husband, who manipulated and mistreated her. And Jordan got the girl he'd always loved. I didn't begrudge them anything.

"I don't need a soulmate to be happy," I said.

Jordan crossed his arms, as exasperated as he ever got. "Well, it couldn't hurt your attitude to get laid."

I felt my jaw clench again and worked to loosen it as baseball practice finished up and the players went into the dugout to grab their gear and bags.

Seth made his way over to us, for once not already on his phone. "Pizza at Apollo's?"

Jordan feigned shock. "What? With us old people? You don't have youngsters your age to run off with?"

The nearly six-feet-tall baby brother rolled his eyes and grabbed Jordan's hand to pull him to standing. "Come on, old man. You too, Will. I'm broke and hungry."

I huffed a laugh at the kid.

Jordan kept up the act. "Oh, I see how it is. Fine. I'll buy you some pizza. Chloe's in Asheville anyway."

The truth was, Jordan would have done anything for Seth—had done *everything* for him. Their father had died unexpectedly when Jordan and I were sophomores in high school, and Mrs. Rockford had a newborn at home. My best friend had helped raise Seth. He'd done the daycare run as a teenager. Played babysitter more times than I could count. When other kids our age were out partying or getting up to no good, Jordan was home every night helping his mother get dinner on the table and reading Seth bedtime stories. He came home from college nearly every weekend to make sure Seth always had a supportive figure in his life. And a lot of that support came in the form of nurturing Seth's love and talent for baseball.

He would have done a lot more than take Seth out for pizza. And I knew, inside that big heart of his, he was probably grateful that his little brother picked him over his friends tonight. Jordan would probably slip him a couple of twenties later to get the kid through to payday from his part-time job at the coffee shop downtown. Jordan took care of the people in his life. He made his loved ones priorities and wanted nothing more than their happiness.

As I took in the two brothers and their good-natured bickering through the high school parking lot, I couldn't help but think back to Jordan's nagging earlier about teeth-grinding and dating. That was probably his roundabout way of taking care of me too.

Jordan slung an arm around his brother's shoulders as they walked. A moment later, he reached his arm back and pulled me to his other side. I didn't grumble the way I should have, letting my friend have his moment.

We took three separate cars down six blocks and across 3rd Street before finding parking spots on Main.

Apollo's was pretty busy for a Thursday night. Leafers were in town, and a steady stream of autumn-loving tourists would be around for at least the next two months. And even some of those out-of-towners were smart enough to realize what excellent food Apollo's had. Plus, it was right smack in the middle of Main Street. You couldn't miss it among the popular storefronts, local hangouts, art galleries, and antique shops.

But Seth wanted pizza, so here we were, surrounded by people.

Magdaline Kouides, the daughter of the owners and a former high school classmate, ignored the quartet of dude bros in their ironic flannels milling over the menu and led the three of us to a booth in the back.

"Thanks, Mags," Jordan called with a grin as she sped off in her black sneakers to return to the kitchen.

"I hate when it gets like this," I said, tugging down the brim of my cap, practically able to feel the din of unfamiliar voices in the busy restaurant.

"Well, tourism *is* kind of our thing," Jordan said easily, scanning the menu.

I knew that. Hell, tourism was my family's business. I saw more than my fair share of strangers every day for nine months out of the year. But sometimes I just needed a damn break.

My mind strayed to Becca, the long-term tourist. I'd seen her working in front of the Bake Shop again today—once in the morning when she'd waved at me and again in the afternoon when she'd been so focused on her laptop screen that she hadn't noticed Carl drooling like a lovesick fool at her feet.

She'd been in Kirby Falls for weeks now. It made me curious about what she did for work. How could she just pick up and leave her life in Detroit? Did she travel a lot and work from wherever she wanted? After the tree incident, I was pretty sure she worked with kids. With her child-friendly vocabulary and her bouncy personality, she looked and sounded like a preschool teacher. To me, at least.

But it was September, and most school systems were back in session. Unless she taught at some sort of weird private school that did online classes or maybe had a year-round schedule with different breaks.

"Will?"

My attention snapped up to Jordan, only to see Seth and Magdaline staring at me too. I guess I'd been lost in thought.

"Sorry, what was that?"

"What can I get you, Will?" Magdaline was obviously repeating herself, but she didn't look put out as she held her pen poised over her notepad.

I cleared my throat and quickly rattled off a beer I knew was on tap and the toppings I wanted in my calzone.

"You okay?" Jordan asked, his dark brows furrowed in concern. Seth was back on his phone, ignoring us.

"Yeah. Fine. Just distracted."

Jordan's brows rose a little at that, and I inwardly cursed myself for making him curious. I wasn't about to tell him I'd been thinking about a tourist. And I definitely wasn't telling him about the tree incident.

So I was infinitely grateful when Seth said without glancing up from his screen, "That was the last practice until February. But I'm organizing conditioning for anybody on varsity and junior varsity who wants to come out." His thumbs stopped moving, and he looked back and forth between his brother and me. "Might be nice to have a little help with that."

I nearly groaned. Picking up the standup dessert menu that stayed on the table, I kept my eyes glued to the surface. I could feel the Rockfords staring at me, waiting for me to answer.

"Yeah, we can probably come out and get our asses kicked by much younger bodies. Sure, why not?"

I glared at Jordan, who'd answered as if my participation was a foregone conclusion. He shrugged and grinned, unrepentant.

"Great," Seth replied and went back to typing.

The drinks arrived, and Seth talked some more about how the team was shaping up for the spring. He mentioned a few notable juniors and even a sophomore who'd made the varsity team. He admitted he was a little nervous since some scouts might be at tournaments and games.

"You're doing good out there," I said as the food arrived, and we scooted cups and silverware around to make room for their extra-large pizza and my meatball, mushroom, and roasted red pepper calzone. "Don't listen to whatever those idiot assistant coaches are telling you."

Seth took a bite of too hot pizza and sucked in a breath as he spoke, "Well, I wouldn't have to listen to Butler's car salesman dad try to coach me if you came out there and helped."

I paused with my knife and fork in hand. "Jesus. Not you too."

Then I stared at my best friend, who simply feigned confusion and defended, "Why, whatever could you mean?"

I pointed first at Seth and then at Jordan. "I know what you're doing. Don't try the meddling-Southern-belle routine with me. Or guilting me with children."

"I'll be eighteen in two months," Seth said with an eye roll.

But I ignored him. "Or reverse psychology or whatever this is."

Jordan had been dropping little nudges and comments about coaching for the past year. Always small things while we'd been in the stands for Seth's games or practices. I mostly tuned him out because coaching had never been my plan. Playing had been my plan. And look how well that turned out.

Seth smiled in a way that was a fucking carbon copy of Jordan's despite the fourteen-year age gap. "Come on, Uncle Will."

I shook my head and went back to cutting into my dinner. "Oh, don't 'Uncle Will' me. You're as shameless as your brother."

Both Rockfords said "thank you" in unison.

Even as I glared, I could feel my lips struggling against the urge to grin at these two boneheads.

But the idea of being a hometown cliché had the reluctant amusement sliding right off my face. Of course they thought I should just go down to Kirby Falls High and ask for a coaching job. I couldn't hack it in the real world as a player, so I should come back home to coach my own high school—where my records were still up in the gymnasium rafters and my picture collected dust in the trophy case in the front hallway.

No fucking thanks.

"I didn't realize this dinner was a setup," I groused. "I thought I'd be able to eat in peace."

Jordan sighed, but I didn't glance away from my plate as I heard him say with quiet resignation, "Forget we said anything."

I snorted. Right.

"It's just something I thought you'd be good at," my friend went on. "Something that might make you happy."

My head did snap up at that. "First, Janna Lewis, and now this coaching thing. Just how fucking unhappy do you think I am, Jordan?"

He looked instantly chagrinned. "Will—I—it's not like that. I'm sorry if I was pushy. I just know how busy you are at the farm this time of year—well, most of the year, really—and I thought you might want something just for you."

"How would asking out Janna Lewis be for me?"

Jordan huffed like I was missing the point. "Forget Janna. I'm sorry I brought her up. But coaching . . . that could be a way for you to be involved. You still love the sport. And we have the rec softball league. But I just thought you'd be great working with the kids. You've always been so patient and knowledgeable with Seth."

I didn't want to fight about this, so I just nodded and went back to eating. I heard Jordan sigh again, but I didn't acknowledge it. I got in crabby moods sometimes, and it never fazed him. He'd text me a dumb meme later tonight and harass me at the farm this weekend, I was sure of it.

We'd been friends for a long time and knew how to navigate each other.

And right now, I didn't want to think about his insistence that I'd be good at working with the kids on the baseball team. I didn't want to hear Jordan's big ideas for keeping me connected to the sport I'd loved since before I could walk.

Right now, I just wanted to finish this meal, escape my crowded hometown, and go home to my dog. Thinking about baseball made me bitter and angry. And I didn't want to ruin Jordan's time with his brother.

What my best friend couldn't understand was just how much I felt like a damn failure. He didn't know what it was like to have your body turn on you, to throw your last decent pitch at twenty years old, to go through rotator cuff surgery and physical therapy, and to never get your full range of motion back. As a well-respected and successful business owner, Jordan had no idea what it was like to have a dream that died before it even got off the ground.

It was humbling and humiliating. And I felt it every time a neighbor or acquaintance wanted to bring up the good ole days: how I'd led my team to the Little

League World Series when I was twelve or those damn records up at the high school or my no-hitter in college. They meant well when they slapped me on the back and said what a talent I *was* before my body had betrayed me. *What a shame,* they'd said with pity. *Too bad about all that.*

So, no. I didn't want to revive my love for the sport by begging for some pity placement on the coaching staff at my old high school. The only thing worse might be asking out my prom date from a decade ago.

I was finishing off my beer when I felt my phone buzz in my pocket. I ignored it and paid the check. We were leaving the restaurant, Jordan leading the way through the crowd lingering by the door for a table, when I felt my phone vibrate again.

Pulling it out on the sidewalk, I saw a text from my mother. *Check your voicemail.*

I groaned.

"What's wrong?" Jordan asked.

"Mom refuses to text. She leaves a voicemail every time and then texts me to tell me to check my voicemail."

"Maybe she thinks her texts are going to be hacked," Jordan joked.

"Maybe she's old and stuck in her ways."

"Don't talk about Maggie like that. Maybe you should just answer your phone."

I gave my friend a horrified look as I typed in my passcode and held the phone to my ear.

"Maybe," Seth piped up, his face still focused on his own device, "someone should teach her how to VM."

I told the Rockfords I'd see them later and listened to my mother's message as I waited for traffic to pass and then hopped in my truck.

"I forgot about the brunch ladies' meeting at the gazebo in the morning. They have a book club starting around ten a.m. for seventeen. Can you take the round tables over and set them up for me? I'll be in early to handle the refreshments. I just forgot to have someone help me with the tables and chairs. Thanks, honey. Love you."

I disconnected and sent my mother a text to confirm I'd handle setting up the white event tables and chairs we used. I sighed and dropped my head. I'd need to head back out to the farm, move the stuff out of storage, and set it up before I'd be done for the night.

As the head baker, my mother would be in very early to get to work on the pastries and bake the bread for the day. If she saw that the gazebo wasn't prepped for the brunch ladies' meeting, she'd try to do it all herself. I couldn't wait until I got to the farm in the morning because she'd take it upon herself to haul and unload it all on her own to make sure everything was perfect. And my mom didn't need to be lifting and moving all that furniture.

So, it would have to be tonight. And Carl had been cooped up in my house for too long. I'd swing by my place, grab the dog, and go prep the gazebo.

I checked the clock on my dashboard. 8:38 p.m.

Well, there was nothing for it. I shifted the truck into drive and turned back toward Clark lands.

I probably could have gotten set up and ready to go for the brunch ladies tomorrow in under an hour. But when I'd opened the storage room inside the barn, everything had been in complete disarray. Mac had covered the last event while my aunt Patty had been under the weather. And my cousin had apparently learned how to straighten up from a toddler.

It was nearly midnight when I'd gotten the storage room in better shape, checked on the apple stock for tomorrow, and then hauled the tables and chairs over to the gazebo.

My great-grandfather's house—my house—was up the mountain on the back side of the property. My grandparents had a home that overlooked the pond at Grandpappy's, but, as retirees, they spent half the year in Florida. My mother and father lived on the four acres beyond the cornfields. My aunt and uncle—Patty and Robert—had built their home twenty years ago on the Clark lands neighboring my parents' place. My other uncle, James, had a plot of land but hadn't done anything with it. He preferred living in his townhouse and distancing himself from anything that involved Grandpappy's Farm.

I'd moved into my great-grandfather, William Sr.'s, home six years ago when he'd gone to live at Legacy Hills, the assisted living facility just outside of town. The Clark homestead was the farthest from the farm and would mean going back out onto the main highway until I reached the private access road that wound up the side of the mountain.

But I was tired and would be right back here in the morning. If I could skip the half hour it would take to get home in the dark, I would. I had a duffel bag in my car with clothes and a toothbrush. I used to crash at the tiny house all the time, back before Chloe moved in this past spring. But Chloe was living with Jordan now, as of this very week. The lovebirds were together, and the tiny house was free.

I took out my keys and found the one I needed before glancing at my dog flopped over in the cool grass. "You ready, Carl?"

His dark head lifted. Yeah, he was ready to call it a night, too.

Decision made, I locked up the barn and grabbed my bag from the truck. Carl and I made our way in the dark around the barn to the front door of the tiny house.

Originally, my parents had it built as a rental for the farm. Something cutesy for the tourists to shell out money for and to fawn over. A few renters had treated the place poorly—some drywall issues here, some water damage there. A couple of drunk bachelorettes had thought that renting the tiny house meant they had the run of the farm in the middle of the night. The whole endeavor became more trouble than it was worth.

Eventually, I started using the tiny house more than any out-of-towners, so my mother had lost interest in renting it out. But it seemed like the perfect fit when Chloe had started working at the bakery and needed a place to stay after leaving her ex.

I attempted to slide the key in the lock and wished for the hundredth time that I'd left those solar pathway lights out here.

"Dammit." I fumbled the key once more before finally getting the door unlocked. I'd had a long-ass day, and all I wanted to do was climb in bed.

But before I'd made it past the unfamiliar welcome mat that read "Hope you like Taylor Swift," the light in the hallway clicked on, and a woman screamed. Carl barked, and I froze as a bag of . . . something smacked against my face, releasing a tiny cloud of sweet-scented powder into the air.

The bag of—I looked down—mini marshmallows fell limply to the floor as roughly one hundred of them escaped their confines and rolled in every direction. I stood unmoving as a blond woman in avocado pajamas relaxed from her crouched position behind the couch, met my eyes, and said, "Oh shoot."

WILL

"I am so sorry, Will."

Becca was shifting nervously before me on her bare feet. "I didn't mean to attack you."

I thought *attack* was pretty generous for what had gone down. But I didn't say that. I glanced to where the marshmallows had been. Carl had hoovered them up and then took off for the bedroom.

I shifted to the side so that Becca had a clear path to the door if she didn't feel comfortable with me here. Rolling my shoulders inward, I worked to make myself less imposing and intimidating to the woman staying alone in this house.

But she didn't seem to notice my efforts to make sure she was at ease.

Becca was still talking. She hadn't really stopped since the shock of my presence had worn off. We were on her fourth apology in as many minutes. "Your mom offered to let me stay here—to rent the house—while I'm in town since I'm at the Bake Shop almost every day. I'd been staying at the Sterling House, but she seemed weirdly opposed to that." She anxiously tucked a strand of long hair behind her ear and kept right on going. "I didn't know I'd be imposing."

I worked really hard to gentle my tone and my features, but I was tired and irritated. Yet none of this was Becca's fault. This had Maggie Clark written all over it.

Plus, I wasn't surprised if Vera Sterling was involved. She flirted shamelessly with my father when they ran across each other and had for years. My dad was too nice to tell her off, but Vera made him uncomfortable and made my mother murderous.

Peeking over to look out the front window, I wondered how I could have missed Becca's SUV sitting in the gravel driveway beside the house. I really did need to get those solar lights back out.

I started to dip my chin and then caught myself. No more bobblehead dumbass nodding around this woman. "It's okay. I didn't realize my mother . . . had done all this. I crash here sometimes when I'm working late. I wasn't expecting you, is all. I should apologize for barging in and scaring you." I eyed the remaining marshmallows in the floppy clear plastic bag. "Why the marshmallows?"

Becca's cheeks went a little pink. "Um. I like to eat them in bed. They don't leave crumbs."

I felt the corner of my lips twitch but I made myself ask, "I mean, if you thought I was someone breaking in, why did you choose that to attack me with?" My gaze touched on objects around the room—a carved solid wood candlestick holder on the mantel, a coffee table book by a local photographer, a metal paperweight on the end table next to the couch and within easy reaching distance.

"Oh, I didn't want to break any of Maggie's nice things."

I stared at her incredulously and then pointed. "There was a fireplace poker right there."

She frowned, a little vee forming between her blond brows. "I wouldn't want to hurt anyone."

I shook myself and rubbed my forehead. How did this girl make it in Detroit?

When I opened my eyes, she was closer—still nervous, though.

Becca was wearing an honest-to-God matching pajama set. A pale pink button-up top and little pink shorts with cartoon avocados on them.

She must have noticed me looking because she offered awkwardly, "I, um, really like avocado toast."

Before I could even begin to know how to respond to that, she hurriedly apologized once more. "I really am sorry for the confusion. I can grab my stuff and—"

"No." I cut her off. "This isn't your fault. You're staying. I'm the one going."

"But it's really late. Why don't you take the couch? That way, you don't have to drive all the way home when you clearly planned on staying here." Becca tilted her head toward the fireplace. "I should have known when I saw that dog bed."

An unexpected laugh huffed out of me as I turned with her to look at the white fleece bed in pristine condition. "That . . . is wishful thinking. He would never use it. He's a warm-spot thief and a bed hog."

Becca shifted again, and I fought the urge to look at her bare feet. Her toenails were painted pink. And there was an awful lot of leg showing beyond those ridiculous pajamas. "Stay, please. I feel terrible for messing up your night."

I sighed. Not this again. "You didn't—"

"But I'll blame myself," she interjected firmly. "Unless you stay, like you planned. I'll feel bad and won't get a bit of sleep."

I could see that she was being serious. This wasn't a manipulation tactic. She was fretting over this mix-up.

"Well, I don't want to ruin your day tomorrow," I said, sliding my sneakers off without untying them. "And you probably have a busy day working as"—I squinted, considering—"an online kindergarten teacher?"

She grinned, full pink lips and those even white teeth. "Is that what you think I do all day in front of the Bake Shop?"

I scratched my beard. "That was one of my guesses."

Becca hummed noncommittally but seemed amused and didn't offer up the truth behind her employment or her continued presence on my family's farm.

I was in charge of a lot at Grandpappy's, safety being one of them. It was important to make sure she wasn't up to something nefarious. She was always on her laptop. Maybe she was a hacker. Criminals could do that from anywhere, right? However, the public Wi-Fi wasn't actually that great.

And if this girl were an evil mastermind computer hacker, she'd have to be an even better actress. As bewildered as I was by her presence here, I just couldn't make myself believe something like that.

She stifled a yawn, and I suddenly remembered how late it was.

"Are you sure you won't feel uncomfortable with me here?" I was a stranger. Did this girl have no self-preservation instincts? *I* knew I posed no threat to her. But she didn't.

That little vee formed again on her forehead. "Why would I feel uncomfortable?"

I rubbed a hand across my jaw absently. "You don't know me, Becca."

Her frown cleared immediately. "Well, of course I do. You're Ms. Maggie's son, and you rescued me from a tree just yesterday."

"I didn't—" I started to argue the rescue thing and then just gave the fuck up. "If you're sure?" I felt the need to confirm.

Becca eyed me for a long moment. "I'm sure you are welcome to stay in this house that your family owns. Yes."

I couldn't tell if she was being a sassy smart-ass on purpose, but I hoped so. It made her less of a good-girl robot.

She straightened out of her thoughtful pause when I shrugged out of my flannel and hung it on the coatrack by the front door. And before I could do more than watch her disappear, she took off toward the linen closet calling, "I'll grab some blankets for you."

"That's alright. I can take care of myself."

But she was already loaded up with two extra pillows, folded white sheets, and a blue-and-gray quilt my grandmother had made.

I moved to take the items from her, and a bit of a tug-of-war ensued, in which we both smiled a little awkwardly. She didn't need to handle this for me. I was going to pass out on the couch in my jeans and then take off in the morning at the crack of dawn.

"I'll go get the dog out of your bed," I offered tightly, moving the short distance to the bedroom. Because of course he'd abandoned me and picked this stranger to curl up with.

For eight years, I'd been the center of that dog's world. Carl had such an attitude and didn't really like most people. I'd gotten suckered into adopting him right after college. I hadn't been in a good headspace and hated everyone and everything after nearly a year recuperating from surgery and then finally being released from the team. Jordan and my family had been the only ones willing to put up with my grumpy ass, and sometimes I'd even managed to scare them off. But somehow, adopting an adult dog who'd been just as standoffish and stubborn as me had worked out. I'd earned Carl's trust and, eventually, his unconditional love.

But I looked at him now. Snuggled up on a bed that was probably warm and smelled like leafer and marshmallows.

Then my eyes snagged on Becca's slender calves as she stepped around me. I told myself to stop being a jackass and look away, and then I thought I really couldn't blame the dog so much.

"Oh, that's okay," Becca said. "If you don't mind, he can stay. I've never had a pet before."

Never had a pet. Never climbed a tree. I was starting to wonder about this city girl.

And then she laughed a little under her breath. "It sounds kind of nice to share a bed with someone. It's been a while."

I swallowed, not knowing what to say to *that*. Because now I was thinking of the pretty tourist in bed . . . and not with my dog.

Clearing my throat, I backed out into the hallway. "Well, just know, he steals the covers."

"Sorry again about tonight."

"It's okay. Good night, Becca."

She smiled softly, looking like she wanted to sneak one more apology in there. "Good night, Will."

Becca needed to stop apologizing. It wasn't her fault. She'd been in the wrong place at the wrong time. Just like me. And in a few hours, I'd talk to the woman who'd orchestrated our little mix-up because I had a feeling it hadn't been so innocent.

"Good morning, Mother."

Maggie Clark glanced up from the mini quiches she was plating on the serving tray—probably for the book club brunch ladies. Their meeting was starting shortly. "The gazebo looks great. Thanks for taking care of that for me, sugar. Want a quiche? They're ham and swiss."

"No, I do not want a quiche." Okay, I did want a quiche. My mom was a damn good cook and baker. I grabbed one off the tray. "Why didn't you tell me you had someone renting the tiny house?"

She removed her oven mitt and adopted a confused expression. "Oh, did I not mention that Becca Kernsy was staying there for the next little bit?"

"No, Mom. You didn't." I popped the quiche in my mouth and chewed in what I hoped was a disapproving manner.

Eyeing me in confusion, she grabbed a bowl of fruit salad from the walk-in cooler. "Well, she is. There. Now you know. Why does it matter? Haven't you met Becca? She's as sweet as pie."

I didn't really want to admit that I'd walked in and scared the hell out of Becca last night, so I grabbed another quiche and chewed instead of answering.

But I still didn't trust that my mother wasn't trying to play matchmaker. She made no secret of the fact that I, her only offspring, should be settled down at the advanced age of thirty.

"Hi, Will," Chloe greeted with a smile while she operated the espresso machine. "Want a coffee?"

The morning rush was over. I'd waited to question my mother until I knew things would be settled down a little.

I'd woken up on the short sofa in the tiny house before six, shoulder stiff and legs cramped. After a silent conversation with stern eyebrows and threatening looks, Carl had finally stretched and slid off the bed where Becca was covered entirely by blankets—the one on top was a colorful crocheted throw I didn't recognize from the tiny house. I could only hear her deep breathing as the covers rose and fell over her balled-up form beneath the covers. That was probably for the best. I didn't need to get caught watching her sleep like a creeper while, in reality, I'd just been trying to pry my ungrateful mutt away from her side.

"Hi, Chloe," I finally responded. "I'll take some coffee in a to-go thermos. Thanks."

"You got it. And don't forget about trivia on Monday."

I resisted the urge to groan. Trivia Night at Trailview Brewing was on my weekly calendar thanks to her and Jordan. I figured they were attempting to socialize me like a misbehaved puppy or a homeschooled adolescent.

"Right," I muttered, accepting the green travel mug from her.

"Bring those math skills and sports knowledge," she added with a wink.

Baseball stats were why I was a math nerd in the first place. Math had been my best subject growing up. I liked numbers and percentages, and it came easy to me. When it was time to pick a college major—something I'd never given much thought to since baseball had always been my end goal—I'd picked accounting. I'd been surprised by how much I liked it. That was probably the only reason I managed to finish my degree and graduate following my injury and exit from the majors.

When everything went to shit, coming back home to the farm was supposed to mean taking over the administrative side of things—managing the books, dealing with buyers and vendors, and anything money-related. This was my family's farm. Whether it had been in my life plan as a twenty-one-year-old or not, I was responsible for it.

Nearly a decade later, everything had changed, including my obligations. My responsibilities had grown and expanded a lot over the years. Now I handled whatever needed doing.

"I've gotta get this stuff over to the gazebo," Mom said, interrupting my stumble down memory lane. "Is there a problem with Becca staying in the tiny house?"

"Becca's staying in the tiny house?" Chloe inserted herself in our conversation, blue eyes bright with interest. *Shit.*

"No, it's not a problem," I replied to my mother, ignoring Chloe. "I just wish I'd known before I tried to crash there last night after setting up the gazebo."

Mom set down the chicken salad croissants she'd been packing up. "Oh? What happened?"

Chloe looked equally invested in my response, and I took a step back toward the exit. I peeked out front, but, luckily, I didn't see Becca out on the covered porch yet. It was a little early in the day for her to be here. "Nothing. I just surprised her is all." My mom raised her eyebrows expectantly, but I wasn't about to say that I'd slept on the couch or seen Becca in her avocado pajamas. So I made sure my tone conveyed disappointment and amended, "And it looks really unprofessional for us when you don't communicate properly about rentals."

The women were standing next to each other now, and both wore identical expressions—the trying-not-to-laugh kind.

"You're right, Will," my mother said in a surprisingly serious tone as she nodded sagely. "Very unprofessional. I'll try to communicate adequately in the future."

Chloe covered her mouth with her hand as my mother smiled indulgently.

"Okay, fine. Never mind." I tugged my hat out of my back pocket and pulled it on. "Forget I said anything."

They were both giggling as I snatched up my thermos, two more mini quiches, and strode through the half door of the Bake Shop.

I made my way around the back of the building I shared with the bakery to my cramped office, where Carl was snoring on top of the dog bed in the corner. While drinking my coffee, I worked at my desk, doing the accounting for August, making sure all invoices were paid, the event deposits were sent, and all the upcoming vendor orders were placed. With the Orchard Festival in a couple of weeks, I decided a last-minute merch order of Grandpappy's tee shirts would probably be wise.

An hour later, MacKenzie radioed for additional help at the pond where the apple cannon and hayride were stationed. It was a Friday, and tourists seemed to start the weekend whenever they felt like it. Laramie responded and said she'd be right there, but I figured I could take a break and mosey on over to make sure they had coverage and the lines didn't get too long. I'd peek in on the gazebo while I was at it to make sure everything was under control over there and the brunch ladies had enough chairs.

Carl stayed behind, barely giving me a head raise as I stepped out into the midmorning sunshine of another fall day on the farm.

As I strolled around the building and onto the main path, I glanced toward the front porch of the Bake Shop and the table closest to the electrical outlet, but I didn't let myself think about why.

She wasn't there anyway.

I tugged my hat lower on my forehead and walked on. There were several things I needed to do today, including prepping the produce for the farmers' market tomorrow. I needed to check in with my aunt up at the General Store. I was pretty sure we had an event she was organizing after closing on Saturday night—an engagement party or something. I was still busy running through my mental to-do list when I approached the gazebo and heard loud laughter.

My boots slowed in the surrounding trees as I saw Becca, of all people, seated among the brunch ladies. They crowded around her, ignoring the four tables I'd carefully arranged the night before. They'd pulled their chairs over to be closer to her and whatever she was saying. Her face was expressive and smiling. She spoke with big sweeping hand movements, and I stared for a moment in confusion.

Becca was almost always smiling, and if she wasn't, she was right on the edge of it. Just waiting for someone to give her the opportunity.

She was the youngest woman present by at least twenty-five years. But the ladies were hanging on to her every word, smiling and nodding along. With her long blond hair loose in the breeze, Becca held up a book and flipped through the pages. Finally, she found her place and looked like she was reciting from the text.

Not wanting to be spotted, I backed up slowly into the tree cover as the discussion continued. And if I stayed there longer than necessary, it was because I was confused, not annoyingly intrigued by whatever Becca was doing here. Maybe I stood listening to the breeze carry her voice closer because I was working through solutions in my head. When I hadn't reached any logical conclusions, I made myself ignore the irritating, attractive mystery of it all and turned away.

I had to admit that everything looked like it was well in hand.

Actually, it looked like a tourist who'd been in town a handful of weeks was leading a local book club, and they'd welcomed her like a long-lost granddaughter. But what did I know?

As I redirected to where Mac was working at the pond, I remained baffled about Becca's presence at the event this morning. Maybe she *was* an author. That would explain her remote work schedule at the Bake Shop. And maybe the brunch ladies found out and featured her book for this month's pick. That all seemed very implausible. But maybe?

Yet it was far more likely than a random leafer being invited to participate in a meeting for local grandmothers.

"Will!" my cousin MacKenzie called as I approached the covered area that housed the apple cannon. "We're low on the ugly apples. Can you bring us a pallet over?"

I snapped out of my weird thoughts about Becca, the tourist, and took in the busy line where my other cousin, Laramie, sold tickets to visitors of all ages for a chance to shoot five apples out of the cannon over to a red-and-white bullseye positioned in the middle of the water.

"Yeah," I told Mac. "I can do that."

It was a good thing I'd wandered over to check on things. During the busy season, something always needed to be done on the farm. My dad and his staff generally handled all the produce and plantings, but the business side of Grandpappy's Farm had a hundred working parts. Hiring a general manager would probably be a good idea. That wasn't the role I'd been brought in to fill, but here I was, doing my best to keep everything together.

Later that afternoon, after delivering apples and then holding down the fort at the pond so that my cousins could take lunch breaks, I finally made my way back toward the Bake Shop, intent on finishing the day in my office, barring any more emergencies on the walkie.

My attention was on the ground as I ran through the remainder of my immediate tasks when I caught sight of a four-leaf clover in the grass. I paused and reached down, plucking it from the patch of clover. I'd always been good at spotting them, and several areas around the farm seemed to produce them pretty regularly.

I held the tiny clover in my hand and continued walking, mind on a dozen things at once.

Maybe I could stop by and see if Mom had any little quiches left since I'd missed lunch. My eyes sort of drifted of their own accord to the picnic table near the wall of the building. Becca was sipping an iced coffee and reading over something on the screen of her laptop. Carl sat beside her on the bench, and she absently stroked a floppy black ear.

I sighed. I guessed I should go retrieve my wayward dog.

Becca noticed my approach. Her blue eyes lit behind dark-framed glasses, and I was, once again, struck by her genuine warmth. We hardly knew each other, and each interaction had been more awkward than the last. But here she was, smiling as bright as the sun like we were old friends.

But then I saw her features change, and I just *knew* she was about to apologize . . . again.

"Hey."

She placed her iced coffee on the table next to her computer. "Hi, Will. I'm so sorry again about last night."

I held up a hand. "Not necessary. You don't have to keep apologizing, especially for something that wasn't your fault."

"Okay. Sorry." Then she winced, and I felt my lips twitch. "I'm really done now."

"Good." I nodded and then caught myself. What was it about this woman who made me nod my head like an idiot all the time? I'd never had a nodding problem before this week. Shaking myself, I pointed at Carl. "Sorry if he's bothering you. I'll take him back with me."

"Oh, he's not bothering me at all. He's my buddy." She turned on the bench and used both hands to rub Carl's doggy face. His tail wagged in traitorous ecstasy, and I fought my eye roll. "I've been meaning to ask, what's his name?"

"It's Carl."

She blinked. "Your dog's name is Carl?"

I shifted and slid a hand into my pocket, wondering what was wrong with that. Carl was a good name. "Yeah."

Becca grinned. "Are you a fan of *The Walking Dead*?"

I stared at her, not getting it before shaking my head in the negative.

"You know, 'get in the house, Carl.'" She said this in a really terrible Southern accent before laughing.

I had no idea what she was talking about.

"Oh well," she finally said, cheeks getting a little pink. "It's a nice name. I like it."

"He doesn't usually take to people," I admitted. "Are you sneaking him table food?"

Becca's features morphed into abject horror. "I would never. I don't know his allergies or his favorite foods or what might make him sick. I've never had a dog, but I know enough to recognize that you have to ask permission for those sorts of things."

I nodded again. Dammit.

"Carl just likes me," Becca murmured sweetly, her gaze back on my dog. He gave a happy bark before licking her face.

Her grin was triumphant like she'd won an argument we weren't even having.

I knew Carl liked Becca. That wasn't in question. I was just curious why my typically aloof-with-strangers sidekick had taken to her so easily without food as a bribe.

"I guess he does," I admitted, reaching up to scratch my beard.

Suddenly, Becca gasped, and I froze. "Is that a four-leaf clover?"

I realized I still had the tiny green stem in my hand and glanced at the clover. "Uh, yeah. I found it while I was walking."

She sat up straight and stared with such amazement that I didn't know what to think.

Tentatively, I held it out to her.

Becca accepted the clover like it was a newborn, grinning and marveling all the while. "This is so amazing. I've never seen a real four-leaf clover."

I took in her blue eyes, bright with wonder over something so minor. Of course, this was the same girl who'd gotten all moony-eyed over climbing a tree. Seriously, was there nothing green in Detroit?

"Well, you can have it," I said. She started to protest but I went on, "I find 'em all the time. If you want to keep it, just make sure you flatten it in the pages of a book or something. You've got about ten minutes before it starts to shrivel up."

She was already digging through her laptop bag on the table, pulling out what looked like a planner or notebook. I watched in amusement as she carefully smoothed the leaves between two pieces of lined paper before gently closing the book. "Thank you so much, Will."

I cleared my throat. "It's nothing."

Eyeing her laptop, I wondered again what she was up to. Her laughter down by the gazebo floated back to me. I hadn't gotten a good look at the cover, but I was relatively sure I could find out what this month's book club pick was. My mom probably knew, if nothing else. "How's work going today?"

Both Becca and Carl looked up from their seated positions across from me. Amusement sparkled in the woman's eyes, and the dog just looked embarrassed for me. "Productive," she finally replied, giving nothing away. And then she grinned. "Those kindergarteners won't teach themselves."

"Alright, so you're not a teacher."

Her smile widened. "Nope." But she didn't offer up any alternative career choices. It was like she could tell I was curious about her, and that made me take a sudden step back. No sense in wondering about Becca Kernsy. She was a tourist. She'd go back to her real life when the charm of autumn in Kirby Falls wore off. Like some small-town fairy tale, by the time the last leaf fell, she'd be a goner.

"I'll let you get back to it," I said, tugging my hat low. Patting my leg, I called Carl to my side.

Becca gave him an ear-rub goodbye, her face going soft around the edges. "Thanks again for my four-leaf clover. I'll see you later."

I caught myself mid-nod and then hightailed it toward my office. Carl plodded dejectedly along behind me. I didn't bother stopping to beg quiches off my mother. The sight of her grinning at me through the half door had my appetite abruptly departing. The last thing I needed was for her to be encouraged by my interactions with Becca.

I wished she and Jordan would give the matchmaker thing a rest. Things were just fine the way they were.

Two days later, I had the evening off. Grandpappy's Farm closed at five on Sundays, and at least once per month, I visited my namesake, Grandpa William, at the Legacy Hills assisted living facility between Kirby Halls and Miller Creek.

My great-grandfather was a widower, and about eight years ago, he got a difficult dementia diagnosis. It wasn't until nearly two years later that he willingly went to live at Legacy Hills and insisted that I move into his house to help keep it up and take care of it.

William Sr. was a proud man. Stoic and steady, he was the patriarch of our family. He'd always been someone I respected, so when he'd entrusted me with the upkeep of the family homestead, I'd gladly taken it on. The house was old and too big for one man. But I'd been slowly rehabbing it and fixing whatever saw fit to break down at any given time. But I hadn't done much in the way of modernizing or making it my own. I figured I'd get around to it someday.

Of course, I liked the convenience of the tiny house. The proximity to the farm didn't hurt either. But the homestead off the winding roads of the Appalachian Mountains was part of my heritage—my great-grandfather Clark's legacy. I'd had many a family dinner at the sturdy wooden table in the dining room. I'd learned to work on cars, clean a fish, and build things with my own two hands under Grandpa William's watchful eye.

The house was, at times, a painful reminder. It was also one more thing tying me to my hometown. Another responsibility, another obligation.

But I pushed away the familiar guilt that accompanied those ungrateful thoughts as I went through the automatic front doors of Legacy Hills.

The front desk staff recognized me beneath my ball cap and buzzed me in through the locked doors leading to the long-term-care wing. The nurses did a good job with their patients, and our family was grateful that Grandpa William received a high level of care at Legacy Hills when living home alone was no longer safe.

My great-grandfather rarely recognized me or even spoke during my time here, but the staff said he always had a good day following my Sunday evening visitation.

I greeted several of the nurses and assistants at the desk before making my way to Grandpa Clark's private room. He was by the window, seated in his cushioned glider, gazing out over the well-kept grounds. The light grew dim as the sun worked its way behind the hills in the distance. But he didn't seem to mind. He didn't acknowledge me as I spoke and settled in the chair across from him.

Reaching for the book on his bedside table, I frowned when I noticed it had an unfamiliar blue-and-white cover. *A Collection of Poems* by Robert Frost. "Huh. I thought we were in the middle of that John Grisham novel."

I flipped through the pages until they parted helpfully around a bookmark from Paperback Writer, the bookstore and gift shop downtown.

Without giving it too much thought, I cradled the leather-bound book in my hand and read aloud the poem on the page, *After Apple-Picking*.

" . . . This sleep of mine, whatever sleep it is.

Were he not gone,

The woodchuck could say whether it's like his

Long sleep, as I describe its coming on,

Or just some human sleep."

Grandpa had ceased his rocking about two lines in. When I finished, I noticed his gaze was still fixed on the setting sun in the distance.

As they often did, my eyes lingered on the collection of framed photographs in the room. There was one with Grandpa and his wife who passed away before I was born. In it, she was playing the piano that still sat in the formal living room of my great-grandfather's house—my house. He sat stiffly beside her on the bench, but a small smile lifted his lips. In another photo, they stood on the front porch of the homestead. Her lined face was bright with laughter while Grandpa Clark stood stoically by her side. Another image showed a much younger version of the man before me seated on a tractor in a freshly plowed field. A handful of memories caged in four-by-six-inch frames. A long life lived over ninety-four years. One that had worked the land, raised a family, and started a legacy.

I knew I was lucky in a lot of ways. My history and my family being a big part of that. This town, too.

I continued reading out of the collection of poetry for the next hour until the nurses came in to help my great-grandfather get ready for bed.

Briefly, I considered asking one of the nurses about the mysterious book, but in the end, I decided not to bother the hardworking caregivers.

Instead, I took myself home to the land my great-grandfather had built.

BECCA

"Can you believe these tourists?"

Laramie Burke's aggravated exclamation jolted me from the book cover design I was working on. So much for that spine alignment.

She sat down across from me with a hard thump. "They asked me if I could gift wrap." Her tone was incredulous. "This ain't Macy's!"

I resisted the urge to smile and instead nodded in companionable agreement with the vibrant young woman. Laramie Burke—Larry, to nearly everyone—was in her midtwenties and, by all accounts, a Grandpappy's Farm employee since she was a teenager. She was Will's cousin on his grandmother's side. I wasn't super clear on the family tree dynamics. But I did know that the spunky, opinionated woman was only allowed to work with the public for two hours a day. She must have been scheduled in the General Store this morning.

"So entitled," I murmured in commiseration.

"Exactly!" Larry pointed at me enthusiastically. I was quickly learning that worked up was Laramie's default setting. "That's exactly it. They are so entitled. Damn leafers." And then she seemed to remember that I wasn't a local and glanced my way. "No offense, Becca. You're not like the rest of these ungrateful city people."

I hadn't heard the term *leafer* until a few weeks ago when Will's other cousin, MacKenzie, had explained it was a local determination she and other residents used for the out-of-towners who visited Kirby Falls to enjoy the fall foliage. I'd run across *leaf-peeper* and *leaf-peeker*, but never *leafer*. Maybe it was vocabulary exclusive to the tiny North Carolina town. This place was full of delightful surprises.

"Thanks, Larry," I replied with a grin. "You taking a break to calm down?"

She nodded, her chin-length black hair shifting with the movement. Larry looked like a punk rock pixie princess. Her eye makeup was all expertly applied with dramatic winged liner, and her hairstyle was edgy and fun. On her petite form, she wore ripped black denim and a forest-green Grandpappy's tee shirt knotted just above her navel. I envied Larry's straightforward attitude and her general vibe of a cool chick who didn't give a flip.

I could never be like that. I gave a flip. I gave all the flips. But being around Larry gave me a goal, something to strive for. And she never made me feel like a goody-goody loser. In the weeks I'd been visiting the farm, we'd struck up an unlikely friendship. On day four of my time in front of the Bake Shop, she'd sneaked a peek at my laptop screen and stopped to ask me about the alien romance book cover I'd been working on. Then we'd talked about books for half an hour before our discussion got her paged on the walkie by Will, wanting to know why she hadn't relieved Mac over at the corn maze.

Larry had come by the next day on her lunch break, and we'd talked some more. I usually saw her at least once a visit when she was working. And I liked her more and more all the time. She reminded me of my friend Cece, totally confident in who she was and always willing to speak her mind.

Having friends in real life was a new concept. Most of my friends were online, fostered through a love of reading and my career as a graphic designer who focused on indie book covers, promotional graphics, marketing, and branding.

My childhood hadn't particularly lent itself to having close friends. That had been hard to manage when my parents were frequently in and out of jail. There weren't sleepovers or birthday party invitations for kids like me, not when all the parents of my classmates found out about mine.

"I think I'm going to grab a pastry before I take over for Mac on the hayride.

Carbs always help when I'm feeling disappointed in the human race as a whole. You want anything, babe?"

"No, thanks," I replied with a smile. "I've already had my pumpkin bread allotment for the day."

I watched Larry stroll through the half door of the Bake Shop like she owned the place and heard Maggie's cheerful voice welcoming her.

Before I got the chance to focus my attention back on the screen of my laptop, Will came walking out from behind the building. I considered sitting on my hands to keep from waving like a dork again. But then Carl raced over, eager for pets, and, well, that took priority. I greeted Will's sweet dog before a short whistle had his ears drooping.

Smiling, I watched a resigned Carl trot off toward his master. And then all of a sudden, I was looking at Will in a dark green tee shirt, light-wash denim, and a backward ball cap. He did that cool-guy chin-lift thing as he waited on the pathway for his dog to catch up.

My right hand rose without my permission, going rogue and waving in Will's gloriously bearded direction. I watched his gray eyes narrow, but he didn't look upset. In fact, he was smiling. Teeth were visible and everything. His head dropped for a moment when Carl finally reached his side, but Will was definitely still smiling when he looked up again and met my gaze.

Another chin lift and he was off.

Vaguely, I could tell that my hand was still in the air, but my brain was trapped in some sort of alternate reality limbo where I'd just made Will Clark smile—a real smile. Not a grudging one or a polite half smile. This one had been bright and genuine and absurdly beautiful.

In all of our strange interactions up to this point, he'd been . . . not unfriendly, per se. More like distant. A tad grumpy. A big, bearded crab apple. Like he was giving me a wide berth just in case I couldn't be trusted around the steak knives.

But today, I'd gotten a real grin out of him, and something a little unsteady was happening in the general area of my middle.

"Were you waving like that at Will?"

Laramie's words and sudden presence at the end of my table had me jumping in surprise.

I slowly lowered my hand and turned to watch her sit down with a blackberry Danish and a bottled water.

"Waving like what? How was I waving?"

Dark eyes bright with amusement, Larry bit her lip momentarily before answering. "Becca, you did a royal wave. Like a *Princess Diaries* wave. Miss America on stage. Queenly. Majestic as all hell."

"No, I did not."

She laughed.

I looked down at my right hand in horror. It hadn't betrayed me like this since I tried to fist-bump someone at a conference instead of shaking hands like a normal person. "Did I really?"

"Oh, honey." Larry laughed again and then straightened. "Wait, are you nervous? Do you like Will?!"

My eyes darted to the side to make sure Maggie wasn't at the order window. "What? No. And you're making me sound like a high schooler."

"Um, try middle schooler. Your cheeks are so red, I could roast marshmallows on them." She smiled, one part devious, the other delighted. "It's okay. I won't tell."

"You're his cousin," I said distractedly before whispering, "And I don't *like him* like him. I barely know him."

It was true. I didn't know Will at all. Not really. One smile, a four-leaf clover, a treetop rescue, and a failed breaking-and-entering attempt did not a relationship make. But it didn't stop me from admiring the way his tee shirt stretched across his bulging biceps. And it apparently didn't prevent a delicate little newborn baby crush from growing into a toddler.

"Second cousin, once removed," she corrected around a mouthful of Danish. "I really wouldn't say anything to him," she asserted, completely ignoring me. "I respect people's privacy."

I didn't mean for my facial features to be so disbelieving, but I could feel my eyes narrowing.

"What? When it matters, I can keep a secret. Believe me."

I wondered at Larry's words and what things she felt the need to hide. But before I could ponder it too long, she changed the subject. "Are you coming to Trivia Night at Trailview?"

"I'll be there," I said. The awkwardness of our previous conversation was already dissipating. Laramie had this way of seeming unaffected by the world around her. There couldn't be lingering awkwardness because Larry was too cool to allow it. "Chloe asked me to join her team while I'm in town." And I was pretty excited to be included in the trivia night at a local brewery with the friends I'd made here.

She licked a dot of blackberry filling off her finger. "Good. They could use you. I play on a team with Mac and Bonnie, Bonnie's husband, Danny, and my best friend, Kayla. We would have asked you, but we already have someone for the art stuff. Mac's sister, Bonnie, is an elementary school art teacher."

"Oh, that's so cool. If she ever wants a guest speaker or anything, I have a lots of cool presentations and lesson plans I can do. Mostly art therapy from when I volunteered with the Boys and Girls Club of Southeastern Michigan."

"Great! I'll introduce you tonight. She'll love you." Larry's words made me feel chest-achingly warm. "And y'all can plan an activity for her classes. I'm sure she'd love that."

Before I could ask more about Bonnie or Trivia Night, Garrett, the UPS driver who I chatted with several times a week, approached our table, smile locked and loaded as he called out a greeting.

Once again, he positioned himself across from me and propped his shoe up on the bench seat, his half-bared leg on full display.

Only this time, Larry eyed his fabric-covered crotch in proximity to her face and said conversationally, "Wanna put that thing away, Gare?"

The delivery driver laughed like Laramie was an improv champion but straightened away to stand. Crossing his arms, he kept his warm brown eyes on me but addressed my companion, "Larry, tell Becca to put me out of my misery and go out with me."

I kept my smile friendly but could feel my shoulders stiffening at Garrett's attention. I was flattered. He was a nice guy—totally harmless. But, honestly, he seemed like a player. I got the impression that I was a shiny new toy that landed in Kirby Falls, and he wanted to add me to his collection.

Laramie's perfectly sculpted dark eyebrows lifted. "Wow. Considering Becca is a grown-ass woman and highly capable of making her own decisions, I think I'll let her speak for herself."

Garrett kept right on grinning, undaunted by Larry's less-than-enthusiastic endorsement. "What do you say, Becca?"

My smile wobbled a little at the edges. This wasn't how our midmorning banter typically went. Garrett was supposed to flirt with me. He'd never come right out and asked me on a date before.

Larry watched me carefully while she polished off the rest of her Danish.

Maybe this was a good thing. If I went out with a nice guy, had fun while I was in town, Laramie wouldn't be so convinced that I had a crush on Will. I mean, I did have a crush on Will, but that was between me and my horrible track record with men.

Besides, my . . . infatuation was totally one-sided and equally ridiculous. He probably thought I was insane. Between the tree incident, the marshmallow incident, and the very recent waving incident, we had enough disastrous encounters to fill out a police report.

It was probably a good idea to nip this little crush in the bud before I embarrassed myself any further.

"Sure!" I said, maybe a touch too loudly. "That sounds great."

Garrett seemed thrilled, and we exchanged numbers and tentative plans for the upcoming weekend to grab drinks at a Kirby Falls cider mill and bar. I hadn't been to Firefly yet, but I'd heard great things from the locals and the Google reviews alike.

Laramie drank her water and watched our exchange with an amused expression that I didn't want to examine too closely. And when she and Garrett left at the same time, I couldn't help the sense of relief that came with their departure.

My phone gave a quick buzz, indicating a new text notification in my group chat with my friends.

Cece: How's North Carolina? Still the best thing in your life besides us?

I grinned.

Me: Still amazing. You should have seen the sunset last night.

Cece: I did. You sent us 800 pictures.

Pippa: Very gorgeous. We approve. What else is going on besides the revolution of the planet around the sun?

Me: I actually just got asked out.

Cece: Ohhhhh! The hot lumbersnack who rescued you from the tree?!?!

I winced. Relaying the tree incident to my friends might have been a mistake.

Me: Please stop calling Will a lumbersnack.

Me: And no. The UPS guy asked me out for drinks this weekend.

Cece: *crying emoji*

Cece: *stump emoji*

Cece: *ax emoji*

Cece: *GIF of a woman fanning herself*

Laughing to myself, I typed, *You need to stop objectifying people via text.*

Pippa: LOL

Cece: Fine. Tell us about the UPS guy. Does he have a big package?

Pippa: ba-dum-tss

I snorted despite the terrible joke. And then I realized the thought of gossiping with my friends about Garrett and our upcoming date didn't sound very appealing. Without Larry's accusations regarding Will staring me in the face, I wasn't so sure I'd made the right decision agreeing to get drinks with the flirty delivery driver.

Me: I'd rather hear about what's going on with you guys? How are your deadlines for your next books going?

That got them going, and we texted for the next twenty minutes about their current writing projects before saying goodbye.

I couldn't help but feel like I'd dodged a bullet by avoiding a conversation with my friends about Garrett. I probably would have admitted that I'd agreed to the date while I'd been distracted and experiencing latent embarrassment from waving like an idiot.

The reprieve was short-lived because moments later my phone buzzed again on the wooden tabletop. The caller ID had my stomach clenching uneasily and my blood pressure skyrocketing.

With a deep breath, I snatched up the phone and accepted the call. "Hello."

"Becs, listen. You know I wouldn't ask if it wasn't important, but I need some cash."

My sister's voice was dry and rasping. I could practically smell the smoke from the cigarette she was undoubtedly smoking on the other end of the line.

"What happened?" I asked quietly, glancing around the covered porch to make sure no one was within earshot.

"Dad got picked up on the riverfront. He had that thing in the spring, and the piece-of-shit cop recognized him. They're holding him on a fifty thousand dollar surety bond, the fuckers. Mom's liquidating a few things, but she only has part of it. If we could get three thousand from you, he could be out in time for supper."

I listened to my sister's defensive speech pattern and translated. Our father had been out panhandling on the streets of Detroit, down near the river where tourists frequented. A police officer recognized him due to his frequent-flier status with the Detroit PD, and arrested him for an outstanding warrant pertaining to a felony assault charge from a bar fight back in March. With that type of bond assigned by the judge, $5,000 would need to be paid to a bail bondsman in order for my father to be released. Mom was selling drugs they had on hand to make a quick two grand, and they needed me to make up the difference.

"Heather, I don't have that much in cash on me right now."

"So go to the bank and get it."

I swallowed against my suddenly dry throat, reluctant to admit my whereabouts. "I'm not in Detroit. I'm out of town for work."

A painful beat of silence passed, during which I glanced around again. This time, I spotted Maggie watching me from the open half door. She looked . . . concerned, dark brows furrowed and a question ready and waiting on her lips.

I forced a smile and a little wave—normal this time—and then stood.

"Where are you?" Heather demanded.

"On a work trip," I repeated, unwilling to give her my exact location. "I can't get you the money right now," I added quickly, making my way to the farm's main path. I knew I could leave my belongings. Maggie wouldn't let anyone touch my computer or my bag. And honestly, escape was my priority at the moment.

"Then wire it to me."

This was the first time I'd heard from my older sister in four months. But this was how our interactions always went. She only called when she needed something, usually money. Typically, it was something small: Forty bucks to make it until payday. A broken washing machine. Could she have money for the laundromat? She'd gotten mugged over in Franklin Park, and they'd taken her rent. Could I float her a loan? This was how it was with us.

I'd been estranged from my parents for years, and my sister knew that. There was a boundary in place, and I didn't cross it. But Heather, well, I'd never managed to draw a line in the sand where she was concerned.

It was a heck of a lot harder to tell her no when she was standing on my doorstep, her skin pale, her frame painfully thin.

However, I found the wherewithal here and now, six hundred miles between us. "I'm not going to do that, Heather. Mom will have to find another way to come up with Dad's bail."

She started yelling then. Words I'd heard my whole life. How I was an ungrateful shit, undeserving of all the money I had. Next would come the accusations about how I thought I was better than everyone, with my job and an apartment paid for by someone else. If I didn't hang up right away, Heather would tell me I'd always been the worst part of our family. Disloyal. Garbage. A waste of everything they'd done for me.

I watched my white sneakers move quickly down the dusty path to the field in the distance. I needed to put space between my sister and the comfort and solace I'd found on the farm. My hands shook as I listened to her berate me through the tiny speaker at my ear.

How could someone be so far away and feel like they were standing in front of me? Dragging me kicking and screaming to an uncomfortable childhood. To the sad, lonely kid getting picked on and teased. I longed for nicknames and inside jokes, playdates and sleepovers. Instead, I wore hand-me-down clothes and cried in the middle school bathroom.

My memories of being dirty and hungry flooded my system as my sister's anger breached the distance between us. I felt consumed by remembered neglect and indifference and a thousand other things I never had any control over.

I was an advocate for therapy and had attended off and on since adolescence. I knew the names of what I'd lived through. I also knew that none of it was my fault. But sometimes knowing and believing were miles apart in your heart.

No matter how quickly I walked, I couldn't stay grounded in the here and now. My sister's words transported me back to a dingy, cold apartment in Marygrove, north Detroit. To feeling shame and neglect, and then later, to knowing that my parents weren't good people. And my sister, with eight years between us, was on the same path, unable and unwilling to abandon that unhealthy lifestyle of crime, petty theft, and dealing. They were all criminals and users. Con artists and grifters who took advantage of the innocent. Money and drugs were the only things they cared about.

I'd been lucky. I'd found a way out through chance or fate or whatever you wanted to call it. A guardian angel who'd taken me in. Mrs. Walters had been my saving grace.

When I was six, my parents tried running a con on a little old lady they'd seen in the park. It wasn't the first time they'd targeted someone in such a way. Usually, they'd tell me to wander around and look lost. Once the mark approached, talked to me, and established a connection, my mother or father would rush in and thank them, then explain how they were down on their luck. Living in their car. Or I was sick and needed treatment of some kind. Whatever story they came up with. And then, the good Samaritan would hand over money to help.

Except my parents hadn't anticipated brash and bold Mrs. Walters or the fact that she'd been meeting her police detective son in the park. Dressed in plain clothes, he'd threatened to bring my father in, which would have resulted in jail time and fines from outstanding warrants. Without bothering to consult her son, the older woman had taken one look at me and said she'd let us go if they let her take care of me after school two days a week.

My parents hadn't trusted Mrs. Walters, but they were more than happy to get me out of their hair.

I didn't find out until much later that Mrs. Walters's son, Jamie, didn't approve of the deal she'd struck, but his mother was formidable and no-nonsense. He'd known better than to argue with her.

And so, two days a week, I didn't ride the bus home to our small apartment. I'd walk and take public transit with Mrs. Walters—a sixty-five-year-old retired elementary school principal—to her third-floor apartment in Highland Park. She'd give me snacks and help me with my homework. I hadn't been a strong reader until Mrs. Walters came along. It was also the first time anyone bothered teaching me right from wrong.

As I got older, I spent more and more time with the older woman. By high school, I was practically living in the spare bedroom of her home. And for the first time in my life, I had someone who cared about me beyond what I could do for them.

Mrs. Walters was like a grandmother to me, and I loved her very much.

Heather hadn't been so lucky. She'd never even wanted a different life. My older sister had never known the kind of selfless love I'd experienced. There'd been no help with her math or after-school treats. No movie nights or shopping trips. No tough love and no one to set her on the straight and narrow. Heather had kept right on following our parents to her own detriment.

I lived with that guilt, which was probably why I kept giving my sister money. She didn't love me, but I could still try to help her in the only way she'd allow.

With memories swirling and painful grief threatening, I said, "I have to go," quietly into my phone. It was unlikely that Heather heard me over her own ranting. Her rage had always been a well-placed arrow, and circumstances painted me the biggest, weakest target every time.

My hand still clasped my phone in a death grip, and I moved through the sunflower field in brisk, determined strides. My feet must have carried me here on instinct because I couldn't recall the path I'd taken.

Slowly, my racing mind calmed, and my thrumming pulse slowed to something less fight or flight. This was one of my favorite spots on the farm, so I knew the small maze made of sunflowers by heart at this point.

Several weeks past their peak season, the large blooms were shriveled and drooping, but they still reached over five feet tall. I didn't mind that the sunflowers were mostly dead. There was something comforting about being fully immersed among the dark leaves and wilted blooms. Like they'd done their job, given their beauty to making people happy, and now they got to rest until next year.

I liked the solitude I found here, winding my way around the heavy stalks. It helped to quiet my mind, and, right now, I needed that.

My history and my family felt like the definition of complicated. Part of me—the guilt-ridden and self-loathing part—wished I could abandon my mother and father and sister. Just leave Detroit without a trace. Change my number and be a different person. Someone who didn't have a family who regretted her and had nothing in common with her. A confident, independent woman like Cece or Laramie. Not one with an apology ready and waiting on the tip of her tongue.

I'd lived my whole life being sorry for my existence, feeling like I never fit in the life I was born into. An inconvenience, a liability. My childhood and adolescence translated into an adulthood rife with anxiety and fear. I hovered in the background of every office party or art show, like an extra on a movie set, desperate for a bigger role. Yet knowing I'd only be in the way.

All I'd ever wanted was a place I could belong.

Finally, my steps slowed to a meandering pace. The conversation with Heather was fading into memory, another drop in a very large bucket.

When I turned the next corner, my hands trailing the lifeless leaves, I jumped in surprise. "Will!"

"Hey. Sorry, I didn't mean to scare you. I called your name."

My smile was weak—more of an attempt, really. "It's okay. I was in my own little world."

I scrutinized his tight features and uncomfortable stance before saying, "Did your mom send you after me?"

Will's lips parted, and he stuck one hand in the pocket of his jeans.

I smiled softly, charmed by his unease and his willingness to indulge his sweet mother. "I'm alright. And I appreciate you checking on me. I imagine she caught my expression when I was on the phone with my sister."

His dark brows furrowed. Whether in confusion or question, I didn't know.

But I answered him anyway. "Things are complicated there, and something came up back home."

"Do you need to go back early?" he asked, the concern still lingering in his deep voice.

"No. It's nothing that would be helped by my presence." Just my money, I didn't add. Because nobody needed to deal with all my baggage and drama. It really wasn't sexy. I'd rather be mysterious than mentally gawked at. Or worse, seen as pitiful and pathetic.

"Oh." Now both hands made their way into his front pockets.

Gesturing at the area around us, I admitted, "I like it here. Helps me clear my head."

Will's gray eyes glanced at the dead and dying scenery. I supposed it wasn't your typical soothing space. There wasn't a peaceful babbling brook or layers of mountains to gaze upon. The vibe in the sunflower maze was more haunted farm or horror film. Tim Burton light, at the very least.

"It's quiet here," I added, feeling the need to defend my choice.

Those pale eyes strayed back to mine. "I suppose I can see the appeal of that."

"Did you know that sunflowers always face the sun? And when they can't find the sun, they face each other?"

"Uh, no. I did not."

"I just love that," I admitted.

Will watched me curiously. I couldn't place his expression. It was something similar to when you see a spider in your car, but before you can do anything about it, it sneaks away. Will was watching me like I might escape or potentially jump out when he least expected it, bite him, and cause a ten-car pileup.

"Where did you learn that?" he asked, still tentative.

"From a meme on the internet."

Will's laugh sort of erupted out of him. His lips parted around a burst of air and amusement, and I didn't know who was more surprised by it—him or me.

I grinned in response. "See, it's neat." Playfully, I wagged a finger at him. "Now, don't get ideas about stealing my favorite spot."

He smiled. "Mine is the corn maze actually. I walk it at night sometimes if I'm here after closing."

"Wow. That sounds terrifying. Very *Children of the Corn*."

Will's smile widened. "There's just something calming about the wind moving through the stalks. I like getting lost there sometimes."

I squinted. "And that is precisely why I don't go in. I have a terrible sense of direction. I'd need a search party."

I'd only tried completing the corn maze once in all my time on the farm. I hadn't enjoyed walking the paths without a map or a clear direction. The uncertainty had not been fun for me. When the worn dirt track I'd been on had gotten close to the perimeter of the maze, I'd simply stepped out through the corn into the open and worked my way around the outside until I'd returned to the entrance. I hadn't really felt the need to try again.

The sunflower maze was a fraction of the size of the cornfield, and everything was planted in straight lines that turned inward until you reached the center. Between the flowers, I could see beyond it in nearly every direction. I'd never be in danger of getting lost here.

Losing myself had never held any appeal. I wondered what made Will seek out the feeling.

He squinted right back. "You know little kids go in the corn maze."

"I am aware of that, yes."

"Just checking."

I was still grinning at him when he added, "I figured you'd be into that sort of thing. Had it on your wish list of climbing trees and finding four-leaf clovers."

Will probably thought I was some weirdo who didn't have a normal childhood. He was right, but I definitely didn't want to draw attention to it. "Well, I did try the corn maze once. Maybe my first week here, back in August. It just wasn't for me. Now I do other things for fun."

As we talked, we'd drifted a little closer. Will stood just a few feet away.

"What other things have you tried in Kirby Falls for fun?" Will asked, keeping the conversation going.

I was a little surprised that he was interested. Maybe he just felt sorry for me after finding me upset and stumbling through a dead flower patch. But okay. A conversation! Not exactly my time to shine, but I could do this. Probably.

"There have been so many wonderful sights to see." I told him about checking out some of the local vineyards and breweries. The playhouse, the restaurants, the farmers' market, of course. Visting Asheville and seeing the touristy things there. I mentioned a few of the trails I'd hiked and waterfalls I'd seen. "Aside from Grandpappy's, being outdoors has really been my favorite part of exploring Kirby Falls. I'd never really been hiking before this trip. Now I want to go every day. Your hometown is so beautiful. I love it."

Will watched me curiously the whole time I spoke. I couldn't say for sure, but his expression showed a bit of surprise as if he'd never considered some of those sights worth visiting.

"I bet you and Carl head out on trails all the time."

Will glanced away briefly. "It's been a while actually."

"Oh."

An awkward moment passed when I hadn't hidden my disappointment well enough, and maybe Will didn't know how to handle it.

Then, surprising the caffeine right out of me, he said, "There's a trail for locals. It's on private property and it's by reservation only, so that the path doesn't get overrun. But I could take you if you want. I've known the owner since I was a kid."

Excitement welled in me like that middle schooler Laramie had unearthed with her crush accusation. But I told Inner Becca to play this cool like coconut water. I smiled and said evenly, "That sounds like fun. Thank you, Will."

He nodded slowly a few times and then stopped abruptly. With a jerky movement, he reached up and spun his backward ball cap around, tugging the bill down over his eyes. "Yeah, okay. I'll get in touch with Mr. Abrams and let you know. It might be early, before work one day, if that's okay."

"Sure!" I scolded Inner Becca and then, after taking it down several notches, amended, "That won't be a problem. I'm an early bird."

Will's lips quirked the barest amount. "I figured."

This seemed like the least amount of awkward I could hope for at this point. We were making plans to go hiking together. He hadn't asked me to prom or anything. I should get out of this conversation now before I tripped and fell into his crotch or blurted out my inexplicable love of the Jonas Brothers.

"Well, I'll let you get back to work. Thanks again for checking on me for Maggie. I'm going to wander for a few more minutes before I make my way back to the Bake Shop."

"Okay." Another tug on the bill of his hat. I was sensing a pattern there, and it would be painfully adorable if that, in fact, was big, crabby Will's tell of uncomfortable nervousness. "I'll see you soon."

Fifteen minutes later, when I got back to the Bake Shop and my computer, I saw a bright green four-leaf clover waiting on the table for me. The stem was secured beneath the edge of my coffee mug to keep it from scattering in the midday breeze.

My lips turned up in a small, shy smile as I stared down at Will's kind gesture. The unexpected nature of it caused my stomach to flip.

I tucked the clover carefully between the pages of my notebook and didn't let myself think about the fact that my junior high crush had definitely bumped up a grade level.

six

WILL

Trailview Brewing was loud. Voices rose over one another as the deejay and host for the evening set up his sound system and laptop at a table beneath the awning.

I wound my way through the grid of wooden picnic tables arranged in the outdoor seating area of the bar. A few firepits glowed along the perimeter, surrounded by customers or tourists who weren't here to participate in Trivia Night.

Perry MacArthur's food truck, Hogs Wild, was parked at the curb. The line was long, so I kept moving, looking for Jordan, Chloe, and Seth. I'd grab some barbecue and coleslaw later when it cleared out a little.

Finally, I spotted the back of Chloe's bright red hair, high in a ponytail. Jordan was across from her running his mouth, like usual.

Someone crossed in front of me, and I pulled up short. Beer sloshed over the rim of the glass hovering in the air and onto the toe of my boot. I shot the owner of the hazy IPA a look before he mumbled out an apology, then took off.

Realistically, I knew Kirby Falls survived on tourist dollars. But sometimes, I really just wanted to enjoy my town without dude bros crowding my favorite spots.

I eventually made it to Jordan's side of the table where, thank you, Jesus, a beer already awaited me. Before I greeted anyone, I sat down, snatched up the cold glass, and took a quick gulp, grumbling, "You'd think these people could let us have one place in town not overrun by their tourism bullshit."

"Will."

Chloe's sharp tone had my gaze snapping up. And that was when I noticed it wasn't Seth Rockford seated beside Chloe. Instead, I felt myself staring at long blond hair and a big-ass smile.

"You know Becca," Chloe said pointedly. Her blue eyes were sharp little daggers that told me to be nice *or else*.

Jordan sighed next to me.

For the life of me, I couldn't get my brain to understand why Becca, the *leafer*, was sitting at our Monday night trivia table. It was one thing to see her at the farm day in and day out. I'd come to expect her there. But this was something else.

"Hi, Will!" the interloper said, her small hand with pink-tipped nails rose in a short wave before she appeared to wedge it deliberately between the bench seat and her thigh.

I finished swallowing the beer in my mouth. "Hey," I managed, sounding a little choked.

"Seth couldn't make it tonight," Jordan offered. "We invited Becca here to join us."

"Right," I replied for no other reason beyond the awkwardness that had descended like a damn elevator.

Becca picked up her drink and took a sip. Her curious eyes moved around the outdoor space and all the people gathered.

Jordan said, "Becca's going to help us out with geography."

The geography expert in question frowned and then glanced at Chloe. "I . . . don't think . . . what?"

Chloe rolled her eyes at her boyfriend. "I didn't invite her because of your trivia player wish list, Jordan. Besides, with Becca's job, she'll be great at fielding the —" I sat up straighter, and Becca noticed.

She interrupted quickly, "I'm knowledgeable about lots of things."

Chloe shot her a confused look, but Becca just smiled before saying, "But geography isn't really one of them. Sorry, Jordan. And Will has been trying to figure out my job and how I can be a lazy tourist at Grandpappy's every day. He still hasn't guessed it."

Jordan laughed loudly while I gave Becca a flat stare. "Ohhhh. What's he guessed so far?" my friend asked.

"I never said you were a lazy tourist," I insisted, ignoring Jordan's question.

Her grin was practically incandescent beneath the warm glowing bulbs overhead. "You didn't have to," she teased.

I could tell she wasn't actually upset. Or maybe Becca never really *got* upset. But then I thought back to the sunflower field earlier today. She'd been distracted and unsteady. I'd seen her hands shaking where she clutched her phone. It hadn't been my place to ask, but whatever that conversation with her sister had been about hadn't been anything good. If it was enough to turn the perpetually cheerful Becca into a shadow—a ghost—of herself, it must have been pretty serious.

Seeing her so off-balance had been jarring. It was probably stupid to have left the clover for her to find, but I'd done it anyway. And seeing her now, back to her sunny self, I couldn't make myself regret it.

"He thinks I'm a kindergarten teacher," Becca finally answered Jordan without looking away from me.

"I could see that," Jordan agreed.

I pointed his way. "Thank you."

"Yeah, but you're both wrong," Chloe said matter-of-factly.

Becca's eyes sparkled. She looked pretty pleased with herself, and despite my initial annoyance with her presence here, I found myself smiling back. Maybe her answers would give her away tonight, and I'd be able to figure out what she did for a living. Not that it mattered. I didn't care.

But I *was* curious.

The intro music started up, and Becca's bright blue gaze found the main table and the emcee. She held her drink—a red ale, maybe—but it was still practically full. Her clothes were different. She usually wore practical things to the farm. Jeans and tee shirts, hoodies, sneakers. But tonight, she wore earrings and a gold necklace that rested across her collarbones in the open vee of her peach-colored button-down. Her hair wasn't up in a bun or ponytail like usual. It was long, a stream of loosely styled blond waves that came to nearly her elbow. And it looked like she was wearing makeup. Definitely lipstick or gloss or what—

Jordan elbowed me, drawing my attention away. I could feel my cheeks heating beneath my beard at having been caught staring.

My friend's dark eyebrows were raised. "You ready?"

I realized abruptly that they'd already introduced the participating teams, and the first question was coming up.

"Yeah," I mumbled, taking another bracing swig from my glass.

Thirty minutes in, and things were going . . . fine. I'd answered one geometry question and another about the winners of the 1938 World Series (the New York Yankees in a four-game sweep). Chloe and Becca had fielded the pop culture segment save for Jordan who had successfully completed the lyrics to a Taylor Swift song. Becca had offered up a friendly high five for that one.

We'd hit the mid-point break, so when Jared, the emcee, put on some music for the intermission, I stood and asked if anyone wanted anything from the bar.

Chloe stood too. "Why don't you and Becca bring back another round of drinks while Jordan and I place an order with Perry? We should have it before Mac and Brady go at it, and Jared calls it a night."

Becca looked confused, but Chloe just patted her shoulder and smiled, "Trivia Night always ends in bloodshed. You'll see."

We all exchanged orders. Then Becca and I took off for the bar. It was still pretty busy, so I placed a guiding hand gently on the small of her back, keeping a vigilant eye out for the asshole who'd spilled beer on my shoes.

Becca fielded calls from Mac and Larry's team. She waved back and promised to come by after trivia was over to talk. I didn't have the heart to tell her that my cousin MacKenzie would probably get hauled out of here by a bartender and would, therefore, be unable to chat.

When we made it under the awning and up to the bar, I removed my hand from Becca's lower back and tugged the bill of my hat down a little lower over my eyes. Going out usually meant at least one friendly neighbor would try to talk baseball with me. A handful of times during the busy season, I'd have strangers recognize me from my short-lived career on the field. If I could make it through tonight without either, I'd call it good.

The bartender was busy with other patrons, and it was loud with everyone talking and the music playing. Becca leaned toward me to say, "What do you recommend? I'm not a big beer drinker."

During trivia, I'd noticed her glass hadn't dropped below three-quarters. And every time she took a sip, her nose did this crinkling thing that was borderline adorable.

I tilted my head toward her ear to answer, doing my best not to bump her with my hat. "Try a cider from Firefly. They have the fall harvest one on draft"—I pointed at the numbered board listing all the beverages on tap—"or honeycrisp is a pretty safe bet."

She squinted to read the text, and I wondered if she needed her glasses. Becca sometimes wore round tortoiseshell frames when she worked on her laptop.

After a moment of looking, she leaned back into me, her lips going next to my ear to speak. I missed the first part because I could feel her breath ghost across my neck, warm and unexpected. But then I swallowed and caught back up. " . . . Jordan's place, right?"

Clearing my throat, I ignored the scent of honeysuckle drifting from her hair, working its way beneath my skin. I remained a safe distance away and spoke loud enough to be heard, answering, "Yeah, Jordan owns Firefly."

I was grateful when Benny noticed us waiting and motioned us up to the bar. "What can I get you, Will?"

I ordered another round for me and Chloe and Jordan and then indicated that Becca should let him know her choice.

She smiled at the bartender. "I'll have the fall seasonal from Firefly, Don't Fear the Reaper."

He grinned back, eyeing her for a little longer than was strictly necessary to take her drink order. "Nice choice."

"That'll do it." I cut in before he could get down on one knee. "Thanks, Benny."

He wandered off to start on our drinks, and before I could ask Becca why she'd ordered a beer the first time if she didn't like it, someone came up and clapped a hand on my shoulder.

Jesus. *Here we go.*

"Hello, William," said the elderly man attached to the hand.

I'd known Nelson Ammons since I was a kid. He was in his seventies now and retired from teaching high school biology. He wasn't usually one to stop me and reminisce about my athletic past, though. I couldn't actually recall any conversation we'd ever had about my failure of a career. He usually asked after my parents and grandparents if I happened to see him around town. But my shoulders still tensed just the same, bracing for a trip down baseball memory lane.

"Good evening, Mr. Ammons," I replied stiffly.

But then something different happened. Instead of awkward conversation that made me want to yank my own teeth out, Mr. Ammons moved by me using the wrinkled hand on my shoulder and came to stand beside Becca.

"Nelson! What a surprise seeing you here." She took his offered hand and shook it gently.

He smiled at her, warm and friendly. "How are you enjoying the Merlin Bird app?"

I stared in utter bafflement as the two people at my side had an entire conversation in English that I didn't understand at all. Something about birds and . . . that was all I got. They were both animated and excited, and I had no idea what to do. I'd been neatly—but not unkindly—excluded from the conversation. After a moment, I looked around to see if anyone had noticed. But Benny was placing the fourth glass in front of me, so I paid for the drinks instead.

Mr. Ammons wished Becca a good night and inexplicably said he'd see her on Thursday before shuffling off to his table of other elderly men and women.

Becca turned back to me, still wearing her smile for Mr. Ammons. When she caught sight of my expression—undoubtedly confused—she offered, "They let me join their bird-watching group at the park. Nelson is helping me be a junior ornithologist."

I blinked.

Why in the world would a tourist be joining the local bird-watching group? And why did my former high school teacher greet Becca like *she* was the long-lost student?

Now that I considered it, I thought Mr. Ammons's trivia team was on the board as *Me So Orni*.

I mean, I was grateful. I'd been anticipating one thing—a well-meaning but painful conversation about baseball—and had experienced something very different instead.

The music must have changed to the intro jingle for the next round of trivia, but I couldn't say I noticed. I was still staring at Becca in stunned bewilderment.

But she hurriedly grabbed two of the glasses and said, "We better get back before they start without us. And honestly, Jordan really needs the help."

I snorted a surprised laugh at that, and Becca grinned in response.

A moment later, I managed to get myself together and snatched up the two remaining beers, weaving through the tables and following Becca through the crowd. We made it just in time for Jared to announce the topic for the new round: Dolly Parton. A cheer rose from the locals.

Everything was going pretty well until the final trivia round twenty-five minutes later. And honestly, that was further than we usually got. It was almost nine o'clock.

We'd all eaten pulled pork sandwiches from the food truck and shared our sides between questions. An art history question for Becca. A British history guess from Jordan that ended up being correct. And an enthusiastic response from Chloe for a round on true crime. Becca had declared my coleslaw the best she'd ever eaten, so I'd nudged the container a little closer in her direction.

Jared announced *Cinema* for the final round, and half the teams present groaned in unison.

I heard my cousin MacKenzie say, "Come to momma. I've got this," loudly from two tables away.

And then from somewhere near the front, Brady Judd called, "What you've got is no chance whatsoever."

"Oh, Lord," Chloe muttered.

"It's eight fifty-six p.m. That has to be a new record," Jordan said brightly before finishing the rest of his beer.

Becca watched people start to gather their paper and pencils and pack up. "What's going on?"

But before anyone could reply, Mac yelled back, "Yeah, well, that's what I heard Caroline Jennings say when you asked her to prom senior year."

A chorus of *ohhhhs* sounded.

Chloe sighed and reached for her purse, finally explaining to Becca, "Brady and Mac get way too into Trivia Night. It always ends early because they start slinging insults."

"At least one of them—usually both—ends up getting kicked out," I added.

"But they typically shout from the parking lot and ruin the vibe for the rest of us," Jordan said. "So we all usually pack it in and head home."

Mac and Brady were both standing now. My cousin was yelling, as was her way, while Brady mostly smirked in her direction. It never failed to rile her up.

"Why do they hate each other?" Becca asked, obviously distressed but strangely compelled by the unfolding drama.

Chloe and Jordan and I all sort of glanced at one another before I admitted, "You know, I'm not really sure. They were a couple of years behind us in school, and I just assumed something happened back then. They've just never gotten along."

Jordan chuckled. "Remember that time Brady taped a strip of condoms to her back?"

"Oh, and when Mac drew a penis on his forehead when he passed out at Jolly Adams's divorce party." Chloe was cackling.

Becca looked horrified. "People have divorce parties?"

"Sometimes," Chloe said easily enough, "a divorce is a reason to celebrate."

Jordan reached over and squeezed her hand. Becca looked like she was about to apologize, but Chloe continued, unbothered, "Besides, Jolly was married to Buck Adams for thirty years. She deserved an all-expenses-paid cruise for putting up with that ornery asshole."

The commotion got louder, and we all looked over to see Benny trying to keep an irate Mac from charging over to Brady's table. With one arm locked around Mac's middle, he pointed at Brady, "You're out too. Come on."

Amid Brady's loud argument against his ejection, Mac's table and teammates continued drinking and chatting. Bonnie saw me looking and gave me a friendly wave, completely unbothered that her little sister was causing a public spectacle. It would undoubtedly be in the town's Facebook group within the hour.

Several tables had already cleared out, and I polished off the rest of my beer, content to get home to my dog.

Becca still looked a little bewildered. "I have so many questions."

"You get used to it," Chloe consoled.

Why would Becca need to get used to anything about Kirby Falls?

Before I could ask what she meant by that, Chloe said, "C'mon, Becca. I'll take you over to meet Bonnie. Larry said y'all were going to plan a lesson together."

Frowning, I met Becca's gaze. Bonnie was a teacher at Kirby Falls Elementary School.

"Still not a teacher," she said smugly, and I shook my head, fighting a laugh.

Chloe led Becca over to Bonnie's table, where she and her husband sat talking. Larry was there too with her best friend, Kayla. Everyone made room for the new arrivals as Becca got enveloped in the regular chaos of a Monday night in my hometown.

"Why is she here?" I asked when I could feel Jordan watching me.

"Seth is less reliable because he's a teenager. So Chloe invited her."

"I know, but why would you invite a leafer?"

Jordan looked confused by the question. "She and Chloe are friends. She's a nice girl."

I narrowed my eyes. Why was he being deliberately obtuse? "But she's on vacation. She's going to leave."

"So what? She's here now, and everyone likes her. Why do you care? And why are you staring at her so much?"

I gave him a withering glare and ignored the part I didn't want to think about. "It's a waste of time to include someone who's just going to turn around and leave. She's not a local."

My friend turned on the bench to face me more fully. He propped his elbow on the table and scrutinized me like he could see inside my damn brain cells. "You know it doesn't have to be an *us* and *them* sort of thing. It's not *West Side Story* or Jedis versus the Sith. Plenty of nice tourists come through town."

"Exactly," I argued. "She's just passing through."

Jordan deliberately widened his eyes. I could practically hear the *BIG FUCKING DEAL* he was mentally shouting at me. "And while she's here, she can come to Trivia Night."

And bird-watching, apparently. And Grandpappy's Farm four days a week. And brunch lady book club. And Kirby Falls Elementary School with my cousin Bonnie.

"And maybe softball," Jordan added quietly.

I groaned. "Come on."

"Just give her a chance. She's sweet."

That was not the argument. Becca *was* nice. Probably too nice.

I just didn't understand why she was suddenly in every aspect of my life. Lurking around corners and popping out when I least expected her. My mother was well-connected, but this went beyond her desire to set me up with a nice girl.

And I'd gone ahead and invited her hiking with me because I was an idiot and just as bad as everyone else. I didn't have a leg to stand on. I'd seen her wave at me like a pageant queen and thought she was fucking adorable. My dog loved her probably more than he loved me at this point.

And something about seeing her so completely off-balance among all those dead sunflowers she loved had given me a funny feeling in my chest. I'd wanted to cheer her up and make her happy again. So I'd asked about the places she'd visited. And she'd sounded so excited about the town that I thought I could show her a few more places she'd love—places only the locals knew about. Places I hadn't thought about in years. I was just as bad as Jordan and Chloe and old Mr. Ammons.

"Fine. Whatever." Annoyed with myself more than anyone else, I stood and started buttoning my flannel. The night air was getting cooler. Pretty soon, I'd need the jacket draped across the back seat of my truck. "I'm going home. I'll see you later."

Jordan sighed, but he got to his feet, too. "Listen, if you don't want her at Trivia Night, find someone who's good at geography, and we'll replace her."

I ignored my friend's smug, grinning face and walked to the parking lot, where Brady Judd stopped bickering with Mac long enough to tell me good night.

For the most part, the rest of my week was more of the same.

I was still putting out fires around the farm. Chipping in where I could and managing the day-to-day life at Grandpappy's during high tourist season.

But on Tuesday evening, I'd managed to get away for a few hours to help Seth and Jordan with offseason conditioning. Nothing more humbling than doing cardio with a bunch of teenagers. At least most of them were incapable of growing a beard as full as mine. It was a small consolation when I'd been huffing and puffing up the hill behind the high school as we finished up our five-mile run. Jordan offered to sneak away once everyone got on the road and circle back to pick me up in his car next week.

The twenty minutes of yoga following our run had been surprisingly nice. Several of the stretches helped my shoulder feel looser. I'd done physical therapy for a long time following my surgery, in the vain hopes I'd be able to return to the roster. So it had been years since I'd given up on any of the suggested exercises my very patient PT had encouraged me to do. It might not be a bad idea to incorporate some of these yoga moves into my daily workout routine. Couldn't hurt, I supposed.

On Wednesday, I heard about some vandalism over at Judd's Orchard. It was across the highway from Grandpappy's and catered to tourists much like we did. However, Judd's didn't pull out all the bells and whistles to tempt out-of-towners. They ran a pretty standard pick-your-own-apples operation with less variety than we planted and on a smaller acreage. No apple cannon or hayride. Just a playground for the kids, a small stand for refreshments, and a gift shop for merchandise. They weren't open year-round like our General Store and bakery. From what I'd heard through the grapevine, the vandalism sounded like some kids messing around on their property after closing.

I hoped that was the end of it. The last thing anyone needed was someone destroying their livelihood. And I didn't want one more thing to worry about. A smashed pumpkin patch or spray-painted buildings in the middle of September would be a headache I didn't have the time or energy for.

I'd spent an hour after closing on Wednesday pulling security footage from the main gate that caught anyone coming and going onto the highway entrance. Judd's Orchard was directly across the road, and the cameras stretched far enough that you could see their gate as well. I texted Brady about it and told him I'd drop off a copy of the footage to see if it was at all helpful for the police department.

It was Friday afternoon, and I'd just finished pulling together the produce that my dad would haul over to the Kirby Falls Farmers' Market tomorrow morning. I liked to help prep and load the truck so that everything was ready to go.

Carl and I were walking back toward my office behind the Bake Shop when I noticed Becca standing beside her table. Her glasses were back on, and she was wearing an orange flannel that looked brand new. She leaned from side to side and twisted, stretching her arms skyward. The soft-looking fabric of her shirt lifted, and I had a moment to admire the top of her button-fly jeans and a section of pale, smooth midriff. Then she placed her hands on her lower back and arched, grimacing, and I found the wherewithal to glance away.

The picnic benches weren't comfortable by any means. There was no back support to speak of, and the wooden seat was hard. Of course she needed to stand and stretch. She didn't need me to be an asshole about it.

With a pat on my leg, I called for Carl, and we took a detour out to my truck, where I grabbed a padded cushion I used when I went to high school football games.

When we made it back to the Bake Shop, Becca was, once again, in front of her laptop. Carl made a beeline for her, and after she greeted the temperamental beast, she scanned the space until she found me.

It was innocent and completely innocuous. Cause and effect. I knew she'd done it because Carl had run over, and she associated the two of us together. But there was something to be said for having someone look for you in a crowd—to seek you out with their eyes and smile when they found you. I refused to focus on the way it made me feel to have her grinning my way.

"Hi," Becca said when I reached her table.

"Hey. Can I sit?" I indicated the bench seat opposite.

"Of course," she offered and then smoothly slid her laptop closed.

Guess I wasn't getting a peek of whatever she was working on.

I placed the cushion on the table surface and slid it over to her side. "I brought you that. Thought it might be easier to sit on than hard wood."

"For me?" Becca reached for the thick stadium cushion and squeezed the edge.

"Yeah."

"Don't you need it?" She looked like she'd rather die than inconvenience me, a worried frown forming that little vee between her brows that was so rare to see.

"I have another one," I lied. Jordan had one I could borrow before the next home game.

Her finger was still tracing the dark edge of the cushion. "Thank you, Will. That's really nice of you."

It wasn't that big of a deal. She sat out here for hours. I was a little disappointed in myself for not considering it sooner. But then again, she was a visitor. I didn't usually make a habit of seeing to their individual needs here on the farm.

"It's no trouble," I finally replied.

Carl gave an annoyed woof at being ignored and hopped up on the seat next to her. Becca gave a delighted laugh and lavished the grumpy dog with attention and ear rubs.

I caught myself smiling and looked down. When I glanced back up, she was already watching me, so I blurted out, "Cheese is his favorite food." I didn't know why I was bringing this up. "You mentioned before that you didn't want to accidentally give him something he might be allergic to. Well, cheese is really the only people food he cares for, so you don't need to worry about that."

"That is good to know." She was pleased.

I tugged on the bill of my cap and eyed her closed laptop. "Busy day?"

Her grin was knowing. "Yep."

I squinted, considering, and then gave up and just flat-out asked, "Are you a librarian?"

She laughed. The sound was bright and happy like I'd just told a joke instead of tried to guess her career. But there was no mean edge, no amusement at my expense. The way she lit up made me want to laugh with her.

I waited instead.

"Sorry, no. Not a librarian." Her fingers still scratched absently over Carl's head, but it was me that had her attention. It wasn't a terrible feeling. "Did you guess that because it's the closest thing to a kindergarten teacher you could think of on the wholesome scale?"

Yes.

"No," I replied.

Her blue eyes sparkled, too pale to be sapphires but too dark to be topaz. They were the saturated middle blue gray of the mountains in the distance. The layered hills that drew spectators from all over the world.

"Maybe," I admitted finally.

Becca laughed again, pushing a strand of hair behind her ear. "Is it the glasses?"

Since she offered, I let myself look. As painful as it was to admit, I usually had to make a conscious effort not to stare at her too long. Becca was objectively pretty. The petite, slender body. The long blond hair. The bright eyes and warm, friendly expression. She was welcoming to the eye. And I thought, initially, I was trying to find the lie. I'd stared and scrutinized, looking for the fallacy in her genuine nature. I'd watched and waited, sure I'd see the real Becca lurking beneath the surface. It was hard to accept that there was a person in the world this guileless and open. But I was starting to believe it.

Now, my eyes roamed her features because I wanted to—because I liked it.

I shook my head. "Not the glasses."

Although the naughty librarian thing had its merits. Briefly, my caveman brain envisioned Becca in the role. Propped up on a desk, short skirt, cardigan sweater on, shirt dipping indecently low, and her nibbling on the tip of a pen between full red lips. But the image wouldn't stick. I couldn't see Becca playing that part, faking some sex kitten routine when she was perfect just how she was—sweet and lovely, real in a way that you didn't see very often.

"I guess you'll just have to keep guessing," she said, still amused.

"I guess I will."

But as I watched Carl lick her face to get her attention, and Becca laugh and indulge him, I wondered how many more guesses there'd be. She was leaving—probably when the season ended. Knowing her career wouldn't put me any closer to knowing *her*. And I'd have a brokenhearted dog on top of it.

I stood from the picnic table abruptly. "I better get back to it."

"Thanks again for the cushion."

"No problem."

I ignored Carl's dramatic sigh as he followed me back to the office. And I didn't take it personally when he spun around and faced the wall as he lay on the dog bed.

The following day after closing, I made my way over to Firefly to meet Jordan. He was filling in behind the bar, but we would still be able to catch the Braves game he'd have on the televisions there. Plus, the drinks would be free, so I was willing to risk Saturday night socializing. The majority of the people at Firefly this weekend would probably be tourists anyway.

When I arrived, I found Chloe and her friend Andie hanging out on barstools while Jordan stood nearby with a towel slung over his shoulder. Andie was another high school classmate who'd grown up, gotten married, had a few kids, and stayed in Kirby Falls. I slid onto the stool beside Chloe and ignored Jordan's dramatics at seeing me in public on a weekend.

"Well, look who graced us with his presence," Jordan called.

I rolled my eyes but said hi to Andie and Chloe. "You invited me, you dumbass."

"I know. But I'm never sure you'll really show up. What do you want to drink?"

"The blackberry one," I replied.

"You got it."

Jordan walked off toward the taps on the other side of the bar, and I called, "And can you turn the game on?"

He gave me a thumbs-up but didn't turn.

I glanced behind me and took in the busy setting. The interior of Firefly Cider was a lot like a big warehouse. The cidery, along with the canning, keg, and bottling operation were behind huge glass windows in the half of the building located behind the bar. The other side was devoted to the bar top and seating. High-top and low tables filled the space, and tonight, they were mostly full. There was an empty stage at the far end of the room, but I could hear a band performing outside in the covered area. The night was pretty mild, and I knew bonfires would be lighting up the perimeter of the huge lawn and even more patrons filling the outdoor seating area beneath low-strung twinkle lights.

Firefly was in a great location with mountain views in the distance, and I knew Jordan had plans to add an event barn for weddings and parties. He'd accomplished a lot in the past eight years, and in-house event planning was next on his list.

Grandpappy's supplied Firefly Cider with apples—the ugly ones that fell on the ground or weren't up to grocery store beauty standards. Jordan, in turn, had grocery and convenience store distribution to all the surrounding counties as well as local businesses and restaurants. I was happy for my friend. He'd worked hard and built everything here with his own blood, sweat, and tears. Jordan deserved his success.

And that success was apparent when the place was packed the way it was tonight.

In my scan of the interior, my eyes snagged on a moment of stillness coming from a small table in the corner. It was Becca. She was sitting alone at a two-top, alternating between glancing at her phone and keeping an eye on the front door. Her hair was down, and she wore a denim jacket over a red shirt. That was really all I could see with the table in the way.

I frowned and turned back to Chloe. "Why aren't y'all hanging out with Becca? I thought you were friends."

Chloe gave me a surprised look just as Jordan returned with my blackberry hard cider. "We are friends," she confirmed. "I introduced her to Andie when we went over and said hi earlier. But she has a date, so we didn't want to interrupt."

"What?" Sloshing the liquid over the rim of the glass, I cursed, then returned my attention to Chloe. "How does she have a date?"

Becca didn't even live here, and now she was dating.

"You see, William," Jordan began, "when two people like and want to get to know each other—"

I ignored him and tried again with Chloe, "Who is she waiting on?"

"Garrett. The UPS guy."

"That asshole?"

Andie was peeking around Chloe, a delighted look on her face. "He's nice!"

I gave her a flat, disapproving look and then glanced back at Becca. She looked tense and out of place. The first time I'd ever seen her anything but right at home, I realized. Even when she'd been dangling off a tree branch, twenty-five feet in the air, she hadn't looked nearly so uncomfortable. Even in the sunflower patch, when she'd been visibly upset by her phone call, she'd still somehow seemed like she was supposed to be there.

When I faced forward again, Chloe and Jordan were exchanging one of those annoying looks that mind-reading couples seemed to manage easily enough. Then I checked my watch. 8:34 p.m. "What time was he supposed to meet her?"

Another shared glance among my friends. "Eight," Chloe said and then winced.

I shook my head. "Told you he was an asshole."

Garrett, the delivery driver, was at the farm several times a week. He charmed my mother and my aunt and my cousins and flirted with anything that moved. But something about the way he approached women didn't read as genuine. Everything felt like a play he'd rehearsed a hundred times. The same lines over and over again.

I didn't like thinking that Becca had fallen victim to his ways because she was new in town and didn't know that Garrett was just a big flirt. She'd obviously taken him and his intentions seriously if she was waiting for him to show up for a date for over half an hour. She was just too nice.

I briefly considered that Becca was hoping to indulge in a vacation fling with the UPS guy and then discarded the thought immediately. Mostly 'cause I hated it.

"Maybe something came up," Andie argued.

"Maybe he had to work late," Chloe added.

Taking a swig of my cider, I replied to both of them, "Then he could have texted her."

"Maybe he realized his feelings were bigger than he thought and was too scared to confront the very real possibility that he might be interested in someone who isn't planning on staying." Jordan's words had everyone looking my way.

"Yeah, well, he still could have texted."

Jordan sighed deeply. "I'm going to go pour some drinks."

"We're heading out," Chloe said before leaning across the bar to kiss Jordan goodbye. "See you at home." They shared dopey grins, and then Chloe and Andie took off toward the exit.

I made it through a quarter of my cider and half an inning before I peeked back over my shoulder. Becca was talking to Lettie Louise Walker, who was standing beside her table. The older woman was showing Becca something in her purse. It looked like brightly colored yarn—maybe a hat. Becca was smiling and admiring Lettie Louise's knitting. Well, at least she wasn't staring at the front door looking like a kicked puppy anymore.

Another two outs and I looked back to see Becca, once again on her phone. The pint glass in front of her was empty. So, without examining my actions too closely, I flagged down a bartender—definitely not Jordan—and asked for two of the fall seasonals, remembering how much Becca had enjoyed it during Trivia Night earlier in the week.

Then I took both drinks and worked my way through the tables.

There wasn't a good reason for why I was doing this. I told myself she was a nice girl and didn't deserve to be sitting there waiting for some douchebag who wasn't going to show. That I couldn't just sit there at the bar, watching baseball knowing she was alone and miserable. My mother would have been very disappointed in me. That was going to be the official reason for me approaching Becca at her table.

But the real one was a little more complicated. I . . . liked her. She was easy to be around. She smiled often and made you want to smile with her.

Plus, my dog liked her. What better judge of character did you need?

Part of me liked how untethered she was to Kirby Falls's history and gossip. Becca didn't care that I was once a heartbeat and an MRI away from a career in the major leagues. She never asked me about baseball or anything too personal. It was refreshing to have someone respect your boundaries, especially in Kirby Falls, where people tended to plow right through them with a John Deere tractor.

Granted, Becca probably didn't know enough about my past to ask the sorts of questions that my neighbors couldn't seem to resist. I wasn't bracing for a blow or a well-meaning jab. With Becca, everything was easy because she didn't know any different. And sometimes ignorance really was bliss.

"Hey. Mind if I sit?" I asked when I reached her table.

Pretty blue eyes snapped up from her phone. "Will! Hey! Yeah, of course. Have a seat."

"I grabbed you another."

"That was thoughtful. Thank you." She cleared her throat a little awkwardly and shot one more tense look toward the front door. "So, what are you up to tonight? Just out for a drink?"

I successfully resisted the urge to nod and indicated the bar behind me. "Jordan invited me down to catch the game."

She squinted a little over my shoulder, and I briefly thought of her tortoiseshell glasses and our librarian conversation from yesterday. "Oh, baseball. I've never been a big fan. I'm more of a hockey girl."

That had me grinning. "Red Wings?"

Becca brightened. "Yeah."

"I like hockey, too. The Hurricanes are my team, though."

She nodded. "That makes sense, being from North Carolina."

"Jordan and I used to catch games when we were in college at UNC. Short drive."

"That's fun. What did you study?" Becca took a sip of her drink, and I noticed she hadn't glanced toward the front door again. I wasn't about to bring up her date. Hopefully, she'd already given up on the guy. Becca seemed like a smart girl. I couldn't imagine she'd actually fallen for Garrett's ladies' man shtick.

"Accounting."

But before I could ask her where she went to college or what she studied, a person silently approached our table. The lurking figure was too short to be Garrett, but I was still surprised when I looked over to see a kid no older than thirteen or fourteen in baggy jeans and a black tee shirt waiting at Becca's side.

She finally looked away from me and gasped. "Hi, Teddy! Gosh, you surprised me." But her smile was all genuine delight. "Are you here with your parents?"

"Yep," the kid replied. "I just wanted to come say hi."

"How'd your algebra test go yesterday?"

I watched in befuddled amusement as the boy gazed at Becca, paying me absolutely no mind.

"Pretty good. You'll be at the library on Thursday again, right?"

She grinned. "I wouldn't miss it." Her eyes slid to me before she focused back on Teddy. "We can work on that thing I showed you at the end of class last week."

"Cool," he said. "See you, Becca."

She murmured her goodbye and watched the teen return to his table, where his parents waved in her direction.

I propped my chin on my hand and waited for the imminent apology.

"Sorry," she flushed.

"It's fine. What was that all about?"

"Oh." She fidgeted with the third button down on her jean jacket. Her eyes were just about the same color as the denim under her pale hands. "Well, when I first got to town, I went over to the Kirby Falls Library just to look around a little. But Mrs. Crandall was so nice and gave me a library card even though I'm not a resident. We started talking about some of the youth programs, and I volunteered to lead a class for teens once a week."

I'd known Mrs. Crandall since I was five. She'd been the head librarian since the beginning of time. I was sure she enjoyed having someone as enthusiastic and friendly to help with the youth, even if it was temporary. Poor Teddy was going to be disappointed when Becca up and left.

"So are all the attendees teenage boys?"

Becca paused to consider. "Well, now that you mention it . . . yeah. They are."

I fought a grin and smoothed a hand along my beard before reaching for my glass.

"What?" She laughed a little. "What is it?"

"Did you really not see the way that kid was mooning over you? Cow eyes the size of dinner plates?"

Becca looked surprised and amused. "I really don't think so." Her cheeks were pink, and her gaze strayed to her phone on the tabletop as if remembering how she'd ended up here tonight in the first place.

But I didn't want her thinking about getting stood up, and I really didn't want her thinking of Garrett, the UPS driver, when she was sitting here with me. So I asked, "I don't suppose you'd tell me about this class you're teaching to the impressionable Kirby Falls youth?"

Her eyes glittered mischievously. "Nah. That might give it away. Any guesses tonight?"

"Romance novelist," I said evenly.

Becca laughed loudly, but I didn't take offense. In fact, I was smiling too.

We spent the next hour and a half nursing our drinks and talking about the town, our favorite dishes at all the restaurants she'd tried, and all the festivals and events Kirby Falls had to offer.

Becca easily fielded two more interruptions from locals. One from Laiken Scruggs, who supplied Becca with a dozen farm fresh eggs every week and also let her come say hi to the chickens on her farm. And another from Esther Kent who used to be my Sunday school teacher but was apparently on Becca's bowling team down at the Lucky Strike Lanes.

Both women paid me no mind. I got a polite "hello, Will" from their general direction before they eagerly sought Becca's conversation. My companion, for her part, was kind and warm. But she apologized each time we were interrupted. Yet she didn't seem to mind the attention. Instead, she blossomed under their recognition. I could see it in the happiness stealing across her features and the genuine way she conversed with each person, bringing up something about them that she remembered—Esther's granddaughter or Laiken's routine or even Teddy's algebra test.

Becca was making connections here, and while I didn't understand it, I could see she was sincere. This wasn't some game she was using to pass the time. She actually enjoyed getting to know the residents of Kirby Falls.

For every time I tugged down my hat in anticipation of being accosted by a well-meaning neighbor, Becca welcomed hugs and smiles and chitchat from those seeking her out.

I was destined to be surrounded by friendly, extroverted people. It was worse than going somewhere with Jordan.

Becca was a star, and her orbit pulled everyone in. And while they focused on her, they ignored the hell out of me, which was kind of nice.

And maybe I was just like everyone else in town. I couldn't help but admit I liked her too. Her sweetness and bright personality drew people to her, myself included. I was self-aware enough to admit being curious about her. Whatever game we were playing regarding her career and presence in Kirby Falls wasn't keeping me up at night, but it was close. I thought about Becca more than I cared to admit in the light of day.

There were all the things I'd learned or overheard. Her childhood devoid of four-leaf clovers and climbing trees. I wondered over that phone call in the sunflower maze. The one that made her so upset my mother was worried enough to radio me to go check on her. I would have chalked it up to my nosy momma looking to set us up, but I'd seen the tremor in Becca's hand and the cornered, wounded look on her face.

When I was being honest with myself, I thought about her dazzling eyes, the shape of her body against me following the tree incident, how she always seemed so damn happy to see me, and the way she treated my dog.

I never expected to wonder about a tourist on the farm. And I sure never expected to be sitting here having a drink with her very publicly on a Saturday night. But here I was, having a good time, anticipating her smiles, and learning the different ways she laughed.

And it wasn't until the following morning that I even thought to check the score on the Braves game that I'd missed while I'd been enjoying her company.

seven

WILL

Grandpappy's Farm typically closed early on Sundays. I didn't always get out of there when I was supposed to, but sometimes the stars aligned and tourists got the hell out without needing to be herded to the exit or recovered from the corn maze.

Today was one such occasion. So I was headed out to Legacy Hills to see my grandpa William.

When I entered the long-term-care wing, one of the nurses—Tanisha—flagged me down. "Hi, Mr. Clark. We finished dinner early tonight so the residents could listen to a little music from one of our volunteers. Mr. William is in the large group meeting room at the end of the hall."

"Oh," I said. "Thank you." That wasn't typical. Usually, my grandfather was already in his room, and I spent the evening reading to him before bed. But now that I considered it, I could hear someone playing the piano. The melody drifted down the corridor, and I let my feet guide me across the wooden floors in that direction.

Upon reaching the doorway, my gaze searched the room, wondering how Grandpa William might react to the music. With his late-stage dementia, he could sometimes be combative or resistant to new situations. It was difficult to see him that way, and I didn't want an upset in his schedule to make him angry.

But then I remembered the piano in the formal living room, out of tune under my wayward ownership, and the photo of the great-grandmother I'd never met, playing for a much younger, healthier William.

My eyes found him first. Grandpa wasn't among the other residents in the periphery. He wasn't in a wheelchair near the piano. And he wasn't one of the few elderly people swaying with nurses and assistants in the center of the room on what looked to be an impromptu dance floor.

Grandpa sat on the piano bench, in profile from my position. His focus was on the keys, and his hands were resting placidly atop his thighs, but the little finger on his left hand tapped in time to the beat. I was so surprised that I just stood there staring.

It wasn't until the song ended and a new one started that my gaze landed on the person beside my great-grandfather. The person making the music. The woman smiling and mouthing words or notes along with her not entirely fluid playing.

Long blond hair in a thick braid rested over one shoulder, and elegant fingers pressed the black and white keys. I sighed out a slow breath at the realization.

Becca Kernsy just kept right on surprising me.

Every few moments, she'd raise her head to scan the room, grinning and making eye contact with the men and women listening to her play. Her energy was upbeat and positive, and when she missed a key, she leaned her shoulder gently against my grandfather's and said "whoopsie" in an exaggerated whisper. But no one minded. It was clear from the faces of most of the residents that they enjoyed Becca's playing. The music made them happy and so did the smiling woman who chose to spend her evening with them.

I was reluctant to interrupt. My great-grandfather was content, and my presence wouldn't improve anything. It had been at least six months since he'd recognized me during one of my visits. He rarely spoke anymore, and he needed help from the staff of Legacy Hills for even the most basic care. Rationally, I knew—as did the rest of my family—that Grandpa William didn't have much time left on this earth. If he was comfortable here and now, I wasn't about to disturb him.

Eventually, a male staff member who had been swaying gently on the dance floor with Mrs. Charles got Becca's attention and held up a hand showing five fingers. Becca nodded and transitioned into the next song.

I recognized the opening chords of "Imagine" by John Lennon.

She seemed to know this song pretty well because she didn't need to focus on the keys as much. On one of her scans of the room, she caught me loitering in the doorway. Happiness lit her features from the inside out. I felt like I'd won a prize to be able to put that kind of smile on her face.

Briefly, I wondered if she was remembering last night at Firefly. Because suddenly, that was all I could think about. The easy conversation, her teasing grin, and the parade of Kirby Falls residents who'd fallen under her spell.

Becca tilted her head and motioned me toward the old upright piano facing the large room. Reluctant to get in the way, I slowly inched forward as she played the song's final notes.

When I reached her side, Becca beamed up at me. "Will! What a surprise to see you here."

"You too," I replied quietly. And then I focused on the man still seated calmly beside her. "Good evening, Grandpa."

Becca's eyes widened, her mouth dropping into an "o." I could see her mind turning over as she looked between us. The gray eyes we shared and his salt-and-pepper hair that had once been the exact shade of near-black as mine. My great-grandfather had thinned and stooped with age, but at one time he'd been a larger-than-life presence.

Becca's look was pleading, an apology waited its turn right there on the tip of her tongue. But she had nothing to be sorry about. Circumstances were what they were. I appreciated that she was here visiting the patients in long-term care. I knew several of the residents didn't get many visitors.

Before she could offer any sort of consolation, the male nurse hurried over. "Okay, thanks, Becca. I'll take over now." And then his sly glance cut to me. "Why don't you take her for a spin on the dance floor? They'd get a kick out of the two of you. And she gets mobbed as soon as she's done playing anyway. You'd be doing me a favor for crowd control."

He . . . wanted me to dance . . . with Becca in the meeting room at Legacy Hills for the dozen residents gathered?

"Oh, no," Becca was saying before the man had even finished speaking. "Will doesn't need to do that."

Well, it wasn't what I'd anticipated when I'd walked in here tonight, but it seemed like an easy crowd. And the idea of having Becca in my arms for a few minutes wasn't a terrible one. Plus, I would still have a chance to visit with Grandpa William once the music and dance portion of the evening was over.

So I leaned down to my grandfather and said, "I'll see you in a few minutes, Grandpa."

And then I held my hand out to Becca, who looked horrified.

"I'm not that bad," I teased. "I *can* dance."

Maggie Clark and two years of middle school cotillion had made sure of that.

"I don't want to force you into doing this. I don't think—"

But the male staff member was already nudging her off the bench and launching dramatically into a modern song that I vaguely recognized.

Becca stood, and I wiggled my fingers in her direction. "You gonna leave me hanging?"

Immediately, she slipped her hand into mine. "Of course not."

She was tentative, but her soft hands were firm in my grip. Our eyes met as she stood, and I wasn't romantic enough to say a spark lit between us, but it was *something*. Less of a firework, more of an ember.

I led her around the piano and onto the open floor, not missing the smiles on several residents' faces. I recognized Mrs. Atherton, one of my grandmother's friends. They'd been close before an Alzheimer's diagnosis several years ago. I knew my grandma Nola visited when she and my grandfather were in town during the spring and summer. If swaying offbeat with Kirby Falls's new favorite visitor was enough to make her smile like that, then it was alright with me.

With a bit of space between us, I put my hands on Becca's waist as she dutifully placed hers on my shoulders. She was as stiff as a board, and I felt like I was at a middle school dance.

"I'm sorry you got coerced," she whispered, avoiding my gaze.

"Hey. Stop that," I said quietly. "You have nothing to apologize for. And this isn't as much of a hardship as you seem to think it is."

She glanced at me quickly and then away, shy and uncomfortable, but I caught how the corner of her mouth lifted.

"How often do you volunteer here?" I asked conversationally. It was one more extracurricular activity for Becca's extensive Kirby Falls résumé. I still couldn't figure out her motivation. Why invest your time and energy with people who weren't yours?

"Oh, just about once a week. So I've been out here four or five times. Not always playing the piano. That's pretty new. Usually, I just visit with the residents. Talk and read. Look at pictures of their family. Stuff like that."

An image of the mysterious blue-and-white book of poetry from my grandpa's room flashed in my mind.

My eyes narrowed. "You've been reading to him? My great-grandfather."

Becca's cheeks were already pink from the forced dancing, but the heat in her face deepened to a rosy glow with my question. "I didn't realize who he was to you. The nurses just call him Mr. William. I didn't put two and two together until you called him Grandpa. I can stop if you like. I didn't mean to overstep."

"You didn't," I interrupted. "I'm grateful. I try to visit when I can. And so does my family, but he seems comfortable around you. I—thank you, Becca."

"He likes the music, I think," she said, ignoring my praise.

"His wife used to play for him," I admitted.

Becca was looser in my arms and less tense now that we were talking and dancing at the same time. It had been the same last night at Firefly. Once she warmed up with some conversation, she was more relaxed.

"I saw the picture in his room," she confessed. "It's where I got the idea. I asked the staff if I could play a little, and they were enthusiastic and supportive."

Her hands moved around to the nape of my neck as she spoke so that we were a bit closer; only a few inches separated our bodies. But we could talk quietly like this while we swayed slowly to the piano playing behind us.

She met my eyes and asked gently, "How long has your grandpa been here?"

"Six years. He got an early-stage dementia diagnosis a few years before that. He wandered away once while he was at the farm. Mac was a teenager and found him out in a field while she was driving the tractor for the hayride. When he started leaving the stove on and having difficulty remembering things, he moved himself in here. Grandpa William is a prideful man, but he was also very insistent that he not be a burden on anyone else."

Becca's hands were cool as they clung gently behind my neck, and I fought my instinct to lean into her touch. "And your great-grandmother?"

"She passed away before I was born."

"I'm sorry," Becca said, her blue eyes full of emotion. "Loss is never fair. Whether you had them your whole life or barely at all."

I nodded because that was true. And from the look of it, Becca had firsthand experience with grief.

The man at the piano moved into an upbeat Bruno Mars song, but I was not about to change the rhythm of our movements. So I inched a little closer to be heard better and caught a hint of Becca's sweet honeysuckle scent and had to keep myself from leaning closer still.

I cleared my throat and changed the subject. "It's nice that you play for them."

She smiled. "I'm not very good. Mrs. Walters tried. Oh, she tried so hard to make piano a strength of mine, but the lessons didn't really take. Especially as I got older."

"Was that your music teacher?" I asked as I turned us slowly to face the opposite side of the room.

Becca's steps faltered, and I gripped her tight to me to correct the misstep.

"Sorry," she breathed. But when she straightened, she didn't move away, and I didn't take a step back. Our sway continued, just in closer proximity. Becca was tucked up against me, her chest brushing my upper abdomen and my chin beside her ear. I couldn't see her face, but it felt nice to have her in my arms. And something about her reaction to my question told me she needed the support.

"Um, no. Mrs. Walters wasn't my music teacher. She—she was like a grandmother to me."

I moved my hands from her waist to her back in an approximation of a hug, even as we moved. It felt like the right thing to do.

Becca sighed and then admitted, "She actually raised me."

I opened my mouth to ask . . . something. Was she a neighbor? Where were your parents? Did they pass away? Is Mrs. Walters your foster mother? But all those questions seemed too forward and me too curious. Becca was none of my business.

I heard her swallow roughly a couple of times, so I didn't push. Eventually, she offered, "My parents aren't dead. If that's what you were wondering. They were in and out of jail a lot. Still are, actually. And Mrs. Walters wasn't my official guardian or anything. She worked out an arrangement with my parents when I was little. They'd tried to con her and got caught. She didn't press charges or have them arrested, and in exchange, they had to send me to her a few days a week."

Becca let out a humorless huff of laughter. "They didn't even care. My dad still says that's the best scam he ever pulled off."

My chest ached at her bitter admission. I'd never heard Becca be anything but happy or sweetly self-deprecating. She complimented any and everyone and spread joy like wildfire. To hear the bitter edge creep into her voice was a stark contrast to the Becca I'd come to know.

And at that moment, I hated these careless parents she spoke of. People who didn't appreciate her or protect her—people I didn't even know.

The tightness that accompanied the realization didn't loosen, so I asked instead, "And she was good to you? Mrs. Walters." What kind of parents sent their kid off with a stranger? Someone who could have done damn near anything to their child.

I felt Becca nod, her hair grazing my jaw. "Yes. She was amazing. She took this foul-mouthed six-year-old girl who was basically feral and didn't know any better and gave her a home. A retired elementary school principal who'd already raised one son to adulthood. She helped me with my reading, got me back on track in my studies, and kept me there until graduation. She gave me a safe environment where I was fed and cared for and guided on the path to right and wrong. Those things weren't important to my family. Mrs. Walters had this gruff, no-nonsense way about her, but she loved me. She saved me." Her voice was shaking by the end of her speech.

My hand on her upper back moved counterclockwise in what I hoped were soothing circles while my other hand on the small of her back kept her close, tethered to me. I didn't have a lot of experience taking care of people. Providing comfort wasn't really one of my strengths. But right now, I wanted to give Becca a sense of security—a crutch, if she needed it.

"Your sister? Did Mrs. Walters raise her too?"

Becca sighed deeply, the movement bringing our bodies that much closer. Heat and desire and the need to protect this woman from a past that had already formed her made the disquiet in my chest constrict tighter.

"No," she finally said. "And that's a big part of why Heather and I aren't close."

My hand on her back paused. I considered the call Becca had taken at the farm. The one that had made her so upset she'd retreated to the sunflower field to find solace. I wouldn't forget the vulnerable look in her eyes or the way she'd clutched her phone in desperate hands.

After a moment, Becca answered my unspoken questions. "She calls, but it's never for anything good. She usually needs money for her habits or for my parents."

God. What this woman had been through. Yet you'd never know it. If I'd been pressed to hazard a guess, I would have said that Becca had been raised in a loving two-parent household with two point five kids, a dog, and a scholarship to an Ivy League college after she'd graduated at the top of her high school class while also being the homecoming queen and head cheerleader.

I'd been an ass to make assumptions based on her cheerful demeanor and perky attitude. She was all those things *despite* her life growing up. Becca wasn't some one-dimensional tourist I could judge from afar, telling myself I knew everything I needed to know about her.

Not anymore at least.

Maybe I wanted to regret dancing with her—holding her in my arms and offering her comfort the only way I knew how. It was sure as hell easier to think I *didn't* know her. That Becca was just some stranger I was crossing paths with for a few months out of my life.

But none of that was true. I *did* know her. I'd danced with her and held her. Shared a drink with her and gotten to know her . . . the big things like Mrs. Walters and her history, and the small things—that she wore pajamas with avocados on them and loved the hell out of my spoiled dog.

After tonight, I feared that Becca Kernsy would become even more present in my mind. She was real. No longer a leafer. Not an outsider. She was someone who loved and appreciated my hometown, probably more than I did.

I didn't know why I'd resented her so much initially—showing up in every corner of Kirby Falls and weaseling her way into my life and my friends' lives.

No, that wasn't true. I did know why. She'd made me uncomfortable. But I didn't want to consider all the whys. I probably wouldn't like the answers.

Tonight had changed something in me, and I wasn't sure what to do about it.

It was unbearable to look at her but nearly impossible to look away.

Becca

Why did I tell him that?

Why did I tell Will *any* of that?

We'd been having a nice time. There was the surprise dancing that Will had just rolled with. And I had been relatively normal up until that point despite accidentally trying to hijack Will's great-grandfather away from him.

I closed my eyes in mortified frustration as the music drifted around us, and Will kept up the comforting back-rubbing thing he had going on. He probably thought I was in need of calming touches, what with the childhood trauma I'd just spewed like Old Faithful.

My past wasn't a secret. Not really. Pippa and Cece knew, but I hadn't really broached the subject of my life back in Detroit with any of my new Kirby Falls friends—not even Chloe or Laramie. They knew surface things like how I killed houseplants by accident and wanted a pet but felt too guilty to keep a dog cooped up in Mrs. Walters's cozy apartment.

Mostly, I hadn't mentioned my family or my past because when was the right time to do that? There was no graceful segue into "Hi, my parents were all too happy to abandon me to a stranger. Also, they're lowlife degenerates who get picked up for possession occasionally and don't give a crap about me. Oh, and my sister resents me and uses me for money."

Then there was my fear that the truth would change how people looked at me. It had happened before when I'd worked in an office and with some of the people I met doing volunteer work. Knowing how I'd been raised made others feel sorry for me or borderline distrustful—like misdemeanors ran in the family.

Rationally, I knew that everyone had something. No pasts were perfect, and no families in real life resembled the ones portrayed by sitcom actors. I *knew* this, but it never seemed to ward off the feelings of shame and embarrassment when I considered my own messed-up situation. Not to mention how discouraged I felt that Will seemed to be constantly exposed to the worst parts of me. The incapable pieces. The less-than bits that never measured up.

Finally, I got the nerve to open my eyes, but I kept my gaze trained on Will's strong shoulder clad in navy-blue waffle print. This close, he smelled good—sweet and smoky. I wondered if he'd mind if I just face-planted right into his firm chest and stayed there until they invented a time machine so I could go back a half hour and never overshare my life story.

"I'm sorry," I said quietly to the dark blue fabric. "That was way more of an explanation than you were probably looking for. Can we rewind and just pretend I said, 'Yes. Mrs. Walters was my piano teacher'? Because that is technically true. She was my teacher for a lot of things. Piano was just one of them, and honestly, it stuck the least."

I felt Will's cheek press against my hair, and my heart tripped over itself. I could imagine how we looked from the outside. Two people, barely moving on a makeshift dance floor, curved around one another. It was intimate and intoxicating. It was also not a very accurate representation. Will was comforting me because he felt sorry for me. And I was accepting it because I was a weak, weak woman.

Due to our proximity, I could feel his jaw working. Eventually, he said, voice as soft as I'd ever heard it, "I'm sorry you had to go through that with your family."

It was almost funny because there were so many things I hadn't told him. The things only my therapist knew. How my parents had ruined my credit score by the time I could walk. How, as an adult, my sister had shown up at two different jobs and made a scene and gotten me fired. One was a marketing firm I'd really liked working for, and the other was a part-time volunteer position at a food bank in Detroit. It was why I worked remotely now, for myself, so they couldn't ruin that too.

I didn't curse or use bad language because it had taken Mrs. Walters years to break me of the habit. My parents sounded like sailors, and they never cared that my sister or I were young and impressionable and in the room to hear it. I knew I was ridiculous with all the *golly-gosh*es and *goodness graciouses*. But I couldn't go back to how it was before. I didn't want to be tied to them in such a way. A family resemblance was never anything I ever wanted.

Of course there was a time and place in conversation for a well-deserved *fuck*, but I'd rather sound like the preschool teacher Will thought I was than sound anything like my mother and father.

But telling Will all of that would only make his voice go even softer with pity. He'd treat me like a wounded bird and put me back in the nest and hope we never crossed paths again because someone like me was a lot to handle. I had issues and hang-ups and baggage. And Will had the dream family.

Opposites didn't always attract. Sometimes they steered clear to avoid a head-on collision.

"And," he continued, unaware of my inner meltdown, "I'm sorry for your loss."

That had all my frantic thoughts slowing to a grinding stop.

Pulling back to see his face, I tried to remember if I'd explicitly mentioned Mrs. Walters's passing. "How did you know?"

Will looked thoughtful as his eyes moved across my features. "You talk about her like a treasure. Like something missing from your life."

I took in his words, so simple yet so profound. We were just swaying in the middle of the floor, a piano solo of "Someone Like You" playing in the background, staring at one another.

My nose stung, so I knew I was in danger of crying. "Thanks. It's been three years. Mrs. Walters was sick for a while, and I took care of her. There are a lot of bad memories trying to crowd out the good ones." I felt a tear escape as I blinked, but Will reached up and wiped it away with his thumb as I spoke. The tender, casual touch had me aching to reach for his hand, to cover it with my own.

"She left me her apartment in the city, and as disloyal as it is to admit, I just had to get away. I couldn't be there. Couldn't bear it. So I came here. And at the same time, it's why I sought out Legacy Hills. I like visiting with the people here. It reminds me of her."

"I'm glad you're here," Will said quickly as if he was ripping off a Band-Aid.

Despite the heaviness of the conversation, that made me smile. "Me too."

Behind us, the piano playing ended. It took us eight whole seconds to stop swaying. And then another four to untangle and step apart.

Maybe I had been weak to accept Will's comfort. But sometimes it was easier to lean for a while than to pick yourself up off the floor later.

I glanced around us to see only a few residents remaining as the staff escorted folks back to their rooms. Will's grandpa was no longer on the piano bench.

Clearing his throat, Will said, "I'm going to go say good night to my grandfather. I'll come back and walk you out."

I nodded. It felt safer not to speak. Between last night at Firefly and whatever had happened on the dance floor just now, I didn't want to break the tenuous peace we had in place between the local and the leafer.

While Will went off toward the hall housing private rooms, I visited with each of the patients waiting for their turn to be helped out by the nurses and staff. I told them how nice it was to see them and wished them all a good rest, promising to return and play for them again soon.

I was gathering my bag and sheet music when Will appeared at my side. He casually took the tote from my hand and fell into step beside me. We made our way past the nurses' station and through the security doors out into the main lobby.

When we hit the pathway in front of the building, I paused and inhaled the night. Cool air filled my lungs, and I wondered how I'd ever gone twenty-nine years without taking a full breath. Everything in Kirby Falls felt bigger and brighter and just . . . more.

I glanced at Will, who was watching me with an amused expression. He was hat-free tonight, so I could see the subtle softening around his gray eyes and the relaxed line of his lush mouth.

To keep from noticing anything else about his handsome face and blushing like a preteen, I asked rather abruptly, "Have you ever thought about bringing Carl here to visit the residents?"

Will hummed. "Not sure Carl has the right personality to entertain the masses. Too bossy and opinionated. Too much attitude."

I squinted thoughtfully and then stepped off the sidewalk. Will followed.

"I don't know," I mused. "You do alright."

Will huffed a surprised laugh from beside me. I liked how rough and unused it sounded. And the fact that I'd drawn it out of him. "Are you comparing me to my dog?"

"Noooooo. I would never. I'm comparing your dog to you."

I wasn't quite sure where this confident woman had emerged from—the one sassy enough to tease the perpetually serious-faced Will Clark. But I had to admit, getting a grin out of him sure felt nice.

The smile still lingered on Will's face by the time we reached my SUV, parked in the back row of the lot. He opened the driver's side door and passed me the tote bag, waiting for me to climb in.

I stood in the space between, fiddling anxiously with the end of my braid, and said, "I'm glad I ran into you tonight. Thank you for the dance."

Will's face wasn't exactly relaxed, but it was thoughtful. "Anytime."

For the first time, he was looking at me like he really saw me. Not this person he had to handle. Not a situation or an inconvenience. Not one more thing occupying his time on a never-ending to-do list. And not like a tourist on the farm.

The hopeless crush I'd been trying desperately to ignore made my heart beat a little faster.

Will was looking at me like I was *someone*. Whether it was from repeated exposure or all the personal information I'd shared tonight, I couldn't say. But he watched me like he might want to know more.

BECCA

I checked the sign on the table just to make sure I wasn't in the wrong spot. But there it was. *Becca's Table, Reserved Indefinitely,* printed on white cardstock and folded so it stood propped in the middle of the picnic table in front of the Bake Shop. It had been there for over a month now.

Everything else was familiar. I could hear Maggie humming and the espresso machine whirring through the open half door. Tourists were milling about, several seated nearby beneath the covered porch enjoying delicious treats and hot cider on this chilly fall morning.

But what I couldn't make sense of was the navy-blue rolling desk chair pushed up to the end of my table or the sweet dog waiting for me underneath it.

With my laptop bag and Will's stadium cushion in hand, I stood staring for a few more moments until Maggie placed a mug down on the tabletop and startled me out of my stupor. "Honey, that's for you."

"What?" I turned to her in confusion. "Why?"

She settled a small white plate with the pumpkin bread I'd ordered on the wooden surface. "Will brought it out from his office. It's on the back side of the Bake Shop."

I glanced up as if I could somehow see through the wall to where she'd indicated. "But why would he do that? Give me his chair?"

She gave me another one of those bless-your-heart smiles. "Was probably tired of watching you sit on this uncomfortable bench all day. And he hardly uses it anyhow. Always on the go, that Will."

Maggie patted me on the shoulder before wandering back inside the Bake Shop. I still stood staring as my mind sputtered uselessly.

Why would Will give me his desk chair?

Yes, of course, the picnic table got uncomfortable after sitting for a while. That's why I stood and stretched and took breaks and went for walks all over the farm. It was why I went to sunrise yoga with the ladies at the senior center a few days per week. But how did Will Clark know my back was bothering me? And why in the world would he give up his own chair to try to make me more comfortable? I wasn't even sure Will liked me most of the time. I sort of thought I was too much for him—a complicated and troublesome woman who smiled too much.

Plus, on the farm, I was a tourist. And I knew how he felt about them.

I thought back to the stadium seat cushion he'd brought over on Friday. And the way he'd sat down with me at Firefly two nights ago.

I knew Will didn't get a lot of downtime. And he'd spent his evening with me instead of at the bar with Jordan and the baseball game he'd planned on watching. Several times I'd opened my mouth to say . . . something. To let him off the hook and to get back to his night. To free him from my presence. But in the end, I hadn't. I'd had fun instead.

In fact, two minutes after Will had joined me, I'd forgotten all about getting stood up. I'd already regretted agreeing to the date with Garrett before I'd even arrived at Firefly. Flirty, charming men were not my type. And something about Garrett's attention was off-putting. Like he only saw me because I was new and interesting. I thought it might be nice to be seen for who I was.

Then there was the dance and conversation with Will at the assisted living facility last night. I hadn't let myself think about it too much. It made me wish for something that I had no business hoping for. More dances. More conversation. A warm, calloused hand on my waist and a deep, gentle voice in my ear.

Someone to know me—all the ugly, inconvenient parts—and to want me anyway.

I didn't need this crush to get out of control. But a part of me knew the effort was in vain. Kirby Falls already had a piece of my heart. Would Will Clark end up with the rest?

Eventually, Carl stood and stretched, coming over to nose at my hand. "Why did he do this, huh, Carl?"

The dog didn't answer. So, I dropped my things on the table and moved behind the chair. Swiveling it in the direction of the path, I started pushing, intent on returning it, when Maggie called from behind me, "Might as well keep it. He's filling in for Otis on the tractor this morning. He'll be on hayride duty until lunchtime." And then her head disappeared back inside the half door but not before I caught the edge of her satisfied expression.

Sighing, I returned the rolling chair to the end of the table and sat. Carl dropped his head in my lap. With guilt and confusion swirling, I drank my cinnamon bun latte and got to work.

By midmorning, I had to admit that the new chair was infinitely more comfortable than the wooden bench seat my butt had been occupying for many hours per week. I was even so cozy in my sweatshirt and comfortable in Will's chair that I hardly minded when Garrett, the delivery driver, approached and propped his leg up nearby.

"Becca, I am so sorry I missed our date," he said, dark eyes wide with remorse. "It just slipped my mind."

Smiling, I ignored the sting of his thoughtlessness and replied truthfully, "It's okay. I think it actually worked out for the best. I had a great time at Firefly."

A tiny frown caused a ripple across his forehead. "Oh, yeah?"

"Definitely," I said brightly. "The bar was great, and I ended up running into several people from town. So, all in all, a wonderful night."

"Oh. Well, I'd love to try again. I think you'd have an even better—"

"No, that's alright," I interrupted, proud of myself for being assertive for once. Cece and Pippa would have high-fived the heck out of me. Especially since they'd gotten a text update on my date fail. Many emoji and exclamation marks were used in our group chat. But, for some reason, I hadn't told my friends about Will sliding into the seat across from me and turning my Saturday night at Firefly into something better. I wanted to keep that to myself.

Giving Garrett a genuine smile, I added, "I think we're both in different places, and I'm not really looking to date." *A player who lacked common decency* went unsaid.

"Right. Okay." He looked so out of sorts that I almost felt bad. But then I remembered our date had *slipped his mind,* and he hadn't bothered to at least text and cancel on me.

"Have a good rest of your day!"

Garrett lowered his leg and stood awkwardly. "Yeah. Thanks. You too."

I watched him make his way down the path toward the parking lot and smiled to myself. As a people-pleaser since birth, it was difficult for me to say what I meant. I was proud of the way I'd handled the situation with Garrett. If I'd been forthright initially, I could have avoided this whole fiasco by saying no to the date in the first place.

But part of me thought I might not have ended up at Firefly on Saturday night, and then I would have missed out on an evening with Will. Seemed like a fair trade-off.

So what if my innocent little crush was growing butterfly wings and flapping around in my belly whenever I thought of the tall, quiet man who ran this farm? It would be fine. If I could keep my cool and stop waving at him like a dork, we might even get to be friends. And I could always use more of those.

Following Garrett's departure, I pulled up my online calendar and double-checked my activities for the week. Normally, I'd have Monday night trivia tonight, but there was a private event at Trailview Brewing, so it was canceled this week. I needed to finish a cover for one of my authors and a set of new release graphics for another. There was yoga on Tuesday and Friday mornings. Knitting lessons on Wednesday with Lettie Louise at her shop downtown, Weaverly Place. Then I had my graphic design class at the library with the teens on Thursday afternoon followed by bowling league. Bird-watching was slated for early Saturday morning. And the Orchard Festival planning meeting was one week from today. I was looking forward to that. My first big festival in

Kirby Falls, and it was the seventy-fifth anniversary of the event. I couldn't wait.

Carl hopped up and raced off with a quiet woof, drawing my attention away from my screen. Will was walking up the path, and his dog ran to meet him. Will's hat was turned backward, and his jeans had a smudge of grease across his broad thigh. His gray flannel looked warm and inviting and so did the smile he gave his dog. Much to my surprise, when he straightened from greeting Carl, he met my gaze across the distance, and the grin stayed firmly in place.

Apparently, our tentative truce was still holding, and I hadn't scared him off last night with my overshare of epic proportions.

I smiled back, eager to thank him for his chair and offer it back since he was probably returning to his office. But before he'd taken more than a step in my direction, a man approached and clapped him on the shoulder.

I didn't recognize the elderly gentleman, but he seemed to know Will. He smiled and spoke like they were well acquainted. It was something I loved about small-town life—the camaraderie, the familiarity, and the willingness to be neighborly.

In Detroit, the lady who lived in the apartment across the hall darted in and out whenever she saw me to avoid any conversation. In my experience, people didn't talk in elevators, and they wore earbuds to escape any sort of chitchat. I thought there was definitely something to this Southern-hospitality thing.

Except Will's expression didn't look particularly welcoming after a moment. He'd flipped his hat around and tugged it low, something I noticed he did when he was uncomfortable. He was being polite to the man who'd approached him but nothing more. Nodding along to whatever was being said, Will looked slightly pained as his gray eyes narrowed and his mouth went tight beneath his beard.

What was that man saying to him? Was he complaining about something that happened at Grandpappy's?

I was standing before I realized it. Confrontational was not my default. I had three unanswered texts from my sister asking for more money on my phone to prove it. But I just couldn't stomach the scene before me. I didn't know what I'd say when I got over there, but *something* to distract from the conversation would surely be welcome. I would be rude if I had to. I'd interrupt—anything—to get that look off Will's face.

"Sit down, killer."

I paused at MacKenzie's pleasant demand. She and Laramie were in the process of sitting down at my table, and I hadn't even noticed. Mac dropped a large pizza box from Apollo's on the surface. "There's nothing you can do. When Old Man Armstrong gets going about Will and baseball, there's no stopping him. Best to just let him wear himself out. Have some pizza with us."

"What are you talking about?" I was still standing.

Larry patted the tabletop. "C'mon. Eat a slice. We'll explain."

I turned back to Will, but he was striding off behind the building with Carl at his heels. And Mr. Armstrong was ambling down the path back toward the main gate. Their conversation was thankfully over.

I sat and accepted the slice of mushroom-and-olive pizza Larry handed me. "What did that man say to Will?"

Mac was sucking in a breath after a too hot bite of cheese. When she recovered, she said, "Will used to play baseball."

I waited. "That's . . . nice?"

Larry added, "Professionally."

"Oh." I considered Will's size and build. He was tall and strong but lean and tapered at the same time. I guess I could see him filling out a baseball uniform nicely. And he sure could wear a baseball cap. "Sorry, I'm not big into baseball. I didn't realize."

"He grew up playing. Even before he could walk, he was throwing a ball," Mac said. "Will used to eat, sleep, and dream baseball. He could have signed a contract right out of high school. He was that good. But there was a pitching coach at UNC he wanted to work with, so he got drafted after two years of college. He played rookie ball and moved through the minors pretty quickly. But he was injured as soon as he got pulled up. Pitched two whole games in the majors before he messed up his shoulder. Then he tried to keep practicing and made it worse. Finally fessed up and went to a doctor to repair his rotator cuff.

He went through endless physical therapy only to be unable to return at the same caliber."

Mac took another bite, and Laramie took over the story. "The team released him before his twenty-first birthday. His career in the major leagues was over. He managed to return to college and finish out his degree with an extra couple of semesters. He graduated and then came back home to work on the farm. That was nine-ish years ago. If you think he's grumpy now"—she whistled—"he had an even shittier attitude for a long time after returning to Kirby Falls. Finally, he got himself under control, adopted Carl, and settled in."

"Settled, period, is more like it," Mac argued, her gray eyes—so much like Will's—going fierce.

"Yeah, but you can't tell him anything," Larry said, her two pizza slices already demolished. "He thinks we can't possibly survive without him. That the farm would just up and fall apart. And while he does a lot here . . . he could do more somewhere else. Especially if it actually made him happy."

My heart ached suddenly. Poor Will. I couldn't imagine working that hard and coming so far, only to have circumstance and rotten luck take away your dream so viciously.

"And the man talking to him today was a local?" I asked quietly, the realization making my voice sad and small.

"Yeah," Mac confirmed, tucking a strand of her dark hair behind one ear. "People come up to him and bring up the good ole days all the time. They want to relive his moments at ballparks and talk about his no-hitter in college or gossip about his time on a major league bench." Her pretty face twisted in a disgusted sneer. "They just can't seem to let him be, and he's too polite to tell 'em to go to hell and mind their own business."

I thought about Will at Firefly the other night, hunching in his seat and tugging his cap low anytime someone approached the table. And during trivia at the bar. He'd been anticipating—bracing for some well-meaning but thoughtlessly intrusive person to ruin his night. Instead, they'd ignored him and talked to me.

Despite how I longed to hear the details about Will and his life, the uneasy feeling in the pit of my stomach intensified. I'd opened up to Will about my family, but he hadn't exactly reciprocated at the assisted living facility. "Should you have told me about Will's past?" I said worriedly. "I didn't mean to gossip. I just wondered about—"

MacKenzie frowned. "Will's our family. We can talk about him all we want."

But I'm not, I wanted to say. And then I felt another guilty pang that I didn't *really* belong in Kirby Falls as much as I might want to. And I shouldn't be privy to the knowledge regarding its hometown heroes.

"But other people can't." Larry nodded decisively. "Not Old Man Armstrong or Vera Sterling or all the other busybodies who want to think they have some in with a famous athlete."

Mac snorted. "Plus, it's all stuff you can find out from his Wikipedia page anyhow."

"He has a Wikipedia page?" I blurted.

Larry and Mac shared an amused look.

"It's okay for you to know, Becca," Larry added. "I saw the way you were ready to march over there and defend his honor or at least bail him out of an uncomfortable conversation. You're a good one. You may not be here for good, but while you *are* here, you're one of us."

Laramie couldn't know how much I wanted those words to be true—how deeply they affected me. In all my twenty-nine years, I'd never truly found a place where I belonged. Definitely not with my parents or my sister. And while I'd loved Mrs. Walters and continued to be grateful for all she'd done for me, I'd had so many moments of feeling like a charity case, a debt to be repaid.

As I watched the two women bicker over the remaining pieces and eventually polish off the rest of the pizza, I fought the sudden urge to cry. My new friends would just think I was weird for getting emotional over shared secrets and an impromptu lunch break.

I shook my head and handed over my uneaten slice to Larry, who clapped in delight while Mac sneaked in and ripped a huge piece off the crust.

If I could belong anywhere, I'd want it to be right here.

I worked late into the afternoon, hoping Will would come out of his office. I wanted to return the chair and thank him, but I didn't trust my face not to go all soft and sympathetic when I saw him—my knowledge of his past leaking out of every pore.

But all that worry was for nothing because when I packed up at seven that evening, I hadn't seen a single sign of Will or his backward hat. I rolled the desk chair around the corner of the Bake Shop and found the door to Will's office, but it was locked, and all the lights were off inside. I guess I'd missed him.

Disappointment rose within me as I pushed the chair back to my table and made the walk across the farm to my rental house. Inwardly, I made plans to chat with Pippa and Cece later. They were so good at cheering me up.

The sun was low in the sky, and the shadows were long. I was glad I'd put my sweatshirt back on. The autumn evenings were growing chilly. In another half hour, it would be fully dark. I bet the fireflies were already out in the field behind the tiny house.

When I rounded the corner behind the big barn, I stopped in my tracks. There, lighting the pathway to the front door of the tiny house, were solar lights. They were placed equally and shone warm golden light over the pavers that led to the entrance. And they hadn't been there before tonight.

I sighed.

Will Clark might not be the friendliest, and he might not put those straight white teeth of his to good use very often. But he was a doer. He showed people he cared by showing up. He worked tirelessly at the farm when he'd been deprived of the career of his choosing. Will visited his great-grandfather and worked to honor his family legacy when it probably wasn't always easy. The quiet, stoic man gave his time and his energy. And every now and then, some sweetness sneaked in around the edges.

I could see it as clear as the lights on the pathway. Not to mention the rolling chair that had supported my back all day long. And the four-leaf clovers he'd left for me just because they were exciting to this city girl and made me happy.

Will was a top secret sweetheart. A good-guy spy with only the best of intentions. And his reluctance to be friendly only made me want to try that much harder to get a smile out of him. If I had to pull out another Miss America wave to do it, then I would. Because that man deserved some goodness and levity in his life.

Did Will have anyone who tried to make him laugh? Was there anyone brave enough to risk his glares and crabby attitude?

I knew he had Jordan and Chloe and a whole town full of people who respected him.

But who was taking care of Will's heart? Who was cultivating that sweetness that he couldn't seem to banish entirely?

Everyone needed something from Will, but who made him *feel* needed? Because those were very different things.

Tugging my laptop bag higher on my shoulder, I made my way to the front door of the tiny house and did my best to remind myself that Will was none of my business. And his heart wasn't my concern. But as my feet passed through the glowing circles cast by the outdoor solar lights—the ones I was convinced he'd installed with his own two hands—it became harder and harder for my brain to listen to rational warnings.

I didn't want to get my heart broken while I was on vacation. But an instinct within told me this crush of mine was well on its way to something else, something bigger and brighter and louder than a city girl and country boy with no future. And I'd never been very good at forcing myself to stop caring—even when it was probably the smart decision.

The key turned in the lock, and suddenly, I was home.

I dropped my bag by the sofa and left my shoes on. Making my way to the back door, I slipped out to the patio to catch the last rays of sunlight dipping over the mountains.

The fireflies were out, or lightning bugs as Mac called them. A sense of peace settled over me as I watched them blink in and out of existence. The air was cool but not unwelcome. And the night sounds buzzed and chirped, making me feel less alone in this land that was not my own.

My home back in Detroit was too tangled up with loss and grief. I felt guilty for how much I loved this tiny house. How right it felt to be here—to escape my life and my family and everything that tied me to the city.

Mrs. Walters had left her apartment to me. After her year-long battle with cancer, it had been the only thing left. Jamie, Mrs. Walters's son, had died in the line of duty when I'd been in high school. She didn't have any other family. In most ways, that two-bedroom apartment had been the only real home I'd ever known. My relationship with my parents had always been volatile and neglectful. But Mrs. Walters had given me stability and consistency, something I'd desperately needed as a child, an adolescent, and an adult.

She'd owned her apartment and willing it to me ensured I'd always have a place to call home. It also afforded me the luxury of traveling and this extended stay in Kirby Falls. I didn't have to worry about making rent. My clients, steady income, and savings had me living comfortably. I didn't spend excessively and lived simply. This trip to North Carolina was the first thing I'd splurged on in a very long time.

I loved Mrs. Walters's apartment. But even after three years of grieving her loss, the third-floor residence still felt like *hers*. It carried the memories of her cancer diagnosis and slow decline. Of appointments and hospice. Feeling utterly helpless to care for the only person who'd ever cared about me.

I'd been feeling the need to get out of Detroit for a while. The guilt that followed was a nagging ache, always with me and within easy reach.

Loving Kirby Falls and this tiny house felt like I was dishonoring Mrs. Walters's memory, not to mention abandoning my sister. But I couldn't help the way my soul seemed to sigh out in relief when I sat here watching the mountains in the distance. I didn't know what that meant or what to do with it.

Closing my eyes, I breathed in cool, clean mountain air. I didn't try to stop the tears that came. I just let them fall.

Sometimes grief—even years old—was something you had to take a day at a time or the enormity of it would swallow you up.

WILL

The Saturday crew at Grandpappy's had things well in hand when I took off just before lunchtime.

My cousin Mac needed coverage at the farmers' market downtown today. She had to leave around noon, so I was handling the last two hours in the booth and then packing up any leftover produce and merchandise and hauling it back to Grandpappy's. I might even get home early enough to strip the wallpaper out of the upstairs bathroom if things stayed calm at the farm this evening. Only time would tell. All it would take was one lost toddler in the corn maze to mess up the delicate balance of entertaining the public.

Carl knew the drill and ran up to our booth halfway between 2nd Street and 3rd Street. He slipped under the table and settled in.

"Where's Mom?" MacKenzie asked when I ducked under the rope securing the white tent and took the empty seat beside her.

Mac's mother, my aunt Patty, was busy meeting a bride. "She had to go over the plans for the wedding ceremony next month with Stacy Fuller and her momma."

Mac frowned. "If I'd known she was going to send you, I would have canceled."

I was scanning the apples to see what had sold and not paying much attention. "Canceled what?" I asked absently.

Just then a man I didn't recognize walked up. He looked like a financial planner or, maybe, an orthodontist. "Hi, MacKenzie. Are you ready to go?"

My cousin stood and offered the stranger a demure smile that looked out of place on her face.

"Sure, David. Let me grab my things."

Turning, I gave Mac a flat look. "Did you really need coverage so you could go on a date? Seriously, Mac?"

She had the decency to look chagrinned. "I'm sorry," she whispered. "I thought Mom would be the one coming to take over. She likes working the farmers' market."

My aunt Patty usually handled things in the General Store with her husband, Robert. They were great with tourists and upselling and all the stuff I typically avoided. But Patty was also the event planner for the farm. She coordinated weddings and parties, another side of the business I tried to steer clear of.

"Who's this, Mac Attack? Your new boyfriend?"

I closed my eyes and shook my head at the sound of Brady Judd's delighted voice coming from the next booth over where he was seated with Mark Mercer, one of the farmers over at Judd's Orchard.

Brady and Mac had probably bickered on and off all morning. Poor Mercer.

Honestly, I didn't know why our vendor tables were always beside one another. Probably because Eloise Carter, the head of the Kirby Falls Agricultural Committee in charge of the farmers' market and festival planning, couldn't wait to see Mac and Brady come to blows. The footage might get captured on video and go viral. Then Kirby Falls would attract even more tourists thanks to Grandpappy's Farm and Judd's Family Orchard.

The thought had me grimacing.

Mac glared at the middle Judd sibling, but the David guy missed the torturous glee in Brady's tone and stepped over to shake hands with the immature bonehead.

"Hi there. I'm David," he said. "Are you friends with MacKenzie?"

"I sure am," Brady replied.

At the same time, Mac said, "Hell no."

"Known her my whole life," Brady continued, unbothered.

I rolled my eyes and went back to taking inventory. The strawberry balsamic preserves were all gone as well as the white chocolate raspberry scone mix from the Bake Shop. Momma would be pleased.

Mac was growling quietly at my side as Brady continued chatting with her date.

"A daytime date is pretty ballsy," he said. And then turning to Mac, he called, "This guy already knows you turn into a gremlin after dark, right?" Brady didn't give her a chance to answer, just cheerfully slung an arm over Mercer's empty chair while he bagged up some apples for a customer. "Whatever you do, David, don't give her food after midnight or spill water on her."

"I am going to murder you in your sleep, Brady Judd."

The idiot smiled like Mac had just told him he'd won the lottery.

"Let's go," she snarled before tugging away a very confused-looking financial planner . . . or orthodontist.

Carl huffed out a beleaguered sigh from beneath the table, and I leaned back in my chair in silent agreement.

"You know, she really is going to kill you someday," Mark Mercer said in his low voice from Brady's other side. The farmer was a quiet guy, several years younger than me. I think he was in Laramie's grade in school, so he must have been twenty-five or twenty-six now, but he'd gone to college for agriculture science and was a good addition over at Judd's Orchard. Mercer was also one of the only employees they had who wasn't a blood relative. They ran a smaller scale operation, so I'd never considered us rivals like Mac and Brady did. There were enough tourists to go around. I didn't begrudge Mercer and the Judd family their fair share.

"It's okay," Brady murmured. "You'll avenge my honor."

Mercer huffed out a dry laugh. "Doubtful. No one will say a word about it because when Mac murders you, your pointless and idiotic feud will finally be over. The town will breathe a collective sigh of relief."

Brady gasped, clutching imaginary pearls to his chest. Without missing a beat, his long, lean form peered around Mercer to meet my amused gaze. "Will, can you check"—he pointed over his shoulder—"just there?"

I shook my head and watched the overgrown frat boy stand and turn, giving me his back. "Here?" I asked, indicating the spot between his shoulder blades.

"Yeah, just a little lower," he confirmed. "Is there a knife sticking out from Mercer's betrayal?"

Mercer tilted his head to the sky and chuckled from beneath his ball cap. "Brady, you are an idiot."

But the bozo was grinning, pleased with himself.

My smile lingered as I focused back on Main Street, closed off from vehicular traffic for four blocks for the weekly farmers' market. The crowd of people had thinned a little, but there would probably be another rush after the brunch crowd finished up at the restaurants downtown.

I noticed workers hanging a new sign over Apollo's. Frowning, I said, "What's going on over there?"

Brady answered, "Becca Kernsy—this leafer who's been hanging around for a few weeks—helped design a new logo, and Magdaline loved it. It's the only thing her parents have agreed on in their whole marriage. So they had a new sign made up . . ."

Shock at hearing Becca's name come out of Brady's mouth had my gaze snapping to him. But he was watching the installation across the street.

The new design *was* eye-catching. I liked how it used the colors from the previous logo, so it was familiar . . . just upgraded, I supposed.

I considered the fact that Becca had helped with the new logo. What did that mean? Did she draw it? Was she an artist?

I thought of her many notebooks, all the time she spent on her computer, and the way she seemed to always have her phone out snapping photos of Carl or her lattes or apples on the trees. I'd seen her on her walks, in her own little world, taking pictures of everything at Grandpappy's. I'd chalked it up to standard tourist behavior, but maybe there was more to it.

Brady was still talking. "Sheila Jessup even asked Becca to be a guest on her podcast. That girl gets around."

Yeah, she did get around, I silently agreed. I didn't demand to know how Brady knew her . . . but I wanted to. Becca was all over Kirby Falls, getting absorbed into the fabric of the town. She had a bird-watching group and helped design logos for my favorite pizza restaurant. She talked to my own neighbors like she'd lived here her whole life. I didn't understand it. Who got so bored on their vacation that they volunteered to teach a class to teenagers at the local library?

Her constant involvement with all things Kirby Falls was confusing. I didn't know what it meant. Was she really a tourist? Or was she scoping the town out and planning on moving here?

That was the question I never let myself think while I was with her. When we spoke on the farm, when she was making me laugh, I didn't want to consider what would happen if the question slipped out. What if she stayed?

Yes, I was attracted to her. She was beautiful. Of course, I liked her. She was kind and thoughtful and funny. And after our recent interactions at Firefly and Legacy Hills, I knew enough about her that I couldn't accurately consider her a stranger anymore. She was fully formed in my mind and seemed to be occupying plenty of time there.

But it all came back to one thing. She was a tourist. If I found out she was staying, what would I do with all the *what-ifs* invading my brain every time I looked at her?

"Hey, there she is."

Brady's big mouth drew my attention once again.

I tracked the line of his gaze, and there was Becca, across the street and two booths down, browsing at the Bramble Pottery table.

Her hair was long and loose, nearly to her waist, and as bright as a beacon in the midday sun. She wore a long floral skirt and a tee shirt tucked casually in the front. She was smiling softly as she looked at every vase, mug, and place setting inside the tent. Her hand would hover over the clay pieces as if she might touch them but then lost her nerve at the last moment. Becca lined up shots with her cell phone and photographed the table from several angles before approaching Agnes Devon, the ceramic artist who ran Bramble Pottery.

I watched as they spoke, my eyes tracking between pedestrians still wandering up and down the aisles of the farmers' market. I wondered what Agnes and Becca were discussing. Was she signing up for a class on the pottery wheel? Designing a logo for her too? Maybe she was offering to help in some other way. As confounding as that was, it seemed to be her thing—making an impression and endearing herself to strangers.

A few customers wandered up to my table while Becca and Agnes smiled and laughed through their conversation. I was distracted, taking money and bagging items. I'd never been good at upselling or chatting with tourists about our farm and plantings anyway. But I was even worse now, waiting to see what Becca might do, where she might go. If she'd catch sight of me and cross the street. Smile and wave. Get flustered if I grinned back.

And then I felt like an idiot when she kept right on moving down the street. She wandered on the opposite side of the road, dipping into booths to check out their wares.

I shook my head at how ridiculous I was being. She hadn't even seen me.

I looked down at Carl, fast asleep by my feet, knowing he'd be disappointed that he missed his new favorite human. And I didn't quite understand it, but I was disappointed too. Like the anticipation had been a balloon inflating inside my chest only to loosen its hold and collapse at the last minute.

There was no logical reason to feel that way. I'd seen her several times this week at the farm. Becca had caught up with me on Tuesday and thanked me for the desk chair, and then tried to give it back.

In the spare moments I actually got to use the office, I was just fine with the folding chair I had in there. Plus, it was a relief knowing she wasn't killing her back at that uncomfortable picnic table. On Wednesday afternoon, I'd happened upon another four-leaf clover and gave it to her. Becca had been just as awed and excited as the last time. She'd carefully flattened it in her notebook, and I liked knowing she had a collection of little things that made her happy. She'd thanked me again for the use of my chair, and I had to stop her before she offered to return it once more.

Then yesterday, when I'd sneaked a Danish and some coffee from the Bake Shop, she'd invited me to sit down and have breakfast with her. So I had. We'd talked about the places we'd traveled and the sights we'd seen. She asked me a little more about my family while Carl sat happily by her side. I'd guessed—incorrectly—that she was a YouTuber, and she'd bitten her lip and looked down at her plate, trying not to laugh.

Becca was clever and witty. But she was hard on herself, self-deprecating in a way that made me wonder if she saw herself differently than how I saw her—capable and sweet and open and accepting.

Yesterday, the breakfast—and the conversation—had been nice. *She* was nice. It was nice talking to someone who hadn't known me since the third grade. Who didn't think they already knew every single thing about me and all I had to offer. Sure, maybe *nice* wasn't what some guys were looking for. But I'd never been the kind of person who needed angst and drama and a whirlwind to shake me up. There was something to be said for steadfast and dependable. Becca was a breath of fresh air on a fall day. She was someone I could see myself being friends with, a person I wanted to get to know.

Right now, she was a mystery in that nebulous space where I was eager to learn more about her. See her. Hear her voice. Make her laugh. Know what she liked. How she'd react.

She was a million firsts waiting to happen.

Just not for me.

Ignoring the urge to track Becca's progress farther down the street, I tugged the bill of my cap down lower on my head and got back to work.

No sense in watching her walk away now when, in a few weeks, she'd be walking away for good.

Monday rolled around, and I thought I'd gotten out of socializing because Trivia Night was canceled, but then my dad reminded me that it was called off because of the Orchard Festival planning meeting.

I dropped Carl at home and made the drive over to the Kirby Falls Public Library. Mrs. Crandall, the ancient librarian, had the back door propped open for all the business owners, vendors, planning committee, and volunteers required to attend the meeting.

The Orchard Fest was a big deal and would be held this upcoming weekend. Our small county in North Carolina produced the most apples in the state and the eighth highest in the country. Over two hundred farms supplied apples and apple products nationwide to grocery stores, restaurants, markets, and everywhere in between. Kirby Falls celebrated all things apple every September with a three-day festival. All of Main Street would be closed off and lined with vendors and farmers. Every year, there were tables for local artists and authors and craftspeople. Several antique dealers would be on hand to entice out-of-towners with their goods. Then you had bands and performances. Some poetry and storytelling set up in one tent. And fair rides for the kids, and as much carnival food as you could eat. There would be a local food truck rodeo on the end of Main Street and a fun run as well.

Farms like Grandpappy's and Judd's would have booths selling apples and apple-adjacent items. We were one of the festival sponsors, so we'd have a pretty big booth with five to ten employees working steadily all weekend to cater to the thousands of tourists who would flock to the area.

And this year was the seventy-fifth anniversary of the event. They anticipated record numbers in town.

To someone like me who'd been working the Orchard Fest for nearly a decade, a planning meeting seemed like a waste of time. But Eloise Carter, the committee chair, was holding court at the podium near the front of the library's large meeting room as people milled about talking and grabbing some store-bought cookies someone had brought. As the representative from Grandpappy's, I was required to attend tonight, but this whole thing probably could have been an email.

It looked like Joan was the designated employee from Judd's Orchard. "Will," she murmured and gave me a brief nod.

"Joan," I replied, "how've you been?"

Joan Judd had been a senior when I'd been a freshmen back in high school. She was a straight shooter, and we'd always gotten along. When your farms were across the highway from one another and your town was the size of a postage stamp, you tended to know most people in your line of work. And Joan was a farmer, born and raised.

Tonight, she looked annoyed. Her chin-length hair had gone gray in her twenties, but it suited her. She could often be seen running around town or in the 5K held this weekend. Joan usually had a ball cap on her head and a don't-fuck-with-me expression on her face. Right now, it was dialed up to I-don't-have-time-for-this-bullshit.

But she replied easily enough, "Can't complain." Then she caught sight of something over my shoulder and rolled her eyes.

I glanced back to see a tall young woman with brown hair in a fancy updo wearing a pale pink pantsuit, blazer and everything. It had been a while, but I thought I recognized her. "That Candy?"

Joan sighed, eyes still fixed behind me. "She goes by Candace now." The eye roll was implied this time.

"I thought she was in New York or LA?" Candy Judd had lit out of Kirby Falls on graduation day. Her daddy liked to joke that she'd left skid marks on the auditorium stage after she grabbed her diploma.

"Yeah, well, she's back now," Joan admitted, her pale blue eyes finally coming back to me. "And she's involved." She said involved like Candy was a toddler who thought she was helping when, in reality, she was just making a bigger mess for someone else to clean up.

I was not touching that family drama with a ten-foot pole.

"Well, have a good night," I mumbled and then darted for the back of the room, away from the crowd.

But then I saw Jordan waving frantically at me from the third row. I just stared until he finally called out, "Saved you a seat!"

Sighing, I worked my way through the sea of neighbors. A few moments later, I made it through relatively unscathed with just a few hellos and nods. I slid into the uncomfortable folding chair next to Jordan and crossed my arms.

"You ready for this?" my friend asked.

"As I'll ever be," I replied.

Lazily, I scanned the folks in the rows ahead of us. My gaze snagged on a curtain of blond hair, and I straightened in my seat against my will. Becca was front and center, jean-clad legs crossed with a notebook in her lap and a pen poised and ready to go.

Jordan must have noticed where my attention had strayed because, for once, his big mouth told me what I actually wanted to know. "She volunteered for setup."

"Of course she did," I mumbled, forcing myself to relax back into my seat. She looked like the star pupil ready to make her favorite teacher proud on exam day. It was annoying how fucking adorable it was.

"The other volunteers voted her their leader, so she's here at the meeting on their behalf to take notes and communicate what needs to be done."

"God." I sighed. "Why is she like this?"

"What?" I could feel Jordan's eyes laser-beaming the side of my head. "Helpful? Involved? A damn delight?"

I turned to face him, eyes narrowed. "Why is she taking such an interest in the town when she's here on *vacation*? It doesn't make any sense."

"Chloe thinks she's going to move here." Jordan said the words casually, yet my reaction was anything but.

"What?" My voice was sharp and too interested, impatient in a way that Jordan noticed immediately.

His eyes searched my face before he said slowly, "She loves it here. Chloe says her life back in Detroit doesn't seem like it makes her happy. She's been encouraging Becca to stay, to really get to know the town, and then make a decision. Plus, she did alright at trivia. I'd be happy if she stayed permanently. She and Chloe are getting close."

My friend fell silent as we watched Eloise Carter open her binder and get behind the microphone to start the meeting.

It was difficult to focus on the specifics of what was being discussed. I was distracted by Becca's presence as well as Jordan's offhand comment about the possibility of her staying. It was pointless to dwell on those same *what-ifs,* especially when I was in the same room with her.

As much as I didn't want to consider it, something in me wanted this girl. Wanted her smiles and her attention and her sweetness. Like a greedy bastard, I could feel myself getting my hopes up. Despite our circumstances and the fact that we were dancing around something, Jordan's gossip and Chloe's hearsay worked its way beneath my skin, making me wonder about Becca Kernsy over and over again.

The meeting seemed to take a lifetime. I didn't retain much in my distracted state. Jordan gave up listening halfway through and played *Candy Crush* on his phone. But not Becca; she took diligent notes and nodded along to Eloise's long-winded remarks. I knew the volunteers would be in good hands because Becca didn't do anything halfway. She was dedicated and enthusiastic, even when there wasn't anything in it for her.

During Eloise's final reminders, a text came through on my phone. It was Mr. Abrams returning my message about hiking the private trail on his land. My eyes scanned the reply quickly, and as the meeting finished up, I watched Becca stand from her seat.

I considered my schedule for the following day and nudged Jordan. "Meeting's over."

"Huh," he mumbled, thumbs still moving over his brightly colored phone screen. He finally glanced up to see people milling about and making for the exit. "Oh, thanks, man. Conditioning tomorrow afternoon?"

I resisted the urge to groan, but nodded instead. "Yeah. Tell Seth I'll be there." The exercise was good for me. So was getting out and doing things, even if it was subjecting myself to teenagers for a few hours every week.

I waited until Jordan headed out and then sat back down. Becca had packed up her notes and was introducing herself to Eloise Carter. She was networking and charming the typically stuffy older woman. It was interesting to watch it happen in real time and I wondered what I looked like mid-conversation with Becca Kernsy.

Probably like an idiot bobblehead. But hopefully not as bad as the cow-eyed teenagers.

By the time the women finished their conversation, the meeting room was practically empty, so I wasn't surprised when Becca's blue eyes found me seated only a few rows away.

Her smile bloomed wide and lovely, and my own emerged without conscious thought.

"Hey, you. I didn't see you there," she said, tucking a strand of blond hair behind her ear. I'd noticed the nervous habit before, and I wondered what it would feel like if I did it for her—touched her soft hair, ran my finger around the delicate curve of her ear. Would that make her more nervous?

"Yeah, businesses and vendors are strongly encouraged to attend. Heard you were volunteering," I said, rising to my feet and skirting the end of the row to walk to the front of the room to meet her.

"Yeah," she confirmed, stepping closer until we were only separated by a couple of feet. We weren't in dancing range, but it was close. "I wanted to help out." Then she straightened as if she remembered something.

"If you're about to thank me for the desk chair again, I'm going to go out and get a recliner and put it in front of the Bake Shop for you instead."

She laughed, her expression equal parts sheepish and embarrassed. "Busted."

"Busted," I agreed, but my tone was warm, unbothered by her persistent gratitude, and amused by it instead. "Hey, so I finally heard back from Mr. Abrams about that hike on the private trail. He offered up tomorrow morning if you don't have anything on your busy schedule."

Becca's face brightened. "No, that sounds great. I'd love to."

Squinting, I asked, "Is six thirty too early?"

"What? No! That's totally fine."

My dubious squinting intensified.

"Seriously, I'll be up. I'm an early bird of the highest caliber," she assured me loftily, upturned nose high in the air.

I thought of her buried under her covers in the tiny house while I'd tried to cajole Carl out of bed with her and smiled.

"If you say so," I replied, still grinning. "I'll get you back in time to work on . . . your . . . " She watched me struggle through another fumbling career guess with giddy amusement. "Content as a food blogger?"

Even white teeth bit down gently on her lower lip, and I got distracted at the sight. But she was shaking her head slowly. "Are you just googling 'work-from-home jobs for nice girls'?"

I shifted a little on my feet. She wasn't too far off.

"Oh my gosh, you are!" Then she reached across the distance and whacked me on the arm.

I laughed, enjoying her casual touch. I fought the urge to snag her hand out of the air and tucked mine in my pockets instead. How the hell would I explain wanting to hold her hand? "Well, if you'd just tell me."

"No way. This is too much fun."

Eyeing her happy face, I considered that brand-new sign over Apollo's restaurant on Main Street. "What about marketing? Brand analysis?" *Was that a thing?* "An artist?"

It was clear by this point that I was the only one she was withholding this information from. I'd tried asking Chloe in a roundabout way last week at the Bake Shop, but she'd just smiled knowingly and shoved a cinnamon roll at me. Jordan wouldn't tell me because he thought it was hilarious that Becca was "keeping me on my toes."

Truthfully, I was glad she thought this little game between us was fun because I did too. It made me think about what else might happen between us if we let it. I wondered what Becca would do if I leaned in close and made my growing interest known. If I tucked some of that soft hair behind her ear. If I got close enough to touch. If I let my lips—

"What made you guess those?" Becca asked, interrupting the direction of my highly inappropriate thoughts.

I went to tug down the bill of my cap but remembered I wasn't wearing one, so I ran my fingers through the strands that were too long and curled along my nape, in need of a trim. "I, uh, heard about you helping Madgaline at Apollo's with their new sign."

"Ah," Becca replied knowingly.

"You didn't really answer."

"No, I didn't." But she didn't look sorry about it at all. She looked pleased, her eyes soft as they traveled over my face. Her lips were still tilted in a smile but it was less amusement and more anticipation.

We stood staring at each other for a long moment, one in which I considered taking another step closer. I remembered how the dip of her waist felt beneath my fingers.

But then the lights in the meeting room clicked off, and Becca made an alarmed sound. Mrs. Crandall appeared in the open double doors at the far end of the space, silhouetted and backlit by the harsh fluorescent lights of the hallway. "Oh! I didn't realize there was anyone left. Becca honey, is that you?"

"Hi, Mrs. Crandall. Sorry, we were just finishing up."

It's Will, too, I wanted to say. You know, the person you gave a library card to when he was five years old. Or the guy who helped you load your groceries in your giant Cadillac a week ago at the Winn-Dixie.

But then I pushed away the annoyance at being overlooked and interrupted and thought it was probably a good thing Mrs. Crandall had intervened when she had.

I'd been distracted, staring at Becca's lips like I'd lost my damn mind for a moment. There wasn't a point in thinking misguided romantic thoughts . . . unless Chloe was right and Becca was considering staying in Kirby Falls.

I wasn't interested in a fling. I was thirty years old and past that phase in my life. A part of me saw the easiness between Jordan and Chloe and wanted that sort of relationship for my future. But those two had a bond that came from friendship and a long history.

Finding something meaningful seemed nearly impossible. I didn't have the patience for most people and the thought of playing games or wasting my time with someone just didn't do it for me.

And even if I wanted a casual hookup, I didn't know if Becca was capable of a short-term arrangement like that anyway. She had monogamy and matrimony stamped all over her.

There was also the fact that we were dancing around each other like freshmen in homeroom. But there were moments. Like when she blushed and got flustered or embarrassed around me. The pageant wave flashed adorably across my mind. But Becca was kind and sweet and friendly with everyone. I'd only ever seen her less-than-upbeat following that phone call with her sister two weeks ago and the night she'd told me about her family.

I wondered how many people got to see her that way—vulnerable and off-balance, less than perfect. I nearly cursed my relentless curiosity aloud as Becca gathered her things, and we hurried toward the exit.

Would I always find myself wondering about this woman? Was that how you knew someone was important? Because you couldn't seem to stop thinking about them? I didn't know. The only thing I had experience thinking about this often was baseball.

With a sigh, I watched as Mrs. Crandall retrieved a book she'd set aside for Becca. They chatted for a moment while I hovered nearby. Then Becca thanked her and apologized again for keeping her late.

We escaped through the back door and into the parking lot. Only three vehicles remained: my gray truck, Mrs. Crandall's Caddy, and Becca's dark blue SUV.

I walked her to her car, keeping a safe distance between us that didn't feel safe at all. I wanted to carry her bag and hold her hand and drive her wherever she wanted to go.

God, Jordan would have given me endless shit for such ridiculous romanticizing.

When we reached the driver's side, Becca broke the silence. "So, I guess I'll see you bright and early in the morning?"

"Maybe not bright. The sun probably won't be up until we're driving over to the trailhead," I said. "I'll have a backpack with some emergency gear just in case, but it's a pretty easy four miles roundtrip. Dress in layers and bring a water bottle."

Becca nodded. "I can do that."

She was leaning against the back door, and I dipped in close to open the driver's side for her. I caught a hint of honeysuckle sweetness and heard her sharp inhale at my sudden nearness.

"Thanks," she murmured unsteadily once she realized I was being a gentleman and opening her door for her. Then she bit her lip and shook her head, and I found myself desperate to know what she was thinking. I didn't make it a habit to feel desperate about anything, so I was a little unsteady myself as I took a step back so she could climb into the vehicle.

"Drive safe. I'll see you in the morning," I said before closing her door gently.

She smiled behind the dark glass before carefully reversing out of the parking spot.

I watched until her taillights disappeared from view. Then I waited for Mrs. Crandall to lock up and made sure she was safely on her way too.

Tomorrow, I would show Becca a part of Kirby Falls that wasn't on any tourist map or in any online article. It was a firsthand resident-only experience. A part of my adolescence. A part of me.

It had been quite some time since I didn't know what the next day might bring. My hometown return hadn't been the kind with fanfare and applause. It had been marred by regretful glances and sympathetic smiles. The life I led now was the same thing, day in and day out. But Becca Kernsy was a change, for sure. I hadn't decided whether it was a good or bad one yet. She was popping up everywhere, infiltrating my life and leaving a mark on Kirby Falls.

I had no idea what sort of mark she'd leave on me, but I wasn't going to find out by sitting in this parking lot worrying about tomorrow. So I put my truck in gear and let myself feel excited about something for the first time in a long time.

WILL

The sky was going gray in the east when Carl and I reached the tiny house the following morning.

Becca opened the front door before my boots even touched the solar-lit pathway. It looked good. I was glad I'd put those lights in the other day.

"I have on sunscreen and bug spray already. I brought a hat, if needed. And I have bear spray in my bag that you can borrow if you want."

I smiled. "Good morning."

"Right." She winced. "Sorry. I got ahead of myself. Good morning, Will."

Carl was at her feet, gazing adoringly, and she bent to give him attention. I took in her long hair in a high ponytail. She wore a half-zip fleece pullover on top of a soft pink shirt and dark pants with several pockets. The cool, foggy morning was supposed to lead into a relatively mild mid-September day. Becca would be fine in what she had on, weather-wise. Her hiking boots were worn with a few mud stains. That was good. She didn't need blisters from brand-new shoes while she played local. A small bag was slung across her back with a water bottle tucked in the netted side pocket. She looked ready to go.

"Bears are a lot more likely to dig in your trash. If there is one out in the woods, in all likelihood, it'll hear us and take off. Black bears are pretty shy."

"Gotcha. Okay," she said, straightening. She seemed just a touch nervous, making the anticipation flowing through me glad to know it had some company.

"You ready, City Girl?"

Her grin was broad in the dim morning light, but I could see it just fine. "You bet."

We climbed into my truck and there was a bit of readjusting as Carl tried to squeeze in the passenger seat with Becca, but I moved him to the back amid some grumbling and dirty looks.

The drive to the trailhead wasn't far, but Becca seemed to need to fill the quiet with helpful observations and questions. I didn't mind. As surprising as it might be to literally everyone—myself included—I liked talking to her. And listening to her ramble nervously was pretty cute too.

But when I used the code from Mr. Abrams and unlocked the gate to the trail, Becca's voice dropped away, and we just hiked.

Our quiet footfalls were the only soundtrack to the early morning. Gray light filtered through the canopy of leaves overhead. Birds and the occasional squirrel rustled in the bushes lining the trail. Becca stopped occasionally to take pictures with her phone. I didn't mind. I pulled out my water bottle while she did her thing.

Something I'd always liked about this trail was the sudden change in surroundings when you hit the end of it. Watching Becca take in the unexpected view was worth it.

We broke through the steady incline and the line of low-hanging trees onto the hard rock that jutted over the hillside. Suddenly the world expanded, and the mountains spread out before us.

Becca placed her hands on her head and said a breathless, "holy cannoli," into the quiet. I smiled to myself as she carefully stepped out onto the dark gray stone, inching close—but not too close—to the edge.

The fog was sitting low and thick, filling the valleys between all the peaks in front of us, working its way in among the mountaintops. The landscape resembled a pale ocean with dark blue cresting waves just breaking the surface.

Turning back to look at me with an enormous smile was Becca. "This is amazing. I've never seen anything like it."

It *was* beautiful. And it had been a long time since I'd made the effort to really look. I hadn't hiked this trail with any regularity since I was a teenager. So much of my life in Kirby Falls was tangled up with regrets and failures. But there had been a time when I'd loved my hometown—before it had become a fallback plan.

Maybe I'd taken the simple things for granted. Things like the land and the beauty of my surroundings. The things that Becca was devouring with feverish intensity in her efforts to get to know this place. Seeing it through her eyes was somehow better than remembering it through my own. It was all wide-eyed innocence and awe.

My own youthful experiences had gotten clouded by time and space and distance. I'd gone away to college, reaching for new and different. Baseball had been my whole damn life. Kirby Falls was always supposed to be the place I was from. A hometown listed in my bio. A stat. Not the place I returned to when I was out of options.

Now, breathing in the cool morning air, seeing my surroundings the way Becca must see them . . . it was a bittersweet ache. Dawning nostalgia that made my heart feel tender, if not bruised.

After a moment, she sat down on the rocks and simply gazed out over the hilltops. You couldn't understand this kind of beauty unless you'd seen it firsthand. I was fortunate enough to have this backdrop just driving down the road. The long-range views from my own back door were stunning, but I couldn't remember the last time I'd stopped to take note of them.

Before moving to the assisted living facility, my great-grandfather William used to love to drink his coffee out on the screened porch in the morning and just listen to the birds and look out over the land. A prickle of guilt had my gaze dropping to the tops of my worn hiking boots. I wondered if he'd be disappointed in me.

Carefully, I moved closer and lowered myself down beside Becca.

She looked over and smiled when I settled next to her. "Thank you for bringing me here."

"You're welcome." It was easy to accept her gratitude for this. I'd made the right decision inviting her. Anyone could see how much she loved it and appreciated it.

Reaching into my backpack, I pulled out my insulated thermos and two cups. Then I found the paper bag and placed it between us on the rock face. Before picking Becca up this morning, I'd swung by the Bake Shop and gathered some breakfast for us, ignoring my mother's knowing grin all the while.

Now, I poured out the cinnamon bun latte she liked and passed her a cup. "Here you go. There's pumpkin bread in that bag if you want to get some out."

I was suddenly nervous about the innocent gesture. It felt like this was some sort of date, and I was trying too hard.

But Becca's warm expression and obvious pleasure helped ease my worries. Her eyes were impossibly blue when she looked at me this way. "That's my favorite."

"I know," I replied, taking a sip of my coffee so I had something to do with my hands.

"Thank you. This is perfect."

I told myself to ignore her praise, but that didn't stop me from returning her small smile with one of my own.

She passed me a slice of bread, and we settled in, sipping our drinks and enjoying our breakfast.

"Have you been to Bella's downtown?" I asked as I brushed crumbs from my hands.

"No," she answered. "What's that?"

"It's on a side street off Main, but they have really good avocado toast for brunch. Thought I'd mention it."

Becca grinned. "You remembered."

I nodded, then busied myself with taking a too large swig from my cup. Hopefully, my beard hid the heat I felt creeping up my neck. Those avocado pajamas were kind of hard to forget for a variety of reasons.

"What's some more Kirby Falls insider info that only a local would know?"

"Let's see," I said, stretching my legs out and considering. "There's a chocolate shop two blocks away from the library. They don't have a website and close whenever they feel like it, but they have the best sweets. Mom loves them, and I get her a box every Mother's Day." It was getting easier to think of things that Becca might enjoy, so I added, "There's an artisan market that rotates to different locations all over town every Saturday. Random candles made from vintage beer cans. Everything handmade or sewn or drawn. You'd love it."

"I *would* love that." Her smile was pleased.

"Oh, there's tubing on the Sage River. And horseback riding just south of here in Clemmons at the Ecusta Farm. They even let you take care of the horses that you ride. Brush them down and feed them. That sort of thing."

"I've never ridden a horse."

Somehow I knew she'd say that, and the knowledge made my chest tighten, especially now that I had a glimpse of what her childhood had been like. "And if this didn't put you off hiking, in mid-May, you can go on the Blood River Trail in Miller Creek and the whole mountainside turns bright red from all the rhododendrons blooming at the same time. It's something to see."

Truthfully, I hadn't thought about hiking that trail in a long time. There was an aged photo on my great-grandfather's mantel of my cousins and me posing in front of the bright blooms. Bonnie and I were probably eight years old in the picture and Mac around six, all of us sunburned and wearing gap-toothed grins.

"Is Blood River the name of the water nearby?" Becca asked curiously.

"No," I explained. "The rhododendron variety is called blood moon. Plus, the blooms blow onto the path, covering the hiking trail in red. That's really why they call it that."

Her horrified expression made me chuckle. "Goodness gracious. Who would call something the Blood River Trail? You guys should have workshopped that to come up with a less off-putting name."

"Well, we voted on it, and Slaughter Hill was the runner-up, followed by Massacre Mountain."

Her laughter was loud, echoing in the stillness of the morning, multiplying my joy. "What? No Scarlet Stream?" she teased. I shook my head, grinning. "Or Satan's Eyelids?"

That had me cracking up. I leaned inward, and our shoulders pressed against one another. I could detect her laughter too. It made me feel good to make her happy. I wasn't a funny guy nor was I easy to get along with, but Becca . . . everyone loved her. And for some strange reason, she seemed to like me.

We stayed close, our shoulders still touching. While we'd eaten and spoken about the Kirby Falls sights, the bright sunshine had burned away the hazy fog. Layer after layer of mountains spread out as far as the eye could see. Leaves were changing in the higher elevations. In another month, it would be all golds and reds and oranges.

Knowing the setting would be evolving just reminded me that Becca might not be here to see it. And I didn't know what I'd been thinking, telling her about the rhododendrons blooming in the spring. She wouldn't be here for any of that. She couldn't go tubing on the Sage River. She'd be back in Detroit well before summer.

I needed to keep things in perspective. Becca was a visitor. I was stuck in Kirby Falls. Maybe it wasn't the worst place to have family ties and obligations, but that didn't make Becca any more permanent. It was undoubtedly a bad decision to get too attached.

Clearing my throat, I leaned away from her. "Yeah, maybe if you make it back this way next year, you can check out that trail."

I could feel her eyes on me as I packed up our trash and closed up the thermos. When I was brave enough to meet her gaze, I could see that her expression had dimmed, whether by the change in me or the fact that she'd also suddenly remembered her own looming departure.

"Yeah, that definitely seems like something worth seeing."

It was on the tip of my tongue to ask. To just show my hand and blurt out, "Are you thinking of staying?" But I didn't. It wouldn't be right to put that pressure on her, and it was none of my damn business. There was also the fact that I was a huge chickenshit because instead, I said, "We should get back."

I got to my feet and offered Becca my hand, pulling her up to stand. She watched me carefully before turning to take a final look at the landscape. She produced her phone from a zippered pocket and snapped a quick photo. Then she turned and moved back to the tree line behind me.

Backpack on, I gave the mountains one more glance, promising myself I wouldn't let another decade go by before I returned to this view.

"What are you doing?"

My cousin's sudden appearance startled the hell out of me.

I was bent over, staring at the ground, and I hadn't heard MacKenzie approach.

Straightening, I shot her a glare. "Just checking on something."

Mac's suspicious gray gaze looked to where I'd been stooped over staring before she asked slowly, like I was suffering from a head injury, "You know we grow apples, right? They're in trees, not in the dirt. Do you secretly want to be a potato farmer?"

"We have potatoes in the field behind the barn," I grumbled.

"No shit?" Mac exclaimed. "Well, you learn something new every day."

It seemed better to distract my cousin than tell her the truth. I sure as hell wasn't going to admit that I'd been scouring this patch of grass looking for another four-leaf clover to give to the pretty tourist I couldn't seem to stop thinking about.

It had been two days since our hike, and we were back to dancing around each other. I'd seen her working in front of the Bake Shop, just like always. But now she was sitting in my chair, usually with my dog at her feet. We'd smile and speak, but I had no idea what to do with this restless energy I felt where Becca was concerned. I wanted to ask her to go on another hike but I didn't know where any of this was going. Spending time together, getting to know her, and liking her more and more felt like a wasted effort. If she just up and left in a few weeks, where did that leave me? I couldn't see the future, so it made me reluctant to act in the present.

And I hated feeling so unsettled and off-balance. I thought about Becca a lot—to a distracting degree. There was a slight chance I was extra irritable from so much upheaval in my typically ordered existence.

So I wasn't surprised when I snapped out an impatient, "Did you need something, Mac?"

"Dad sent me to find you. He said there's a thunderstorm warning and that you might need to call Uncle William so he can tell the farm hands to take cover. I'm going to herd the tourists up to the General Store to wait it out. There aren't many this late in the day, but I wanted to mention it."

"Okay, I'll handle it."

"Thanks, Will," she replied cheerfully, dark ponytail swinging as she strode down the path. My cousin was probably hoping to get out of here early if the weather stayed poor.

I glanced back toward the grass at my feet. Knowing I needed to deal with this weather situation, I figured I could find Becca a clover another time. Hell, I'd brought her one just yesterday. But I hadn't seen her reaction or made sure she got it. Glasses on and gaze fixed, she'd looked really focused on something on her laptop. I hadn't wanted to interrupt, so when my mother asked me to deliver her afternoon tea, I'd hidden the four-leaf clover sandwiched between the bottom of her cup and the saucer it rested on.

With a sigh for this incoming weather, I abandoned the clover patch and made my way back to my office. My father never kept his radio on him, so I'd need to call his cell phone. And if I couldn't get him on his cell, I'd need to take the ATV and track him down in whatever field he was working in today.

When I passed by the Bake Shop, I didn't see Becca at her table. That was good. Maybe she'd already packed it in for the day—it was nearly six—and gone back to the rental. Part of me wanted to swing by and make sure she was settled in and safe from the storm, but visiting her at the tiny house seemed intrusive. Or maybe it would reveal too much about how I was feeling, and I couldn't even seem to pinpoint that myself.

Luckily, back in my office, my dad picked up on the third ring. He said he'd take care of notifying all the workers in the fields. I glanced at the weather report on my phone just to confirm what Mac had told me, and it did look like we were in for some foul weather. There was a chance of hail, which was always dangerous on a farm or when working with the public. I made an announcement across all the radios to take shelter as soon as possible.

I left Carl in the office and went around the corner to check on Mom. Chloe was done for the day and my mother would be closed up but prepping for tomorrow. But when my boots hit the wooden porch in front of the Orchard Bake Shop, I noticed what I hadn't before—while the desk chair was empty, Becca's computer was still at her table, along with her laptop bag beneath. My steps slowed as I scanned the area, sure she must be nearby.

But I didn't come up with blond hair or bright smiles in any direction. I knocked on the restroom doors nearby but got no response.

Dark clouds were rolling in, and the wind had picked up. I had on a long-sleeved thermal and could detect the chill in the autumn air, definitely more pronounced in the last twenty minutes.

"Mom," I called as I approached the half door.

She poked her head out. "Hi, honey." Her eyes strayed to the table behind me. "Have you seen Becca?"

"No, I was going to ask you that. There's a storm headed this way."

"I know. I just got off the phone with your dad." She looked troubled before admitting, "She got another phone call. Like the one that made her so upset a couple of weeks back."

Frowning, I felt unease tighten a band around my chest. "What happened?"

"I don't know." But my mother's dark eyes were worried. "It didn't feel right to butt in."

That surprised me because nothing seemed off-limits to Maggie Clark.

"But I could tell she was upset. She wandered off with the phone to her ear just like last time."

Immediately, my mind went to the sunflower field. Becca had said it was her favorite spot. It was quiet and helped her think.

"I'm going to put her stuff in the office and then go look for her. Radio me if she gets back before I do, okay?"

My mother nodded. "I'll keep an eye out. Be careful, sugar."

I gathered Becca's belongings and hurried them around to the office, making sure Carl stayed inside. While the porch in front of the Bake Shop was covered, I worried that rain might blow in if the storm was bad enough.

Clipping my radio to my belt, I took off for the sunflower maze. It wasn't far, and I really hoped that I'd find her there again. But a few minutes later, when I stepped off the worn path toward the dying flowers, I didn't see anyone moving about.

"Becca!" I called, just to be sure.

No response beyond the rustling of leaves and the sway of the corn stalks in the distance.

With my hands on my hips, I paused to consider where Becca might have gone. There were just too many places. I should have gotten the ATV, but I'd been so sure that history would repeat itself, and I'd find her distracted, wandering between dead blooms.

I unclipped the radio. "Anyone have eyes on Becca Kernsy?" I didn't take the time to explain who she was. Most Grandpappy's employees had run across her at one point or another. Plus, I doubted anyone would forget her.

The tiny speaker crackled a moment before I heard Laramie's voice. "She went into the corn maze about an hour ago. She was on the phone and barely noticed me. I didn't see her come out before I had to go get folks off the hayride. Do you want me to take a pass?"

Shit.

I was already moving. "No. Thanks, Larry. I'll go get her."

What had Becca said about the corn maze when I'd told her it was my favorite spot on the farm?

I have a terrible sense of direction. I'd need a search party.

What had made her venture in there in the first place? And what were these phone calls that made her so distracted and on edge? Was her sister calling and asking for more money?

Five minutes later, the sky neared darkness from the impeding cloud cover, and I was climbing the tower in the middle of the cornfield. We used it to get a better vantage point when kids got lost inside the maze and to keep an eye on things when we switched over to the haunted maze in October. But when I rose above the stalks, I noticed the first drops of rain, cold and hard against the top of my hat. Movement to my right had me turning into a roaring gust of wind. It was Becca, moving frantically, darting down one path before pivoting back the way she'd come.

Relief flooded my system. I hadn't let myself consider what my next steps would be if she wasn't inside the maze somewhere. But she was here. She was okay. The tightness in my chest loosened like a strained seam unstitching itself.

Descending the ladder, I lowered to the ground and took off in her direction. "Becca!"

In the distance, I saw a flash of red—her sweatshirt—move between the tall corn stalks, and I called her name again. This time, I saw her body pause. "Stay there!"

Glancing up, I could see the gathering storm clouds. A flash of lightning and then an echoing crack of thunder had me jogging to get to her.

My dad had taught me as a little kid that you could count the seconds between lightning and the answering thunder to figure out how close a storm was. And there had been no delay in the loud rumble that had reverberated in my chest.

The pelting rain was coming a little faster, but I was almost to her. Her voice, high and frantic, whipped along with the wind, "Will?"

I rounded the corner, and there she stood, ten feet away. She looked small and lost among the surrounding corn stalks. Her hands were clenched at her sides, and her hair was starting to darken as the rain fell harder and faster. I saw the relieved breath she took as our eyes met. She pressed a hand to her chest, and her lips formed my name.

And that was when the sky opened up.

BECCA

He was here. Will was *here*.

Thunder crashed overhead as I took another grateful breath, willing my heart to slow down. Except Will was standing *right there* and my heart always seemed to be a step ahead where Will Clark was concerned.

But then he was striding up and hugging me hard. My arms went around his waist, and I clung to him as rain poured from the sky. I buried my face against his warm chest, moisture trickling down my neck and into my hair.

"I'm sorry," I said, loud enough to be heard over the splash of water and the rumble of thunder. "I didn't mean—"

"It's okay," his deep voice interrupted. "Let's get back and get out of this."

His urgency was enough to cut through my humiliation and self-recrimination, but just barely.

Will took my hand and pulled me along behind him. I kept my head down, focused on his boots in the muddy earth as rain dripped into my eyes. Eventually, we stepped out from between the corn rows into ankle-high grass surrounding this side of the maze.

The rain continued to lash us as we hurried along the main path through the farm, my hand still engulfed in Will's strong, sure grip. In minutes, the long, narrow building that housed the Bake Shop came into view. But Will darted around to the far side instead, leading me into his office.

It was warm inside but shadowed. Will flipped the light switch on and off, but the power must have been out. I could still hear the rain outside, loud against the tin metal roof above us, but it had quieted enough for my thoughts to intrude.

As my embarrassment surged back to the forefront, I felt Carl's fur move beneath my hand and then his impatient nose prodding me when I'd ignored him too long. I petted his head and stroked his ears as he did his best to lick the rain dripping down my arm from where I still had my sleeves pushed up. Will was moving around in the dim office while I stood rooted to the floor, the only light coming in weakly from a window near the door.

Straightening, I blurted, "I'm so sorry. I don't know what happened."

But Will was pulling a towel from the supply closet in the rear of the office and not listening to me at all. With the towel in hand, he moved to stand in front of me with a quiet but firm, "Carl, enough," that had the dog slinking back to his bed in the corner.

Will gently swiped the terrycloth across my forehead and cheeks, taking great care in his movements. I started babbling so I wouldn't burst into tears. "I was distracted, not paying attention to where I was going. My sister called again, and I just started moving. I didn't notice how dark and cold it had gotten."

He ran the towel down one exposed forearm and then the other, intent in his focus.

"The wind was picking up, and I could hardly hear Heather on the other end of the line," I continued my story. "By then, I realized I was in the corn maze, and I got off the phone, but I was upset." At this, Will's eyes found mine, a concerned edge drawing his dark brows together. "And not thinking straight."

But I didn't want to talk about the phone call. I didn't want to get into the mess with my sister or how she needed my money, but never me.

Will wiped the soft edge of the towel beneath one eye and down to my jaw. The drag of the fabric along my neck had me sucking in a sharp breath. "Thank you for finding me. I just panicked when I heard the thunder, and I couldn't get the map for the maze to pull up on my phone. I tried to go in one direction and push through the stalks, but I came out in waist-high grass on the back side of the field. So I went back in to try the other direction, and that's when I heard you calling for me."

He was using the cloth to dry the wet ends of my hair and still hadn't spoken.

Closing my eyes, I admitted, "I feel so stupid. Why can't you ever see me being totally capable, having it all together? It's always when I'm failing at something a child can manage that you—"

"Hey, stop that," Will finally said, low and firm.

I opened my eyes to his intense frown. But his hands were gentle as he passed the towel back across my forehead and hairline.

Swallowing, I insisted, "Admit it. That is what you thought."

"Maybe. Back when you were stuck in a tree," he said, but he softened the blow with a gentle swipe of the towel along my ear. "But that's what humans do, honey. We make snap judgments in the first five minutes of knowing someone. It's called a first impression for a reason. That doesn't mean it's a lasting one."

The deep timbre of his voice combined with the sweet endearment turned me inside out. I knew I shouldn't ask. It was borrowing trouble. But I asked anyway, "What *was* your first impression of me?"

Will focused on dabbing the skin of my collarbones and the base of my neck dry, but he smiled, this soft, tender thing that made my stomach flip. "I thought you were friendly. Talkative. A hugger."

Groaning, I covered my face with my hands.

A soft huff of laughter met my ears before Will gently pried my hands away from my overheated cheeks. He set about drying each finger carefully, his gaze focused on his task. "I didn't think I'd ever seen someone so genuinely happy to see me."

It was my turn to frown. "That's not true, Will. Your family. Your friends. Jordan and—"

"I don't know if you've noticed, but I'm not a friendly guy. I'm stubborn and not easy to get along with." He glanced up from where the towel was wrapped around my right hand and squeezed softly. "'Pain in the ass' has been bandied about. I'm the kind of guy people put up with. Yet you were so genuine and warm when you didn't even know my name. It threw me off. I was confused and distrustful. *That* was my first impression."

I wasn't sure how to respond. I felt sad at Will's self-assessment. Sure, he could come across as a crab sometimes, but he cared so much about the people in his life. He was an acts-of-service guy all day long. And being on the receiving end right now was as wonderful as it was foreign.

Before I could mount an argument regarding the inaccurate way Will saw himself, he asked quietly, carefully, "And what was your first impression of me?"

My mind drifted back to the day of the tree incident and then further still. I'd seen Will around the farm several times prior to our first meeting, always quiet, stoic, and frowning. Forever busy and on the go. Untouchable and unhappy.

Instead, I answered, referencing our first real encounter, "Capable. Reliable. Like there was no chance in the world you'd ever let anyone, even me—a clueless city girl—fall out of that tree." Then I paused dramatically before adding, "And you really wore the heck out of that backward hat."

"Yeah?" His gray eyes sparkled, catching every bit of light in the dim room and holding it hostage.

I liked the way he was looking at me. I liked how close we were in this dark room and the thoughtful way he'd dried my skin. I didn't think I'd mind it if Will wanted to take care of me for a very long time.

I grinned, unable to look away. "Oh yeah."

Will reached up and slowly grasped the wet bill of his ball cap, turning it to face backward. His gaze stayed playful and trained on me as he leaned in, so close I could feel his breath ghost across my still smiling mouth. I met him halfway, disbelieving and pretty sure this was an alternate reality where Will Clark was going to kiss me. But here we were, and it was happening.

I closed my eyes just as his nose brushed mine in a sweet caress.

At the first touch, I couldn't help but notice how unbelievably soft his lips were. Surprising for a man who was so rare with his smiles. I expected hard lines and firm coaxing, but Will's mouth greeted mine, warm and welcoming. He was all give and no take.

I could feel and taste the rainwater lingering on his lips because he'd taken care of me and didn't even bother wiping the moisture off himself. It was obvious Will was much better at taking care of others and ignoring what was best for him.

And then I couldn't think anymore because his calloused hand was cupping my cheek and sliding into my damp hair. I tilted my head, chasing the touch, pushing into his waiting grip.

My lips parted, inhaling a bracing breath as his tongue stroked a delicate path along the seam. Even as we deepened the kiss and our connection, Will kept the pace slow and steady. His other hand was flirting with the hem of my wet shirt before he trailed fingers beneath the fabric and up my spine. The confidence of his movements and his unhurried pace had me shivering as Will reached the band of my bra. His warm hand flattened against my back and urged me closer.

So I raised my arms and wrapped them over his shoulders. He felt so solid and present. I was protected and cared for. There was something intoxicating about the way he held me.

Will Clark kissed me like he did everything else—with single-minded attention and utter proficiency. I couldn't say I was as skilled or focused. I was caught up in his touch and his taste and how he made me feel.

When I shivered again, Will loosened his hold and sucked on my bottom lip until I groaned out my approval. But then he was pulling away.

"Arms up," he directed.

Distractedly, I opened my eyes and lifted my boneless limbs as Will snagged the hem of my red sweatshirt in his big hands.

He kept his gaze trained on my eyes as he lifted the soaked fabric up and over my head.

"Oh, okay," I said as cool air met my damp skin. "Yeah, we can do that."

I mentally considered what bra I'd put on that morning and nearly winced when I remembered the plain white cotton. Why couldn't I be wearing something sexy and see-through when Will rescued me from a rainstorm and peeled my shirt off while we made out in his office?

Will grinned and kissed me on the nose. "Good to know." But his eyes never dropped below my face.

I felt the drag of soft, dry fabric slide over my skin as Will carefully guided my arms into a worn blue flannel.

He didn't look down or away as he deftly did up the buttons until he reached the sensitive skin of my throat. I was encased in Will's dry shirt—one he must have retrieved along with the white towel now at our feet—while he stood before me, dark hair still dripping and his long-sleeved shirt wet and clinging to every part of his body.

"Thank you," I whispered, breathing in the scent of him—maple syrup and wood smoke—within the soft cotton.

"You're welcome," he replied as he reached over and pulled my long, damp hair out from inside the collar of my borrowed shirt. "You were shaking. I wanted to get you warm."

I could have corrected him, told him that I'd been shivering from his touch and how good it had felt to be in his arms. But instead, I reveled in the feel of Will's limitless care and concern.

The way he'd undressed and then redressed me had every feminine part of me swooning. He hadn't sneaked a single peek at my chest. Will had stopped kissing me to make sure I was comfortable. He'd respected boundaries when I'd been ready to hurdle over them like a track star.

That was maybe the sexiest thing that has ever happened to me.

"You're still all wet," I noted.

"I'll be okay. It's slowing down out there anyway." But he did take his hat off and brush a hand through his hair, the ends coming away damp.

I glanced toward the window. Listening, I did notice that the patter of raindrops was markedly less violent against the metal roof. And the sky was lightening as the storm gradually blew past.

"You should still probably get that wet shirt off," I said.

In reality, I was not this sassy, confident woman suggesting Will get undressed. But I figured I could fake it till I made it.

He raised a brow, his gaze knowing. But he didn't call me on it. "Oh, should I?"

I bent down and grabbed the towel from the floor. "I wouldn't want you to catch a cold."

Will grinned. "You've been in the South too long. That's just an old wives' tale." But he didn't wait for me to argue. He just reached back with one arm and did that hot guy thing where the shirt comes up and over with minimal effort and a single flexing bicep.

He watched me take him in, a roguish lock of black hair falling enticingly over his forehead.

I would like to say I exhibited Will's respectful restraint, but I did not. I ogled his fine form. And then I ogled it some more.

My greedy gaze moved over his leanly muscled body, taking in his firm chest with a smattering of dark hair. Briefly, I noted a scar on his rounded right shoulder, but I didn't let my eyes linger there. Instead, they skimmed the ridges of his taut abdomen and the very enticing vee that sliced into the waistband of his worn jeans. When I was done enjoying the return trip to Will's face, I found him looking on in amusement.

Taking a step closer, I tried to play it cool as I lifted the towel and started working it over his damp skin.

"I gave you my only backup shirt," he said, lips still tilted in a grin.

His hands came to rest on my waist while I leaned closer, running the terrycloth smoothly down one strong forearm.

"I don't mind," I offered magnanimously, and he laughed.

I made it to his belly button before Will gripped my fingers. He took the towel from my hands and tossed it on the chair behind me. Then we were kissing again, my arms wrapped behind his neck and Will's hands on my back guiding me in close.

The softness was still there, but we skipped right over the exploratory touches. I opened for Will as his tongue stroked into my mouth. He made a sound that I felt low in my belly when his warm palm gripped my waist beneath my borrowed shirt.

My fingers toyed with the wet ends of his hair. They were long and curling around the nape of his neck, and I liked scratching my nails against his scalp. Another low groan met my ears, and I thought it was okay that Will was a man of few words if he kept encouraging me like that.

But then static squawked from somewhere between us, and we both startled. A voice emerged, tinny and small but undeniably Laramie Burke. "William Jeffrey Clark the Fourth, did you or did you not find Becca? Are you both dead somewhere, struck by lightning?" Larry demanded over the radio.

Will cursed, and I stared in horror. Did everyone know that I'd wandered off like an idiot?

Shirtless Will gave me an apologetic wince before unclipping the walkie-talkie thing from his waistband and speaking. "Becca's fine. I've got her. We're both fine."

"Oh, well, gee. Thanks so much for letting us know. We've been worried sick but so glad you're—"

Will turned a dial on top until Larry's voice cut off abruptly. "I'll apologize later."

"They all knew I was missing?"

With a sigh, Will admitted, "I didn't know where you were. I came back to check on Mom after I saw the thunderstorm warning and saw all your stuff still out on the table." I straightened, remembering my laptop and bag. Noticing my alarm, Will squeezed my arm gently. "I brought it in here."

He pointed at my things sitting on a folding chair behind the desk.

"Thank you." My voice was thick with gratitude, not only for saving my computer but for rescuing me too. For caring enough to notice I wasn't safe and for tracking me down.

"I tried the sunflowers first, but when I couldn't find you there, I knew I didn't have much time before the weather turned. I radioed to see if anyone had seen you. And Larry had caught you going into the corn maze on the phone."

"My sister," I confirmed, looking down at where my fingers were nervously worrying the buttons along the flannel I wore.

I felt a finger beneath my chin. Raising my gaze to his, Will said, "I'm sorry she upset you again."

There was a question in his voice. Will knew that my relationship with my family was complicated, but I didn't want to talk about the phone call. I didn't want to talk about my sister or her increasingly heated demands for money. And most of all, I didn't want my crappy family history to sneak into this room with us and change the way Will was looking at me.

He was finally noticing me. Finally acting on our slow-simmering attraction despite his cautious nature. It felt tenuous, this thing happening between us. I didn't want to lose it.

"It's okay," I murmured.

Will scrutinized me for a moment before nodding. He glanced toward the window and the bright sunlight shining beyond the glass. "Looks like the storm moved on."

Disappointment threatened. Maybe the kissing had been madness-induced—a spell cast for only a moment. A literal perfect storm of circumstance, heightened emotions, and rain-slicked bodies. Part of me worried that Will would remember I was a tourist and pull away. And then my lips might never taste his again.

He roughly dragged the towel over his wet hair. "I should get out there and assess any damage. Make sure we don't have any downed trees and help Dad in the fields."

I nodded, already backing away. My fingers continued fidgeting with the buttons on my borrowed shirt, and I stared awkwardly for long enough that a star was probably born somewhere in the galaxy . . . maybe two.

"But I'll see you tomorrow?"

Will's question had me halting in my tracks. "Yeah." I cleared the high-pitched surprise from my voice. "I'll see you tomorrow."

"Good." He smiled.

Maybe the spell hadn't been broken.

Maybe Will would keep on looking at me like I was something special after all.

TAKE IT OR LEAF IT

The following morning was cold. It was the first time I'd had to switch the heat on in the tiny house. I thought of the fireplace in the living room and looked forward to snuggling up there tonight with a book and a glass of wine.

The thunderstorm had cleared out the evening prior, but it left cooler air in its wake, and when I made my way to the Orchard Bake Shop the following mid-September morning, I had to admit that it was a bit chilly for working outdoors.

I wore a striped beanie and several layers of warm clothes, but I knew that sitting outside for any length of time would cause the morning chill to seep through.

When I arrived at my table beneath the covered porch, Will's desk chair was waiting on me. And in it was a thick blanket. I picked up the soft dove-gray fleece and held it to my face. It was Will's alright. That same inexplicable scent of pancakes cooked over a campfire permeated the fabric and made my mouth water. How did he even smell like that?

I glanced around to make sure Will's mother hadn't seen me huffing the blanket like a lunatic. Then I set my laptop up and wandered to the window to place my breakfast order.

Maggie didn't comment on how I'd gone missing during the storm. She greeted me warmly, like always. Chloe said she'd come take her break with me in a little bit. And no one made a big deal about what had happened yesterday.

Huh. If no one else was going to give me a hard time about my mistakes, maybe I didn't have to beat myself up over them either.

The time away from my life back in Detroit had been good for me. I didn't have my grief staring me in the face every morning when I woke up in Mrs. Walters's apartment. I could ignore the texts and calls from my sister and the silence from my parents. They didn't even know where I was.

In Kirby Falls, I could be someone different. Someone who tried things and spent my time making an impact. Here, I had friends. Even in the short time I'd been in town—just over a month—I had Chloe and Jordan and Mac and Larry. They were kind, genuine people, and they liked and included me. I had Maggie's sweet mothering and so many new acquaintances from my adventures in town.

How was I supposed to leave in six weeks?

I stared at the blanket in my lap, as secure and thoughtful as the man who'd left it for me. How was I supposed to pretend that Will wasn't one of the biggest reasons I wanted to stay in Kirby Falls for good?

Guilt ate at me as I even considered the prospect of giving up Mrs. Walters's home—something she'd wanted me to have. I didn't know if I was strong enough to cut ties with my sister once and for all. A part of me always hoped for a relationship with Heather that went beyond use and abuse. Besides, if I wasn't there to give her money, who would take care of her when she got herself into trouble.

It was easy enough to ignore Heather's demands for bail money for our father when I was six hundred miles away. I knew that those funds wouldn't help Heather. They'd just further my dad's criminal career. The guilt-ridden, soft spot I had for my sister made the thought of packing up and abandoning Detroit nearly unconscionable.

But when Maggie delivered my latte and apple cider doughnut with a comforting squeeze to my shoulder and a sweet, "There you go, sugar," I couldn't ignore the warmth that flooded me at her genuine care.

What would it have been like to grow up with a mother like Maggie Clark?

A fresh wave of shame had me biting my lip. It was wrong and ungrateful and disloyal to think that way. I'd been lucky enough to find Mrs. Walters. Her unwavering support and gruff love had seen me through to adulthood. Heather had been stuck with only our neglectful parents for role models. No child deserved that. She'd already had a juvie record by the time I'd met Mrs. Walters. If anyone had needed saving, it was Heather.

While I couldn't change the past or my older sister's circumstances, I could try to help her now. Abandoning Heather and up and leaving Detroit to live out some fantasy in Kirby Falls wouldn't make me a better sister. I'd be one more person neglecting her in favor of my own selfish wants.

An image of a rain-soaked Will flashed in my mind. His warm touch on my bare skin. How he'd carefully buttoned me up in his shirt. Will Clark was definitely a want. A loud and insistent part of me fairly shouted that he was a need too.

My thoughts were leading me around in a circle of discontent. I picked up my phone and texted Pippa and Cece a picture of the sunset from the prior evening.

The storm front in the distance had made for some dramatic purples and blues as the sun had gone down. After we chatted back and forth via text for a few minutes, I settled in with my breakfast and got to work.

Chloe joined me an hour later, and we talked about the Orchard Festival tomorrow. I had plans to set up the vendor booths on Main Street bright and early with the rest of the volunteers. Chloe would be helping out in the Grandpappy's tent with Maggie, Will, Larry, Mac, and several more employees.

It wasn't until nearly lunchtime that I was startled out of my work by a strangled voice behind me.

"What in the hell is that?"

I turned to see Will's face hovering above my shoulder, staring in horror at my laptop screen.

Stifling a laugh, I put a hand up to block the character illustration I'd been working on.

But he gently pried my hand away to get a better look. I did laugh now. I guessed the cat was out of the bag, and our game of guess-Becca's-work-from-home good-girl career was over.

"Is that an ogre?" Will's face was a study in confused dismay. "Also, that doesn't seem physically possible."

"Stop." I giggled. "Just sit down, and I'll explain."

Will immediately climbed onto the seat next to me, straddling the bench and sitting close. His eyes finally drifted from the computer screen to scan my features.

"Hi," I murmured, feeling shy all of a sudden.

"Hi," he replied, a small smile tilting his lips up beneath his beard.

"I'm a graphic designer," I admitted, shifting the computer to face him more fully. "I work on book covers and graphics for authors. Sometimes . . ." I indicated the steamy image in front of us. "I make not-safe-for-work illustrations for special editions or swag or other merchandise."

Will eyed the ogre and his human bride, both scantily clad in a hayloft, their bodies frozen in a moment of interspecies passion.

"It's for a monster romance," I explained.

"A . . . monster romance," he echoed.

"Don't kink shame."

Will's eyes flicked over at my teasing. "I apologize to any ogres I offended."

I grinned.

"Will you show me some covers you've worked on?"

Despite his initial shock, Will seemed genuinely curious. So I maneuvered to a folder and pulled up some images, giving him a cross-section of book covers I'd created over the years.

"This doesn't count as you guessing my job," I finally said after Will had watched me scroll through photos for several minutes. "You cheated. You sneaked up on me."

He looked affronted. "I was just walking by, minding my own business, when I saw an ogre with someone bent over a hay bale. I could have been a kid on my way to get a doughnut, you know."

I laughed. "Well, you still didn't win."

"Fine," he agreed, amusement softening the typically firm line of his mouth. Maybe I was noticing his lips a little more intensely since the events of yesterday. Chances were good that was the case. "We'll call it a draw."

"A draw," I confirmed.

"You sticking around for a bit?"

"Yep." I wondered where this was going. We hadn't discussed the kissing yesterday. Will had gone to his truck to grab a dry shirt and then joined his father in the orchard to make sure there hadn't been any damage to the apples or the property. I'd gathered my things and walked in a kiss-drunk haze to the tiny house. Then I'd slept in Will's shirt. I'd considered washing it and bringing it back to him today but couldn't bring myself to actually do it.

"Jordan is bringing pizza over for lunch. Would you like to join us?" Will sounded cautious. He watched my face carefully, like I might try to kiss him again or demand a marriage proposal.

There wasn't really anything to be weird about. Lunch with Will and Jordan and Chloe wasn't, like, a date or something. And honestly, I didn't think Will was the kind of guy who had any intention of playing games with me. We probably needed to have a conversation before any more kissing happened, but I'd worry about that when the time came.

I was on vacation. It wasn't like I could just uproot my life and marry the guy. Not that he was asking to marry me. He was asking me about pizza. Currently. I needed to speak with words, not just obsess inwardly.

"Sure," I replied, pretty proud of how cool and unaffected I sounded. "No pineapple, though."

WILL

"What are you doing? We're supposed to meet Seth and the team in an hour."

I didn't so much as twitch when Jordan came into my living room questioning me. A few minutes ago, I'd heard the security system at the door leading from the garage beep announcing his arrival. I knew we had plans for conditioning this evening with the kids. But I'd gotten home from work forty minutes ago and thought I could sneak in an episode before Jordan picked me up.

Then I'd gotten sucked in, and now, here I was, snuggled up on the couch with a blanket over my workout clothes and an episode of *The Walking Dead* up on the television. Carl was curled up against my thigh with his head beneath the covers as if he, too, was embarrassed for me.

"I'm ready to go. I just wanted to finish this episode."

I felt Jordan sit down on the couch on the other side of Carl. "Are you watching *The Walking Dead*?"

"Yes," I replied, impatient. Then I clicked the volume up on the remote.

A few minutes progressed in blessed silence, and then Jordan piped up again, "But why are you watching *The Walking Dead*?"

I sighed and hit pause on the episode. Turning to Jordan, I grumbled, "Are you going to talk the whole time?"

"Trust me. You're going to want to watch the rest of this one later. I remembered when it aired near the holidays, and I pretty much thought the Governor ruined Christmas."

I threw the remote control at his shoulder. "Hey. No spoilers."

Jordan laughed. "Man, this show premiered over a decade ago. Where were you in 2010?"

Vibe ruined, I got out from under the blanket and stood. "Come on." I grabbed my hat off the coffee table and my water bottle, fully anticipating these high schoolers to run me ragged.

I patted Carl and told him I'd be back later.

"What?" Jordan was still laughing. "I'm sorry. I didn't say what happened. Also, I've never seen you interested in a television show. What brought all this on?"

I paused in the mudroom so Jordan could go out ahead of me and I could lock up. While there, I considered how to handle this. I didn't particularly want to admit that I was watching the show because of Becca. She'd mentioned it when she'd found out my dog's name and then made a joke that went right over my head. So one night a couple of weeks ago, I'd found the first episode on demand and watched it.

And when that episode ended, and I didn't hate it, I kept going. I'd accidentally stayed up until three in the morning. Now I was on season four, and the late-night binge-watching had really cut into my sleep. But I didn't actually mind. Part of me thought maybe I could casually bring up the show to Becca now that I knew what she meant about Carl the dog and Carl the boy from the series. Also, why couldn't that kid just stay in the damn house?"

Instead, I told my friend, "I just happened to catch the first episode and liked it. So now I'm watching it. It's not a big deal."

Jordan eyed me suspiciously as I climbed into the passenger seat of his big black truck and buckled up. "You just *happened* to watch the first episode . . . on demand on your television."

It wasn't phrased as a question, but his curiosity was front and center.

Sighing, I admitted, "Becca said something about it when she found out Carl's name. Asked if I was a fan of the show."

Jordan's gaze flicked to mine as he navigated down the steep incline of my driveway out onto the main road. "Okaaayyy."

I reached for the bill of my hat and gave it a sharp tug downward. "She thought I was being funny. Like, 'Carl, get in the house' because he's a dog, and that idiot kid on the show is always getting told to stay in the house."

Jordan chuckled. "That's pretty good. And it would have been hilarious if you'd done that on purpose instead of just giving your dog the name of a middle-aged human being who sounds like he works on cars in his spare time and chews tobacco."

I sighed again. It was easy to ignore Jordan. I knew he was just giving me shit. And besides, Carl was a good name for a dog. I didn't need to defend it.

"So you got curious and watched it?" he prompted as he maneuvered the vehicle down the winding roads of the mountainside. "Because of Becca, the tourist."

My eyes cut in his direction, but his face was impassive, easygoing. The tourist comment hadn't been an intentional jab, but I could tell he'd said it to make a point. You didn't know someone for twenty-five years without recognizing the meaning behind their words.

"I didn't put a whole lot of thought into it, Jordan."

He hummed noncommittally. "Right. Well, I've seen all eleven seasons and even some of the spinoff series. Feel free to share your *TWD* journey with me. Angry text whenever the need arises."

"I can't imagine the need will arise," I said.

"Or I guess you could talk to Becca, the tourist, about it."

"Stop calling her that," I snapped and then shook my head at how fucking ridiculous I was being.

It was confirmed when Jordan made a pleased sound from my left. "I knew it! I knew you liked her."

"What are we? Twelve?" But I could feel the heat creeping beneath my tee shirt and up my neck.

"About you, William J. Clark the Fourth, being into a girl? Yes. Yes, we are. Because that is how stunted you are. You have never, not once, thought about a woman enough to go home and search out a television show she mentioned." Jordan shook his head in wonder. "This is like Christmas."

My exhalation took my last two sighs and combined them into a mega-breath. "I am not discussing this with you."

"Why not? I'm your best friend. I'm the perfect candidate." He pulled up to the stop sign at the intersection of my private road and the highway. In no hurry, he turned in his seat to regard me, amusement evident in every one of his features. "And I've been waiting a million years for you to be interested in something—shit, anything—that wasn't baseball."

This insinuation that I was so consumed with the sport was . . . okay, accurate. But how else did people expect me to behave when being a major league pitcher had been my only goal in life? That level of compete required work and focus. It was not something you could just stumble into.

So, yeah, I'd gone all-in on a bet that hadn't paid out in the end. Of course I felt like shit about it. Maybe if I'd been a less motivated, less intense person, I would have let baseball run its course. Maybe I would have played in high school and then in college, and maybe that was where my journey would have ended. If I hadn't been so driven, maybe I would have met a nice girl while studying at the University of North Carolina. Perhaps we would have gotten married and settled down. If not for the overwhelming need I'd felt to be the best at every damn thing relating to the sport, I wouldn't be back on my family's farm with nothing to show for it.

Those were all very real possibilities, and Jordan was an asshole to think I didn't consider that every day of my life.

"I don't want to talk about Becca."

Just thinking about Becca was hard enough. The kissing had been good yesterday. Really good. I'd liked having her in my arms at Legacy Hills, doing what barely constituted as dancing. But drying her off after a rainstorm and taking care of her had been a different sort of feeling altogether. And then she'd been playful and sweet, responsive in a way that told me we'd be plenty compatible in other areas.

But the feeling of fear when I hadn't been able to find her during a dangerous situation had been unexpected and troubling. My worry and panic had gone beyond losing a wayward leafer in the corn maze. I'd been concerned about Becca—desperate to find her and make her safe. It had gone well past feeling responsible for a tourist at Grandpappy's. And the stark relief at finally locating her had been enough to rattle me.

I didn't need to take one failed obsession and replace it with another. I couldn't get so invested in this thing with Becca. Despite how I felt about her, she was still a visitor to Kirby Falls. And she was going to leave. Until I heard different, it was better to keep myself grounded and rational. Manage my motivations and expectations to something realistic.

Even if he was trustworthy and practically my brother, gossiping with Jordan wouldn't help with all the complications surrounding Becca.

I needed to have a conversation with her, but I was dragging my feet on it. It seemed pointless to ask her what she wanted when I didn't even know that myself. But some instinct told me to proceed with caution.

My friend gave me a pass and changed the subject. But I was mostly quiet on the way to the high school.

We did a four-mile run with the dozen boys present. I enjoyed it for the simple fact that it kept Jordan winded and unable to question me any more about Becca.

After twenty minutes of plyometric exercises, Seth called me over to a bucket of balls and one of the juniors on the varsity team. Mason Gentry played first base, but he also pitched when needed. Seth wanted me to advise him on a few things. The kid was big for his age and could throw hard, but his control was shit. But that was something that could be taught and managed. I watched him pitch to Jordan behind the plate for several minutes before I talked him through some things he could do to help the ball stay in the strike zone.

He made adjustments and pitched a few more with marked improvement. Gentry seemed like a good kid. He took direction well and asked the right kinds of questions. But more than that, he listened.

When I looked around, I noticed all the other players were still in the stands watching. I thought they would have packed it in.

"Thanks for taking the time to train with us, Mr. Clark. And thanks for the pointers. I'll work on it," Mason said quietly, drawing my attention from the onlookers.

"It's just Will," I said. "And it's no problem. You'll get there."

Seth and Mason took the balls and left the infield as Jordan jogged up to the mound from home plate. He looked smug, and I knew what he was going to harp on.

"Not a word," I groused as he tossed me his mitt, catching me off guard.

"What?" He grinned. "I wasn't going to say anything."

But I knew it was a lie. Jordan was dying to bring up the coaching thing again.

I eyed the boys still gathered on the bleachers as they finally stood, laughing and messing with one another and made for the parking lot.

I'd liked being part of a team at one time. It was different as a pitcher. I'd had my own pitching coach, and practices weren't the same for players in my position. But the camaraderie had been one of the things I'd always loved about baseball. I hadn't always been driven by the control and the challenge of pitching a great game. In the beginning, it had been about being a good teammate and earning a win for the players I shared the field with.

"But that had to feel good, right?" Jordan said, ignoring my threat.

I sent him a glare, but admitted, "Yeah. He seems like a good kid with talent."

"And you could help him," Jordan insisted. "You're patient and they respect the hell out of you."

Reaching down for my water bottle in the grass, I snorted in response.

Jordan grabbed his mitt out of my hand and whacked me in the stomach with it. "Shut up. They do."

There wasn't anything about my situation that should make those kids look at me starry-eyed. I was a cautionary tale accompanied by a mournful headshake. Jordan was supportive but misguided.

I didn't even know what it would take to be a high school coach—even if I wanted to. Which I didn't. I knew the assistants didn't need to be teachers at Kirby Falls High School, but I wasn't sure about the head coach.

Briefly, the idea of volunteering as an assistant coach flitted through my mind. The games. The kids. The teamwork. The camaraderie.

But a whole boatload of painful reminders accompanied the good aspects. I still felt like a failure. Adding hometown cliché to my résumé left a bitter taste in my mouth.

"Let's go," I said, deliberately trying to get Jordan off this topic. "We have the Orchard Festival in the morning."

"Okay, but let's finish that episode when we get back to your house."

Jordan was digging his keys out of his waist belt, a.k.a. fanny pack that I gave him relentless shit for, and didn't see me roll my eyes.

"Fine. But just watching. You don't get to commentate the whole episode." I pointed in his direction. "And no more spoilers."

"Cross my heart," Jordan swore with a grin.

And I just knew I was going to regret this.

I'd made it my goal to get down to Main Street early enough to set up our own tables for Grandpappy's and the Bake Shop beneath our big white tent. But when I arrived to see all six tables already arranged in an organized U-shape, complete with chairs for all employees, I knew the volunteers had gotten to us first. And when I'd found a small cooler filled with bottles of water hidden beneath the corner table, I'd known which helpful volunteer had taken care of us.

I glanced down the street to see if I could spot Becca in her lime-green volunteer tee shirt, but she wasn't anywhere nearby. So I got to work unloading the produce in the back of the truck instead. The rest of the crew would be along within the hour and then things would really get going.

Mom and Chloe would be under the tent with the rest of the Grandpappy's staff, serving apple cider slushies and all manner of baked goods. They'd even recruited Laramie to their side to assist in the prep work so that Mom and Chloe could handle the face-to-face with the customers. I was a little jealous that she'd thought of that while I had to be public-facing, selling Grandpappy's merchandise and fifteen varieties of apple on the farm side of things with Mac, my father, my aunt and uncle, and a handful of other farm employees.

The Judd's Orchard tent was right next door, as to be expected, and I shot Joan a salute when I noticed her arrival a few minutes after mine. She had her sister, Candy—right, *Candace*—on her heels, awkwardly carrying some sort of cardboard cutout. It looked like a giant apple with a cowboy hat. That was . . . different. But maybe kids would be into a photo op with a cartoon apple. I didn't know what the cowboy hat was all about. This was North Carolina, not Texas.

That reminded me, I needed to talk to Mac about social media crap. She handled that for Grandpappy's Farm, and Eloise Carter had given us strict instructions for tagging or hashtagging or something. I had the email on my phone.

When Mac strolled in, dark ponytail swinging, ten minutes before the start of the festival, I resisted my eye roll and pulled her aside. "Hey, so for social media, you're supposed to take photographs throughout the day and tag @TheOrchardFestival and hashtag a bunch of things so that Eloise can share them across their channels. I just forwarded you the info to the farm email address."

"Hello, William. Yes, I'm doing well, my dear cousin. I hope you are too," she replied dryly, shoving her giant purse under the table in the back.

"Just do it, Mac Attack."

"Don't you dare," she growled.

I grinned, unrepentant. "What?"

Her gray eyes—near replicas of my own, passed down from our grandfather—blazed fire. "You better not use that stupid nickname that Brady calls me."

"Which one?" I teased. The guy had about ten that he cycled through regularly. Mac Attack. Big Mac. Maxi Pad. Mac Daddy. Mac Truck. Mac and Cheese. Mac Book Pro. Brady Judd just never knew when to give up.

But I did, so I left Mac alone before she got her revenge on me. "Truce," I said, holding up my hands. "Just do the social media thing so I don't have to worry about it."

"Social media is my job, so, of course, I'll do it. You're not the only capable person under this tent, Will." Then she tightened her ponytail and shot me a glare before going over to talk to Larry and Chloe.

Frowning, I wondered where that snipe had come from. My cousin was a sassy firecracker any day of the week, but I hadn't meant to indicate that she couldn't handle herself. Sure, sometimes I didn't like how she shirked her responsibilities—requesting time off for arbitrary day dates or showing up on time by just the skin of her teeth. But I knew Mac was good at her job. I should apologize to her later.

Soon enough we were so busy that I didn't have time to think about the way I'd irritated my cousin. We sold apples by the bushel, peck, and half peck. My dad fielded questions about the farm while I bagged produce. I could see Mom and Larry and Chloe doing a brisk business from across the tent. They ran out of boxed apple cider doughnuts by noon. I knew because I sneaked over there to grab one for lunch, but I was a half hour too late.

Just after 1:30 p.m., I happened to glance up from the restock I was doing on the Mutsu apples when I noticed a lime-green tee shirt hovering at the corner of our table. Becca stood off to the side so that she wasn't in the way of any of the customers crowding around.

She wore a royal-blue Burke Hardware hat with her long blond ponytail snaked through the hole in the back. When she met my gaze, her face split into a wide smile.

I set down the crate I'd been grabbing yellow-green apples from and met her near the tent pole. "Hey."

"Hi, how are you? You guys have been so busy all day."

It was good to see her. I could tell from her rate of speech that she was just this side of jumpy. I felt that same happy dip in my belly that likely afflicted her, but I was better at hiding it. Becca rambled when she was nervous, and it was fucking adorable.

"Yeah, it's packed this year," I agreed. "You've been busy too, I bet."

She nodded. "Oh yeah. We got through setup surprisingly quickly, but I've been checking in with Eloise often to help out with whatever she needs."

I frowned at the thought of Eloise Carter wielding her influence and cornering Becca into overworking herself. "Have you gotten a break? Did you eat lunch?"

Becca brightened. "That's why I was loitering. I'm taking my break now, and I wanted to see if you or your mom or anyone else needed me to pick up anything."

She'd been working hard since six in the morning. Setting up tables, lugging equipment around, and running all over Main Street to make sure everything was perfect. And when she got a minute to herself to refuel, she'd come here instead.

"Becca, you don't need to—"

But I was cut off by Larry from over my shoulder. "Becca! We love you! Could you grab us something from the Empanada Shack?"

I watched incredulously as Mac joined in begging for food. "That would be amazing."

"Of course!" Becca said.

"I'll write down our order and grab you some cash," Mac said and then returned to my mother behind the cash register.

"You don't have to take care of them," I said as soon as my cousins wandered off. "They're adults. They can get their own lunch."

"I know." She smiled. "But I like helping. And they've been working so hard all day."

Debatable.

Before I could argue further, I felt my mother step up beside me. "Hey, Becca honey! You're not working too hard, are you?"

"No. Not at all. My shift is over at three, and I'll be able to go around and enjoy the festival after that."

"Well, good," my momma said, smiling at Becca. And to me, she instructed, "Here's some money and our order. Why don't you go with Becca over to the empanada food truck and help her bring everything back?"

It was phrased like a question, but I could read between the punctuation.

"That's okay," Becca was already protesting.

Mom's eyes narrowed at me, waiting for my argument. I sighed but didn't call her on the blatant setup attempt. I actually wanted to go with Becca.

"Sure thing," I replied, taking the list and the money and ducking beneath the rope holding the corner of the tent in place.

"Thank you, Becca! We appreciate you, sweet pea!"

Becca smiled at my mother's parting words, but then she looked at me and opened her mouth, the apology practically preparing to high dive off her tongue.

"It's okay," I said, gently grabbing her arm beneath the edge of her shirtsleeve. "They can spare me."

"Are you sure?" she murmured worriedly.

"Yep."

I kept the hand at her elbow to guide her between festivalgoers. The street was packed with people, and Becca was petite. I didn't want her to get run over by some rude tourists. However, my size and general facial expression afforded me some space among the folks circulating.

After working under the tent all morning, it felt nice to be under the September sun.

Becca said, "I'm looking forward to three o'clock when I can take my time and go visit all the booths. Since you're the insider, is there anywhere in particular I should be sure to hit?"

I watched a little boy come racing up with a stick of cotton candy that was bigger than he was. I reached down to grab Becca's hand to tug her to the side to avoid the undoubtedly sticky kid as he brushed close by.

It took me a minute to consider her question and then another minute to finally let go of her hand. "It's been a while since I've done more than work the festival," I admitted. "I'm probably not the best person to ask."

"Oh, okay," she said, nodding around a half-hearted smile that she tried to pass off as normal. But I'd seen her when her grin could hardly contain her joy. I was familiar with the difference.

I didn't know how to explain my complicated feelings surrounding my hometown unless I told her about baseball, and this wasn't really the time or the place. It wasn't her fault or anything she'd said.

Nowadays, when I thought of the Orchard Festival, I only associated it with work. But there'd been a time when the biggest event in Kirby Falls hadn't been all duty and obligation and my ass parked behind a table for eight hours.

At one time, the Orchard Fest had meant giant bags of cotton candy and weaving through pedestrians. When I'd been little, my dad had propped me up on a stool so I could grab the apples for him while he and Mom had sold to the tourists. I remembered liking the attention from the strangers. I'd felt special to be a part of the magic of my hometown.

Later, the event had meant riding in the parade on Sunday with the rest of the baseball team. It had felt like a lot of nonsense and small-town hero worship but the support and the applause had been nice to receive from neighbors in the crowd.

I couldn't remember when the Orchard Fest went from a fun weekend in mid-September shared with family and friends to something I dreaded on my calendar, but seeing Becca take it all in with fresh eyes made me feel a bit ashamed.

I didn't want to disappoint her even more, so I didn't say any of that. I just let it go.

It was important to remember that this was all new and exciting to Becca because she wasn't from here. Her status as a tourist just reiterated the fact that she wasn't staying.

No matter how much I'd liked kissing her and holding her and even dancing with her, she would still leave. It wouldn't do me any good to think about how good she'd tasted, how soft she was in my arms, and the sweet sounds she'd made against my lips if it had a big expiration date on it. We definitely needed to talk about where we went from here.

BECCA

The line at the Empanada Shack was long, but Will told me it would be worth it. We chatted while we waited, but I could tell Will was skirting around something. He'd tugged on his hat no less than four times, and by now, I knew what that meant.

When he'd first seen me outside of the Grandpappy's tent, he'd looked . . . I didn't know. On anyone else, I would have called their expression pleased. But Will's face was typically so stoic and reserved that the change was a stark contrast. One that had filled me with sunny warmth. He'd looked like he wanted to tug me by the waist and kiss me right there on Main Street.

And then he'd guided me through the crowd and even held my hand. But as we'd walked and talked, a change had come over him. Something I'd said or done had made him pull back.

Maybe he hadn't wanted anyone to get the wrong idea about us. Will was practically a celebrity in his hometown. It could have been that he didn't want to be seen holding my hand.

I ignored the spike of disappointment that thought caused and did my best to focus on the present, not my best second-guessing of the recent past.

"What do you mean my dad let you drive the tractor?"

I couldn't help but laugh at his incredulous expression. "I don't know! I was walking near where he was working, and he told me he wanted to show me something. So he led me through the plantings for the Christmas trees you all sell in the winter, and I'd asked about a million questions. He was patient and kind, and the next thing I knew, he was letting me drive the tractor."

Will shook his head, bewildered. "He didn't let me—his own son—drive a tractor until I was fifteen and had my learner's permit."

I laughed again as the line shifted forward a foot.

"I must look more trustworthy than a teenage boy, I guess."

"No doubt he was charmed by you and thrilled to have an avid audience to discuss Fraser firs."

I grinned. Then my eye snagged on something amazing over Will's shoulder.

Grabbing his arm, I practically squealed, "Oh my gosh. Look at them."

Will glanced backward but then turned back. "What am I looking at?"

"Them!" I whisper-yelled, my eyes going wide. "The elderly couple in the matching shirts. They are so adorable."

With another look over his shoulder, Will finally zeroed in on the couple meandering down the center of Main Street. They were both gray-haired and a little stooped with age. But they walked arm in arm and seemed to delight in the whole spectacle of the Orchard Festival. They were enjoying themselves. And why shouldn't they? She wore an orange tee shirt that said "He's My Sweet Potato," and his matching shirt said "I Yam."

I was still watching them pass by, but I could feel Will's attention on me. Shaking my head ruefully, I said, "They are so cute with their gray hair and wrinkles. You never see stuff like that in Detroit. I love this place."

Partway through my little overshare, I realized that I maybe should have kept that sort of stuff to myself. Admitting to the guy you'd kissed a few days ago that you were into matching outfits was probably the quickest way for him to lose interest.

When I got the nerve to meet Will's eyes, his were thoughtful and shadowed beneath his ball cap.

"Y'all want to scoot up?"

A voice from behind jolted us forward as the line for empanadas had progressed without us.

"Sorry!" I apologized brightly to the middle-aged man.

When I faced forward again, Will said quietly, "You seem really involved with Kirby Falls. All the groups and the volunteering. The bird-watching and the bowling league. You must be part of so many things back home. What do you do back in Detroit?"

My mind went blank, and I had to swallow a few times before it re-engaged.

What did I do back in Detroit?

Well, there had been the failed book club attempt at my local library, and I'd been trying to decide on a hobby to take up for a few months now.

The embarrassing truth was I didn't go out of my way to join things and meet people in Detroit. But I was doing it in Kirby Falls, and I didn't know what that said about me. I had this idea in my head that people here were friendlier and more accepting, but that couldn't be true of the hundreds of thousands of people who lived in my city. Something about Kirby Falls gave me confidence and made me fearless. I felt freer here than I did in Detroit, so I'd branched out and made myself available to new experiences.

For a moment, I considered Will's reluctance to go out and take part in his town. Maybe hometowns were just complicated when you didn't feel like you belonged there. I could understand Will's lack of enthusiasm. He probably felt trapped. Being back in Kirby Falls hadn't really been his choice.

This place was different and exciting to me—a girl from the city, a tourist experiencing so many new things. Will had a whole lifetime to experience the reality of Kirby Falls. He had to deal with nosy neighbors and people who reminded him of all the things he'd lost. I could definitely see how that might not be all sunshine and rainbows.

I was enamored with the novelty and newness of rural North Carolina. I loved that it was so different from the life I'd led thus far. Detroit made me feel trapped in a lot of ways too.

"I . . ." I began finally, but before I could admit the sad truth—that I was a lonely hermit who hid herself away and braced for encounters with her family, my phone buzzed in my hand.

Wow. What perfect timing.

My sister's name flashed across the screen, and the resulting dread crept up my spine. I thought about it for a fraction of a second before I sent it straight to voicemail.

Her calls and texts had been gaining in frequency and fury. The afternoon I'd gotten lost in the corn maze, I'd tried to endure her accusations (that I didn't care about her) and her anger (that I was a huge snobby bitch who thought I was better than everyone). I knew whatever Heather had to say today would be more of the same. She wanted to know where I was and when I was coming home. And I just couldn't bring myself to tell her.

If I knew the money she kept demanding was for her and not my dad, I probably would have already wired it to her. I'd never been very good at setting boundaries the way my therapist always encouraged. But I could, however, separate Heather's needs from my parents'. They'd ruined enough. Wasted enough. *Destroyed* enough.

But I owed it to Heather to help her, to improve her life, when I'd been the lucky one. I'd escaped and been unable to take her with me. So a part of me would always feel responsible for my older sister.

Will's tall frame cast a shadow over my phone screen, so I knew he'd watched as I hit the red button, declining the call. The guilt was a slow, steady rise that painted my cheeks hot with shame.

"I'll call her back," I said, pasting on some approximation of a smile or what I could manage of one.

I moved forward, and Will followed. We were next up in line at the food truck window.

Quietly, from my side, Will murmured, "I'm not trying to butt in, but it's okay to want to protect yourself, Becca."

Unable to meet the knowing in his eyes, I settled my gaze on his beard-covered chin. It looked like he'd trimmed it a little since yesterday, and we were close enough that I caught a hint of his sweet, woodsy scent.

I nodded, but my voice emerged small and remorseful all the same. "I know. It doesn't make the execution any easier, though."

"Next," a friendly voice called from the window.

I breathed a sigh of relief that we could put that awkward conversation behind us in favor of ordering an unholy number of empanadas. Will suggested I try one of each of the five varieties to figure out my favorite. "They're always at Firefly on Wednesdays, so you can order your favorites for next time."

Then we ordered for the crew at Grandpappy's and paid in advance before stepping to the side and waiting for our number to be called. It didn't take long at all, and soon we were on our way back to the big white tent on the corner of 3rd and Main.

"Here," Will said, passing me an empanada from the bag. It had a C stamped into the flaky, golden crust. "It's corn, onion, potato, and cheese. It's my favorite."

I waited for a family with two strollers to pass while I took a big bite of the filled pastry. "Holy cannoli," I breathed, sucking in air to cool my mouth. "This is amazing. The filling is so hot and creamy." I moaned around another bite, and the woman with one of the strollers gave me a look.

Maybe I'd groaned out my approval a little too enthusiastically.

Will coughed into his fist and drew my attention. His neck was pink below his trimmed beard.

Fighting embarrassment, I finished the empanada in two more bites as we continued walking. But when the Grandpappy's tent came into view, Will snagged my hand and pulled me to the side of all the foot traffic in the middle of the street. We emerged behind the vendor tents on a side lane closed for the festival, and he released me.

I felt the surprise and confusion on my face as I turned to look at him.

Will cleared his throat and said, "I just thought we should talk for a minute . . . about what happened. About the kiss."

"Oh. Right." Nerves had my fingers tightening on the paper bag in my hand.

"The thing is . . . I like you, Becca. But I know you're just here for the season, and I'm not really in the market to be anybody's vacation fling." He sounded tired but earnest, and every single one of my hopes regarding further kisses with Will Clark basically plummeted to the pit of despair. I definitely should not have mentioned the old people and their adorable matching shirts.

"I think," he continued, "that it might be better for both of us if we just stay friends while you're in town."

My head nodded along because it felt like the right thing to do, and I desperately wanted to react appropriately here. I didn't feel like crying or anything so dramatic, but I *was* disappointed. The ache of it left me hollow.

"Yeah, of course. Friends. Friends would be great," I said decisively.

His gray eyes searched my face, likely hunting for a sign that I might turn into a clingy, crazy person and go rogue. But I wouldn't do that. I knew what Will had suggested was the smart way to proceed. I *was* a tourist, and starting something with him would only lead to complications and messy endings. I knew it in my soul. Leaving Kirby Falls in six weeks was going to shatter something inside me. Dragging home a broken heart would only make it worse.

My life—as messed up as it was—was back in Detroit. A temporary fling wouldn't be satisfying for either of us. Well, it would probably be satisfying. I mean, I'd seen the size of Will's hands. But there was no reason to make things weird. I was happy to be Will's friend. Honestly, that seemed like a pretty short list, so maybe this was the better deal anyhow.

While I could definitely understand where Will was coming from, I had a sense of losing something significant. Hovering on the precipice of adventure. The delicate feelings of liking a person and having them like you back but you never really got a chance to get off the ground. I'd been in standby mode since we'd kissed two days ago, and now the airline was telling me they didn't have a seat for me after all.

"We should get this stuff back," I said when I realized I'd been quiet for too long. I hoisted up one of the two giant paper bags we were carrying as proof, and I made sure to hold Will's steady gaze while I did it.

"Sure." He nodded and led me back to the tent.

When we arrived, I passed over the empanadas. Will pulled out mine and put them on a paper tray before handing them over. My appetite had abandoned me, but I smiled and thanked him nonetheless. I wasn't about to eat here with his family. I was a party crasher—someone who'd overstayed their welcome. The Clarks would never make me feel that way, but it was what my anxiety was shouting loud and clear.

Unaware of my inner turmoil, Maggie strolled up with a bright smile on her face. She handed me a plastic container filled with six apple cider doughnuts, rolled in cinnamon sugar and sparkling in the midday sun. "For you. For dessert. Thank you for fetching lunch for all of us."

Will eyed his mother. "Are those the same doughnuts that were sold out an hour ago?"

"What?" Maggie challenged. "I was saving them for our girl here."

Our girl.

The mood shifted with Will's mother's statement. Looking quickly away, he appeared as let down as I felt. Weirdly enough, that gave me some small consolation. But before Maggie could notice how heavily her words had landed, a customer called her name and drew her attention away.

I mustered up a smile and offered, "I'll share with you if you'd like."

"Oh yeah?" Will replied, and my traitorous mind flashed back to when he'd been rain drenched and beautiful, saying the exact same thing in his office before he'd flipped his hat around and kissed me.

"Yep," I replied quickly, already snapping open the plastic and passing him a circle of deep-fried heaven. "That's what friends are for."

WILL

Tuesday night's conditioning practice with the baseball team ended up being more one-on-one time with the kids than I was expecting. But the boys were eager and hungry, and I could understand wanting to learn all you could. I'd worked with Mason Gentry a bit more, the pitcher I'd shown a few pointers to last week. Once I'd focused my attention on one kid, it seemed the others wanted their five minutes with the has-been too.

Overall, I didn't mind. They seemed like good players. And they were out training of their own volition. Motivation wasn't something teenage boys were born with, so it didn't feel like a wasted effort to take some time out of my day to talk to them about the sport.

When we finished up, Jordan managed to get Seth to agree to come to dinner with him and Chloe. He invited me, but I thought it best to let them have some time to themselves.

As everyone packed up their water and gear, a middle-aged white man approached me from where he'd been parked on the bleachers for much of the unofficial practice. He wore khakis and a button-up and looked like any other baseball dad hanging out in the stands.

The man caught me throwing on a hoodie as the night air dipped, cooling the sweat lingering on my skin from our earlier run.

"Hi there! I wanted to introduce myself," the stranger said, a pleasant smile easy on his face.

"Will Clark." I shook the hand he extended, feeling my muscles go tight as familiar tension took hold. I wondered what this guy wanted.

"I'm Jim Gentry. Mason's dad."

My shoulders relaxed. "Good kid you got there."

Jim smiled like he knew it. "I'm lucky. He doesn't give me much trouble. I wanted to thank you for taking the time to work with him."

I reached for my duffel bag and straightened. "It's no trouble. He's talented and a good listener. That's a rare combination."

The man nodded. "I'm hopeless at baseball. Never played in my life. But we go out and throw a lot, and I come to his games. It doesn't count for much, but it's something."

I thought about my own dad. He'd encouraged my love of baseball from a young age. We'd played catch out on the farm, and he'd even driven over to Chapel Hill to see some of my college games. I remembered my family in the stands when I pitched my first start in the majors. My dad had a whistle you could hear from anywhere, and when I'd taken the mound, I'd heard it, as sharp and supportive as a slap on the back. Sometimes the best thing you could do was show up, and I'd been lucky as hell to have a father who supported me. Mason was clearly in the same boat.

"That is something," I finally replied.

Jim Gentry fell into step beside me as we made our way off the field and out to the parking lot behind the high school. Mason was ahead with a group of boys, laughing and horsing around. Seth and Jordan were gone already.

"I'm also the principal here at Kirby Falls High," Jim said suddenly.

I'd known that my old principal, Carlton Early, had retired a few years back, but I hadn't heard who replaced him. I knew they'd brought in a new hire from Georgia or somewhere.

"You like it?" I asked to be conversational, not entirely sure where this was going.

Jim chuckled a little under his breath. "I do. I've been here three years now, and I finally feel settled. Mason likes it, but I try to give him his space. We moved here from Savannah."

My mind chose that moment to conjure up Becca Kernsy—fitting in and flourishing in Kirby Falls in only a few weeks. Becca had already settled in and she hadn't even moved here. And then I told my brain, for the hundredth time since Saturday, to stop thinking about Becca. But it had been difficult. She hadn't shown up to Grandpappy's on Monday, and I'd wondered if that had been my doing.

Clearing my throat, I offered, "Yeah, I spent a little time in Georgia. Beautiful place." But I wasn't going to expand on my very short stint playing in Atlanta. It didn't seem like what Jim wanted to talk about anyway, which was a relief.

"Well, I'll leave you to your night, Mr. Clark. I just wanted to introduce myself and express my gratitude."

"Call me Will," I offered, turning to shake his hand once more. "It was nice meeting you."

We parted ways, and I made the drive over to Montell's Sandwich Shop. I figured I'd grab something to take home while I was in town. Maybe eat while I watched another episode of *The Walking Dead*. I was somehow on season six.

I placed my order and paid at the counter, then slid into a booth to wait. Pulling out my phone, I figured I should check to make sure Mac did the tagging and hashtagging thing for the Orchard Festival.

After bringing up the app, I could see that the Grandpappy's account had several new posts from the past weekend. One featured a colorful row of apples packed in white paper sacks, ready and waiting for tourists to take them home. Another shot showed my mom smiling broadly while she served a cup of apple slushie to a young girl. I'd have to ask Mac to send me that one to print out. My dad would like it.

Then I navigated over to the Orchard Festival's account to see if they'd featured the farm at all. There was Mac's pretty row of apples reposted and shared. Mac had even gone in and answered questions in the comments section from people too lazy to go over and visit Grandpappy's website to check hours of operation and apple varieties. I'd clearly been wrong to give my cousin shit about the social media stuff. She obviously had it handled.

I scrolled through a few more of the photos on Eloise's Orchard Fest account. One photo had far and away more likes and comments than any of the others. It was an objectively gorgeous shot of Margaret Mahroney's flower booth. The warm light was hitting the autumn bouquet just right, deep golds and maroons shining. I didn't know a lot about photography, but the background was blurry in such a way that the focus was entirely on the bright blooms and the rays of sunlight working their way across the flowers in their Mason jars, even reflecting off the water in the base. The whole thing looked atmospheric and uplifting. The photo made a statement. I tapped the caption to read . . .

Reposted from @Snap.Bam.Bloom

Come by and see us today at the 75th Annual Orchard Festival! We have gorgeous fall floral arrangements of all sizes. Special thanks to @TryBeccaKernsy for this lovely photo and her enthusiasm. She's our favorite Orchard Fest volunteer! Becca even set us up with a web designer to get us into the 21st century. Coming soon from @UngoliantWebServices, you'll be able to order your Snap Bam Blooms from anywhere in the continental U.S.!!

The post had over six thousand likes and hundreds of comments asking to buy and what Margaret's shipping options would be. There were so many compliments about the gorgeous photo and even several other local businesses chiming in about Becca being the Orchard Festival's MVP volunteer. My uncle George from Burke Hardware had something nice to say too. I didn't even realize he knew how to social media.

I wondered how Eloise decided which businesses to feature. And even more nagging was my curiosity over Becca's guiding hand. Had she known that Snap Bam Bloom had been struggling since the death of Margaret's husband last winter?

My thumb hovered over Becca's social media handle for all of a second before I tapped. My grip tightened involuntarily at the explosion of Kirby Falls on her feed, all through Becca's artistic eye. There was a gorgeous sunset from a week ago that I knew was taken from the back patio at the tiny house. Scrolling, I found myself face-to-face with so much of my hometown. There were local businesses and restaurants on display. The new sign above Apollo's with Magdaline Kouides and her parents beneath it, arms thrown wide, huge smiles on their faces. Becca had an entire ten-photo carousel featuring the food of Hog's Wild food truck. Perry McArthur, the owner and proprietor, had even commented on the post that Becca "was the best and got free food for life."

My fingers scrolled through weeks of photos—a visual diary of everything familiar but through Becca's lens. Everything about my hometown looked brighter and shinier. Was this how she saw it—how she saw all of us?

I paused when I got to an image from our hike on Mr. Abrams's trail from exactly one week ago. The caption was simple: *What a view.* In the background were the endless layers of hazy blue mountains, and just shy of center was the back of a lone figure, mostly in shadow. The hills were lit up by bright sunshine with only the barest hint of fog lingering in the deepest valleys. So the contrast between the tall form of a man and the landscape was striking. Just a dark silhouette with a backward cap framed on either side by drooping branches and all that bright space in front of him beyond the rock-edged cliff. Save for my momma, no one would even be able to tell it was me. I hadn't realized she'd snapped a photo.

Something warm and weighty had me rubbing absently at my chest. I didn't know how to feel about the picture, but some masochistic part of me wanted a version where Becca stood next to me, arm around my waist while I kissed her forehead. That wasn't something a friend should be thinking, but I was the dumbass who'd set the new rule. But it was better this way—for both of us. Silly daydreams and romantic notions wouldn't make either of us happy in the long run, and it definitely wouldn't protect my heart.

Just when I thought I had this girl figured out, a brand-new layer revealed itself. It hurt to think that I'd been so judgmental and stupid during our first meeting. My first impression of a hopeless city girl had been wrong. She was a grown woman with a life, a complicated family, and the biggest heart of anyone I'd ever met. She loved my town, and she connected with my neighbors. And I wanted more of her—more smiles and sweetness and my arms wrapped around her.

I wanted her to stay, I realized selfishly. I wanted the chance to take her back to that trail, to look out over those mountains and pull her against me while a self-timer captured an image of us both.

A comment below the post caught my attention. I tapped the screen to expand. Two accounts dominated the conversation with a little of Becca sprinkled in. I recognized the handles from comments on several of Becca's Kirby Falls photos.

A smile curved my lips as I read.

@CeCeSlater: IS THAT TREEBEARD?

@PippaNoStockings: I thought we were going with Lorax?

@CeCeSlater: Only because she made us stop referring to him as Lumbersnack.

A short bark of laughter emerged, but I didn't look around to see if anyone had noticed. You could not have pried the phone out of my cold, dead hand.

@TryBeccaKernsy: OMG STAHHHP you two

@PippaNoStockings: It's mostly Cece

@CeCeSlater: What? It's not like he's going to see it. He's too busy saving women from his forest. And too busy chopping all that wood. That hard, hard wood.

@TryBeccaKernsy: @CeCeSlater I'm going to murder you

@TryBeccaKernsy: I'll video call you both later if you promise to be good and stop now

Amusement threatening, I rubbed a hand down my beard, wondering what they said about me on that video call. They obviously knew about the tree incident that brought Becca into my life.

Scrolling further, I found a drought in the photos—a three-year break. There were a few coffeehouse images with twinkle lights and designer lattes. Going further, a colorful crocheted blanket that looked familiar spread across an empty twin-sized bed, then an elderly woman working on a puzzle, only her gnarled hands visible among the pieces.

Becca didn't have any selfies, but four years ago, there was a point-of-view shot of two people sitting side-by-side on a couch, the same crocheted blanket covering two pairs of legs propped up next to each other on a worn floral ottoman. *Wheel of Fortune* was caught in a frozen moment in the background behind their feet. The caption read: *Mrs. W and me on a wild Friday night.*

Now my chest ached for an entirely different reason, and I felt like an asshole for invading her privacy despite her account being public and available to the world.

Becca's mourning was right there between the borders of her photos. Her life had practically stalled out following the death of Mrs. Walters. Knowing what she'd been through with her family and how important the old woman had been made me immeasurably sad for Becca's loss.

But now, this resurgence in Kirby Falls brought light and happiness back into her life. She was taking the town by storm, impacting residents left and right. Becca was happy here, and I knew she'd be happy if she stayed. But that wasn't my choice to make.

I closed out of the app and looked up to see my sub wrapped and waiting for me on the table.

Head rising, I met the gaze of the kid behind the counter. He shrugged. "I said your name a couple of times, but you didn't answer. I dropped it off a while ago."

No, I hadn't noticed. I'd been staring at my phone, too wrapped up in the life of Becca Kernsy to notice anything else.

Jordan: Friday Night Outdoor Movie, 8pm, Harry Potter and the Sorcerer's Stone

Me: No.

Jordan: Come on. Firefly is sponsoring. And I'm fully staffed so I'll be watching the movie with Chloe. Come with us.

*Me: *GIF of a tricycle**

Jordan: I'm proud of your relevant GIF usage, but you will not be the third wheel. Becca is coming too.

Me: Fine.

. . .

The space in front of Firefly Cider's main outdoor stage had been cleared of tables and chairs. They'd been shifted to the perimeter so folks could gather on the lawn with their blankets for the outdoor movie. This was the last one of the year. Kirby Falls Parks and Rec planned them for every Friday, all summer long, and Firefly was hosting tonight.

Someone had set up a projector and a screen beneath the covered awning of the stage, and the sun was about ten minutes from setting. The mid-September weather would get chilly tonight, but most people were decked out with sleeping bags and big quilts to keep warm.

Folks gathered with ciders in hand and plates from the food truck parked out front. Kids ran feral and screaming through the lawn dotted with a patchwork of blankets. And there, in the front row, was Jordan and Chloe and Becca on an unzipped sleeping bag.

I made my way through the crowd, stopping to speak to my cousin Bonnie and her husband, Danny. Bonnie was a sweetheart and didn't seem to mind all the kids—probably her students from the elementary school—who ran up and interrupted. Danny seemed oblivious. It looked like he was watching a football game on his phone.

Jordan spotted me first and held out a cider as I dropped two of my own sleeping bags on the ground. "Glad you could make it."

"Didn't have much choice," I grumbled. But that wasn't entirely true. I could have blown off movie night. But once my friend mentioned Becca's presence, I knew I'd be spending a Friday night in town being sociable.

Things had been . . . off since the "just friends" conversation during the festival last week. Becca finally came back to Grandpappy's on Wednesday to work in front of the Bake Shop, but I hadn't done more than nod in her direction since then.

"Hi, Will," Becca said brightly.

I realized I'd been staring at her like a moron. "Hey. How are you?"

"Good!" But her fingers were busy on the zipper of the sleeping bag across her lap.

"Y'all want some popcorn?" Chloe asked, drawing my attention as both she and Jordan stood. "We'll get some for everyone."

"Sure," I murmured as I worked to open up one of my sleeping bags and spread it out on the other side of Becca.

"Thanks, guys," Becca said, and Chloe and Jordan made for the popcorn stand.

Becca flipped over onto her hands and knees and helped tuck the edges of my sleeping bag flat alongside Jordan's. Her blond hair was down, dangling past her shoulders as she moved. Her pale pink sweatshirt looked cozy, and a part of me thought it would be nice to lie back on those blankets, all snuggled up with her in my arms.

Instead, I cleared my throat, and she passed me the cider I'd set aside.

"Busy week?" she asked mildly. There was no accusation in her tone, and that just made me feel more like shit.

I *had* been avoiding her, feeling awkward about our conversation and regretting my decision to keep things simple between us. I should have realized that simple was an illusion when you wanted to make out with someone.

"Yeah," I answered. "There's always a rush the week after the festival."

The conversation stayed stilted and stiff until Chloe and Jordan returned with popcorn, refills on cider, and the digital projector clicked on. The speakers they used for bands throughout the week amplified the opening soundtrack, and save for a few rambunctious children, everybody got quiet.

Bunching the flannel fabric beneath my head, I leaned back to watch the show. Becca reclined nearby, on top of the border of my spread sleeping bag and Jordan's. We were separated by a few inches, but awareness stole through me at the promise of accidental contact.

But it never came. Becca stayed contained, shifting carefully so that our bodies never so much as grazed. She sat up a few times to reposition or drink her cider, but each movement was mastered under her control.

I was so aware of her that I hadn't paid any attention to the show, and about thirty minutes in, I abruptly sat up to finish my drink. I stayed sitting, legs stretched out and arms braced behind me. But that was somehow worse because I didn't even need to tilt my head to see her spread out on the patterned flannel next to me. Her arms were behind her head, propping herself up so she could see the screen better. Her jean-clad legs were crossed at the ankle, and her blond hair fanned out in every direction. There was a strand about an inch away from my pinkie that was particularly distracting.

However, a short while later, Becca sat up, gaze fixed on the screen. She glanced over her shoulder and whispered, "This is my favorite part."

My eyes strayed to the film in time to see Harry and Ron celebrating Christmas at Hogwarts. Harry looked down into the common room to see Ron clad in his hand-knit Christmas sweater. "Looks like you've got one too," the red-haired boy said.

Becca grinned and turned back to me. "I love that Ron's mother knitted a sweater for Harry too. Like he's already part of the family."

She returned her attention to the screen, but I continued to look at her face for a long time. My throat got tight as I witnessed Becca's love for the moment when a fictional character felt like he belonged—like he'd been accepted.

Eventually, Becca reached up to wipe a tear from her cheek, and my gaze darted to the screen. She was watching the little boy stand before a mirror, looking at the people he'd lost. The tightness in my throat was growing, making it hard to swallow.

Becca huffed a little laugh at herself before whispering, "I could cry over anything, I swear. They could have played *Ghostbusters* tonight, and I probably would have shed a tear or two."

Grabbing the other sleeping bag I'd unzipped to use as a blanket for when the temperature dropped, I took it and spread it over Becca's legs. "Here you go. It's getting cold."

"Thank you, Will," she said quietly, the light reflecting the moisture lingering in her eyes. She lay back down again, snuggling beneath the warm bedding, and I had to take a long deep breath before I could manage the unspent energy coursing through me.

There was no one to blame and not a soul to punish. But I wanted to.

I thought about the old woman from her social media photo—Mrs. Walters. The gnarled hands separating puzzle pieces and the person beside Becca beneath a crocheted blanket watching *Wheel of Fortune*. I hated that Becca lost the one good person in her life. Someone who loved her.

My fingers flexed at the unfairness of it all.

Raising my gaze from where Becca lay, my attention snagged on Chloe. She was watching me, a sad, knowing look on her face as if she, too, knew of the unfortunate loss that Becca had suffered. After a moment Chloe gave me a weak smile and then lay back, cuddling into Jordan's side and reaching over to squeeze Becca's arm.

I didn't pretend to know what Becca's relationship was like with her sister or her parents, but I knew it wasn't healthy. They didn't appreciate her, and they made her unhappy. And at the very least, there was a long history of neglect and abuse.

I couldn't imagine a world where people had the chance to know Becca but rejected her instead.

I didn't want to be one more person in Becca's life who used her or took advantage. Her family had stolen from her. They'd manipulated her. Her sister punished her for things that were out of Becca's control. But I knew that the tender-hearted woman lying beside me would never voluntarily give up on anyone.

She deserved to have a person in her corner who wouldn't give up on her.

Shame drowned out the movie and the night sounds. All I could think about was how I'd avoided Becca all week in an attempt to, what, sidestep an awkward conversation? To save my pride after letting her down easy? No, I'd been a coward. I'd told her I wanted to be friends and then used that as an excuse to pull away.

I should be a man true to my word. I didn't want to hide from Becca. I wanted to absorb all the time I could. It was foolishness to avoid her and hold on to some wound caused by her impending departure. Becca was not to blame for circumstances beyond our control. Holding her responsible was weak of me.

Of course I wanted her to stay, but that wasn't up to me. From the outside looking in, her life in Detroit wasn't fulfilling, but I didn't know the whole story with her sister, and it sure as hell wasn't my place to tell Becca what to do.

I wasn't about to ask more from her than she was willing to give. I had my life, and she had hers too. If she thought Detroit was what was best for her, then I trusted her enough to know that.

"Are you cold?" Becca whispered suddenly, breaking me out of my thoughts.

She didn't wait for me to answer. Instead, she said, "Here you go," and tugged some of the makeshift blanket over to spread across my legs too.

"Thanks," I replied, voice rough as I settled beside her, careful to keep some distance between us. But it was hard. Beneath our sleeping bag cocoon, it smelled like her sweet honeysuckle scent, and it was warm from the heat of her body.

Every day, there was something new. Everything I learned about Becca just made me want a little more—to know her, to be near her, to touch her. She was kind and thoughtful. Helping Kirby Falls residents and touching lives in this small town. I thought of the way she regularly visited my great-grandfather, playing piano and reading to a man she didn't even know and had no connection to.

For the first time since I'd pushed her away, I was no longer concerned about breaking her heart. I was starting to worry about my own.

BECCA

It had only been a few weeks, but I felt like my surroundings were changing a little bit every day. In these early days of October, more colors were popping up in the mountains. Leaves going gold and orange and some so vibrantly red that I wanted to memorize the color. I snapped photos on my phone all the time. The urgency was there to catch every single phase of this transition and miss nothing.

All the lightning bugs had abandoned the area behind the tiny house and taken a bit of the whimsy along with it. The corn in the distant field had been harvested for feed, I'd been told, and even the pace of the farm had slowed somewhat. I still loved sitting on the back patio, wrapped up in my crocheted blanket, watching the stars wink into existence, but the days were growing shorter.

The weather was getting colder too. Nearly every morning that I went out to the farm, a warm blanket waited for me in Will's rolling desk chair beneath the Bake Shop's covered awning. I made sure to dress in several layers and to always wear a beanie. But most days, the sun shone bright and the tourists still flocked to Grandpappy's to buy their apples and, now, pumpkins and enjoy the entertainment on the farm.

It was hard to believe that this place would shift into holiday mode in a little over a month with Christmas trees for sale and "sleigh" rides to visit Santa. Mac told me that it was really just the same hayride setup they used in the fall but with twinkle lights and greenery decorating the trailer where the people would sit. It still sounded magical to me.

But I wouldn't be here for any of that. I wouldn't get to make s'mores around the bonfire. And I wouldn't get to buy peppermint bark in the General Store or try Maggie's famous hot chocolate. My plan was to return to Detroit right after Halloween, and I needed to stick to that. If I didn't, I'd never leave Kirby Falls. I didn't need to see the future to know that I'd just keep extending my stay indefinitely to keep from having to say goodbye to any of it. Maggie still wouldn't let me pay more than the utilities on the tiny house, but I knew that it was wrong to take advantage of her generosity. I couldn't very well abandon my life in Michigan, no matter how tempting the prospect.

One thing that had remained consistent in the last few weeks was Will. Ever since that movie in the park, I could count on seeing him at least once per day. It was like the standoffishness following our kiss had never happened. He'd sit down with me for breakfast or lunch, sometimes both, depending on how much time he had on his hands. Occasionally, we'd join Jordan and Chloe for a midday meal, but more often than not, Will would arrive early, and it would be just the two of us enjoying whatever Ms. Maggie whipped up.

We talked throughout the day, and Carl often spent time with me while Will was off putting out fires on the farm and assisting where he was needed. I saw him at Trivia Night at Trailview on Mondays. We made plans for drinks at Firefly, and we'd even gone on another hike—this time, a longer trek out to the waterfalls the town was named for.

Will and I were well and truly friends.

We talked a lot. I typically avoided my family stuff, opting instead to tell him all about Cece and Pippa and my life with Mrs. Walters. Will usually skirted around the professional baseball part of his history, but he'd told me funny stories about him and Jordan on the high school team together. And he often mentioned working with the current baseball kids at conditioning every week.

I wondered if Will even realized how much he enjoyed those sessions. It was clear to me that he loved it. Loved being immersed in the sport again. Loved working with the kids. Loved guiding and instructing and being a part of a team. I hoped he'd figure out that coaching might be an option for him, but I'd learned that you couldn't force Will into anything. So I'd kept my mouth shut in that regard and just listened.

Will kept bringing me four-leaf clovers. I now had sixteen little lucky charms pressed flat in my notebook. I didn't know what I'd do with them in the long term, but for now, I'd stopped using that planner as anything but a clover keeper. They were important to me. They'd be a special memory from my time at Grandpappy's and my time with Will.

I was kidding myself if I thought my more-than-friendly feelings were going anywhere. My innocent little baby crush had since graduated from high school and was currently applying for study-abroad programs. But I wasn't acting on those feelings. I was content to be a good friend and enjoy the time I had with Will. And if I got lost in daydreams where I shared the tiny house with a grumpy farmer and his cheese-loving dog, well, that was my own problem.

I had trouble sleeping last night, my anxious brain eager for attention before the sun was even up. I finally gave up around four in the morning and got up and showered. I worked on a few branding concepts I had on my schedule, but when the clock hit seven, I was ready to relocate from the tiny house to the Orchard Bake Shop. There was just something so welcoming about it. I enjoyed chatting with Maggie and Chloe in the mornings, and the coffee and pastries didn't hurt either. Plus, I was just a more productive person away from home. Even in Detroit, I often got distracted when I was alone and found it easier to focus on my tasks while working at a coffee shop or park.

Something I hadn't counted on, however, was how much the temperature had dropped overnight. I shivered as I zipped up my puffy jacket. I eyed the dark and gloomy sky as I walked, laptop bag in hand and yawning, over to the Bake Shop. My weather app hadn't mentioned any chance of rain, but this was shaping up to be one of the least hospitable days I'd experienced since landing in North Carolina back in August.

A chilly, overcast morning awaited me once the sun rose. And there, at my reserved picnic table, sat Will's navy-blue desk chair and thick blanket, ready to keep me warm.

I drank my cinnamon bun latte and ate my slice of pumpkin bread. My fingerless gloves kept my hands warm as I typed until midmorning when the wind picked up. Shivering, I tucked the gray fleece firmly under my thighs to ward off the chill. A more intelligent woman would pack it in and head back to the tiny house. I was even considering it myself.

I hadn't spied Will so far today. Normally, he would have popped into the Bake Shop for coffee by now. It wasn't until another frosty half hour had gone by before Carl came bounding up to me, eager for attention and ear rubs.

"Hey, bud. I missed you all morning. Where have you been?"

The dog didn't answer, but his whole body shook with excitement, and I took that to mean he'd missed me too.

I glanced up to see Will striding down the path from the direction of the General Store. He'd swapped out his ball cap for a maroon beanie. His dark hair curled around the edge of the fabric. He wore a tan work jacket with the collar turned up at his throat to block the wind. He caught sight of me and frowned.

I smiled. "Hi."

"What are you doing out here? You'll freeze."

"Not your best greeting," I teased. "But I suppose almost surprising me out of a tree was arguably worse."

Will ignored me and proceeded to circle my chair and grab the backrest.

"Whoa!" I flailed, grabbing the armrests as Will rolled me backward over the wooden planks of the Bake Shop's front porch. "What are you doing?"

"Warming you up."

Before I could protest, he wheeled me around the corner of the building to his office. He opened the door, and Carl zipped in, excited about whatever game the humans were playing. Then Will delivered me in my workplace chariot to the quiet interior of his small space. He pushed me right up to the desk and told me he'd be right back.

I sat in stunned silence before looking at Carl. "Your dad is so bossy."

Will came back into the room with my laptop and bag. "And you're going to catch pneumonia out there."

"I thought that was an old wives' tale," I countered with a raised eyebrow.

Will shot me a sharp look, and I wondered if he remembered repeating that phrase before he'd peeled the wet shirt off his rain-soaked body after we'd made out, right here in this very office, weeks ago. If he made the connection, he didn't comment on it. Instead, he carefully placed my computer on the desktop before me.

"I thought you'd stay home today," he finally said, straightening away.

"I'd rather be here," I said, feeling heat creep into my cheeks at the admission. "But I draw the line at stealing your entire office." I shifted the blanket aside and stood to emphasize my reluctance to be an inconvenience.

Already shaking his head, Will moved to intercept me. "I won't be here to use it. We're short-staffed today and have a surprisingly big crowd for a Tuesday in spite of the weather."

"I can't work in here, Will."

"Why not? I can turn the heat up if it's not warm enough."

"It's not fair to put you out. You're right, I should just pack up and head back to the tiny house."

Will reached out and gently snagged my wrist as I started to turn. "Stay. I want you to. And you can keep Carl company while I'm filling in at the General Store."

I did my best to ignore the way my stomach swooped at Will's casual touch. We were friends, and friends occasionally—innocently—touched. Every now and then, we leaned our shoulders against one another when I showed him something on my phone. I playfully swatted Will sometimes when he teased me. And there were times when the backs of our hands brushed when Will joined me on one of my daily walks around the farm. I wasn't surprised by Will's touch, but I sure was affected by it.

When I frowned up at him and made no move to return to my seat, Will gathered up my other wrist and encircled it with his warm, calloused fingers. "Stay. It'll make me feel better. And I'll come back when I get a chance and bring us lunch."

He was so close, and he smelled so good. The maple-sweet wood-smoke scent made me lean in closer.

There was a mischievous grin lurking beneath that dark beard. "Besides, there are a lot of kids running around today. I wouldn't want them to stumble upon one of your not-safe-for-work aliens or gargoyles or goat men doing something naughty on your computer screen."

"Is that right?" I asked mildly.

Will nodded, but his fingers tightened on my wrists as his smile finally let loose—like he knew I wanted to whack him on the stomach for teasing me.

"That only happened once," I argued as he pulled me in a little closer until the toes of our shoes touched. "And it was just the one big baby who saw the ogre in the hayloft."

He laughed, and I could feel his exhale. "Did you just call me a big baby?"

I grinned, butterflies rioting in my stomach. "Maybe."

There was something about the combination of Will being playful mixed with the way he wanted to take care of me. It made me careless and suddenly forgetful of the rules of friendship.

Without thinking, I turned my wrists within his grasp and laced my fingers through his. It felt as natural as breathing to slip my hands in his. And for his part, he curved his large hands around mine too, welcoming and sweet. I didn't realize the danger I was in until we were already leaning in toward one another, the smiles still on our faces.

Our lips met, and good sense still didn't kick in. Instead, I tasted the mint of Will's toothpaste and felt his beard tickle my cheek. Our hands untangled suddenly as Will wrapped me up in his arms. I snaked a hand beneath the back of his jacket and felt warm, smooth skin. He nipped my bottom lip in return, eliciting a sound from within me that broke the spell.

We froze, conscious of the fact that friends didn't put their tongues in each other's mouths. But we didn't pull away. Not yet.

I was still snug in Will's embrace, breathing the same air, my eyes good and closed, letting the daydream last a little longer.

"I'm sorry," I whispered, just as his forehead pressed gently to mine.

"Me too," he sighed, and I felt his mouth shape the quiet words.

Neither one of us moved to unwrap ourselves, so I finally ordered myself to get my hand out of Will's shirt. But on the way down, my nails scraped lightly against the firm line of his spine.

Will groaned out a needful sound, so I did it again.

I wasn't an idiot. I knew that keeping our distance was for the best. But I liked having my hands on Will, and I liked the tortured sound coming out of his throat as I scratched up and down his back. It was proof that I affected him as much as he affected me. I enjoyed getting those reluctant smiles out of the typically controlled man, but this reaction—this raw display—was even better. That groan, so deep and rough, gave me the confidence to ask for more.

My nipples tightened beneath all my layers, and I licked my lips. But Will was still *right there*, so I licked his lips too.

And then, despite our apologies, we were kissing again, harder and deeper than before. I felt my beanie tumble somewhere as a strong, sure hand threaded into my hair and another landed on the curve of my backside.

There was a relief in giving in. After weeks of being careful and controlled, I felt like I was catching my breath above rough water, taking a long, shuddering gasp as the weight of our actions settled with bone-deep clarity. I wanted this man, and temporary was never going to cut it.

But it was all we had.

I kept one hand on Will's back as the other reached around to take hold of his belt buckle. I felt Will's abdomen tighten reflexively against the backs of my fingers, all hot skin and coarse hair disappearing behind his jeans.

Will's grip on my behind urged us closer, and the hard length of his arousal pressed into my hip. His lips left mine, and I made an impatient sound, my grip tightening on the front waistband of his jeans. But before I could complain, I realized Will was placing open-mouthed kisses along my jaw and down the column of my throat. Fingers brushed my hair aside, and then he murmured, "You smell so fucking good. Right here," followed by a careful bite on the slope of my shoulder.

I wanted to say that he smelled good too. That I was addicted to the smoky-sweet scent that lingered on his skin and the blanket I inhaled like a lunatic. But the kisses on my neck turned hotter and wetter, and I couldn't articulate anything at all.

A needy tug on my ear followed by a whisper in Will's low voice, "Can I touch you, City Girl? Can I make you feel good?"

A shaky nod was all I could manage as Will's soft beard grazed my skin.

I was forced to remove my hands as Will gently guided my movements. I faced the side of the desk and placed two bracing hands on the smooth surface as I felt his large body move behind me. Will kept his attention on my neck, sucking and licking my skin there, but then I felt his strong hand working the buttons on my jeans.

A gentle scrape of teeth over my earlobe. "Okay?"

"Um. Yeah. Yes." I swallowed. I could feel my heart beating in my throat. Dreaming about Will and having his hands in my pants were two very different things. I was nervous and desperate and aching to touch him in return.

Will's clever fingers sneaked beneath the waistband of my underwear, and I widened my stance.

He made a rough noise as two digits discovered the moisture at my entrance. When those same two fingers glided easily up and over the tiny bundle of nerves where I was most sensitive, I arched reflexively, my backside pressing into the erection behind me.

Will's forehead dropped to my shoulder as he continued massaging my folds. Based on my increasingly inarticulate sounds, it didn't take him long to figure out I liked to have my clit touched but not directly. Those same maddening two fingers alternated between circling my pleasure button and rubbing up and down either side of my most sensitive spot.

Will was patient but insistent. I didn't feel rushed or manhandled. It was all building toward something. The kissing, the touching, the way I was held and supported. Will was there through it all—making me feel good and taken care of.

"Oh!" I sighed out a shuddering breath as the tension coiled tighter and tighter between my thighs. "Right there."

The fingers circling me picked up the pace, and I knew I was close—so very close. My hips worked in tandem with Will's persistent touch, my backside grazing his erection over and over as a result.

"Fuck," Will breathed, his exhale hot and welcome against my neck. Then he was kissing me, trailing a path from the side of my throat to the nape of my neck. When his teeth scraped over the sensitive skin just below my hairline, all that coiling pressure broke in a wave.

A low moan escaped my lips, and I squeezed my eyes shut.

Leaning my weight more firmly on the desk, I rode out the pulsing pleasure of my release.

Will's stroking fingers gentled and finally stopped.

I could imagine the sight we made. Me bent over the side of the desk, Will's large frame caging me in with one hand while the other snaked down the front of my unbuttoned jeans. I wanted a mirror. I wanted to tilt my head back and kiss him. I wanted to take Will in my hand and mouth and make him feel as good as he'd made me.

But before I could do any of that, the radio in his back pocket came to life, and Mac's voice filled the small room. "Will, I could use some backup at the pumpkin patch. There's a guy who looks like he's up to something, and I'm going to follow him."

"Jesus Christ," Will muttered before extracting himself from my underwear. With his other hand, he grabbed the radio and replied impatiently, "I'll be right there."

I took a moment to button my jeans, figuring sexy fun time was over for the moment. But I couldn't keep the satisfied smile off my face. That was, until I turned to face Will, who wore an expression best described as abject regret.

"Don't," I got the nerve to demand. "Don't apologize or say you wish it had never happened. Because I don't. I'm tired of tiptoeing around each other. I want to kiss you at Trivia Night, and I want to hold your hand when we walk through the dead sunflower field. And I'd really like to do what we just did and more in bed at the tiny house. I know it's not ideal, and it's not fair. But I want to be with you while I can. It's October, Will, and I'm only here for another month. I've spent all this time *not* kissing you. I really want to make up for that."

Will's gray eyes were soft by the time I finished speaking. He'd set the radio on the desk and stepped forward to cup my cheek. After a tender kiss against my lips, he said, "I don't regret touching you. That's not possible. But we need to—"

The walkie flared to life again, and Mac's panicked voice announced, "Will! I really need some help here. There is an ENTIRE NAKED FAMILY BEHIND THE TOOL SHED."

I met Will's wide, horrified gaze. Grabbing the radio, I thrust it in his hands. "Oh my gosh! Go!"

"I really do not want to."

And then I started to laugh. "Go help MacKenzie."

He sighed and took a step backward, bringing the walkie to his kiss-plump lips. "On my way, Mac."

I covered my mouth with my hand to contain my giggles. What in the world was going on behind the shed next to the pumpkin patch?

Will was at the door to the office, shaking his head. "Hey, we're talking about this later, okay?"

"Yes, please. I want all the details."

Will blinked and then huffed a surprised laugh. "No. You and me. We're talking about you and me later."

Grinning, I replied, "Oh, that. Sure. We'll discuss that too."

Shaking his head, Will reached for the doorknob, and then he was gone, off to rescue Mac and deal with whatever all that was. And we were going to talk about us . . . later. Hopefully, that meant there would be more kissing and more touching and less interruptions.

What was it about this office?

"They did what?" Pippa's blue eyes nearly bugged out of her head on the screen of my laptop.

TAKE IT OR LEAF IT

We were in the middle of a three-way video call discussing this morning's events. Cece was in the upper left corner with a hand covering her mouth in shock.

I nodded, proud of myself for getting the beginning of the story out without spewing my red wine all over the couch. "Apparently, they were trying to get one of those family photos where you put a baby inside a pumpkin. But they wanted to include everyone. So they put the little baby in the pumpkin, had the toddler and the dad holding pumpkins in front of their, you know, nether regions. And the mom posed behind a hay bale to cover her lower half and holding up two small pumpkins in front of her boobs."

"Why did they do this on the farm?" Cece wondered before taking a sip of her own wine.

"I don't know. Maybe they didn't want to pay for the pumpkins or liked the farm's atmosphere. And they needed it to get the pumpkin family photo just right. I don't know."

"I thought you said it was cold there today?" Pippa asked.

I took a sip from my glass. "Oh, it is. But apparently, this was their last day in town, and they wouldn't have another opportunity."

"Lunatics." Cece shook her head incredulously.

It was all very ridiculous. I was glad that Mac had Will for backup. I couldn't imagine stumbling across a naked family of four trying to use a tripod and a self-timer to get the perfect photo op.

"They set everything up behind the shed. Maybe they hoped to be dressed and out of there before anyone noticed. Mac said the dad was acting shifty, and she followed him from the ticket booth," I explained.

"I bet she regrets that," Pippa said, twisting her long, dark hair into a bun as she spoke.

"I bet she'll have nightmares for the rest of her life," Cece amended with a cackle.

After what happened in Will's office, I'd stayed and worked for about an hour before I got worried and ventured over to the Bake Shop to see what was going on. Maggie and Chloe had been eager to share the story while Will and Mac were occupied with providing a statement to the police officers who'd been called to the scene. They figured the misguided family would be let off with a warning and a permanent Grandpappy's ban, but it still meant there had been a lot for Will to deal with.

Eventually, I'd gathered my things and Carl and retreated to the tiny house. I hadn't wanted the dog to be cooped up in the office if Will was occupied for the foreseeable future. I'd also left a note for Will and told him to come over to talk whenever he was ready.

It was now just after nine at night, and I figured Will had suffered a long day of interruptions while short-staffed. That, or he was willing to forfeit his dog in order to avoid a difficult conversation with me.

Getting frisky in Will's office hadn't been the plan. The plan had been pretty clear: stay friends, avoid hurting one another, and deny any sexy instincts where either one of us was concerned. Obviously, we'd failed, considering I'd had an unexpected orgasm with my pants still on.

I hadn't told my friends about the office incident, as I was now referring to it. Cece thought Will and I were crazy for going the friend route. She thought we should "seize the lay" as it were, and spend what little time I had in Kirby Falls exploring our physical relationship. Pippa hadn't expressed an opinion beyond telling me to be careful with my heart.

I wanted to talk to Will first. We'd been interrupted, and I didn't feel right sharing what had happened with my friends. Part of me was worried that Will would show up here for Carl and let me down easy, reiterating his desire to keep things platonic between us.

I didn't want that. I'd been truthful and upfront when I'd told Will I didn't regret what we'd done. I was tired of holding myself back. I wanted more . . . while I was here to have it.

"Hypothetically," I began, "would it be crazy if I thought about staying in Kirby Falls?"

"Like, extending your trip?" Cece asked, a frown drawing her dark eyebrows together.

Toying with the stem of my wineglass, I admitted, "No. Like if I relocated here from Detroit."

I glanced at the screen in time to see my friends share a look with one another.

"What?" I straightened in my seat, uncurling my legs from beneath me. "What was that?"

Another wide-eyed expression passed between them before Cece said slowly, "We've just been, sort of, waiting for you to bring this up."

"Really?"

Pippa nodded. "Becca, you clearly love it there. You've sent us so many pictures. And they're all wonderful," she hastened to add.

"You're joining all these groups," Cece said. "Making friends. Really getting to know the town and the people. It's been obvious since the beginning that you love Kirby Falls. You fit, babe."

I'd been so careful, never letting myself consider the possibility of staying. Sure, I'd daydreamed about leaving my life in Detroit behind to make my time in North Carolina more permanent and lasting. But guilt usually followed swiftly on the heels of those dangerous thoughts. I had responsibilities back home. Heather needed me. I couldn't just up and leave Mrs. Walters's apartment either. She'd wanted so badly for me to have a place to call home that she'd left me hers when she died. Saying goodbye to her apartment would be like saying goodbye all over again to the one person who ever really cared about me.

Yet the temptation to give those daydreams room to grow was admittedly strong. My friends were right. I did love it here. I loved the land and the people, all the weird little quirks of this town that wasn't my own but somehow made me feel like I fit. Belonging was something I'd searched for my whole life. But I didn't know how to make the dream a reality.

"Talk to us, Becca." Pippa's gentle voice had me focusing on the screen.

"I *am* happy here." The confession felt like a punch to the gut. Admitting I was happy in Kirby Falls implied that I wasn't happy in Detroit. The two felt mutually exclusive, and in acknowledging the truth, I was shining a light on the things wrong with my life back home. I felt disloyal to my sister, who needed me and relied on me. And I felt disloyal to the memory of Mrs. Walters.

"I think that counts for something," Pippa replied.

Cece nodded. "That counts for a lot."

"But it's too much, right?" I hedged. "Who goes somewhere on vacation and actually stays? I can't really uproot and just move here. Can I?"

"You can do whatever the hell you want," Cece replied emphatically. "You work from home. You could sell your apartment. Or rent it out," she quickly added, likely after seeing the way my face crumpled at the thought of selling Mrs. Walters's home. "You could make it work."

"But Heather—"

"Heather is a grown-ass woman," Cece interjected firmly.

I knew how my friends felt about my sister. Pippa was more subtle in her disapproval, but Cece vehemently opposed my relationship with Heather. She thought I should cut her out of my life the way I'd excised my parents—for my own mental health and well-being.

And realistically, I knew that Heather used me. But the part of me drowning in survivor's guilt seemed to be louder than the self-aware side who knew that Heather only needed me for money.

"Has she been bugging you for cash while you've been in Kirby Falls?" Cece asked suddenly.

I looked away from the screen and picked up my wineglass, and Cece had her answer.

She made a rude sound. "Fuck that noise, Becca. I know you have this misplaced guilt where Heather is concerned, but it's not your job to pull her out of the gutter. She likes the gutter. She uses and abuses you. That is not a relationship, no matter how much you want it to be. Getting away from Detroit would be a good thing where your family is concerned."

Cece's face was flushed in anger, her brown skin heated beneath her cheeks. My friend was my champion, and I knew she meant well. But hard truths weren't easier to hear just because the volume was turned up.

I thought about the recent phone calls and the texts I'd ignored from Heather—two from earlier in the day demanding to know when I'd be back in the city. I didn't want to be someone who ran away from her problems. But at the same time, I didn't want to think about what would happen if my older sister knew my whereabouts. I didn't think she had the money or motivation to come all the way to North Carolina, but it was a fear I'd considered. Desperate people did desperate things.

My mind drifted to the two jobs I'd been fired from as a result of my sister's interference. The times she'd shown up at my high school dealing drugs to my classmates. The way she'd fed my anxiety until I had panic attacks.

A ruthless, selfish part of me didn't want her to ruin Kirby Falls too.

"Becca," Pippa said gently, drawing me out of my painful ruminations. "Consider what it would take to make the move to Kirby Falls. Make a pro/con list if you want. But don't rule it out because of some sense of obligation you feel toward your life in Detroit. You deserve to be happy, wherever that may be."

I blinked, nodding slowly along with my friend's words.

What if I stayed?

A little house and some land. Fireflies in my own backyard. Trivia Night on Mondays. Hiking and bird-watching. Friendships and potlucks. Festivals downtown and an everyday life that felt like it was meant to be.

Something desperate and hopeful pierced through the worry. Something I wanted. Something that looked a lot like happiness.

I risked a glance at where Carl's warm body pressed against my thigh.

A dog curled up beside me on the sofa. A man with a beard and a backward hat in my bed and branded across my heart.

The same man visible through the glass of my front door, the porch light illuminating his tall frame, preparing to knock.

"What is it?" Cece asked. "Your face just did a complicated gymnastics routine."

A moment later, Will's knuckles met the wood of the doorframe.

"Is someone there?" my friend gasped.

"Yes, hush. It's Will." I set the laptop aside, placing it on the other side of Carl who dozed on the center cushion.

I jumped up, ignoring Cece's squeals of delight and Pippa's face leaning so far forward that she was going to hit her nose on her tablet screen.

Opening the door, I smiled. "Hey."

"Hey. I got your note." Will swallowed, the movement pronounced along the strong column of his throat. I briefly wondered if he was nervous. If he could feel his heart beating wild and erratic, the way I could. "Thank you for looking after Carl."

At the mention of his name, the dog sighed heavily from his flopped-over position on the couch. We watched as he raised his head to greet his owner with a single tail thump before reclining once more.

"Well, that was some reception," Will mumbled, and I laughed softly. I loved that Will's dog felt so comfortable with me.

But then I noticed Will's gaze stray toward the laptop screen where my two friends were waving like dorks.

He straightened and shot me a glance before raising a hand in their direction. "Uh, hey."

Darting for the laptop, I heard Cece and Pippa speaking over one another rapidly, their voices emerging from the tiny speakers.

"Hi, Will! We've heard so much about you!"

"So nice to finally meet you."

"Our girl Becca is the best."

"You're our favorite lumbersnack!"

Cece's last comment before I snapped the lid shut seemed to echo around the room. Facing away from Will, I kept my eyes closed for a moment, hopeful that a wormhole to another dimension might open up beneath my feet. Maybe it would swallow the couch too so I'd have Carl for company in the alternate timeline.

My eyes opened when I felt Will pry the laptop out of my frantic, clutching hands. I risked a glance and found him grinning at me, the tips of his ears a delightful pink.

"Sorry about them," I said sheepishly.

"Don't be," he said, running an absent hand over Carl's head. "They seem fun, and they obviously care about you." I nodded. "And they clearly have great taste since I'm their favorite lumbersnack."

I groaned and hung my head.

Will's low laughter rumbled against me as he wrapped me up in a sudden hug.

Content to ignore that embarrassing encounter ever happened, I clutched the soft flannel at his waist and mumbled against his chest, "I'm sorry you had a crappy day with the nudists."

"You heard about what happened?" His hand was rubbing up and down my back.

"Yeah, Chloe and your mom gave me the scoop."

Shaking his head, I felt his beard brush the top of my head. "People are wild. You'd think I wouldn't be surprised at this point, but that was a first."

"I bet."

Will reached down to nudge Carl over and then tugged me down next to him on the sofa. "I figured I should come by so we could talk."

Nerves flooded my system. And so did images from this morning. Will's persistent touch. A slow slide into pleasure. Someone taking their time with me. How good it felt to be held by him. The fear and panic in his eyes afterward.

"Right."

Will picked up my hand and laced our fingers together, but his gray eyes stayed locked on mine. "I think you're right. I know I said being friends was probably best for both of us, but we sort of blew right by that line today. And I don't regret it, you know. Touching you felt inevitable."

Relief coursed through me at his admission. "I wanted you to. I want . . . you." Bravery was not my default. Asking for what I wanted didn't come naturally either, but the words emerged steady and strong. Likely because of the way Will was looking at me—like he *wanted* me too.

"So maybe we stop holding back and do what feels right." Will's gaze searched mine before he added, "While you're here."

The conversation with my friends from moments ago pushed its way forward like a battering ram. The sweet encouragement from Chloe to make this place my home joined in the chorus. All those secret daydreams about picking up and planting roots in Kirby Falls coalesced in my mind, and I blurted, "I really want to stay."

Will's attention sharpened, and his lips parted as if he might speak.

But suddenly, I was the one talking, laying it all out there. "I love this town, and I've been happier here in the last six weeks than any time in my life. I don't know how to make it work, but I want it. And I'm not trying to scare you off." I realized this wasn't something I'd addressed with my friends. My brain was processing in real time the fact that I might come off as an insane clinger-wannabe girlfriend. "I don't want you to feel pressured. I'm not trying to pull a relationship out of you by moving to your town. God, that sounds crazy. I'm sorry—"

My apology and instant mortified regret were interrupted when Will's lips met mine. A surprised squeak left me as his hands cradled my jaw, and he kissed me like he meant it.

He broke off just as suddenly and said, tone earnest, "Don't be sorry. I . . . want you to stay, Becca. I haven't said it because I didn't want to bring up something I had no business asking for. Your life is your own. I know things are complicated back in Detroit. But the possibility of you staying here in Kirby Falls is the best thing you could have said."

I could feel disbelief pinching my features. "Really?"

Will's thumbs stroked over my cheekbones and he smiled—just a bit before saying, "You fit here. You belong. Don't you feel it too?"

Sudden emotion filled my throat, and I couldn't speak, so I nodded instead—a jolting, broken thing within Will's calloused hold.

He kissed me again, and my eyelids fluttered closed. Relief and happiness warred with the constant tug of guilt telling me I didn't deserve any of this, not a place to call home nor the man beside me. That now that I'd put my desire to stay in Kirby Falls out into the universe, something or someone would come along to snatch it away. Or more likely, I wouldn't have the courage or the strength to actually go through with it.

"Will you stay tonight?" I said a short while later. "Just to sleep. You've had a wild day, and I'd really like it if you spent the night."

Will nodded and let me pull him to standing.

After a quick walk outside with Carl, Will returned with an old duffel bag slung over his shoulder. I could feel the night air, cold and clinging to his skin. When he slipped under the covers in boxer briefs and a white undershirt, I caught him casting a sly glance at my leggings and long-sleeved lounge top.

"What?" I asked, snuggling up to his side like we did this all the time. Contentment made me brave. And the way he was looking at me didn't hurt either.

Will turned off the lamp on the bedside table before bringing an arm around my shoulders and pulling me to his chest. "I was kind of hoping for the avocados."

I laughed, pressing my face to his tee shirt and twining my legs with his. "I can change," I said into the quiet darkness.

Tightening his hold, Will's lips grazed my temple as he replied simply, "No, don't. You're perfect."

WILL

"Batter up, Kernsy. You ready?"

Becca's already blissful smile widened further at Jordan's question. I'd noticed she loved it when he called her by her last name. Like a nickname was just as new and exciting as the rest of her Kirby Falls experiences.

"You betcha," she practically squealed as she made her way off the bench.

It was Thursday, the night of our adult rec softball league. I played on the Bar Hoppers' team, and we invited Becca out to join us. The Bar Hoppers consisted of players from Firefly Cider, Mattie B's, and Magnolia Bar—three of the more popular local hangouts and bars in town. But none of it was very official. We mostly just had fun.

Chloe was in the stands with the other girlfriends, wives, husbands, and family members, cheering on the team, and she whistled like a pro when she saw Becca coming up to bat next.

I stood just inside the dugout, watching the action in the third inning. We had Rhonda Coates on first after she had a solid hit that had sneaked past the Teachers' Lounge's shortstop out into left field. We were up against the school system's team, made up of elementary, middle, and high school teachers and coaches. I recognized Mason Gentry's dad playing second base.

"Hey," I said, drawing Becca's attention as she made to pass by me, headed for the on-deck circle.

She turned to me excitedly, her blue eyes as bright as a summer day. "Hey. I'm up. I hope I don't throw the bat. I've never played softball before."

I smiled, pretty much expecting that this was something new for her. "You'll be fine. Just keep your eye on the ball." Without making a big deal about it, I reached for the bill of my hat. It was one I kept in my truck and wore on occasion, the baby-blue color still bright and the white script lettering that said *Grandpappy's* still vivid. "You need a hat. Every ball player needs one."

After tightening the strap a little, I popped the hat onto her blond head. And I couldn't ignore the way it made me feel to see her smile up at me, so ridiculously happy over something so small. My chest felt warm at the sight of her. "There, now you're ready."

"Thanks, Will," she replied around her grin.

I thought how good she'd look in a real baseball jersey, maybe one with my name and number on the back. Then I shook my head and told myself to cut that shit out.

Jordan moved to stand beside me as Becca went up the steps and on to the field. I watched her take a few practice swings in the on-deck circle and fought my smile. She looked endearing out there—totally charming with zero athletic ability.

It would be fine. The teachers weren't a competitive bunch, and no one on the Bar Hoppers would make her feel bad her first time out. And if they did, I'd make them regret it.

"So, that's happening, then?" Jordan said quietly, nodding toward the blonde swinging her heart out. I could hear the smug smile in his voice.

"Yeah," I said, leaving it at that.

Our attention was drawn to the field at the crack of the bat, but Matilda Bartholomew's pop fly was caught neatly by my cousin Bonnie just behind third base. Rhonda drifted back to first to stay put on first. Bonnie had a good arm and played softball growing up.

And then Becca was grinning over her shoulder at me before she hurried up to the batter's box.

I could feel my smile lingering on my face as I watched her widen her stance and raise the bat. Her right elbow could be a little higher but she looked good out there in her jeans and her white rec league tee shirt. Jordan had surprised her with a Bar Hopper's uniform tee with her last name on the back. She'd clutched the shirt to her chest and given Jordan a huge hug, thanking him genuinely.

I tried not to focus on all the little things that made Becca so happy. If I thought about how much she'd missed out on and all the simple joys she'd never experienced as a child, I'd start grinding my teeth again.

"So you and Becca . . . " Jordan mused, fishing for information. "I'd have to check the date, but I think I owe Chloe twenty bucks."

I ignored my friend as the first ball came in low and outside. Becca didn't even flinch.

"Way to watch it," I called.

Becca grinned over at me again before spinning back, ready for the next pitch.

"You think it might be serious? I'm getting a vibe," Jordan said, his amusement plain.

I slid him a glance as Becca swung high for the first strike.

"I don't need your vibes, Jordan."

"No, you have plenty of your own. This is like watching the Grinch's heart grow three sizes."

I rolled my eyes, then returned my attention to my girl. She swung hard on the next pitch and connected. I watched the ball sail up and over the reach of Jim Gentry, and I knew the centerfielder was too far out. In my periphery, Rhonda was on her way to second, but Becca was stationary at home plate.

"Run to first, Becca!"

She jolted into motion, sprinting up the first base line, carrying the bat with her. Everyone on the bench was up and cheering as were the folks in the stands. And my smile felt too big for my face—for the first time in a very long time.

Clapping, I jogged over to first base. When I got there, I eased the bat from her grip. "Nice job, City Girl."

She beamed. "Oh my gosh! I can't believe I forgot to run."

"You did great."

I gave her a few pointers about when to head for second as Jack—the bartender over at Magnolia—came up to bat.

Making my way back over to Jordan, I leaned against the chain-link fence separating the bench from the field. I could feel his attention on me.

"What?" I said without looking.

"You seem . . ."

I frowned at the way he trailed off. Finally turning, I was surprised to see Jordan looking faintly concerned, his dark brows pulled together over knowing brown eyes.

"I seem what?" I asked.

Jordan glanced toward the field before returning his attention to me. "Just be careful. I don't want you to get hurt."

"I thought this was what you wanted. Playing matchmaker. Trying to get me to date."

He shook his head a little. "The way you're looking at her . . . Just watch yourself."

I could have told him I would be fine. That whatever he was reading on my face was my own damn problem. I could have given him shit for trying to act like a mother hen. But part of me recognized that I was getting in deep with Becca already. I didn't know if keeping things casual was possible at this point, and I didn't want to think about what would happen if she changed her mind about staying. And Jordan was a good friend.

So I nodded. "I will."

Our attention snapped away when we heard Jack connect with the ball. The bartender had hammered it over the right field fence and three runs would score as a result. I watched Becca round the bases, a huge smile on her face. My cousin Bonnie even sneaked her a low five when she rounded third.

Our bench cleared to come out and celebrate because adult rec leagues were anarchy and there were no rules.

After Becca touched home plate, there was the instinct to march over and pick her up, maybe swing her around and plant a kiss on her lips. But she looked so happy high-fiving everyone on the team, accepting congratulations and back slaps, and getting positive attention for her accomplishments.

I'd done a pretty good job of sharing Becca since I'd woken up wrapped around her yesterday morning. I kept waiting for it to be weird that night at the tiny house, but between our conversation and sharing her bed, none of the strangeness ever seemed to kick in. Maybe because I'd spent so long trying not to kiss her or touch her, but instead of awkward newness, I just felt relief.

It had been natural to climb beneath the covers and pull her against me. Just as it had been easy to wake up spooned behind her with thirty pounds of dog passed out across our feet. She'd stretched and turned to face me, and it felt so damn easy to welcome her—like I'd been waiting my whole life for the shape of her in my arms. We had coffee together before I'd showered and headed off to work. And that had been effortless too.

"She's a good luck charm," Jordan murmured, drawing me out of my thoughts of yesterday.

Becca finally caught my eye and started making her way toward me on the periphery.

"Yeah. It sorta feels that way," I replied quietly.

Turned out I didn't have to deny myself the urge to pick her up after all. As soon as she got close, Becca put her arms around my neck. I straightened, lifting her feet off the ground.

"That was so fun," she whispered against the shell of my ear, like she had a secret, like she couldn't believe it.

"You did good, honey."

Leaning back to face me, she said sweetly, "Thanks, Will."

"We still have a lot of game left. You ready?"

"I can't wait."

The Bar Hoppers eked out the win. Becca got on base once more in the sixth inning, and we had fun playing in the outfield together. She worked hard and tried her best at something totally new for her. And she was positive and upbeat, all the while cheering for her teammates and never once putting herself down. She was perfect.

For the first time in a long time, I didn't wish I was on a bigger field in a bigger stadium with a bigger crowd. I was happy playing left field in my hometown. I didn't feel so much like a washed-up wannabe when I had Becca grinning at me like she'd won the World Series.

After play finished up, both teams were in good spirits and decided to grab drinks together over at Mattie B's. It was the closest bar to the field, and the owner, Mattie Bartholomew—our star pitcher—invited everyone to come spend their money at her place.

I was up at the bar getting a cider for Becca and an IPA for myself when Jim Gentry—the high school principal and Mason's dad—sat beside me amid the chaos of both teams' arrival and attempt to order.

"Good game out there," Jim said after a handshake.

"Yeah. Nice job at second."

He laughed good-naturedly. "It's a good thing Mason inherited his athletic talent from my wife because I'm pretty hopeless."

I smiled. "I think the league is mostly for fun. And the beer afterward."

"Yeah, luckily, no one takes it too seriously," Jim replied.

I nodded as the bartender got a little closer to us.

"It's none of my business," Jim began, his gaze suddenly more direct than it had been, "but I have a bad habit of recognizing talent and seeing where I could utilize it. You're so good with the kids at those conditioning practices. And you were great out there, encouraging your teammates and helping out the new girl. The boys' baseball team could use your guidance and experience."

My finger traced the smooth woodgrain of the bar top while I tried to decide how to respond. I wanted to sigh and tell this guy to mind his own business. I liked his kid, but we didn't know each other. He had some nerve saying he wanted to "utilize" me.

But before I could formulate a response, Jim continued, "I know I'm out of line here, but I think you could do a lot of good. Inspire those kids."

I resisted the bitter laugh that threatened. I was a cautionary tale, not an inspiration.

Instead of arguing the point, I said simply, "You already have a coach."

The principal lowered his voice. "Between you and me, Whitaker hasn't been much of a coach or an educator since my arrival here three years ago. I've heard that's been the case for much longer. But he's retiring at the end of the school year. And North Carolina is one of the few states that doesn't require coaches to teach. It would just be a couple of certifications on coaching education—player health, first aid, concussion protocol. That sort of thing. Anyway, just something to think about, Mr. Clark. Have a good night," he finished quickly, dropping his bomb and then vacating the premises to avoid the resulting damage.

He was gone before I could remind him to call me Will. He hadn't even ordered his drink.

Before I could puzzle over his out-of-the-blue offer, Jordan slid into the seat the principal had vacated. "Saw you talking to Jim Gentry. He's a good one."

I cleared my throat. "Yeah, he introduced himself the other week after conditioning. Mason is his kid. The junior with the arm."

"Yeah. He comes into Firefly at least once a month with his family. They get dinner from the food trucks and listen to whatever band is performing. He's got a wife and two twin little girls too. Seems like a real nice guy."

I eyed Jordan for any ulterior motive, but he seemed more interested in the bartender who was getting blessedly closer.

"Becca's the belle of the ball," Jordan said with a grin and a tilt of his head.

I was further distracted from Principal Gentry's offer when I turned in my seat to see Becca crowded around a huge table, smiling and chatting with a mix of people from both rec teams.

"Yeah, I don't think she'd had much of that before coming to Kirby Falls," I replied quietly.

"Yeah," Jordan agreed.

The bartender approached and grabbed our orders, and we returned to the big table that butted up against where several of my teammates were playing pool. Jordan broke off to sit with Chloe, and Becca waved me over to an empty seat she appeared to be guarding.

I mostly listened and sipped my beer as the conversation continued in little groups among the softball players. Becca had plenty of people vying for her attention, but she pressed her thigh to mine while she chatted, and mouthed "you okay?" at least three times before I gave in and laced my fingers with hers beneath the table.

When her cider had nearly reached the bottom, I leaned in and whispered, "Do you want to come over? I can make you some dinner, show you the house?"

I wanted to spend time with her and let whatever was happening just . . . happen. I'd been foolish to think I could stop it. Maybe it wouldn't be forever, and maybe Becca's plans would change, but I wanted her here in my space—in my life, in my heart, in my bed.

So when she responded to my invitation with a wide grin and a quick nod, it felt right.

It wasn't until forty minutes later when I was letting Carl out into the yard and guiding Becca into the kitchen at the homestead that I felt sudden nerves. I wasn't uncomfortable to have her here. I just became suddenly aware of how my great-grandfather's home didn't feel much like mine.

Since I'd moved in six years ago, I'd mostly been handling the upkeep of the big house. Improvements and modernizing had taken a back seat to putting out fires. Things that needed doing like replacing the roof or updating the plumbing and furnace as well as the water heater.

Taking in my great-grandparents' photographs in gilt-edged frames and the faded wallpaper and the old furniture, I felt uncomfortable at the lack of progress I'd made on the place. I had ideas and plans, but I'd avoided making the house a home for myself in favor of keeping it a museum to Clark ancestry.

"It smells good in here," Becca said as she wandered over to the worn countertop.

A full kitchen remodel was on my to-do list. It had been for a while now. I'd replaced the appliances a couple of years ago as they'd all been old and well used. But I planned on painting the room a brighter color and updating the cabinets and counters, maybe adding a granite island with tall stools in the center of the space. The kitchen table in the breakfast nook was one that my grandpa William had made by hand. It was a testament to his woodworking talent, but it was scratched and scarred from decades of use. I wondered how it looked through Becca's eyes—if she only saw the age and the wear and not the love and years.

"What?" I finally replied. "You think Maggie Clark raised a son who can't cook for himself?"

Her blue eyes sparkled. "Oh, I'm sure she taught you a thing or two."

Becca went back to examining the bubbling crock pot filled with tender beef and onions, carrots, and potatoes in a savory sauce.

"I can meal prep with the best of them."

She laughed, and I was continually amazed that I could get that sort of happiness out of her. I was often too serious for my own good. Not soft enough for someone like Becca. But when she smiled like that, I thought I might just be soft enough.

"I'll pop the bread in to warm and then show you around."

"I can't wait."

Taking the French bread out of the bag from the bakery, I turned on the oven and put it inside. When I spun back to face Becca and get this tour started, I saw her fingers trailing over the oak surface of the kitchen table. She traced the woodgrain reverently, a small wondering smile on her face.

I swallowed against the sight of her in this space filled with so much Clark history, and thought, she might not mind the worn edges after all.

We worked our way through the main floor. Becca lingered over the piano in the formal living room and the pictures on the wall. I showed her the photograph of me and my cousins from the hiking trail I'd told her about. Her eyes happily scanned the image of my younger self and the brilliant path lined with red rhododendron blooms.

Becca exclaimed over the powder room beneath the stairs and the light fixtures in the hallway. Her hands traced over everything that caught her eye. She asked me all about the table in the dining room and what family dinners were like back when my grandpa William had lived here. Her gaze took in the room like she could envision the laughter and the conversation from four generations of Clarks, the hands held over prayers, the meals prepared in celebration. Becca smiled at me like she could see it all, and my heart ached knowing she'd asked because she'd never had that for herself.

It made me want to invite her to my parents' house for family dinner tomorrow. She deserved to experience the boisterousness and the familiarity of a family who meddled and overwhelmed but who loved fiercely. But before I could ask, Becca's voice drew my attention.

"Look at this!" she exclaimed when I tried to lead her up the staircase to the second floor. She was marveling over the doorframe and I realized what had caught her notice. There, carved into the dark wood, were lines marking the height of many a Clark descendant. I saw initials and scratches for myself and my cousins, Bonnie and Mac. But older lines captured the growth of my father and my uncles, Robert and James. And even more worn and dated were the markings for my grandfather William Jr., the only son of our shared namesake and the great-grandmother I'd never met.

Becca's touch smoothed gently over the history and progression of my lineage, something I'd long since ignored every time I came up and down the weathered staircase. "This is amazing! R.C. is Robert?"

"Yes. Bonnie and Mac's dad."

"And J.C.?"

"My uncle James," I explained. "You haven't met him yet." Her eyes met mine on the last word, but I didn't let myself regret the implication. "He doesn't involve himself with the farm. Works and lives in town."

"I see," she said, back to tracing the lines. "And Jr. is your grandfather who lives in Florida part of the year?"

"Yeah. They have the big house overlooking the pond."

"Ah." She nodded. "How long have you lived here, Will?"

My hand tightened on the top of the newel post. "Six years. When my great-grandfather moved into Legacy Hills."

Becca nodded again as if she'd expected that.

I felt the need to explain myself. "I have plans to remodel and update the property. I've stripped some of the wallpaper here and there. One of the bathrooms on the second floor even had it on the ceiling. There's just a lot of little things—"

"I think it's the most wonderful house I've ever seen," she interrupted. "Things like this"—she stroked the doorframe—"make it this living, breathing thing. There's so much of your family's history here. It's beautiful and well-loved. This place is lucky to have you looking after it."

Her praise heated my cheeks. I wanted to argue and say I didn't deserve the soft way she was looking at me. Sometimes I felt overwhelmed by the responsibility I'd been entrusted with. Even more times, I felt resentful and saddled with something I'd never asked for. Becca gave me too much credit, painting me with all these shades of unfair devotion.

But before I could correct her or alter the tenderness in her gaze with my blunt honesty, she took my hand and said gently, "It's full of possibility, and when you're ready, you'll make it into something for the next generation. Now, let's go rescue the bread from the oven and eat that pot roast. You can show me the upstairs later."

"Shit," I murmured, noticing the smell of bread just this side of burnt.

She grinned and tugged me in the direction of the kitchen. And I thought I might follow this woman damn near anywhere.

Becca

We ate at the nook in the kitchen. Will gave me an honest-to-goodness cloth napkin for my lap and served me a hearty portion of comfort food while Carl lay at our feet.

The pot roast was delicious and the bread crusty and warm. We'd caught it just in time. But I was happy for the distraction.

The deeper into the house we'd wandered, the more uncomfortable Will had become. Tension radiated from him—jaw clenched tight and shoulders stiff. I imagined I knew what had put him on edge, judging from the way he'd tried to hurriedly explain away the lack of renovation he'd done.

I'd wanted to put him at ease. I loved this house, but it was obviously an undertaking. Will had been entrusted with something massive, and once again, it was another Clark legacy that he hadn't asked for, but had inherited just the same. As he did with the farm and the business, Will was honoring and nurturing his family and his responsibilities. I ached for him in this life he hadn't really chosen for himself.

But the meal had seemed to put him at ease. We'd talked and teased, and I was happy to be back on surer footing.

After dinner, we'd washed the dishes together. Will had done his best to discourage me, but I'd had none of it. I was a guest, but I didn't feel like one. Not really. I felt like I belonged.

I wanted to be elbow deep in soapy water, right beside him. I loved the domesticity of it and how comfortable I felt in this house with this man. From the rich history to the easy conversation, contentment settled deep in my bones.

If you'd have told Becca from a month ago that she'd be sharing dinner alone with crush-worthy Will Clark, she probably would have hyperventilated at the prospect. But something had shifted, bringing everything into clearer focus. If I wanted a future with Will, I needed to be brave, and that was all there was to it.

This whole evening felt like a favorite book I'd picked up from the shelf, worn and beloved. The words came easy and made my heart feel full. Dazzling and familiar all at the same time.

I'd be lying if I said I hadn't come here tonight without expectations.

I wanted to stay. I wanted to be bold and fearless and offer Will my body and my heart. And I wanted Will's offering in return. It seemed like the next logical step, a progression toward the *more* we were trying to achieve. Staying in Kirby Falls was ultimately my goal. I'd tentatively begun the planning stages by looking into the real estate market around town. I still wasn't ready to consider selling Mrs. Walters's apartment, but a decision would need to be made sooner rather than later.

"You ready for the rest of the tour?" Will said, taking a kitchen towel and carefully drying my wet hands.

"Yes, I'd love that," I replied, unable to hide my smile.

Will grinned too. He leaned in close to hang the towel on the handle of the oven door behind me. As he did so, his nose nuzzled against mine before he pressed a quick kiss to my lips.

When he pulled back, he was still smiling. Then he held out a hand and led me back toward the staircase. The hardwood creaked as we ascended, Carl racing up ahead of us.

"You've seen everything down here except for the screened porch, but it's too dark to appreciate the view. But you can check it out in the morning."

Will didn't say it with a presumptuous leer or with any expectation whatsoever. It was just a statement of fact—something understood and defined. A truth that I belonged here tonight and tomorrow too.

"Sounds good," I replied, working to make my voice even.

Will was patient as I explored the second floor. There was the large study, and the three guest bedrooms. The wide landing adjacent to the top of the stairs would make a perfect reading nook. It had a tall window to let in plenty of light during the daytime and enough space for a wide, comfortable chair and built-in bookshelves.

More family photos were hung in the long hallway. These looked older and more fragile. I could understand Will's reluctance to change a home that didn't really feel like his. This house had lived a thousand lives, and change was difficult no matter how you sliced it.

Will's room was the largest bedroom at the end of the hallway. He'd made the space more comfortable with an updated bedroom suite. It was pretty minimalist, with a chest of drawers for clothing, two matching bedside tables, and a large mirrored wardrobe in the corner that looked like a holdover from Grandpa William. There was an adjoining bathroom and a walk-in closet. Carl had a dog bed in the corner that looked brand new and rarely used. And when I ventured closer, I noticed a book on the end table next to a phone charger and a bedside lamp. When I got a good look at the book cover, I quickly glanced away and moved to poke my head into the bathroom.

He'd picked up one of the books I'd designed the cover for, and I thought my heart might explode. It was an indie romance title, so it wasn't like he grabbed it while browsing downtown at Paperback Writer. He'd purchased that romance novel online and had been reading it judging by the bookmark sticking out.

Will stayed near the bed while I fought to control my smile and my racing heart. When I returned from checking out the renovated en suite, I noticed that the book I'd spied was suddenly absent. I didn't want to tease him for something so adorable. I wanted to take the knowledge and hug it close before I rolled around in it.

Will was such a sweetheart. I couldn't handle it.

He was sitting at the foot of the bed, watching me.

"That's a good-looking tub," I complimented the restored white clawfoot bathtub that made me itch to pick up a loofah.

His smile was small and pleased. "Thank you. You can try it out if you want."

I came to stand in front of him and his hands immediately rested on my hips. With that big bed behind Will, this felt like a game of chicken, only I didn't think I'd mind being the loser.

"Maybe later," I said as I stepped closer and wound my arms around his neck.

Our lips met in the next instance, a mutual meeting of intent. My bottom lip slotted neatly between both of his, and he bit down gently before sucking it into his mouth.

My fingers drifted into his soft hair as his hands urged me between his spread thighs. When Will's arms closed around my waist, he tipped us back onto the bed, all my softness cradled by his firm chest and thighs. He didn't stop kissing me, just angled for a deeper taste.

I wanted this with him, and I luxuriated in sharing his space. Will was someone who valued his privacy and guarded himself. To be invited and welcomed into his orbit was another layer of acceptance I'd been missing in my life.

Strong, capable hands moved to cup my backside, and I felt the hardness of Will's erection growing between us.

I was eager for his skin and his warmth, but when my fingers closed around the hem of his tee shirt, a faint buzzing met my ears.

Lips locked, and we both paused as the vibration continued.

Finally, Will pulled back. "I think that's you." He removed my phone from my back pocket and held it up.

"Oh."

The screen faced me, and I blinked, surprised to see Laramie's name there. We'd texted plenty, but she'd never called me. I knew how opposed she was to talking on the phone.

Grabbing my cell from where Will had extended it, I wiggled myself back off the bed. I heard Will's tortured groan as I grazed his tented jeans, and I fought a smile, hitting the green button to accept the call.

"Hello," I said, watching Will cover his face with his arms.

My attention was drawn away from the bulge in his pants when I heard a quiet sniffle. "Becca."

Immediately, I became alert. "What's wrong?"

A hiccup and then a slurred, "Can you come get me?"

"Where are you?"

A muffled sob came through the line, and then what sounded like a door closing. Larry's voice echoed, "Magnolia."

Something was very wrong. I could not imagine Will's pixie-sized, butt-kicking, combat boot–wearing cousin crying somewhere in a bathroom. "What happened, babe?"

"I can't—I can't talk right now. I'm gonna be sick. Where are you?"

My eyes sought Will, who was sitting up now, watching me with concern. "I'm at Will's house."

"Oh God," she wailed, crying harder. "Please. Please don't tell him it's me. He already thinks I can't do anything right. I don't want him to know that I—that I—" Larry's words dissolved into hysterical cries.

I shot Will a tense smile. "Okay. It's okay. We'll talk. It'll be okay. Just hold tight for me."

"Thanks, Becca," she slurred, and I heard the phone plunk down on a hard surface.

Quickly straightening, I hung up and hurried over to Will, who was standing from the bed, worry and alarm clear on his features.

"I have to go. I'm so sorry."

"What's the matter? Is everything okay?"

I didn't know why Larry wanted me to keep her secret, but she was my friend, the first one I'd made in a very long time. She'd welcomed me into her life when I'd been an intrusive tourist, and we'd bonded. I cared about her, and if she needed me, I would be there for her.

I didn't want to lie to Will, but in my panic and haste to get to Laramie, I blurted out the only thing I could think of, "Everything will be okay. But I need to head back down the mountain and deal with it. Something important came up back home."

At my final word, the warmth leeched out of Will's gray eyes. His confusion set in the hard lines of his face, and I wanted to take back what I'd said about home.

Reaching out, I clasped his hand in mine. "I'll see you tomorrow at the farm. I promise. I just need to go right now. I'm sorry. Thank you for everything. This has been the best day."

Will nodded stiffly as his hand slid out of mine. "I hope everything is okay."

I forced a smile. "It will be."

seventeen

BECCA

"Larry. Wake up."

I patted Laramie's pale cheek opposite where her face was smooshed against her upper arm. She was flopped over on a chaise lounge in an honest-to-goodness powder room outside the women's restroom.

"Larry." I tried again, pushing dark hair off her face. Her expert eye makeup was ruined from crying, but at least we were alone. The bar was plenty busy, though, and I was shocked that no one had found Larry in here and called for help.

When I'd hurried through the front doors moments ago, I'd been a little surprised by my surroundings. Magnolia Bar was one of the few places in Kirby Falls that I hadn't visited yet. It was on the first block of Main Street and clearly catered to tourists. Everything was polished wood with trendy black and white decor. It looked like a modern speakeasy.

Magnolia lacked the warmth, character, and sticky floors of Mattie B's. It was missing the charm and gorgeous outdoor space of Firefly Cider. But I could see how out-of-towners might be comfortable here—even impressed.

The high-top tables and plush booths were full of puffy vest–wearing outsiders, laughing and drinking men and women who were temporary in the grand scheme of Kirby Falls. I couldn't imagine Mac or Jordan or Chloe ever hanging out here.

So what was Larry doing in this bar?

The tattooed bartender behind the long, gleaming bar top looked intimidatingly handsome. It was strange because he'd seemed approachable and friendly earlier in the day when he'd played with me on the Bar Hoppers' softball team. I was pretty sure his name was Jack. But if he'd recognized me from the field, he didn't say so. He hadn't stopped or acknowledged me as I bypassed the bar and walked right back toward the wooden sign with an arrow that read *Ladies* in elegant script.

"Laramie Jean Burke," I finally said firmly, middle-naming her in an effort to get her up so we could get out of here.

It worked. She groaned and mumbled out between red-smeared lips, "My middle name is Annabeth."

Crouching down before her, I tried to catch her bleary eyes, but they were unfocused and miserable. "What happened, Larry?"

"Can you take me home first? Please, Becca." Her blue eyes welled with tears, and my fear ratcheted up another notch. Larry was the most direct, unafraid person I'd ever met—besides maybe Cece. I couldn't bear that she was hurting, that she'd been desperate enough to need my help in the first place.

"You got it, babe."

Together, we worked to get her standing. I smoothed her short pleated skirt over her fishnet stockings and looped my arms through hers to keep her steady and upright. Then we walked out of Magnolia and to my car in the parking lot across the street. Larry had to stop to puke in the bushes lining the walkway, but she seemed buoyed after that and we made it the rest of the way to my SUV without incident.

She managed to give me her address before resting her head on the cool glass of the passenger side window and falling asleep. I checked her breathing at every stoplight as I drove just to make sure she was okay.

Approximately eight minutes later, my navigation instructed me to pull into a short driveway. The one-story brick house looked like a duplex with two front doors and big bay windows that mirrored each other on each side.

I woke Larry and got her up onto the front porch before I realized she wasn't carrying a purse or any sort of bag. Her phone had been wedged in her bra beneath a low-cut black shirt when I'd found her in the powder room.

"Larry, do you have a key?" I asked.

She was propped up against one of the porch columns, eyes closed. "Under the cactus."

Sure enough, there was a potted cactus to the left side of the first unit. I carefully lifted the planter and retrieved a key. When I stood, I noticed Larry was staring at the door on the right, so I made my way over there to unlock it.

"Shit, no," Larry called in a frantic whisper. "Mine is on the left."

I looked at the white front door that had a 107 on it and then stepped over to quickly unlock 105 as she'd indicated.

Larry's apartment was a little like Larry herself—sleek and stylish but chaotic. I ushered my drunken charge past boots and high heels piled by the front door, beyond the low black leather couch, and back to a bedroom that had a huge bed framed between two tall windows. Stray clothes covered nearly the entire surface of her fluffy white duvet. It looked like she'd been trying to decide what to wear and needed to try on everything in her closet.

"You sit," I ordered after grabbing an armload of shirts, dresses, bras, and jeans and clearing them to a desk chair in the corner. I flipped on the desk lamp while I was over there so I could see better to get her settled.

In the bathroom, I found a dark washcloth and then a bottle of aspirin in the medicine cabinet. After a quick detour to the kitchen for a glass of water, I returned to find Larry sitting dutifully on the edge of the mattress. Her eyes were closed.

I unlaced her shiny boots that went up past her ankles and slipped them off. Then I took advantage of her closed eyes and started wiping away the smeared mascara and eyeliner.

Larry surprised me when she started speaking unprompted, "I went to Magnolia to hang out with Kayla." I knew that Kayla was Larry's best friend. They'd gone to high school together, and Larry had mentioned Kayla playing on her trivia team as well, but I'd never met the woman myself. "She was working tonight, but I didn't mind. I've sat at the bar plenty of nights while she served the tourists."

I tried to be gentle as I forced the dark makeup from her pale skin. But I ignored the red staining her lips because I thought Laramie needed to get this off her chest and I didn't want to interrupt.

"But there was some hipster-looking guy flirting with her all night. He had this dopey mustache that curled up on the ends, and she just kept drifting over to chat with him. I guess I was irritated because here I was, after she'd invited me, sitting on a barstool all by myself so she could get cozy with this—this *guy*." She said *guy* like he was the heir of Slytherin or a Kardashian.

Finished with the washcloth, I moved to sit beside Larry on the bed. In silent support, I pressed my shoulder to hers.

"Then Kayla told me she was getting off early. Jack was back behind the bar, and she could take off, but she was going home with the hipster, and she'd see me later."

"I'm sorry. That was a crappy thing to do after she'd invited you to the bar," I said gently. But something about Larry's hurt led me to believe this wound went a little deeper.

"I guess I took it bad because I started drinking. Not just nursing the beer I'd had all night. But taking shots people bought for me. Jack cut me off and told me to call for a ride, and I thought, I can't call Kayla to come and get me because she's off—she's off banging some guy at his Airbnb."

"Does she pick up guys a lot?" I asked, testing a theory.

Larry shook her head and then stopped herself abruptly, as if the movement might cause all those shots to perform an encore. "No. She actually dated the same guy since high school. They broke up this spring because long distance wasn't working anymore, and I thought. Well, I thought she . . . "

Her voice trailed off, and my heart ached for this tough girl who maybe had an unknown soft spot. "And you thought she might start looking at you."

Larry turned to face me, her eyes bloodshot and full of tears.

"Oh, honey," I murmured and then wrapped her up in my arms. "I won't tell anyone." Suddenly, her assurance from weeks ago that she could be discreet and wouldn't tell Will about my crush made a lot more sense. "I can keep a secret too."

Larry cried sloppy on my shoulder for a time, and then she warned me that she needed to puke again. So I helped her to a bathroom that was covered in cosmetics and held her hair back while she emptied her stomach of alcohol. She mumbled drunkenly about how she'd been in love with Kayla since high school and that her family didn't know she was bisexual. She kept going on dates, hoping to meet someone and get over her best friend, who also happened to be her neighbor and completely heterosexual. They'd shared a wall and a duplex for over four years.

I didn't know what to say or how to reassure Larry, so I listened, and I wiped her mouth with a towel when she couldn't manage it herself.

When all that was done, I got Larry into some pajamas and made her take a couple of aspirin with a full glass of water. Then I slept beside her to make sure she didn't need me again.

The following morning, Larry's alarm sounded at eight, and I figured she was supposed to be at the farm by nine. She grumbled and groaned but made her way into the shower. Maybe not fully functioning but hovering at a solid sixty percent.

I got up and found my way around her kitchen. After making some coffee, I went simple with some buttered toast and hoped she could manage to keep it down.

She fell on the impromptu breakfast with reckless abandon, considering I'd had a front-row seat for how unstable her gastrointestinal system had been a mere six hours ago.

"Thanks for riding to my rescue last night, Becca. I hope I didn't pull you away from anything."

Clearly, she hadn't remembered the phone call and me telling her I was at Will's. I took a sip of coffee before admitting, "I'm glad I could help you when you needed it. I was actually having dinner at Will's place. You told me not to tell him it was you when you called."

"Oh shit," she said around a triangle of toast. "I vaguely remember that. I'm sorry I messed up your night. What did you tell him?"

Uneasiness had my stomach clenching when I thought of Will's reaction to the way I'd hurried off last night. "I told him something came up with my family that I needed to take care of. It wasn't that far-fetched. But I think he was hurt that I rushed off like I did."

"I'll talk to him," Larry said decisively.

"No, it's okay. Last night was your business, and you don't owe an explanation to anyone. I could see why you wouldn't want Will to know, but I don't think he truly considers you incapable or bad at your job. I can't imagine he'd hold a drunken Thursday night against you."

Larry laughed a little bitterly. "Will lives by the hard truth that if you want something done right, you have to do it yourself. He thinks Grandpappy's would crumble and blow away without him there to keep it all together. It's like he took all his baseball drive and determination and put it into being a martyr for the farm."

I frowned at her interpretation. She saw it and raised her hands, saying, "Calm down, tiger. I know he works hard, and I know he didn't ask for any of it. If Will had his way, he'd be in the middle of the playoffs right now, throwing strikes and kicking ass. He's just an intense personality. Always has been. I guess my drunk ass didn't want to give him any more ammunition in thinking I'm an incompetent waste of space."

I agreed with part of Larry's assessment of her cousin. He did put too much on his own shoulders, but he put it there himself. Will wasn't someone who asked for help, and he didn't expect anyone to do things on the farm that he wouldn't do himself. It was why he helped out and provided support wherever he was needed—on the tractor, in the fields, or even with the catering and events.

But part of what Larry said rubbed me the wrong way. "There's no way he considers you an incompetent waste of space, Larry. He's never said one bad word about you to me. And I can't imagine he even thinks those things where you're concerned."

Larry smirked. "Getting to know my dear cousin so very well, are you? Y'all finally stopped dancing around each other?"

I felt heat make the journey from my neck to my cheeks. "We're working on it."

"What does that mean?"

"It means we're trying."

Larry's eyes narrowed, and she took a thoughtful sip of coffee. "Are you staying in Kirby Falls?"

I thought about the emails I hadn't answered from a real estate agent in town and how I was dragging my feet deciding what to do about Mrs. Walters's apartment. Then there was the panic I felt at abandoning my sister to her dangerous lifestyle. "I want to," I said quietly, unable to meet the accusation in Laramie's gaze.

"You know everyone loves you, and we'd support you moving here without question. But you need to decide what you're doing. Will's life is here whether he wants it to be or not. He's too loyal to ever leave the farm and the Clark legacy. I imagine it's hard to be with you in this in-between, undecided state. Obviously, he cares about you, but if you're just going to up and leave when the apple cider doughnuts run out and the corn gets harvested, then what's the fucking point? Will looks at you like you're endgame, but if you bail on Kirby Falls, he'll be left the loser."

I swallowed the lump that had swollen in my throat as Larry spoke. I didn't want to hurt Will. I knew that if I broke his heart, I'd destroy my own in the process. But I was scared too. I couldn't deny that. I had obligations and responsibilities the same way Will did. Sure, mine weren't as noble or flashy, but there were things about Detroit that it would kill me to abandon. It would mean giving up on my sister once and for all. Because when I was out of sight, out of mind, and never coming back, Heather would no longer seek me out for the bare minimum. And while that might sound like a good thing to a normal, well-adjusted person, to me, it just meant that I wouldn't have any family left. I'd be alone, and that would be it. Giving up Mrs. Walters's apartment would be like saying goodbye to her all over again.

But Larry was right; I needed to figure out exactly what I wanted and make it happen. The back-and-forth, wishy-washy indecision would only make things harder in the long run.

"I don't want to hurt anyone," I confessed.

"I know," Larry said, her face softening into a tired smile. "Big changes are scary and hard. I'm a hypocrite to sit here and tell you to throw caution to the wind and take what you want." I started to protest but she waved me away. "I'm tired of whining about me. What I'm saying is, it might be terrifying to reorder your life for Kirby Falls and us and Will"—she fluttered her lashes dreamily—"but it'll be worth it."

Smiling her direction, I nodded because I did know that.

Larry shook her head, amused. "Will is one of the best people I know. He'd stop and help a stranger change their tire on the side of the road or give someone the shirt off his back. He'll do anything for you, Becca babe. He just won't smile while he does it."

I grinned. I knew that too.

"Did you ever hear how he ended up with Carl?"

I straightened, immediately interested in the story. "No. How did that happen?"

"Years ago, after Will graduated and came home. He was bitter and angry for a long while. It was during one of the summer markets downtown. The animal shelter had a booth set up for a big adoption event. Will was breaking down the Grandpappy's setup at the end of the day. Afterward, he walked by the pens and cages the shelter was packing up and saw they had one dog left. It wasn't particularly friendly. Not jumping around, eager for attention. An adult dog who didn't give a shit if anyone picked him or not. They told Will they'd had this dog for six months and not a single taker. He sat in his cage with his back to everyone, unimpressed with the prospect of trying to get adopted. Will took him home that day. And now Carl rarely leaves his side . . . except to seek you out apparently." I grinned. "There's a moral in there about patience or obstinate males or worthiness or something, but I'll let you figure it out."

My heart felt like it might burst thinking about a grumpy man and a grumpy dog trying to find their way together. It sounded like Will had needed someone when he was hurting and forced to return home. I was glad Will and Carl had found each other.

"Well, I better get to work. Hopefully, I'm not on hayride duty this morning, or I'm going to barf all over the leafers."

I laughed.

"Thanks again for taking care of me last night, Becca. I owe you."

"You don't owe me anything. That's what friends are for."

I thought about what Larry had said as I drove to the tiny house. I did need to decide what I was going to do. No more dragging my feet through indecision valley.

I was staying in Kirby Falls. I'd rent out the apartment. I'd tell my sister goodbye and hope she'd want to keep in touch.

Sure, I'd have to go back to Detroit at some point to pack up my things and meet with potential tenants for Mrs. Walters's apartment, but now that I'd settled on this course of action, I felt lighter, freer, braver.

I'd work at the tiny house today and get my plan together. Then I'd talk to Will, reassure him that I was committed to a future here—with him. I'd do what I could to wipe that look off his face when I'd left last night.

Things were shaping up. Larry was right. It would be scary. Change always was. But it would be worth it in the end.

I smiled to myself as I pulled out my laptop and made another cup of coffee.

I had some real estate agent emails to return.

WILL

Me: Is everything okay?
Becca: Yes! Everything is fine.
Becca: I'm working from the tiny house today, but I'd love it if you wanted to come over later.

It was Friday, and I had a family dinner tonight. I considered inviting Becca. I knew everyone would welcome her around the table at my parents' house. Hell, they'd probably rather have her there than me. And I knew that Becca would love every moment of it. Answering her questions last night about the big table in my dining room made it clear that the concept of a family dinner was foreign to her, but would be very welcome.

But there were other parts of last night that I couldn't stop recalling, like how she'd run away after an awkward phone call and hadn't really given me an explanation.

"Something important came up back home."

Things were complicated with her family, and I got that. And our relationship was new. I wasn't about to make demands of Becca, but I couldn't help but feel like I was missing something about her abrupt departure. Hearing her refer to *home* like that hadn't helped my suspicions either.

I wondered how it would be if Becca did, in fact, end up moving to Kirby Falls. Would her sister continue harassing her for money? Would Becca be able to separate herself from someone who clearly relied on her, even if Heather didn't have her best intentions at heart?

The part of me that was a skeptical asshole wondered if Becca actually planned on leaving Detroit at all. Wanting to do something and actually following through were two very different things.

Eventually, I texted back: *I have plans tonight, but thank you for the invite.*

Becca: Sure. No worries. We can talk later.

I could see her smile in my mind's eye. The one she rushed to put on when she was disappointed but didn't want anyone to know it.

Sighing, I stared at my phone like a coward until the screen went dark, and then I slipped it into my pocket.

My parents lived on a flat four acres that butted up against the mountain I currently lived on. The house I'd grown up in was surrounded by old-growth trees and had a huge barn across the gravel driveway. The backyard still contained a tree house and a tire swing, and a shed was likely still filled with every piece of baseball equipment you could imagine. My childhood bedroom was dusted once a month. Otherwise, it remained untouched. Mom and Dad kept all my trophies and pennants and posters just the way I'd left them when I'd moved out at eighteen.

The sun was behind the hills, working its way toward a dramatic sunset. Plowed cornfields lined the road to the property. Mom typically drove to work on her baby-blue side-by-side UTV currently parked in the barn. The Orchard Bake Shop wasn't far—maybe three-quarters of a mile away—so the commute was convenient. And even if it wasn't, nearly every part of any Clarks' life was tangled up in the farm somehow.

Well, except for Uncle James.

My father's youngest brother was climbing out of his electric car when I pulled up in front of my parents' house just before six o'clock.

"Will," he greeted. "How the hell are you?"

He gave me a quick hug and a slap on the back. He still smelled like Old Spice and looked relaxed in loafers and a polo shirt.

"I'm good," I replied. "It's been a while."

James nodded. He and my dad favored one another. Same tall frame, dark hair, and gray eyes that I'd inherited. "Been busy, and I'm sure you have too."

I didn't think I'd seen my uncle since the big Memorial Day party my grandparents hosted every year at Lake Archer. It wasn't unusual to go three months without seeing James around, but it did make me curious how he got away with it.

If I so much as ignored a voicemail from my mother, she'd show up on my doorstep with a Tupperware container full of soup with the assumption that I must be under the weather if I couldn't so much as return a phone call within twelve hours.

But Uncle James missed birthday parties and the occasional holiday. Family dinners on a random Friday in early October probably weren't high on his priority list, but it was nice to see him all the same. I was a little jealous that he'd managed to extricate himself from the Grandpappy's business side of things so cleanly.

To hear my dad tell it, his youngest brother had no interest in the farm or the running of it, even from a young age. He'd gone to college and lived his life as if his own father and grandfather hadn't entrusted the farm to future generations. Grandpappy's was in good hands with my dad and my uncle Robert. I guess the key to avoiding farm life was to have two older brothers who weren't opposed to running it. That wasn't really an option I had though.

"Let's get in there before Maggie comes out here looking for us," James said good-naturedly.

I ushered a reluctant Carl out of my truck and in we went.

We were, in fact, the last to arrive.

Laramie was hunched over at the center island in the kitchen while my aunt Patty, cousin Bonnie, and Mom prepped the meal.

Dad was out on the back deck manning the grill with Bonnie's husband, Danny, my uncle Robert, and MacKenzie. Uncle James slipped out through the sliding door to join them after greeting everyone in the kitchen.

My dog disappeared into the living room to curl up on the couch and be left alone.

I placed the three bottles of red wine I'd brought on the kitchen counter and kissed my mother on the cheek. "Hey, Momma."

"Hey, sugar. Did you bring Becca?"

She was whipping potatoes and didn't do more than glance at me while she focused on the bowl in front of her, but I wasn't really surprised by her question. She saw me with Becca nearly every day at the farm. She'd backed off on the matchmaking, but I still caught her pleased grins when she spied us together. It wasn't far-fetched to imagine I might bring her to dinner, but I still felt the guilty churn in my stomach just the same.

"Not tonight," I said, and pretty much every eye in the room turned my way. "Do you need help with anything?"

"No, they've got it," Larry said from where she was pushing up from her low-backed stool. She looked a little worse for wear. My cousin typically wore dark, edgy outfits and dramatic makeup. But she was in leggings and an oversized sweatshirt, bare-faced entirely, clutching a Gatorade like it was the Holy Grail. "I need to talk to you a minute."

Frowning, I watched her walk out of the kitchen. I looked around the room to see if anyone else thought that was weird, but Bonnie and her mom were chatting while they chopped vegetables for the salad and my mother was still occupied with copious amounts of butter and starch.

"Well, come on," Larry called impatiently from out in the hallway.

I rolled my eyes and followed, grabbing my jacket back off the coatrack as I went. My cousin led me out onto the front porch and sat in a rocking chair.

Joining her in the chilly evening air, I asked, "What's up? You okay?"

Laramie reached over and grabbed the arm of my chair to prevent me from rocking any further. "I can't even handle watching you sway back and forth right now. Just give me a minute."

"Are you sick?"

She sighed and looked out over the fields. "I'm hungover."

"Oh."

"I got shit-faced at Magnolia last night and called Becca to come and get me." Larry turned to meet my gaze head-on now. "I told her not to say anything, just begged her to pick me up and take me home and to please not tell you."

My mind spun at the idea that Larry would call Becca when she was in trouble, and then it landed neatly on the fact that Becca had gone, no questions asked. She hadn't left me last night to take care of something with her sister. She'd ridden off to Larry's rescue because my cousin had needed her. I felt a swirling mixture of pride and familial annoyance.

"Why didn't you want me to know?" I asked.

Larry snorted and then immediately covered her mouth like she regretted it. "Hell, I don't know. Because I was vulnerable and crying my eyes out in the bathroom of a leafer bar, drunk as a skunk. Not really setting a shining example, dear cousin."

"Oh," I repeated. "I would have come to get you. You know that."

Larry sighed again. "I know, William. But I didn't want someone who was going to judge me for being a fuckup."

"What the hell, Laramie Annabeth? I would not—"

"You wouldn't mean to," she interrupted, dark eyes troubled. "But you would. You'd think I was young and emotional and maybe unreliable. Dramatic at best and a drunken embarrassment causing a scene at worst."

"Larry," I breathed. Did she really think I saw her that way?

I thought back to when I'd harped on Mac about handling the social media crap for the Orchard Fest. Maybe I did have high expectations for my cousins, but I just wanted to make sure things ran smoothly at the farm. Sometimes I felt like they were just out for a good time, always joking and having fun—even at work. But Grandpappy's was a business. Livelihoods depended on us. I didn't need them screwing around.

"Sometimes it feels like you stopped being my cousin so you could be my boss, Will."

Her voice was small, and she wouldn't look at me, and it was so unlike my typically brash and bold cousin that I hated it.

I swallowed down a healthy dose of guilt and apologized, "I'm sorry I ever made you feel that way. I just . . . " Hell, I didn't know what to say.

"You're just an intense buzzkill, and you want everything to be perfect," Larry finished for me.

She laughed, and I did too.

"I'm fucking sorry, Larry. I'll do better. You're a hard worker, and you don't deserve to have me second-guessing you or breathing down your neck. But I definitely don't judge you for drinking in your off time unless there's a problem there and you need some help."

My cousin nodded and took another sip of blue drink from her plastic bottle. "I'm not over-indulging, if that's what you mean. I'm only telling you this now because I didn't want to cause trouble for you and Becca."

I'd been an asshole to question Becca's intentions last night, if only in my own head.

Even if she'd needed to leave to handle a situation with her sister and not my drunk cousin, that was her business. It was wrong of me to suddenly assume it meant she'd leave Kirby Falls as a result. I should have invited her tonight instead of expecting the worst and punishing her for it. I was behaving like a distrustful asshat, and I felt sick at the thought of her sitting home alone while I was surrounded by my loved ones.

She should have been here with me. Remorse churned in my gut.

"Why did you call Becca and not Kayla or Mac?" I finally asked.

Larry winced but admitted, "I called Becca because she's a good person. I knew I could count on her, and I trust her. And if you tell Mac I *didn't* call her, I'll key your truck."

"Jesus," I muttered, holding up my hands in surrender. "I swear I won't tell Mac you love Becca more than her."

Larry leaned over and punched me on the shoulder. "Becca was just better suited for the situation I was in. Mac would have wanted to know whose ass she needed to beat. Becca fucking held my hair back while I puked for an hour and slept beside me to make sure I didn't die. She cleaned the makeup off my stupid face and then made me breakfast this morning."

I'd missed out on something with Becca last night. I knew where we were headed when I brought her up to my bedroom. And I still wanted all that with her—her touch and her skin and to see her all spread out in my bed. But I wanted more too. I wanted her to stay, and I wanted a future. Hiking on the weekends with Carl. Showing her more of my favorite places—the ones that I knew would make her face light up with that stunning combination of wonder and joy. I wanted to play softball with her on Thursday nights and watch her work with her glasses on. I wanted to bring her to family dinner and take her out on dates. Read the books with the covers she'd designed on them and walk with her in the sunflower field.

Of course Becca had taken care of my cousin. Her heart was so wide and open, and she was genuine in a way that had confused me at first but only because I couldn't understand it in myself. She loved people and she loved them hard.

"Yeah," I managed before I had to clear my throat. "She's a good one."

Larry sucked in a slow breath before she spoke. "It would be easy to write her off as a walking, talking Barbie. She loves kittens and rainbows and all that shit. She probably enjoys pina coladas and taking walks in the rain, unironically. I bet she sings adorably off-key too."

I could confirm that after a karaoke night at Firefly last week.

"But she's *so* good," Larry went on. "Like down to her bones. She cares. And she listens when so many people don't. And she doesn't seem to mind your grumpy ass." Larry laughed and I smiled, looking down.

"Will, she looks at you like . . . "

I barely gave her time to trail off. "What? How does she look at me," I demanded, voice low and urgent, desperate for the answer. But also dreading it. Fucking pathetic over what might come out of Laramie's mouth.

But then my cousin smiled, a tender thing that was rarely seen on her face. "She looks at you like you're *home*. Like you're everything she loves about Kirby

Falls, wrapped up in a bearded, scowling package. Like you're the reason to stay."

I sat with Laramie's words all through dinner, let them absorb into my skin and settle around my heart. I thought about the idea of home and how mine had been lost to me for so long. Too mixed up in regret and anger to let me appreciate what I used to love.

And then this city girl showed up and made me see what I'd been missing. She'd reminded me that the mountains were home. That the land hadn't always meant Grandpappy's and tourists and obligation. At one time, it had all been simple instead of hard. It had been familiar instead of routine.

Thinking back to our hikes in the country, witnessing her love of the farm. Hell, even the tree I'd met her in had good memories associated with it before I'd locked everything away.

Looking around the table, taking in my family—laughing, talking over one another, dishing up seconds—I realized I had good memories with them too. I'd grown up surrounded by people who loved, supported, and put up with my intense determination and less-than-stellar attitude. How different would Becca's life have been if she'd had the support system I'd been blessed with?

Her kindness and goodness in spite of her history were admirable, and frankly, astonishing. She'd come to our tiny town and looked for ways to fit in and contribute. And here I was, a reluctant participant doing the bare minimum.

But even as I tried my best to avoid participating, I'd still found something that gave me a sense of purpose. Seth and Mason and the other high school kids were showing me that baseball didn't have to be locked up in a file cabinet with *failure* stamped across the front. They didn't care that I'd thrown two games in the majors before my career imploded. It was fucking terrifying to open myself up to more pain and regret but staying so closed off wasn't really working. Maybe that was what Jordan had been trying to tell me for a while now. Maybe I'd been unhappy without really knowing the difference.

"Earth to William," Mac called, drawing me out of my dinnertime introspection. "Pass the rolls."

Grabbing the basket in front of me, I took one of the dinner rolls and chucked it at her head. She caught it, laughing in startled surprise.

As she reached for a cherry tomato out of her salad bowl, my mom said firmly, "Don't even think about it, MacKenzie Eloise."

I grinned and my cousin stuck her tongue out at me.

"So," Bonnie said brightly, in what I was sure was an effort to distract her sister from troublemaking retribution, "we were thinking of planning an anniversary party for Grandma Nola and Grandpa Jr. It'll be their fiftieth in the spring."

"Who's we?" Mac asked, still eyeing me like I might have another dinner roll locked and loaded.

"Oh, me and Danny," Bonnie replied, glancing toward her husband, seated at her side.

But Danny was on his phone and not paying any attention to his wife. Her arm moved under the table and we all watched the big man jolt. "Shit. What?" he demanded.

Bonnie's face stayed smiling but everything about her went tight. "I was just saying how we wanted to celebrate Grandma and Grandpa's anniversary."

Danny looked like this was the first he was hearing of it, but he picked up on his wife's tense expression and glanced around the table quickly before saying unconvincingly, "Oh, right. That."

"I'll help you, honey," my aunt Patty said, giving her daughter a sweet smile.

"Me too," Mac offered.

"Of course we will, Bonnie," my own mother added. "We can plan something big over on the farm. Invite all their friends. Even the Florida ones. They'll love that."

I thought of my grandparents and their long and happy marriage. They'd run the farm for decades. Now, in their seventies, they took their retirement seriously. They spent the fall and winter months at their condo in Florida, the spring traveling in their RV, and the summer here in Kirby Falls.

I could just imagine how my grandma Nola would love Becca. She'd want her help in the kitchen. I could picture both of them with aprons on, making my grandmother's famous peach cobbler.

"I'll help too, Bon," I said. "Whatever you need. We'll make it happen."

My cousin looked momentarily stunned and the table went suspiciously quiet. "Thank you, Will. That would be great."

I guess I *had* done my best to avoid family functions. I really was an asshole. Shame and guilt threatened, but I worked to beat them back. I'd do better. I'd stop lumping in my family—who I loved very much—with my work. It was difficult because it was all so intertwined. But there was no reason to see my loved ones as an obligation or a liability.

Dinner wrapped up in the next half hour. Mac and I worked through washing a stack of dishes while Mom and Patty packed away leftovers.

When my hands were dry and I was itching to be a half a mile south, I told everyone good night and made for the front door. It wasn't that late. Maybe I could catch Becca.

"Here you go," my mom said, cutting me off in the hallway and passing me a stack of Tupperware.

"I'm good, Mom. I have plenty of food at the house."

She smiled like I was her most precious idiot. "That's for Becca, sugar. Next time, bring her with you."

I nodded like a dutiful son, not bothering to mention that I'd already resolved to do just that.

Five minutes later, Carl and I stood before the glass front door of the tiny house. His tail was wagging, and if I had a tail, it would probably be doing the same.

After a quiet knock, Becca emerged from the hallway. She was in those avocado pajamas, complete with long loose hair, and my imaginary tail gave a hard thump at the sight.

Her smile was the perfect mix of happy confusion as she made her way to the door.

"Hey, you," she said . . . to my dog as she bent to rub Carl's ears. After a moment, she straightened, and I could see that the confusion was now winning the battle with the surprised joy she'd displayed at our sudden arrival. Becca appeared wary, and I couldn't say I blamed her. I'd very clearly blown her off earlier. I could have replied to her text, assuring her that, yes, we'd talk soon. But I hadn't. I'd left her wondering.

And now I was off-balance, showing up on her doorstep, hoping for her patience and her understanding . . . and her forgiveness. It wasn't easy being vulnerable, but that was the whole point. You couldn't be brave unless you really meant it. And looking at Becca, so damn gorgeous and suddenly distrustful, I realized I'd do just about anything to put us back on solid ground.

"Hey, City Girl. Can I come in?"

nineteen
BECCA

For once, Will Clark wasn't wearing a hat. But if he had been, he would have definitely been holding it. Well, if not for all the Tupperware. He gave new, beautiful bearded life to the term "hat in hand."

He stood in my doorway, looking humbled and apologetic, and I wasn't entirely sure why. I knew things turned weird after I bolted from his house last night to go pick up Laramie. But he'd told me he had plans tonight, and I figured that had been a result of said weirdness.

Yet here he was, asking to come in.

"Hi, Will. Of course you can come in." I opened the door wide, doing my best not to be self-conscious in my avocado pajamas once again.

Carl raced to the bedroom, and Will stepped inside, pulling off his dark jacket and hanging it on the coatrack. His eyes caught on the mess I'd made in front of the fireplace. There was a long-handled lighter, some pages ripped from a magazine, twigs I'd collected from beneath the trees in the yard, and a beverage pitcher full of water . . . just in case.

"Were you looking to start a fire?" he asked, finally meeting my gaze.

"Yeah," I said. "It's pretty cold out tonight. I thought it would be nice to read in here with a fire going."

He smiled and watched me for another moment.

"Fine," I blurted. "I was in the other room on my computer googling how to light a fire in the fireplace."

His smile grew, and he glanced back toward the firewood stacked, forming a neat base as per the web page instructions. "Would you like me to walk you through it? Or I could just watch if you've got it handled."

"I appreciate the vote of confidence, but I don't really want you to watch me try to do something for the first time. I did get the flue open, though."

He nodded and then offered, "Maybe we could work on it together."

I smiled, feeling grateful. "That sounds good. Would you like something to drink? I have that IPA from Trailview that you like."

I was already walking the short distance to the kitchen as I spoke. I nearly jumped when I realized he'd followed me.

Will held the refrigerator door open for me as I reached inside. "Here are some leftovers from Mom. She thought you might like them."

"Oh." I frowned. "Is that why you came over?"

He shook his head. "No, I wanted to see you."

I traded his plastic containers for the bottle of beer and placed them inside the fridge. That was nice of Maggie to think of me. I guess that explained where Will was this evening. A tiny part of me felt envious. And then another part—a little bigger this time—recognized that I was sad that I hadn't been invited in the first place. But that was silly. Will and I were . . . whatever we were or starting to be. That didn't mean I should be included in dinner with his parents or whatever had gone on at Maggie's tonight.

Will eyed the bottle in his hands. "Did you end up liking this one?"

"No. Still not much of a beer drinker."

"So then why . . . " He trailed off, and my blush filled in the blanks.

But I made myself meet his curious gaze. "I got it for you. In case you ever ended up back over here."

Will's gray eyes lingered on my face, soft and something else I didn't have the courage to name. But Carl trotted into the kitchen a moment later, drawing my attention.

I grabbed the dog bowl from below the sink and filled it under the tap. After placing it on the kitchen floor, I said, "I got some C-H-E-E-S-E for him, if that's okay?"

Will ran a large hand over his mouth and beard, but I could tell he was amused. Instead of answering, he reached for me, looping an arm around my waist and drawing me to him. His smiling lips met my own in a brief kiss, quick and sweet, before he pulled back to look at me.

"I'm sorry. That was just too fucking cute." He kissed me again, grinning all the while. "I'm pretty sure Carl would like some cheese. And I'm also nearly positive that he can't spell."

I raised a brow. "I bet I could say W-A-L-K right now, and he'd know exactly what I meant."

Will swooped in and pressed his lips to mine once more. "You're right," he murmured. "Don't do it. Then we won't have a moment of peace."

My hands smoothed over the soft fabric of Will's shirt, and I wondered what he had in mind for tonight and why he didn't want to be interrupted.

After one more soft kiss that lingered over my bottom lip, Will said, "Let's go make that fire."

I gave Carl his cheese snack, then followed Will into the living room. Kneeling beside him, I thought about everything I'd done today and how I wanted to share it all. I considered Laramie's words this morning, about how I needed to be honest and upfront with Will. Make a decision about staying and stick to it. Last night, I'd obviously given him reason to think I wasn't serious about staying in Kirby Falls. I didn't want him to see me that way—a person who doesn't mean what they say and doesn't follow through. Someone unreliable. The exact opposite of Will Clark.

He passed me the loosely balled-up magazine pages. "Let's put those between the logs at the bottom."

Then he put two more logs on top, perpendicular to the two I already had in place. "Now the kindling goes in the middle."

We worked together to pile the small branches I'd scavenged from outside. When I didn't think I could hold it in anymore, I spoke, "I wanted you to know that I talked to a real estate agent today. Your dad recommended Trudy Caswell, and we've been emailing for a bit. We spoke on the phone this morning, and I'm going to look at some places she thinks might be a good fit this week. Some are long-term rentals that she manages." I focused on the kindling and took a slow breath. "If you'd like to come with me, that would be great. But if it's too weird, then—"

"It's not too weird," Will interrupted. He touched my chin and drew my attention away from the fireplace. "If you want me there, then I want to be there. And I'm sorry I was irritated last night after you left. I talked to Larry. She told me what happened. But even so, I shouldn't have acted like a jealous asshole, jumping to conclusions and assuming you weren't serious about staying."

His expression was severe, but he spoke softly.

I tried to match his tone. "I am staying, Will. I'll have to go back to Detroit to pack things up and rent out Mrs. Walters's apartment, and to—to talk to my sister. But this is what I want. And it feels right." Biting my lip briefly, I admitted, "Well, it feels terrifying, but also right."

"You're scared?" Will asked, face pinched with concern.

Moving on to the last step, I took the lighter and lit the paper in the bottom, watching it ignite and burn. "Of course I'm scared. But I'm also brave." It felt easier to confess this truth to the catching fire. "Some part of me thinks, what's the worst that could happen? I've been rejected by the people who were supposed to love me. I endured watching the person I cared most about waste away, claimed by a horrible disease. So what if I move here, and maybe you get tired of me? I'll survive. I'll still have this town, and I'll still have friends. I'll still—"

"No," Will said urgently and then swallowed down the harshness in his voice. "No, that wouldn't happen, Becca. Couldn't happen. You are . . . home to me. The same way this place is home. It may have taken me time to see it, but I feel it in my bones. Have felt it every time I look at you."

Being the center of Will's attention was an intense experience. His gray eyes were focused, fixated on me. It felt like being in the eye of a storm—the one solid place amid swirling turmoil.

His words made me brave, made me strong. Being home for someone else, when I'd never even expected to find it for myself was a feeling I couldn't name, couldn't even place. It seemed too big and too wonderful. I wanted it too much. But I knew Will meant what he said. He was the one I could count on.

As the fire burned in the grate, I thought to myself that it was probably weird to already love someone you'd never even slept with. But the strangeness didn't make it any less true. I did love Will Clark. He was faithful and dependable, and he'd made the concept of belonging a reality for me. Maybe it was early days, but I knew it was right. The same way I knew that Kirby Falls was home, I could feel it in this man.

"That's, maybe, the nicest thing anyone has ever said to me," I admitted.

With aching slowness, Will leaned over and cupped my jaw. His thumb was gentle as he stroked my cheekbone. Then he lowered his head and kissed me. It was a promise—a vow—exchanged between two people on the altar of honesty and truth.

I let him set the pace and guide our movements, but I knew where I wanted us to end up.

Will's other hand wrapped around my waist, urging me onto his lap. I went willingly, eager to be nearer. I felt surrounded and safe within the hard confines of this man. His firm thighs supported me, and his warm chest pressed flush against mine. I wanted to be consumed by his heat.

Sifting my fingers through his dark hair, we kissed for long minutes until Will's calloused hands skimmed beneath the hem of my shirt. Fingertips dragged up and down my spine, and I relished his touch—skin to skin.

But I was eager for more.

Breaking our kiss, I reached down and lifted my shirt over my head. Now, I was topless on the floor, straddling Will's thighs in my avocado pajama shorts.

Will's eyes stayed locked on mine before dropping down to take me in. In any other situation, with any other man, I might have felt a pinch of fear, the uneasy twist of self-consciousness in the pit of my stomach. But with Will, it just felt like one more truth being revealed amid breathless anticipation.

"So beautiful, Becca." His gaze came back to mine as his hands settled warm and heavy on my back, drawing me closer, pressing me tight to his chest. "You are . . . sunshine, starlight—the brightest thing in any room. And I couldn't look away if I tried."

I smiled against his lips, loving his words—so stark and honest—and the feel of his soft shirt against my bare skin.

He kissed me again, deeper and harder this time. And maybe I poured out some of my frustration, too. For all the weeks I'd wanted him. For all the times I'd reminded myself we were friends and nothing more.

Eventually, our movements grew restless. I ground over Will, eager for touch and friction and just . . . more. And Will must have had a thing for my tiny shorts because his hands were busy making a path over my thighs to my backside and then back again. Tugging me near, keeping me close, and urging me on.

My body was too small—too inconsequential—for the savage beat of my heart. I felt it in my fingertips, in the violent thrumming against my ribs, and in the tremor of my voice when I gasped out brokenly, "Will."

He got to his feet and pulled me along with him, but I felt his hesitation as we stood in the living room staring at one another. So I reached for his hand and beckoned him to follow. The bedroom was dark, but I didn't mind. I drew back the covers and then turned to face Will.

With bravery guiding my touch, I reached for him, unsnapping his shirt from the bottom up. He slid his shoes off, and when I got to the top button of his jeans, he helped me out and pulled them the rest of the way off.

It was a relief to glide my hands over his skin. The firm rounded tops of his shoulders, over the scar on the right, down his strong biceps and forearms. I explored his chest, lightly dusted in dark hair and molded from hard work on the farm. My nails scratched over the lean muscles stacked deliciously down his abdomen. Then my curious grip traced the edges of the vee tapering into his boxer briefs.

When he'd spent the night earlier in the week, I'd wanted to touch him. Of course I had. But I'd stopped myself from doing more than cuddling myself against him.

Now, I had the freedom to look, to touch, to taste.

And so I did. I pressed my lips to the center of Will's chest. I brought my hands to his firm back and scraped my nails down either side of his spine.

He groaned out a needful sound that had me hiding a grin against his shoulder. And then Will's fingers hooked in the sides of my shorts and slid them down my thighs—along with my underwear—until I stood before him completely nude and utterly ready for him to be the same.

But when I reached for his waistband in turn, he urged me to lie back on the mattress.

Soft lips pressed open-mouthed kisses from my neck to the tips of my breasts, across my stomach and to the tops of my thighs. I watched Will kneel on the floor and spread my legs wide before bringing his mouth to my center.

White-hot pleasure seeped throughout my body at a languid pace as he urged me higher and higher. His relentless effort and determined touch had me clutching the sheets for dear life. And when he leisurely slid a finger inside me, my body locked tight around him before releasing all that pressure he'd slowly been building. All at once, my breath rushed out, his name among the exhale, and I didn't think I'd ever felt so cherished.

When he slowly kissed his way back up my boneless body, I loved the scrape of his beard—rough and soft at the same time.

Boldness and a recent orgasm had me reaching for him, using my feet and legs to push his boxer briefs all the way off. His erection settled against the very heart of me, hot and hard. But Will wasn't in any sort of hurry.

His big hands were still moving over my body, touching and caressing every part of me, lingering in the sensitive dip behind my knee and feeling the weight of my breasts. His lips ghosted along my shoulder and up to my ear before he memorized the jut of my collarbones, tongue tracing and making me shiver.

I was squirming again, searching for something I couldn't name. I was ready. I wanted to feel this connection. I wanted to erase the space between us and banish the ache of his absence.

"I'm on birth control," I whispered, adding a little nudge with my heels to Will's backside.

When he raised up on his hands to hover over me, I caught the glint from his amused smile. "Are you in a hurry?"

"No." I rolled my hips, feeling his hardness touch along all my sensitive spots.

"I think you are." In answer, he thrust against me, once again grazing a place that had me trembling in response.

"Maybe I am in a hurry," I huffed out. "But not to get it over with. Just to get started."

Slowly, Will lowered his body more fully to mine. I could feel him from my chest to my toes, absorbing his heat and his weight—every delicious inch.

He pressed a quick kiss to my lips before saying, "Honey, I'm just getting started. And it won't be over anytime soon."

But he did move then, angling himself and inching forward and then inside as we both breathed through the overwhelming surge of connection, and finally —*finally*—reaching this moment and this place together.

A million thoughts flooded my head, but I couldn't grasp a single one. I was too focused on the here and now and the way it felt to have my body accept his.

Our movements turned from questing and searching to utter harmony.

Through it all, Will never stopped seeking my touch and touching me in return. The press of his lips to the inside of my wrist. The drag of my thigh along his hip. He held me tighter, but I didn't think I could ever get close enough.

Will was gentle and worshipful. His gaze made me feel cherished. For some reason, I thought he'd be shy, but he wasn't. He watched me, coveted me. Led one moment and then begged with his next breath. He was comfortable, I realized, in a way I'd never seen him—content in the push and pull of our bodies. Confident in his affection and mine.

I'd never felt so surrounded and engulfed—so very cared for.

I cheerfully thought someone would have to collect all the pieces of me afterward because I was sure to break apart when this was all over with. But that shattering to nothingness never came.

When I came apart at the seams, Will was there to gather me up, to hold me close, and stitch me back together.

Later, with the sweat cooling on our skin and a blanket of star-speckled darkness outside the window, I breathed in the faint scent of wood smoke. And I let myself enjoy this moment.

Will pulled the sheet up to cover us and then propped himself up on his elbow. I looked up and met his gaze in the darkness as his fingers traced a path from my elbow down to my wrist and then back again.

"What is it?" I asked, worried that he was having regrets or second thoughts.

"Is it okay if I stay the night?"

I frowned. "Of course, Will. You can stay all the nights as far as I'm concerned."

His smile was small, just a suggestion beneath his beard in the dim light from the hallway and the shadows from the moon. "Just making sure you wanted me here, in your space."

"Is this all some elaborate ploy to get the tiny house back for yourself?"

I felt his chest shake with laughter from where it rested against my arm. "Yeah. This was my evil plan all along. The hardest part was getting Carl to fall in love with you too."

Too.

I thought that might be my new favorite word. The unintentional implication of what Will had said made me giddy. I could feel my smile threatening to overtake my face, but I didn't want to embarrass him or let on that I'd noticed. It didn't feel like the right time for me to blurt out, "I love you too."

I managed to say, "Well, no backsies. Hope you don't mind that I talk in my sleep and use all the hot water."

"I know. I heard you the other night."

"Wait." I gasped. "Do I really talk in my sleep?"

The fingertips gliding down my forearm slipped easily into my hand, lacing our fingers together. "Yeah. You kept saying 'lumbersnack' over and over again."

I growled and laughed at the same time, reaching over to swat at him, but he already had one hand subdued. When Will grabbed the other, he used my momentum and simply rolled me on top of him as he laughed, low and delighted into the skin of my neck.

"That's not funny," I grumbled, contradicting my words with the huge grin still on my face. Will was being playful and silly, and it was hard to resist this version of him. And we were still naked in bed together, so lying on top of him wasn't a hardship.

I breathed in his scent, and asked before I could think better of it, "How do you even smell this good? It's like butter and pancakes and maple syrup and campfire all rolled into one."

"Oh, um. It's my beard oil. You like it?"

I nuzzled against his chin. "Yes. Goodness, I love it. I want to roll around on your face."

"We can do that," he replied straight-faced and squeezed my butt.

Then I realized what I said and groaned, lowering my head to his chest. His laughter rumbled against me again, and I loved the intimacy of it, naked and vulnerable with nowhere to hide. "Let's just add that to the list of embarrassing things we're never going to bring up again."

Will nudged my chin up so he could see me. "Wait. What's on this list?"

"Well, the tree incident, obviously."

He was already shaking his head. "No way. That tree has a lot of history. You getting stuck in it only improves it. Besides, it's where we met. I'm not forgetting it. What else is there?"

His words about the tree were casual, but they still had my heart tripping all over itself. "The, um, marshmallow incident."

Will snorted. "I call that one the failed B and E in my head."

That made me grin.

"It's not going on the list either. That was the first time I spent the night."

"That doesn't count," I argued.

"Fine. It was the first time I saw you in those avocado shorts. Definitely memorable, and I'll never recover."

Warmth and something a lot like love filled my chest. I hoped Will couldn't see the gooey way I was looking at him. "Okay, so the corn maze incident."

He gave my backside another squeeze. "First kiss. No way is that going on the list."

I nodded, relieved. "How about the pageant wave?"

Will was quiet for a moment. Then he said, "I thought it was stately and distinguished."

I groaned again, but I was laughing, and so was he.

As our amusement trailed away, Will said softly, "I think that's when I knew that I wasn't going to be able to keep you in a box labeled *untouchable tourist*."

My stomach swooped at his admission, something quiet and honest that was all the more meaningful for it. "That's when you knew?"

He nodded.

"When I waved at you like a dork?"

Leaning forward, he pressed a slow kiss to my forehead, his lips lingering against my skin. "Something like that."

twenty
WILL

"I want to start a book club," Becca said while the rest of us were chewing.

It was just after one o'clock, and Chloe's shift was over. Jordan had driven up to Grandpappy's on his lunch break to join us. Mom had whipped up some sandwiches, and we were sitting in the sunshine at one of the picnic tables in front of the Bake Shop.

"Oh!" Chloe swallowed and then added, "I'll be in your book club."

"I thought you were already in the brunch ladies' book club," Jordan asked, licking jelly off his thumb.

"Well, I could do both," Becca replied. "Plus, the brunch ladies mostly meet up to gossip. I'd want my book club to actually talk about the book."

"But we could eat and drink wine and gossip a little too, right?" Chloe confirmed.

Becca grinned. "Oh, for sure."

I took a bite of potato salad to give my mouth something to do besides smile. Then I said casually, eyes on Becca, "I'll be in your book club."

Her megawatt grin zeroed in on me. "You will?"

"Sure," I replied and speared another potato. "I'll read the book, but I won't crash your meeting. We can have our own discussion."

Becca's blue eyes narrowed a fraction, but she was still happy. I could tell. "It'll be romance," she warned.

"That's fine. I liked the ogre book and the vampire one after that. Though I do prefer romantic suspense."

"Oh, good." She beamed. "We can start with something by Catherine Cowles. Small-town spice and serial killers. You'll love her."

I nodded and went back to my sandwich. Truthfully, I liked that she wanted to put down roots in town. That she was already planning ahead for something like a book club was a good sign. It wasn't that I didn't think she was committed. She was. In fact, I'd gone with her to look at several rental properties this week. I'd left work a few times to accompany her to appointments with Trudy Caswell, as the middle-aged real estate agent had some good spaces in mind. Surprisingly, nothing fell apart while I was away from the farm. And it felt good to be involved in the process of Becca moving to Kirby Falls.

I wanted to be supportive. This was a big change for her. And while I knew she wasn't making it just for me, I still wanted her to be happy with the decision. I also felt the urge to tell her she could just move into my house. But I figured she'd probably rather stand on her own two feet for a while. So, for now, I would follow her lead. I'd visit rentals with her and give my opinion when it was requested.

And then I'd trust Becca to do what was right for her.

If that involved packing up all her stuff in Detroit and bringing it back to the homestead with me and Carl, that would be fine too. Better than fine.

It had been good this week, sharing the tiny house with her. Really good. I'd spent every night in her bed, touching and being touched. Reveling in her sweetness and exploring all the ways I could make her light up. Then we'd wake up and have coffee together. I didn't mind squeezing into the shower with her because it meant our hands and lips stayed close and busy.

I'd invited Becca to work in my office again this morning since the temperature had dropped overnight. Before I'd left her to go pitch in over at the pumpkin patch, I'd gotten her off with my fingers. Then she'd dropped to her knees behind the desk and made me wish I didn't have someplace to be.

When I finally glanced up from reliving that particularly pleasant memory from three hours ago, I noticed Jordan and Chloe staring at me in disbelief. Becca was still grinning, so I probably hadn't mentioned the blow job out loud. A piece of bread actually fell out of Jordan's mouth from where it had dropped open.

Oh, right. The book club thing.

"What?" I scowled. "Are you so penned in by toxic masculinity that you can't imagine a man reading a romance novel? Come on, Jordan. Do better."

He recovered enough to look offended. "I will have you know that I am an Emily Henry stan. It's not that I can't imagine *a man* reading a romance novel. It's that I can't, for the life of me, imagine *you* reading one. Non-fiction. Sure. A memoir. Definitely. John Grisham. No doubt."

I pointed my fork in his direction. "Well, maybe you don't know everything about me, Jordan Anthony Rockford."

Picking up her sandwich, Becca interrupted. "Jordan, you can join too. Everyone is welcome. I already asked Larry and Mac, and they're in. Bonnie too. She invited someone named Candace. And I'm going to ask Magdaline down at Apollo's the next time we go for pizza. It'll be fun." She paused to take a bite, and her eyes went wide. "Holy cannoli. What's in this? It's amazing."

Chloe replied, listing the ingredients on her fingers, "Sliced chicken breast, herbed goat cheese, hot pepper jelly, and butter lettuce on homemade focaccia."

"Well"—Becca smiled—"it's my new favorite thing."

Chloe chuckled. "You love everything, Becca."

Her blue eyes flickered to mine briefly before she shrugged. "I guess I kinda do."

My chest warmed. We were hovering on the precipice of something—Becca and me. I knew how I felt. This was never going to be some short-term fling for me. That had been the problem from the beginning. But now that she was staying, all my wants and complicated feelings had permission to spread out and take up as much space as they wanted. My heart felt full of Becca Kernsy.

Clearing my throat, I told Becca, "We have conditioning tonight with the baseball team if you want to come watch. Carl can keep you company."

"I'm going to look at the house just down the road at six thirty, but I'll come by the high school after that. Trudy said she thinks it has too much land for me to manage, but I told her I still wanted to see it."

I smiled. "Sounds good."

The four-mile run and the rest of the practice went well. The night air was cool and felt good on my heated skin. Jordan's brother, Seth, had gradually seen more and more interest for these impromptu conditioning meetups in the last six weeks. I hadn't made it out to every single one, but I'd been pretty consistent this month, and there were at least twenty kids here tonight.

I checked my watch. At 6:55 p.m., the sun was inching toward the horizon. If we were going to keep these up through November, we'd have to start meeting earlier.

The tail end of practice usually devolved into me giving pointers to any of the pitchers present, and there were a few new faces in the bunch tonight. But they all listened when I spoke and asked questions that showed they were paying attention.

I even took a few throws off the mound to demonstrate a particular point I was trying to make. The familiar tightness in my shoulder welcomed me when I tried to overextend my current range of motion. I rolled my shoulders back a few times and stepped away, motioning for Mason Gentry to come up and pitch a few.

I'd noticed his dad in the stands again and given him a nod when we'd made eye contact. He hadn't brought up the coaching thing again, but I couldn't say I hadn't thought about it. I'd even gone so far as to look up the course requirements for coaches in North Carolina. None of it sounded horrible or unmanageable. My hesitancy at this point was how the high school baseball season might impact my time requirements at the farm.

It seemed I was less worried about how it looked for a washed-up has-been to swallow his pride and coach kids from his own high school. Sure, there would probably be a smart-ass freshman down the line who thought it would be fun to run his mouth and bring up my past. And I was pretty positive the parents would talk and whisper in the stands. But so far, I hadn't heard a word. None of the boys who came out here looking for extra practice and guidance had even asked me about my time playing in college or the minors or the majors. I guessed they were too focused on themselves to be worried about me.

It was humbling to consider. Maybe I shouldn't be so damn concerned about myself either.

Seated a few rows down from Principal Gentry was Becca. She'd arrived a few minutes ago, and Carl had trotted over to join her. She'd given me a sweet wave and sat down very casually in the stands. But I noticed she was wearing a gray Kirby Falls Parks and Rec hoodie I'd left at the tiny house the other night. It swallowed her, hiding her beautiful body, but I liked how my clothes looked on her. And I liked that she was comfortable enough to swipe it and wear it in front of me.

A moment later, she stood and wandered away from the stands. She had her phone out, and I wondered if her sister was bothering her again. I knew she hadn't yet told Heather she was leaving Detroit. But she still texted and called with regularity—demanding money, eager to know when Becca would be back in town. I thought it was the simple fact that for the first time in her life, Becca had told her sister no. Despite her denied requests, Heather was persistent. I wished Becca would block her number or refuse to answer. Heather only added to Becca's stress, and I sure as hell didn't like seeing her hurt.

I was distracted and watching Carl trot after her when I heard some of the new boys horsing around, laughing.

"What is she doing?" one kid said.

"Oh my God. What a freak," another added.

"She's hot, but clearly a weirdo," came the last assessment.

I glanced around and followed their gaze to where Becca was next to the chain-link fence surrounding the field. She had her phone in hand, lining it up for a shot of the sunset. The colors were dramatic, reflecting off the low clouds as the sun threatened to shrink behind the mountains.

The mocking and laughter continued until I barked out a sharp, "Hey!"

They all turned to look at me, wide-eyed and expectant. Not just the teenage boneheads but all the baseball players in the infield. Even a few parents glanced my way from the bleachers.

But I directed my attention to the four comedians who thought it was acceptable to mock someone behind their back. "What did you just say about her?"

One kid—an outfielder on the JV squad, I thought—raised his hands in surrender. "I didn't say anything."

In my periphery, I saw Seth and Jordan walk up to where I stood, just off the pitcher's mound.

I narrowed my eyes, and one of the other four players blurted out, "I'm sorry, Mr. Clark. We didn't know she was your girl."

My gaze focused on him—tall and skinny with big floppy hair—and I said, "Well, she is. And she's the best fucking person I know. And if I ever hear you badmouth a woman, *any woman*, you'll think you joined the cross-country team by mistake. Now go run the perimeter of the field until I tell you to stop."

The boys looked stunned. No one moved, and the only sounds were the leaves on the trees beyond the fence, vibrating in the breeze.

The first kid was brave enough to argue. "But you—you're not our coach."

I gave it a moment's thought, enough that it settled something restless beneath my skin, before I replied, "Yeah, well. I will be next year. So pissing me off now is a mistake. Go. Run."

Two of the four took off immediately for the first base line, ready to hustle around the edge of the field. One of the two boys remaining sighed and hit the first kid in the stomach, "Just come on, Nate, before you make it worse."

After my glare followed them for a moment, I felt a grinning Seth slap me on the back. "Try to only use your powers for good, though, Uncle Will."

I tossed him the baseball I still held in my hand. "Get out of here before I make you run too."

He laughed and hitched his bag higher on his shoulder before heading toward the parking lot with the majority of the boys.

Crossing my arms, I watched the four troublemakers jog through the outfield before Jordan stepped directly into my view. His smile was enormous, engulfing his entire face. Brown eyes sparkled, and I thought he might chip a tooth.

"Not a word," I said, shaking my head.

My friend just laughed. "You have to let me have an *I told you so* moment. Because I did. I. Told. You. So. You stubborn, pig-headed pain in the ass."

"There, you said your piece. Let's just let it go." I peeked at the runners who were closing in on the infield. "Pick up the pace, gentlemen," I shouted, and they scurried to do my bidding.

"This is going to be so fun," Jordan said.

"Yeah, I think it is," I agreed. And I might have even believed it.

Jordan headed out and most of the stands emptied.

Following another two laps, my bloodlust was satisfied. They were only idiot teenagers, after all. They didn't know what it was like to look at another person and see anything beyond the surface. They didn't know that weird was maybe the best thing a person could be. Because when you were sixteen years old, all you wanted was to fit in and be exactly like everyone else. Standing out from the crowd in high school was something those boys didn't have the courage to take on. But we'd work on that.

After I released my winded and shame-faced charges, I gathered up my bag and water bottle from the dugout and made my way to where Becca waited with Carl. She was seated on the first row, looking down at her phone. Hopefully, she was oblivious to everything that had gone down in the last fifteen minutes.

"Hey, you," she said when she caught sight of me walking toward her.

"Hi, City Girl."

Grinning, she stood, and I walked right up to her, throwing an arm around her shoulder and hugging her tight.

She sighed against me, her body sagging forward into my touch. I thought that might be the best sort of welcome—someone else dropping their walls and relaxing their shoulders, just for you.

Becca mumbled against my chest, "Why did four sweaty teenagers come up to me and stutter out apologies?"

It was my turn to sigh. "Let's call it growth and forget it ever happened."

I felt her snuggle closer, her hand sneaking under my workout shirt and up my back, seeking my warmth.

Fighting a smile against her hair, I admitted, "You look good in my sweatshirt."

Becca tilted her chin up to look at me, equal parts shy and mischievous. "You don't mind?"

"As long as I get to take it off you later, it's yours."

Her smile widened and she bit her lip to contain it, even white teeth digging into soft pink skin.

"You ready?" I asked, resisting the urge to kiss that bottom lip.

Becca nodded. "You?"

I cast one more glance around us. The stadium lights had kicked on earlier, illuminating the field—green grass, red dirt, and a huge part of my life.

We were the only ones left, not even the distant sounds of car doors shutting in the parking lot beyond interrupted the stillness in the air. Insects chirped and clicked, making their night noises. And I thought, alone with Becca in a baseball stadium might be the most peaceful I'd felt in a long time.

Finally, I released her from my hold. But before she could get too far away, I threaded my fingers through hers. "I'm ready. Let's go home."

When we reached the tiny house, I set Carl up with some dinner and then asked Becca if she wanted to join me in the shower.

"Sure. I'll wash your back." She'd grinned and went to grab some towels out of the linen closet in the hallway.

I stripped off my sweaty workout clothes and turned on the water. Becca was back before the steam could fill the small bathroom. She was naked with her blond hair piled in a bun on top of her head.

Grabbing her, I pulled her with me under the spray, careful to keep from getting her face and her hair wet.

"How was the house?" I asked, referring to the rental she'd visited with Trudy during practice. It was easy to get distracted when her smooth, wet skin was within touching distance, but I made the effort, eager to hear about her afternoon.

"Trudy was right. The yard was more of a two-acre field, with a little creek and everything. I don't think I could manage that much land."

Grabbing the shampoo, I quickly washed my hair. "But you liked the house?"

"It was cute. More of a fixer-upper than I'm looking for, though."

Closing my eyes, I leaned back and rinsed the soap from my hair. With my arms raised and scrubbing my scalp, I could feel the stiffness in my right shoulder from the pitches I'd thrown today. I'd probably overdone it. I might get up early and go through some stretches in the morning.

"You know you can stay here as long as you like," I said once my head was out of the water.

Becca appeared uncertain. "Your mom is too nice. She won't let me pay rent, and I feel like I'm taking advantage."

I reached for the soap and started soaping up my body. "You're not taking advantage. She wants you here. And she's not going to rent it out to strangers anyhow." She didn't look any more convinced. "All I'm saying is, if you don't find a house or a rental you're happy with before moving, you could always put your things in storage and stay here at the tiny house longer."

And because I was a coward, I turned my body into the spray to rinse off, with my back to Becca, and added, "Or you could always stay with me and Carl up on the mountain. You'd be welcome."

Becca didn't speak, and I realized I was holding my breath. Finally, I felt slender arms wrap around my waist, and soft breasts pressed against the wet skin of my back.

"You wouldn't mind having me in your space?" she asked, and I fought to stay focused. She felt so good.

"I've been in your space all week, and you didn't seem to mind."

Her nails scraped along my abdomen, and I jolted at the touch. "You're a pretty good roommate," she offered, and I felt the sudden drag of her tongue up my spine. "You start the coffee, and you do the dishes. I'm not sure what I could contribute if I found myself at your house."

My lips tugged up in a grin as I turned in her arms. "Well, you're pretty handy in the shower."

She smiled. "I am, aren't I?"

Leaning down, I pressed a kiss to her lips. She welcomed me, humming sweetly in appreciation.

We kissed until our bodies grew restless. I cupped her breasts, running my thumbs across her sensitive nipples—petal pink and just as soft. Before I could lean down to suck one of her stiff peaks into my mouth, Becca's hands found their way to my ass, and she pulled me close. All of our slick, wet skin, heated from the water, suddenly touched from chest to knees.

I groaned into her mouth at the feel of her, so near and warm. With little forethought beyond *more* and *yes*, I bent and gripped her thighs, lifting and pressing her into the cool tiles of the shower wall. Becca gasped and then locked her legs tight around me. My dick was trapped between us, nestled between the folds of her pussy. Despite the water cascading over my back, Becca felt hotter surrounding me.

When our kisses resumed, they were sloppier, needier. I had Becca braced against the shower wall, and she ground herself up and down my erection, driving my need higher.

Another gasp and I knew she was getting close. Her head tilted back as she inhaled a shaky breath. So I took advantage and dragged my lips along her jaw and sucked at her throat.

"Will," she panted. "I want to feel you."

Her arms gripped me around my shoulders, and when I didn't stop licking the water droplets off her collarbone, she slid her fingers through my wet hair and pulled. It wasn't enough to hurt, but it got my attention.

Becca's blue eyes were bright, cheeks flushed, and her already full lips were plump and gorgeous from our kisses. "Please."

Desire pitched low in my belly at the plea. With my eyes on hers, I reached down and positioned myself at her entrance. And then I gave her what she wanted.

Her eyes closed as I pushed inside, and so did mine. I released a rough breath at the feel of her. The utter relief and connection at having her like this. Knowing that this wasn't temporary. That she was mine.

My forehead rested against hers as I started to thrust, deep and slow. She was so tight and hot, and despite the midmorning blow job, I knew this wasn't going to last long. Water dripped from my hair and onto my face. It slid into my mouth as I groaned out rough exhalations. *You feel so good* and *stay, stay just like this* and *Becca, fuck, you're perfect*.

I could feel her tightening around me. Her frantic breaths puffing against my lips.

Repositioning my hands, I squeezed the globes of her ass, and she moaned out brokenly that she was coming.

Thank fuck because I was getting ready to lose it. I pumped into her faster, feeling her spasming muscles clenching over and over. The pleasure that had been gathering, steady and sure, finally released. The tendrils of my orgasm unraveled as I locked my hips against Becca, going as deep as I could go and pulsing into her.

Moments passed, and all I could hear was the thundering of my heart in time with the beating of the water all around us. Becca's fingers sifted through my hair as she placed kisses all over my face.

When I could manage it, I straightened from the wall, lowering her body gently to the shower floor. I held her waist and made sure she was steady before bringing her back under the spray and cleaning her off.

Becca's hands and lips moved over me where we brushed. I liked her sweet affection. Over the years, I'd gotten used to a lack of it. It had been my own doing. Sometimes I felt like an old dog that didn't know how to trust anymore— the way Carl had been when I'd adopted him. Becca had never seemed afraid, just persistent and kind, no matter my mood. I wanted to feel her hands tracing down my arms and smoothing over my back. I liked having her lips graze the skin of my chest and neck.

Sometimes affection didn't have to lead to something else, and I'd forgotten that. It could just be a way to let someone know you were on their mind. That touching you made *them* feel better. And so I was generous with my glances. I let my hands linger when I tucked a wayward wet strand behind her ear. My thumb tracing the elegant line of her neck.

Eventually, we dried off. I slid into some boxer briefs and didn't bother with anything more. Becca put on some underwear—yellow daisy print—and grabbed the navy tee shirt I'd slept in last night.

"Do you want a fire?" I asked, eyeing her in my shirt and fighting the urge to strip it off her because she looked too fucking good wearing my clothes.

She shook her head. "No, I want to do something else."

I raised an eyebrow but stayed quiet as she took me by the hand and had me lie down on the bed.

Becca took a bracing breath, and I had no idea where this was going. "So, um, I looked up a few massage techniques for shoulder injuries and wanted to try them out. I noticed your shoulder is pretty stiff in the mornings when you wake up, and I could tell it was bothering you after practice tonight. I could try a few, and if you hate it, I'll stop, or if it hurts, or I've overstepped or—"

"Becca," I said, eager to halt her worried rambling. I grabbed her hand and ran my thumb over her knuckles. "I'm never gonna say no to you putting your hands all over me."

She managed to meet my eyes and smiled, small and shy and breathtaking. It struck me that we could do what we'd just done in the shower, but she'd actually been nervous about bringing up my injury. And here she'd gone to the trouble to look up massage techniques to help me.

My throat felt tighter than my shoulder at the moment.

"Thank you," I said hoarsely.

"Well, don't thank me yet. Let's just see how this goes. Scoot toward the middle and lie on your left side."

I did as I was told, and she inched closer, kneeling, her bare legs beneath my tee shirt resting against the middle of my back.

"This is just lotion," she warned as she squeezed some in her hands and rubbed them together. "It's honeysuckle. I hope that's okay."

I swallowed thickly. So that was where her sweet scent came from. I didn't want to tell her just how okay that was. I could breathe her in all night. "Sure."

Her touch was tentative at first. She explained what she was doing—soft tissue massage—and where her hands would be touching me. But after a few minutes, she grew quiet and focused, her hands surer, her grip firm.

I could feel my arm loosening as her thumb followed the path of the tendons long since healed in my arm. Well, as healed as they were capable of getting. The slow, steady pressure behind my shoulder blade was a good sort of hurt. Becca pressed and held and then gently released. And I sighed out a long breath through my nose.

My mind worked as I closed my eyes, and Becca kept up her patient movements. She and I had never really had a conversation about my life *before*. Sure, I talked about my teammates in high school and college. She knew that baseball had been a big part of my life. But I'd never brought up my injury and how everything had fallen apart—the sharp decline after trying to piece myself back together for nearly a year.

I was sure Becca knew the basics because my town was nosy and my family vocal. Neighbors felt entitled to my business because I was Kirby Falls, born and raised. They wanted to be a part of my journey and my success—or lack thereof. But there was no way for my family and friends and small-town acquaintances to know how crushing the loss of my baseball career had been. Hell, I hadn't even known when it was happening to me. I'd thought I was young and strong. I'd assumed my recovery would be successful because I'd handled it like everything else—by working my ass off through single-minded determination. I remembered the day of my surgery, thinking I'd be back on the field before I knew it.

Only, it hadn't gone like that.

The surgeon had warned me that with my kind of tendon tears—moderate, full thickness—the odds of rotator cuff surgery failure were nearly forty percent. And the possibility of a re-tear after reconstruction, especially in my chosen field, were somewhere in the neighborhood of likely. The long road to recovery had been frustrating. I'd had a team of professionals dedicated to seeing me back on the pitching mound. I'd taken every suggestion. I'd kept my arm in a sling and my shoulder stationary for six weeks post-op in order to give the tendons a chance to heal and reattach. I'd slept uncomfortably in a recliner instead of my bed for months to make sure I didn't roll over in my sleep and reinjure myself. I'd gone to every appointment, met with every physical therapist, and still was not prepared for the six months of recovery time required for an injury like mine.

I watched my team get to the playoffs without me. I endured pitying glances and well-wishes over time, and then eventually, nothing at all as career trajectories changed, and I'd been excluded from that world.

Not once did I beg to be released to play sooner. Knowing what was at stake, I hadn't rushed my progress or my healing. Instead, I'd gritted my teeth, and I'd done what was asked of me, thinking all the while that there was a day when I'd be back to normal.

Only that day never came.

"Do you, uh, know what happened?" I asked stiffly while Becca worked, figuring she deserved some answers.

Her hands paused briefly at my question, but she quickly regained her composure. "Just what I've been told around town. I didn't go look up your Wikipedia page, if that's what you're asking."

"Jesus," I muttered, opening my eyes and sliding her an embarrassed glance.

She winked. After a moment, her voice came quietly, gently—like she was talking to a wounded animal, and maybe to a lot of people, that was what I was. "You don't have to talk about it, if you don't want to, Will. You don't owe me anything because we're—we're together or because I'm trying to take away your pain."

There was no way Becca knew how much that meant to me. The fact that she cared enough to do this, to care for me in such a way . . . it made me want to fall to my knees and wrap my arms around her waist, press my face into her middle. But there was also what she'd said. She'd never once put pressure on me to talk to her about my life before.

Part of me wanted to tell her, though. Maybe because she'd never needed to ask.

"I got hurt when I was twenty. It was spring, and I'd gotten called up from the minors to pitch early in the season. The team had had some injuries and gave me a shot. Anyway, I didn't hear a pop or anything, like what happens to some people. The doc said it was likely wear and tear—a lifetime of baseball, thousands of pitches thrown." I swallowed heavily. There was no way to minimize what baseball had been to me, condensing it down to an injury made me sick to my stomach.

"But once I started having pain," I continued, "I didn't stop or see a doctor. I thought it would work itself out. I kept practicing and pitched another game in the majors. My whole family was there. Jordan, too. The loudest one. I could hear them all from the stands, screaming my name. So fucking proud. I didn't know how I'd manage to throw a single pitch feeling as emotional and grateful as I did during that ball game." Another rough swallow of remembered pain. "But I did. And afterward, the soreness was worse. The team doctor noticed and wanted to take a look. Then I was referred to a surgeon after testing and scans. It all snowballed from there. The long and short of it is: the surgery and the recovery couldn't get me back to where I'd been. And when playing at that level was no longer an option, the team let me go. I went back to UNC and finished up my degree. Graduated and then I came home."

I didn't tell her about the things that didn't matter—the things I couldn't change or get over, no matter how much I tried. How after my surgery and recovery, the stiffness in my arm persisted. My range of motion was limited. And when I finally started pitching again, I'd lost the power behind my throws. My control suffered too, and I was in a lot of pain from trying so hard to be normal again.

Even with a patient coaching staff and a determined physical therapist, the odds were good that I'd never be at the same level I'd been before my surgery. A second surgery wasn't an option. And when the team released me from my contract . . . that was when I let all those bitter feelings overwhelm me. The *why me?* bullshit. The unfairness of it all. The crushing despair that came with losing your identity, the only thing you'd ever wanted—what you'd sacrificed your whole life to achieve.

I'd been depressed and bitter for a long time. Part of me thought I'd only gone back to college to avoid the inevitable return to Kirby Falls.

"I'm sorry that happened to you, Will," Becca finally said into the quiet of the bedroom.

For the first time, someone saying those words to me didn't feel like pity. It sounded like heartbreak. Becca hurt *for* me. She only cared because she cared about me. I wasn't letting her down by leaving baseball. She hadn't been invested in my career since I was a kid. She'd never watched me on television or sat in the stands in any stadium to see me pitch. She was separate from it all, but she still cared.

Because it was me.

"I can't imagine how hard it must have been to go through all that." Her hands kept up their soothing strokes, over and over. "And I know I'm only getting to know you now, following that part of your life. But I can still see parts of it shining through. Like your determination and your teamwork on the farm. Your dedication to your family. And your leadership and guidance on the field with those kids. I know it probably feels like a part of you died when you had to give up your dream, but our pasts stay with us. Who we *were* informs who we are now, and none of it ever really goes away—no matter how much you might want it to."

I considered the truth of Becca's words and marveled over how she saw things so clearly when I'd been struggling with clouded vision for a decade. And then I thought of how her own history might affect the Becca before me now. The kindness and goodness she'd learned at the hands of a stand-in parent. The way she showed everyone around her that she cared after dealing with a lifetime of neglect.

Reaching back, I placed my left hand atop hers and squeezed.

Over the next forty minutes, she worked quietly, moving and positioning my right arm. She had me lie on my side, my back, and then my chest as she stretched, pushed, pulled, and rotated. But through it all, with every pass of her soft fingers, I felt her care, her concern, her love.

Finally, when her hands smoothed away and she shifted to sit beside me on the bed, Becca asked, "So, how do you feel? Was it okay?"

In truth, I felt a little sore, and I probably would be in the morning too. But my joint felt loose and warm—the stiffness lessened drastically.

I opened my eyes and met her worried expression. Smiling gently, I admitted, "It's the best I've felt in a long time."

Her relief was palpable. She took a huge breath and blew it out before grinning at me. "We can do that whenever you want. Whenever you feel like it might help. I'll get even better with practice, I'm sure of it."

My throat went suspiciously tight again, and I didn't think I could manage to speak around the emotion constricting my airway. The thought of her so eager to help and care for me, researching my injury, watching instructional videos on her laptop in secret, giving me her time and energy and heart—it was all overwhelming in the best possible way.

I reached for her and urged her down beside me. Wrapping her in my arms, I held her close. When I could manage to get the words out, I said, "Thank you for taking care of me," my lips brushing the soft, delicate hair at her temple.

She just squeezed me tighter.

What Becca had done over the past hour hadn't been anything that I hadn't already gone through with numerous physical therapists many years ago, but this —with Becca—felt different. Her touch soothed and roused in equal measure.

Her goal here wasn't to get me back to my pre-operative performance. This was more than improving my range of motion and making me a successful athlete. Her touch had nothing to do with the team or management or expectations, and everything to do with me. Not even me, the baseball player. Just me . . . Will Clark. Farmer. Grumpy hermit. And someone who'd take care of her for as long as she'd let me.

Her thoughtfulness was on full display, bright and bold and eager. But that was just Becca—kind and selfless, attentive and generous. She was more than I deserved.

And she'd be the woman who'd held my heart in her hands for the rest of my life.

BECCA

It was Sunday, and with the bakery closing at noon, Maggie had invited us to lunch in her home.

Will's father had taken a break from the fields and would be joining us as well.

Even Will had managed to take the whole day off. He'd still been up with the sun, but I'd slept in while he and Carl had gone for an early morning run.

It was silly, but I was a little nervous about lunch today with Will's family. I saw Maggie and William most days while I worked at Grandpappy's, but this felt a little more official. More like Will was bringing home his girlfriend to meet the family.

I knew Will's parents liked me. Maggie and I talked all the time, and Will's dad had even let me drive the tractor. But I still felt nerves in my belly on the short drive to their home.

As the house came into view, I nearly pressed my face to the glass. A huge front porch appeared to wrap around the sides of the house. Hanging baskets of asparagus ferns were placed equidistant between each white porch column. I counted four ceiling fans along the front and a huge window that looked out over the yard.

The house extended up to two floors beneath a dark shingled roof. The white paint on the wood siding looked fresh with hunter-green shutters on every window, and the front door was painted rust red.

"You're awfully quiet," Will said as he opened the passenger side door of his truck for me. I hadn't even realized we'd stopped.

Carl raced on ahead.

Taking Will's offered hand, I slid down from the cab. "Afraid I'll claim your title?" I teased.

He smiled, keeping my hand in his as we made for the steps to the front porch. "You know it'll be fine."

I glanced at his face before looking down toward the bouquet I held, my thumb absently fidgeting with the elastic band holding it all together. I might have overdone it a little. The arrangement was large and held peach dahlias amid white carnations, greenery, and a sprinkling of baby's breath. Margaret Mahroney over at Snap, Bam, Bloom had fixed me up with the bouquet and had even given me the insider tip on Maggie's favorite flowers.

"I know," I replied quietly. It might not be a first impression, but I still wanted it to be a good one.

Then the door swung open, and Maggie and William spilled out onto the wide front porch.

"Well, hello, sweet pea!" Maggie enveloped me in a warm embrace. I hugged her back and smiled at William over her shoulder.

Will's dad was tall and dark-haired like his son, but William was clean-shaven, whereas Will was bearded. He wore a snap-front western-style shirt in red-and-gray plaid and pale blue denim Wranglers that looked soft and worn from age. He was a quiet man, and I could easily see where Will got his mannerisms from.

"Let the girl breathe, Maggie," William said.

Will's mother straightened and cupped my cheeks. "I'm just so happy you're here."

"Me too," I replied, and then I had to clear my throat. "These are for you," I offered, holding out the bouquet.

Maggie took it, grinning. "Aren't you the sweetest thing? Dahlias are my favorite. I'll get these in water."

"Come on in, you two," William said.

And then we all went into the house. I slowed on the way to the kitchen, peering into what looked like a pristine formal living room before passing into a hallway filled with framed photographs.

Will eventually had to nudge me along. "You can look at my embarrassing Olan Mills glamour shots later."

I grinned over my shoulder. "Spoilsport."

"Becca honey, come help me chop!"

Maggie's request got me moving.

We entered a large, beautiful kitchen that could have been featured in any Southern home magazine. It was painted pale yellow with glass-front white cabinets. A huge island dominated the center of the space and three rectangular skylights let in plenty of sunlight overhead.

There were sliding glass doors that led out to a wide back deck that looked out toward the tree line and the looming mountain in the distance. William was out there with a bottle of beer in hand.

The mid-October day was mild and sunny and it looked like Maggie had us set up on a glass-topped dining table out there for lunch.

She passed Will a stack of floral plates and pale linen napkins. "Grab a beer and go help your father set the table. We'll be out in a few."

Will grabbed a bottle from the fridge, and with his haul secure in his arms, he leaned over and pressed a kiss to my temple. "Don't let her work you too hard." And then he stepped out through the open doorway onto the wooden decking.

I smiled gratefully, thrilled to be asked to help, and also a little surprised—but pleased—by Will's public display of affection. Not that I thought he'd hide our relationship in front of his parents. But I didn't think he'd be quite so open about it.

Maggie got me set up with a cutting board and some washed broccoli and cauliflower. "Just separate the florets, make 'em bite-sized, and throw them in this bowl with the cheese, bacon, sunflower seeds, and dried cranberries. I have the dressing ready to go and then you can toss it all together."

"You got it." I nodded.

Maggie and I chatted, mostly about the farm and upcoming town events like the Autumn Market and trick-or-treating downtown at the end of the month.

Having a task helped settle my nerves. I liked being included. Maggie was always warm and affectionate, but it was different, being here in her home. With a knife in my hand and a job to complete, I felt like I belonged—not like a guest for lunch.

I finished mixing the broccoli-and-cauliflower salad, and, together, we all worked to set the table with the food that had been prepared. There were pulled pork sliders with homemade spicy dill pickles and oven-baked potato wedges with Maggie's famous curry ketchup.

I poured sweet tea for Maggie and myself, and then the four of us settled at the table beneath the pergola to enjoy the meal and the fine weather. Somehow, the warm weight of Carl's paw across my foot made me feel more at ease.

"I'll say grace." Maggie held out her hands on either side, and I watched as her husband slid his fingers through hers. Will collected my right hand, and I straightened and placed my left into Maggie's waiting grasp. I watched as everyone closed their eyes and bowed their heads, and I did the same, remembering how I'd envisioned this very scenario among Will's family.

Maggie's voice was gentle as she spoke, thanking the Lord for the many blessings in her life. She touched on the meal and the beautiful weather, the bountiful harvest of the farm, and the health and safety of her family. And then she gave my hand a gentle squeeze. "And we are so grateful to you for the company we are fortunate to keep. Thank you for bringing Becca into our lives and allowing us to get to know her and share in her joy."

Maggie closed out the prayer while I struggled through a flood of emotions and worked to make sure my eyes would be dry whenever I opened them.

My family had never been religious, and I couldn't remember a single time either of my parents had said grace over a meal. But even if they had, I couldn't imagine an instance where they'd thank any deity for my presence in their lives. The realization was stark but no longer debilitating. It was more the contrast between a family who'd only known me a few months versus the one I'd been born into.

Maggie released my hand, and I heard the clink of cutlery and shifting bodies, but I kept my watery eyes closed a moment longer. I said my own little prayer thanking whoever was listening for the welcome I'd received by the Clarks and the rest of Kirby Falls. And then I asked for courage as I uprooted my life in the coming months.

Opening my eyes, I found my plate already full and Will's tender gaze trained on my face. Maggie and William were in quiet conversation, passing platters and bowls back and forth and clearly giving me a moment to collect myself.

Will's hand, which hadn't relinquished its hold, squeezed as he said softly, "Okay?"

I nodded quickly, offering a reassuring smile.

Then I turned back to the table. "This all looks so wonderful, Maggie. Thank you. Thank you both for having me."

William gave me a warm look, gray eyes full of affection.

"Anytime, Becca honey." Maggie reached over and squeezed my hand before passing me another slider. "Here, we don't want you to blow away when this breeze gets going."

I laughed.

Lunch conversation flowed easily. Sometimes we all joined in, like when Maggie and William were eager to hear about the properties Will and I had been touring during my house hunt. And sometimes William and Will broke off to discuss farm things while Maggie and I had our own little conversation.

The afternoon felt like a dream—one I'd envisioned and longed for my whole life. I knew Will's family wasn't perfect, but to someone like me, it sure felt that way.

Will and his father gathered up all the plates and cutlery and worked on getting them in the dishwasher while Maggie led me back to the hallway.

"I knew you'd want more time with these," she said, indicating the family photos lining the wall.

My eyes traced over the pictures of Will as a baby and then a toddler before noticing several images of him with his cousins as a child. There was little Mac and Larry and Bonnie on bicycles and rollerblades, with sunburned cheeks and big smiles.

The photographs continued displaying the Clarks and their history as I scanned more and more frames. I loved them all but my curious gaze sought out the ones of Will. And he was there, in baseball uniform after baseball uniform. His hair was always on the longish side, peeking out from beneath whatever ball cap he happened to have on. There was one of him and Jordan from high school prom over a decade ago that had me leaning closer to see Will's unsmiling face and Jordan's happy one. Maggie said it was from their eleventh grade year. I grinned at the baggy tuxedo rentals and Jordan's arm slung across his friend's shoulder, boutonnieres pinned unevenly on their lapels.

Maggie led me to the living room as I spied even more family photos. I heard the floor creak behind me as someone approached, but I didn't look away.

My eyes zeroed in on a picture of Will. Carefully, I picked up the frame and scanned the image. He was standing in the woods in front of a bush with small yellow flowers. There was a baseball mitt on his left hand and he had knobby knees sticking out beneath red shorts.

"Will was eight," Maggie offered. "That's the honeysuckle bush over behind Patty and Robert's house. Will would sneak off from playing with Mac and Bonnie when it bloomed in June and July. He used to sit back there and pull the blooms off and eat every drop of nectar he could get his hands on."

My finger traced his little-boy grin.

Then I thought about my honeysuckle lotion and the way Will always held me close and breathed me in.

With a sly glance over my shoulder, I found the grown-up version of the boy in the photo standing behind me, looking a little pink in the cheeks. "Fan of honeysuckle, are you?"

Will ran a hand across his beard before smiling gently. "Aunt Patty used to have to come and fetch me when Mac whined that I wouldn't play with her. Practically had to drag me away."

I laughed quietly.

Maggie excused herself with a squeeze to my arm and a kiss on my cheek.

And then it was just me and Will facing one another. "Thank you for bringing me here."

"You're welcome." He stepped closer and gripped my waist. "I'll bring you back in a few weeks. She makes popcorn balls and apple cider and invites everyone over just before Halloween. Bonnie and Danny will be here and Mac and Larry. My uncles and aunt. You'll love it."

I nodded, not sure if I could manage to speak through the rising tide of emotion. The prospect of sharing holidays and special celebrations and even everyday meals with Will's family felt like too much to hope for. But I wanted it. I wanted everything.

And maybe that made me selfish or invasive, trying to weasel my way in. But it mostly just felt like making up for lost time.

"Dad wants to show you the chickens when you're ready."

"Chickens!" I all but squealed.

Will laughed. "There's a coop behind the barn. They have a pretty sweet setup. He said you could feed them."

I was already stepping out of his hold and toward the hallway, but Will's hands drew me back in. He placed a lingering kiss on my lips. I tasted the sweetness and the love. Maybe we hadn't exchanged the words yet, but I felt every bit of acceptance and emotion when Will's arms tightened around me. I'd never been so at home in my life.

I had a feeling that Will's love wouldn't be loud or messy. I couldn't envision public fights or dramatic angst. Will's love would be quiet but steady. A slow smile pressed into the soft skin of my throat. Holding my hand because he liked the connection and knew I liked it more. It would be snowy mornings with a car already running and warm with a windshield scraped clean. Or maybe something comforting in a slow cooker after he knew I'd had a long day. Will's love would be a thousand little things all together, spun into a web of care and support. A cup of coffee made just the way I liked it or pumpkin bread packed for the end of a long hike. He'd make sure I had everything I could ever need because that's the kind of person he was. And being his would mean being made a priority.

After a moment, he pulled away, sighing a little before brushing his nose along mine. "Let's go introduce you to the chickens."

"Alright," I murmured, finally opening my eyes. Will looked reluctant but amused. Happy. "But don't think I'm skipping out on seeing your bedroom before we go."

He grinned, sliding his hand beneath the hem of my shirt to smooth rough fingertips along my waist. "Yeah, I'll give you the tour."

I didn't make it back inside to poke around Will's childhood bedroom, however.

Carl ended up chasing an angry hen that got too close to me. I'd run after them and ended up flat on my backside, covered in mud and other horrible unmentionables in the middle of the chicken run. Will had laughed at the spectacle until he'd needed to wrestle a squirmy Carl into the bed of his truck. He'd ended up in worse shape than me.

We'd taken off for the tiny house after that, calling our thanks to William and Maggie who'd mostly laughed at us from the yard.

I'd showered and changed while Will had hosed Carl off outside.

It was later, when Will was cleaning up in the bathroom that my phone rang. With a worried glance at the screen, I'd expected my sister. I'd sent her to voicemail three times yesterday and knew she'd be angry the next time we spoke. But when I saw the name on the screen, I tightened my towel around myself and answered with a tentative, "Hello?"

"Hi, Becca. It's Morty Castle."

"Hi, Mr. Castle," I replied, greeting my building super, who handled maintenance for renters and upkeep of the common areas.

Mrs. Walters had owned her apartment, so Morty wasn't around much for things like repairs. Back in August, I'd let him know I was leaving Detroit for a few months just so he had a heads-up in case anything happened in the building. I didn't want a water pipe to burst or a kitchen fire to break out and no one to know I was away. I wasn't close with my neighbors, so I didn't have anyone local to entrust with a spare key. Morty had always been friendly enough, and the middle-aged Detroit native seemed like a decent guy.

"Is everything okay?" I prompted.

"Yeah, I wanted to warn you, though," he said in his usual gruff voice, and dread hollowed out my stomach. "Someone came by—a woman with dark hair, about your height—and claimed to be a friend. She tried to get a key off me for your apartment. Said you'd asked her to water your plants. You've been gone since August. I figured all them plants were long since dead. So I told her to scram."

My mouth went dry, and I forced a swallow. "Thank you. I appreciate that. I didn't ask anyone to water plants for me."

"I'll keep an eye out, but I just wanted you to know that someone was up to no good."

Still wrapped in a towel with my wet hair trailing down my back, I noticed I'd wandered to the glass doors of the tiny house that looked out over the wildflower field. The sun was drifting behind the mountains in a brilliant display. I stared out at the oranges and pinks of the sunset as I clutched my phone in a desperate grip.

"I can't thank you enough, Mr. Castle," I managed in a low voice.

"No problem, Becca. You take care, you hear?"

"Yes, sir. You too."

He hung up, and I closed my eyes.

With a shaking hand, I lowered the phone slowly and placed it on the stool beside me.

My sister had done that. She'd tried to get into my apartment. I knew better than to ever give her a spare key. I'd learned that lesson when she'd borrowed my car in college and hadn't returned it for a week. I'd been lucky that Heather hadn't sold it or crashed it. But it had been filled with takeout trash and cigarette burns. It had smelled like a frat house.

I didn't know what to do with the information from Mr. Castle. I hated that I had a sister I couldn't trust—that I was in this position in the first place, wondering if I should call and confront her. She'd deny it, I had no doubt. And then act like I was a monster for accusing her of trying to get into my place for nefarious reasons.

As the sun moved behind the hills, the room around me got dimmer in the waning light. I heard the shower turn off down the hall and knew I needed to pull myself together. Will would know that something was wrong.

And I was, once again, embarrassed that I might have to explain the deficiencies in my own family to someone who had Maggie and William Clark around the dining table. Sunday lunches and family photos and sweet stories and so much happiness, it was hard to fathom.

The angry, bitter, tired part of me felt helpless when faced with my own family. I'd mostly given up on my parents. We didn't have a relationship anymore, and I'd managed to keep my boundaries in place where they were concerned. But Heather . . . I didn't think I'd ever be rid of her. I'd never be free because I couldn't seem to face the truth. My sister didn't love me. My sister wanted to use me because I was an easy mark. Dependable, reliable Becca. Always guilt-ridden and available to spare part of her monthly income. I'd been deluded to call that a sisterly relationship.

Every vulnerable part of me screamed to go back to Detroit and pack up my life, change my phone number, and never contact my sister or my parents again. To just disappear.

As it always did when I entertained those hopeless thoughts, guilt was swift to fill all my empty spaces.

I felt sad and lost—desperate for a family like Will's. The simplicity. The happiness. The acceptance.

The way it had felt to be included today at lunch and any time I saw the Clarks. I'd never had that before. It was a connection and belonging I'd been chasing my whole life through my attempts with Heather, work, friendships, and boyfriends who used me or discarded me, a city where I never managed to fit in.

But Kirby Falls was different. Will was different.

Warm hands slid over my shoulders and down my arms where I stood facing away. "Hey," Will murmured before pressing wet kisses along the side of my throat.

I closed my eyes and sank into the feeling of being cared for and accepted. "I'm glad you're here," I whispered.

Will's lips paused where my neck met my shoulder. "Everything okay?"

I nodded quickly. "Yes. It's perfect."

His fingers laced through mine. His touch all heated comfort and aching sweetness.

Reaching back, I realized Will was wrapped only in a towel too. The soft cotton was slung low on his hips.

I longed to feel our connection, something deep and profound. So I worked to loosen the edge of the fabric where it was secured at his waist.

Will's arms slid around me as his towel hit the floor. I sighed as he did the same for me, exposing my flushed skin to the evening air. His hands skimmed reverently over my naked form, tracing along all my curves and valleys.

When I angled my hips and Will pushed inside, I felt it. The unbearable intensity. The undeniable fulfillment.

I was losing more of my heart with every scrape of his teeth along the nape of my neck.

And when the sun finally dipped below the horizon, all I saw was our reflection, moving together in the glass.

This. This was what I craved. With every push and pull and roll of our bodies, Will anchored me. I felt rooted in the very fabric of the universe, steady and strong in a way I couldn't be anywhere else. Here and now were exactly where I belonged, with this man loving me—every part of me, over and over again.

twenty-two
WILL

It was only seven o'clock, but the outdoor firepits were glowing along the perimeter of Firefly. People gathered around them in the chilly evening air with fleece jackets and glasses of cider, a lot of tourists in among them.

A band wasn't playing on the outdoor stage tonight, but the empanada food truck was doing good business, and indie folk music played from the speakers. But the low murmur of voices could be heard all around.

I took a sip of my cranberry seasonal cider—Do You Have to Let It Linger Berry—and scanned the wide space.

Becca had texted me this afternoon and asked me to meet her here for a drink. I'd started my night inside, and then grabbed a glass at the bar when I hadn't run across her yet. I'd continued my search outside assuming she was still on her way.

Spotting Jordan working the outdoor bar counter, I wandered up. On the way, I noticed a figure moving among the guests. It looked like a mascot for a sports team. Dark fabric-covered legs sticking out of a big fuzzy body, antennae on top, and . . . was that? Yep, a blinking light on the bottom half of the getup.

"Did you get a lightning bug costume?" I said when I reached the short bar top.

Jordan looked up from where he was restocking pint glasses and grinned. "Isn't it great?"

I eyed the lightning bug in among the families seated at picnic tables, high-fiving kids and posing for pictures beneath the large bulb patio lights. "It's something." But I couldn't help smiling at the firefly's enthusiasm. "Where'd you get it?"

Jordan leaned on the bar, and we both watched the progress of the walking marketing scheme. "You know how Mom is always on Marketplace looking for vintage Pyrex dishes and Fenton Glass for her collections? Well, she saw a firefly mascot on there. Some old high school in Georgia was selling it used for cheap. I made an offer and got it. We had it dry-cleaned and added a blinking light in the ass, and bam! Kids' night at the cidery."

A group of tourists brought the human lightning bug in for a selfie and I shook my head. "Who's the poor sucker in the suit? Seth?"

Jordan pushed up from the counter and busied himself wiping it down. "Nah. He's busy with his friends. Actually, I think he might be dating that Ellerby girl."

My eyes narrowed when I noticed Jordan drifting away from me, acting weird. Then I glanced back at the firefly, still prancing between patrons. "No," I breathed. Then I glared at Jordan.

Dark eyes wide and hands held up in surrender, my friend squawked, "What?"

"Tell me that is not Becca Kernsy in that thing."

"She wanted to!"

My glare intensified, and I plunked my drink down on the surface of the makeshift bar.

"It was her idea to add the light," Jordan defended. "Becca helped fix it up. She's having fun. Look at her."

I turned right as a little kid flung himself into Becca's arms. I could hear her laughter from here as she swung the small boy around in a circle.

"She likes being involved in the town, Will. You know that. Plus, I told her she gets free cider for life, man. She's one of us."

I sighed but didn't argue further. I knew he was right. Becca was probably the one brainstorming the whole *kids' night* thing, luring parents out, and encouraging Jordan to market the hell out of this. She did like being involved in everything Kirby Falls, and I knew she considered Jordan a friend, too.

He gave me a cheerful smack on the shoulder before helping a couple who needed to close out a tab. I watched Becca continue her path beneath the warm glow of the string lights crisscrossing and illuminating the outdoor space.

When I had nearly finished my drink, I noticed her approach. Becca moseyed up and placed her arm through mine. The fuzzy dark gray suit covered her torso. Her slender legs stuck out the bottom through two leg holes. It looked like she was wearing the black leggings she preferred to read in by the fireplace in the tiny house's living room. Similarly, her arms extended out through the armholes of the costume, covered again in dark fabric from a long-sleeved shirt.

A big, boxy bug head sat atop her shoulders with bouncy antennae sticking out the top on what appeared to be droopy springs. I couldn't see much of her face behind the dark netting and large bug eyes, but I knew she was smiling.

The suit stuck out in the back, accentuating her lower half, and every ten seconds or so, it lit up like a yellow fluorescent firefly backside.

Before I could do more than grin reluctantly in her direction, Jordan called, "What's up, Kernsy? You're killing it out there."

She practically vibrated with happy energy at my side.

But I didn't give her a chance to respond. I straightened and spoke up, "She's taking a break."

Then I grabbed her hand—clad in thin black gloves—and pulled her toward the building.

I walked slowly and made sure to lead her carefully up the stairs on the back deck past the covered seating area. We entered Firefly and I tugged her toward the hallway that led to Jordan's office and the entrance to the bottling side of the large building.

"Are you okay in there?" I said once we stopped.

"Yeah!" she replied, her sweet voice muffled. "I've only been at it for about a half hour."

"Can we—" I felt around her neck for the bottom of the giant head piece. "Can we take this off? I can't even talk to you like this."

"Oh, sure."

Becca's hands joined mine as we felt around the base of her neck for where the boxy helmet thing was attached. "Maybe it's stuck," she said after we'd failed to locate a zipper or release after several minutes of searching.

"Hang on," I said.

Becca bent forward at the waist, and I got a good grip on the edge of the bug head. I started off gentle, but that yielded no results, so I told her to brace herself against my legs.

Her small hands pressed against the front of my thighs, and I curled my fingers beneath the edge of the mask. With a solid yank, I heard a series of snaps, like a button-up shirt being ripped open, and then Becca was free, long blond hair spilling out around her.

From the end of the hallway came a collective gasp. Becca straightened from her bent position and I turned to face a group of six feral bar children. With wide eyes and hanging jaws, they stared in shock as I held the bug head in my arms.

"Oh, shoot," Becca said under her breath just as the two littlest girls in the group burst into loud, noisy tears.

"She's okay," I offered. "She's totally fine."

But the crying continued.

Becca tried to smile reassuringly, but in the heat of the costume, her eye makeup must have melted a little. She had black streaks and smudges beneath both eyes, and looked a little unhinged as she did her best to reassure them. "Lamplight the Firefly is just taking a little break, friends!"

She took a few steps toward the children, but they all flinched away.

The older kids quickly ushered away the crying children, and we stood in the hallway staring at the spot they'd occupied.

Finally, we looked at one another and then burst out laughing. Becca grabbed my arm to hold herself up as she wheezed. "I can't believe—I just scarred them for life. They'll probably have nightmares about beheadings or something terrible."

I examined the inside of the bug head and found the row of snaps we'd missed when I'd been trying to free Becca from her lightning bug prison.

She followed my gaze and said, "Chloe helped me into this thing. I totally missed that part." And then she started giggling again, and I couldn't help but smile.

I placed the firefly head carefully on the ground and drew her close to me. "Are you sure you're fine doing this?" With gentle thumbs, I swiped beneath her eyes, trying to remove the smeared makeup.

Becca looked confused. "Dressing up as a lightning bug?"

"Yeah. It's not like you work for Jordan."

She smiled. "Oh, I know. I'm just helping out tonight. He said he'd pay Seth or one of his baseball buddies to do it from here on out. I was just excited after we finished wiring the light and wanted to try it out for Lamplight's inaugural flight around the cidery."

I smoothed back the tiny, sweat-damp strands of hair near her temple. "You sure you're not too hot in it? You can breathe okay?"

Wrapping a hand around my wrist, she squeezed. "I'm completely fine in there."

"Okay," I said, still not totally convinced. But I leaned forward and kissed her. "You do look pretty cute like this."

Her blue eyes brightened. "Oh, are you into the suit?"

I nodded and kissed her again.

"Does this mean you're a furry?" Becca whispered against my lips.

I pulled back, brows furrowing in confusion. "What the hell is a furry?"

Through her laughter, she managed to tell me about furry sex culture.

"You are lying," I accused, dumbfounded.

She was enjoying this way too much. "You can google it if you don't believe me."

I could feel the horrified expression on my face. I would not be doing any of that.

Becca wagged a finger at me. "What did I tell you about kink shaming?"

I gave her a put-upon look, but she only laughed again.

Once again, heat flared beneath the skin of my neck and cheeks. My beard was trimmed and tidy now, so she could probably see it. Dammit.

"Well, I better get back out there," she said, amusement still sparkling in her blue eyes. "Help me get back into this thing."

Working together, we got her bug head balanced and snapped back into place. I peeked around the corner to make sure the coast was clear back into the main room of the cidery.

"Come find me before you leave," she whispered before giving me a quick hug and knocking me in the chin with her mask.

I watched her wave and weave her way among the patrons inside, back to entertaining once more.

"God, you are a sucker."

I started at the announcement from nearby. Turning, I found my cousin Mac, staring at me pitifully, drink in hand.

"You need a bell, MacKenzie. Jesus."

She grinned, red lips stretching wide and pleased. With a few steps in her black-and-white Converse sneakers she came to stand right next to me. For a few moments, we silently watched Becca flit around the taproom, high-fiving and taking photos with anyone who wanted one.

"You're caught in her net just like the rest of us, William."

I glanced over at Mac, who was looking at Becca with a small smile on her face.

She side-eyed me. "What? Did you think you were special? This whole damn town is in love with her."

The thought of being snared by Becca—like any other resident in Kirby Falls—didn't sit right. I didn't want to be just one more person absorbing her smiles and her warmth. Another business owner utilizing her skills and benefiting from her generous heart. I had no desire to be another person in her life sucking up her goodness and her light.

I didn't think anyone took advantage of her . . . not on purpose, anyway. But Becca went looking for ways to be liked and included. She'd give her time and her energy to anyone who needed it. And she'd run herself ragged if it meant helping others.

Plus, I had my own complicated feelings about her sister and how she used her. Just last night, Becca had stepped outside the tiny house to take a call from Heather. It hadn't lasted long, but when she returned to bed and snuggled up next to me, I'd known the conversation had affected her. I'd asked her if she wanted to talk about it, but she'd said it was the same story. Heather was mad that Becca was still away and needed to borrow some money.

She'd shared a bit of their difficult history and I sympathized. But Becca and I were totally different people. I would have booted Heather out of my life a long fucking time ago. But Becca couldn't seem to give up on her—to Becca's own detriment. All these calls and texts were nothing more than cleverly disguised threats and manipulation.

In the comfort of my arms, I'd told Becca she was doing the right thing by prioritizing her own happiness. But that seemed to make her go quiet and thoughtful.

Sadness had clung to her until she'd fallen asleep against me, and I'd felt frustrated and powerless.

I cared about Becca, so I didn't want anyone using her or hurting her. But I knew it wasn't my place to insert myself in her family affairs, so I stayed quiet on the topic even though it pained me to do so. Becca deserved a sister who loved her. Not whatever twisted, unhealthy relationship she and Heather had.

"I'm happy for you, Will," Mac eventually said, drawing my attention. "You've been so obsessed with the farm. You needed this, I think. You needed something —someone—just for you."

Unease tightened a sharp band around my chest at my cousin's quiet, well-meaning words. "She's a person, Mac. Not a puppy you get because you're bored or a sourdough bread fad."

A hard shove came from my left. "I know that, you doofus. But Becca is good for you."

The lightning bug in question chose that moment to wave in our direction before scooting off toward the side door and back outside.

"And you're good for her too."

I heard Mac's words long after she wandered off to the bar to join Chloe and Andie.

It had been nice bringing Becca home with me. Lunch with my parents had been effortless because they knew Becca and already loved her. But I liked having her there as my girlfriend—partner—whatever we were.

We hadn't really discussed it. We were together and that seemed to be enough.

We'd been basically living together for going on three weeks now. I'd made a few trips up the mountain to grab clothes and check on the house. But in the simplest terms, I was happy and so was she.

There were things I needed to say. But something held me back. I wanted her to be in Kirby Falls, settled and permanent. Then it would be the right time to tell Becca I loved her.

I didn't want to put weird pressure on her with the move approaching. I didn't expect her to uproot her whole life only to replant it in my backyard. Maybe she needed space to make her own decisions and live her own life, especially when so much was changing.

We'd figure it out.

I made my way to the bar, eager to close out my tab.

Winding my way through the tables and chairs, I found Becca afterward and told her I was headed back to the tiny house.

"I'm going to finish up here," she said quietly. "Then I promised Chloe I'd have a drink with her and Andie."

I nodded, happy that she was taking time for herself, for her own friendships. I wanted her to find her way here, to establish herself on her terms. I needed her to be happy in Kirby Falls, for both our sakes.

"I'll see you at home," I said and thought how true the statement was.

I felt more at home, cramped in that tiny house with her and Carl than I ever had in my great-grandfather's house. Briefly, I wondered if the old place would feel like home if Becca was there too. I bet she'd have some ideas—ways to renovate and modernize that would not only restore but also honor the integrity of the house, the history of it too.

I could hear Becca's grin when she replied from behind her mask, "I'll see you at home, Will."

Grinning, I stepped away but lowered my voice and said, "And bring the suit."

Her laughter echoed brightly in the night air, and I sensed my answering happiness settle deep inside.

Something warm and heavy and like nothing I'd ever felt before.

twenty-three
BECCA

It was two days before Halloween when I got the call.

Will was already up and out the door, working at Grandpappy's.

The weather was rainy and cold, so Carl stayed home with me.

"Ms. Kernsy, this is Officer Winthrop from the Detroit Police Department."

Heart hammering, I'd forced myself to sit down in the living room and calm my rising panic.

The officer called to inform me that my sister had been arrested while breaking and entering my apartment the previous night.

Maybe my across-the-hall neighbor, Ms. Allen, didn't hate me as much as I thought because she was the one who called it in when she heard sounds coming from the hallway and my apartment beyond.

The officer said Heather was being charged with a misdemeanor, but they needed more information from me as my sister was claiming she had received prior consent to enter my home and that she had no intention of committing felony burglary. Heather told them she'd simply lost her key.

If I hadn't been so disheartened and upset, I would have laughed at that. Of course my sister had broken in with the intent to steal from me. Anyone who didn't believe that, didn't know Heather.

The officer emphasized the seriousness of the offense. He said there were questions surrounding Heather's claim of a misunderstanding. She'd broken in during the middle of the night, which was often punished more severely by the judicial system, and given Heather's extensive record of petty crime sprinkled liberally with possession charges, the powers that be were skeptical.

Officer Winthrop had advised me to come home to Detroit to give my statement and straighten everything out. Plus, I needed to fix the damage to my front door and replace the locks.

I'd promised to be back in Michigan by the evening.

I didn't let myself cry or fall apart once I hung up the phone. I planned instead.

With my computer on my lap and Carl at my side, I found an afternoon flight out of Asheville. I'd go speak with the prosecutor and see what could be done. And then I'd fly back to Kirby Falls as soon as I handled my messed-up life.

By lunchtime I'd cleaned, done laundry, packed my things, and rolled my luggage to the living room. I'd just grabbed my phone off the charger to call Will when he came through the front door in a rain jacket. A brown paper bag was tucked protectively beneath the waterproof fabric.

"Hey," he said, hanging up his wet things on the coatrack. "I brought us some lunch from the Bake Shop."

Before I could thank him, his gray eyes caught on my suitcase near the end of the sofa. "What's going on?"

Swallowing around the embarrassment and unease, I admitted, "I got a call this morning. Heather broke into my apartment last night and was arrested."

Will placed the bag of food on the end table and came to me. Folding me up in his arms, he murmured quietly, "I'm so sorry."

It felt good to sink into his embrace. I'd been holding myself together all morning, desperately trying to just get through this so I could do what I needed to do.

Will pulled back but kept his hands on my waist. "What's with the luggage? Do they need you to come back to testify or something?"

I frowned. "No, I need to clear things up with the police and speak to the prosecutor so that they won't file charges. Heather is being held and—"

"Won't file charges?" Will asked sharply. "Becca, you can't be serious. She broke into your apartment."

Pressure built behind my eyes, and I was desperately close to losing it. "She's my sister," I breathed.

Will released me and took a step back. "She's a felon." I winced, but Will kept right on going. "She uses you and would have robbed you blind if she hadn't been caught. You don't have to run back to Detroit to fix her mistakes. Your sister needs to accept some responsibility and get her life together. That's not your job. You need to stop enabling her."

"Enabling her?"

Will tossed a hand up in obvious frustration. "She's been harassing you for months. Calling and texting. Trying to get money out of you. You keep bankrolling her bad habits and dirty dealings. You make these allowances for her when all she does is take advantage of you and hurt you."

My breath was coming faster, hearing all the ways my sister didn't actually love me or care about me, how I was small and weak for keeping her in my life. No one wanted their faults tossed in their face, especially by someone like Will.

"Not everyone has the perfect family, Will," I snapped. His face registered shock, whether by my words or my sharp tone, I didn't know. "Some of us just get the shitty hand we're dealt, and that's it. It doesn't mean I can just give up on her."

"That's exactly what it means." Will's tone was incredulous.

But I was already shaking my head. "Some part of me will always be that little girl who got a helping hand while Heather got left behind."

"That little girl needs to grow up and realize that you're both adults now, and Heather makes her own decisions. You've spent your entire adulthood trying to help her. How much longer does she need to throw it in your face? You are not responsible for Heather or the way she chooses to live her life. Why can't you see that?"

I stared, stricken. I'd opened up to Will about my family when I typically chose to keep the truth to myself. I'd told him about my estrangement from my parents and the kind of people they were. I'd confided in him about my sister. He was using those things against me—to humiliate me.

The jobs I'd lost because of Heather. How she'd dealt drugs at my high school and gotten arrested for possession. The bail I'd posted over and over again. The loan I'd co-signed and repaid all on my own. The car she'd stolen. The rehab I'd funded only to find out that Heather had checked herself out.

I felt my face crumple in disbelief as Will stared at me.

"You need to stop deluding yourself where your family is concerned," he said matter-of-factly, and it was like a stab to the chest.

"Deluding myself?" I asked incredulously as anger flowed into the wound. All the little jabs, all the hurt had been replaced by hot fury. How dare he tell me how to live my life? "What about you?"

Will's dark brows pulled together. "What about me?"

Lashing out in anger felt preferable to dwelling in his judgment and condescension. I was tired of hearing all the ways I'd messed up in my life. "You. You're doing what your family wants even though it's never going to make you happy. You keep taking on more and more responsibility at the farm and even moving into your grandpa William's house because you can't tell anyone no."

Gray eyes narrowed to slits, and Will shifted on his feet. "I don't really have a choice. Baseball isn't an option anymore, but you know that."

"Maybe not in the way you always hoped, but your life doesn't have to be toiling away at Grandpappy's, doing a job you hate. You could actually find something that made you happy if you'd just be honest with your family. They'd understand."

"Yeah, well, some families are worth the sacrifice. Some people are worth turning yourself inside out for." He paused. "And some aren't."

His implication had me gritting my teeth. Will's efforts were worthwhile because his family was better than mine.

"So that's the difference between you and me?" I asked. "You're a martyr, and I'm just pathetic."

Will sighed like I was a child, incapable of understanding. "This isn't about me. This is about you putting Heather first instead of standing up for yourself. How are you ever going to be able to leave her to handle her problems on her own? How are you ever going to distance yourself and actually move here, huh, Becca? If you keep living in a fantasyland where your sister loves you instead of uses you."

It hurt to hear all my fears and worries coming out of Will's mouth, twisted with anger and contempt. I didn't want to have this fight. I'd just wanted to tell him what happened. I'd sought him for comfort. Not . . . this.

But I guessed that was what you got in a relationship—unsolicited advice and the wherewithal to share it.

"I don't know how to answer that," I admitted. "I was trying. I was trying to do what was right. What made me happy."

Will shook his head. "You're letting her ruin your life because you're holding on to something that's never going to happen."

I slid my phone in my pocket and walked over to my luggage. "Yeah, well, you might want to look in the mirror."

"This is a mistake," he gritted out, jaw flexing beneath his beard.

"Maybe I am pathetic and hopeless, but I'm leaving. My sister needs me."

"If you go, she'll keep her hooks in you and drag you down with her. You'll never come back."

I stared at him, wondering how we'd even gotten here. How did this conversation go so completely wrong? I'd wanted to talk to him, to tell him what was going on. And tell him I was coming back. I'd planned on telling him I loved him. That I thought I'd missed him quietly my whole life. When I'd set foot in Kirby Falls, it had felt right. But when I'd met him . . . *that* had felt like home.

Will's features flattened as we stared at one another, the emotion leaching from his face. "Do you know why I stayed away at first? Why I didn't want to know you? Why I resented you showing up all over town—all over *my* town? Worming your way into Kirby Falls and into my life, my friends' lives."

I felt moisture well in my eyes, and the vision of Will, standing stoic and harsh in jeans and a gray flannel, blurred before me.

He continued when I didn't answer. "I didn't want to find out that I'd found the girl of my fucking dreams when she was just going to leave and take my heart with her. And I was right. It was all a waste of time."

My lips parted, registering the hurt. "Will," I begged.

How could he say something so cruel? Did he really believe that? Even if I left and never came back. Even if Will and I couldn't find a way to be together—which all signs seemed to indicate—I'd always treasure the time we'd had together.

He'd changed me. Couldn't he see that? And I'd changed him too.

I'd never wish it away.

I wasn't capable of forgetting Will Clark, and I never wanted to.

A tear tracked down my cheek as I watched Will ignore my quiet plea, call for his dog, and turn and leave.

Dropping down to the sofa, I put my head in my hands and cried.

I replayed every part of our fight. Maybe pieces of it had been a conversation, but sitting here now, feeling weary and lost, I was convinced it had been a battle. And I'd lost.

In a way, I wasn't surprised that Will would rather wish me away that ever have to deal with any sort of heartbreak or disappointment. He'd handled baseball the same way. It was a topic he avoided at all costs. I was certain he thought all those years he'd dedicated to the sport were wasted because it didn't get him to where he wanted to be. Except, that wasn't true. He had gotten there. He'd reached the pinnacle . . . he just didn't get to stay. It wasn't fair, but life rarely was. Instead of being grateful for the lessons he'd learned or the person he'd become, Will would rather forget it all. He'd pack it away in a box in the attic and never look at it again.

And now I had a box of my own in that lonely attic. Cast aside and forgotten.

When I could pull myself together, I canceled my flight and packed up the rest of my things. I cleaned out the fridge and took out the trash. I erased my presence from the tiny house as if I'd never been here at all. I took the coward's way out and left the key on the kitchen counter with a note for Maggie.

I didn't say goodbye to anyone, not the friends I'd made or any of Will's family. No part of me could explain my situation or discuss what had happened with Will.

With one last glance around the tiny house, I closed the door on that part of my life, not knowing if I'd ever be back.

It took nearly two weeks, but I got Heather out of jail and off the hook for the charges against her, Will's voice echoing and guilt eating me every step of the way.

By the time I'd made it to Detroit and spoken with Officer Winthrop in person, the prosecutor had already filed charges. Heather had an initial hearing and bond set in the days following.

Then I was able to confirm my sister's story of a misunderstanding with the prosecutor. Both she and Heather's court-appointed public defender didn't look particularly convinced, but they took my statement anyway.

When Heather was released, I waited outside the county jail where she'd been held since her arrest. I stood when she emerged through the glass-front double doors looking worse for wear. I was sure she was eager to get back to her own apartment, but we needed to have a conversation.

Heather stopped short when I approached, confusion scrunching her hard features.

My sister and I didn't look alike, not really. She was eight years older and had lived a pretty rough life. She appeared older than thirty-seven. Her brown hair hung limp around her pale face. We were about the same height, but where I was petite with subtle curves, Heather was painfully thin. Even now, the jeans she wore hung low on her hips and her collarbones jutted sharply beneath her thin shirt. She wore only a denim jacket several sizes too large to ward off the November cold.

"What are you doing here?" Her voice was sharp, rasping from decades of cigarette smoke.

I frowned. "What do you mean? Are you surprised to see me since you broke into my apartment and tried to steal from me?"

Heather rolled her eyes. "No, I meant where are Mom and Dad?"

Realization sank in, and I stared at her, incredulous. For as unwilling as I was to give up on Heather, she was equally as misguided about our parents.

Was this how Will had felt when he looked at me? Was I this oblivious person who ignored the truth?

I feared I knew the answer to that.

"Mom and Dad left you to rot in here, Heather. I'm the one who came. I'm the one who lied to the police and the prosecutor and got you out of this mess. I'm always the one who shows up for you. I'm the one who ruined everything to make sure—" I cut myself off. I didn't want to think about leaving Will and Kirby Falls right now. My sister was good at zeroing in on a wound and pushing it to see where I might bleed. She didn't need to know how beaten down I already was.

But it was enough. Heather huffed a mocking laugh. "Oh, did I mess up your little vacay?" Another eye roll. "Of course you could bankroll a months-long trip to who knows where, but *I'm* the asshole for trying to borrow your apartment for the night."

I wanted to wince at the accusation, but I'd financed my trip through regular employment. My sister had never held down a job.

A tiny voice whispered that maybe I should ask Heather what had happened to her apartment, find out if she'd been evicted again or kicked out by her roommates. It was habitual to wonder, to offer money, to try to fix whatever might be going on in her life. Whether true or a blatant lie from my sister's mouth. But that wasn't my responsibility. None of this was.

As painful as it was to admit, Will had been right.

He definitely hadn't gone about it in a good way. Things had gotten heated and emotional between us. And he'd hurt me badly in the process. But with some time and distance, I could understand that Will had just been trying to open my eyes to the imbalance in the relationship I shared with Heather.

Since leaving Kirby Falls, I'd had time to think about my sister and where I wanted to go from here. It had been painful, but I knew I couldn't keep this up. And deep down, I knew Heather wasn't going to change. Escalating to breaking into my apartment had been stark and eye-opening.

"If you had just helped me out while you were gone, none of this would have ever happened," she spat angrily.

"Maybe that's true, but I'm not sure why you feel like your little sister needs to take care of you."

Her dark eyebrows drew together in confusion, likely shocked that I'd back-talked her for once.

I continued, words coming fast and furious now that I'd given myself permission to speak up at all, "You've never called me on my birthday or invited me to get dinner with you or even asked about my day or my life or anything at all, Heather. You don't want a sister. You just need a payday. And I can't do this anymore. I can't pick up your pieces when all you do is break me apart. I'm selling my apartment, and I'm leaving Detroit. I'm changing my number, and I'm not coming back. I hope, for your own sake, that you get your life together. But I won't be here to see it."

Blue eyes so much like my own grew hard as I spoke. Heather opened her mouth, likely to spew more venom or accusations or horrible truths. I would never know.

I turned and walked away from the only family I had left.

WILL

"Dammit," I muttered, fumbling the paintbrush as the door to the garage opened and then slammed shut.

I caught the bristly end fully loaded with Whisper White in my right hand and cursed again.

I'd just steadied myself on the fourth rung of the ladder and finished wiping what I could of the white paint off my hand when Jordan strolled in.

"Wow!" he said, eyes wide as he turned in a circle, taking in the room—what would be the office on the second floor. "It looks great in here."

When I kept right on painting the trim and ignoring the trespasser, he spoke up again. "I love the built-in bookshelves and how you lined the backs with wallpaper. Really complements the rest of the house."

I focused on my task, making sure my lines were straight.

"Actually, the whole house looks amazing," Jordan continued. "I noticed the fresh paint on the siding and the navy shutters outside. And the kitchen and the dining room look like they could be in a magazine. What do you have left to do since this is apparently where you've been spending all your time?"

"Here we go," I grumbled.

"What? Just wondering where you've been hiding out for the last month since I can't seem to catch you at the farm, and you haven't been to Firefly or Trivia Night or softball or conditioning practice or any-fucking-where, William."

I finished the section I was painting and then stepped down from the ladder, not particularly in the mood to have this conversation. I hadn't done all the renovation work myself. Crews had been in and out, but I had been keeping busy with most of it.

As I shifted the ladder over another few feet, I noticed the tightness in my shoulder from having my arm raised all afternoon. I hadn't stretched it out in a while. And, of course, there hadn't been any more massages. Not since Becca left last month anyway.

I didn't really want to think about that either. But I figured it was the real reason Jordan was seeking me out.

But I wasn't about to rehash Becca's departure from Kirby Falls. The thing with her sister was private, and I didn't feel comfortable sharing. And I really didn't want to talk about the fight we'd had that day. Or how I'd come back after work to try to catch her before she left, only to find a key and a note for my mother waiting on the countertop in the kitchen. I hadn't even been able to bring myself to read it. All her stuff had been gone, and I'd been a fucking idiot.

I was pretty sure Jordan didn't want to hear about how Mom had stomped up to me the following day with the key and note in hand, demanding to know what had happened and why Becca had paid Merry Maids to do a move-out clean on the tiny house and deliver those items to Maggie's doorstep.

"I've been busy," I said instead as I climbed the ladder to repeat the process all over again with the trim.

"What's going on, Will?" Jordan's voice was soft, and I hated that even more than the bossy demands. The disappointment I heard was somehow worse. "You've had this house for six years. Yet you just decided in the last month to bust your ass every free moment you had to fix it up. The remodeled guest bathroom?"

"There was a leak," I argued.

"Yeah, and you needed to put in a fancy bathtub with jets and a huge shower with double showerheads?"

"It'll increase the value of the house."

"And all the new furniture that's actually from this century?" he questioned.

"It's comfortable," I replied, exasperated. Why the hell couldn't I buy a nice couch or chairs for the dining room?

"This place has been like a museum since you've moved in, but *now* you decide to remodel. Don't you see any sort of"—he motioned around with big, annoying hand movements—"correlation? That maybe you're doing this all for a reason?"

I sighed, placed the paintbrush on the tray, and turned to face Jordan.

I didn't have to wait long.

"You're doing all this for her!" he practically exploded and flung his arms out wide.

Gripping the edge of the ladder, I felt the metal bite into my palm. "I don't know what you're talking about, man."

Jordan dropped his head back to stare at the ceiling. "Becca. It's for Becca."

I forced myself to take a breath. "Even if I did remodel this house to make it more of a home. And even if I had done all this work for Becca . . . she's not fucking here, Jordan."

"Well, maybe she should be. Did you ever think of that?"

I fought the urge to roll my eyes and scream into the void.

Did I want the woman I loved to be in my life? Was he insane?

Of course I'd thought about calling her and apologizing every damn day. Of course I missed her. It was why I'd thrown myself into work on the house in the past month. Thinking about her had been too hard. When I dropped into bed at night, I wanted to be so exhausted that I couldn't remember the feel of her skin. When I closed my eyes, I didn't want to be reminded of her smile. Wishing for another outcome just made me angry and frustrated.

But Becca had her life, and I had mine. She'd made her choices, and it clearly wasn't my place to insert myself. Look where saying my piece about her sister had gotten me.

The way things had ended . . . hadn't been good. I'd said things I could never take back. And she'd thrown my whole life back in my face. I never should have forced my opinion on her. She hadn't been ready to face the truth about Heather. And she never would have been happy abandoning her for a life here, with me.

So, no, I hadn't really pushed her away. Not when she was never going to stay in the first place.

"She was a tourist," I finally said, keeping my voice even. "I should have remembered that."

I knew how to move on from disappointment. I'd done that for years. I would be okay. Baseball didn't break me, and I wasn't going to let losing Becca shatter me either.

"Did you ever ask her to stay?" Jordan asked.

"I can't make that decision for her. No one should be manipulated or forced into a situation like that. Not like I—"

Jordan's face went slack. "Shit, Will. I know—I know coming back here wasn't in your five-year plan. I hate that you feel trapped."

"I don't feel trapped," I said automatically.

But my friend kept right on talking as if I hadn't even spoken. "But you never looked for another way. You acted like there was only one path available to you and that was to come back home. You're my best friend. Of course I want you here, but I would have understood if you'd needed to find a job somewhere else. If you needed space. You never grieved for what you lost."

I frowned. "You make it sound like somebody died instead of just my career."

"Part of you did die. The part that dreamed and hoped and worked your ass off your whole life. You took baseball and all your memories and accomplishments and lumped them in with your injury. And then you shoved everything in a box and hid it away. You stood over it, snarling at anyone who got too close."

I looked away, unwilling to acknowledge how painfully accurate that description was.

Jordan continued. "You can't just shut off parts of yourself. You did it with baseball. Are you going to do that with Becca too? That's not how feelings work,

Will. What if I died tomorrow? We had twenty-five years of friendship. Would you shut it all down? Never think of me. Never let anyone talk about me ever again. Would you avoid Seth and Chloe so you wouldn't have to think about me? You'd throw away all the good just because you got hurt in the process?"

It sounded dramatic, but I could see the parallels. When I could meet his eyes again, I admitted, "That part of who I am is over and done with. I can't be Will, the ball player, anymore. And I was short-sighted enough that that was all I ever was. It's easier to just forget about it."

Jordan's words were imploring. "You're not just Will, the baseball player. You never have been. You're Will, the son, the nephew, the friend, the cousin, the partner, the coach."

Realistically, I knew my family was a big part of my life. But I knew how they saw me too. I harped and nagged my cousins about their work ethic. I was too intense, a perfectionist. I worked too hard. Things had to be my way. And so much of that was the truth.

While I did love the farm—its history and legacy—I didn't want the position I had there. I didn't want to be Will, the person who put out the fires and handled anything thrown his way.

Maybe I *had* grown because I didn't want to put everything about Becca in a box and hide it away. It was because of Becca that I could see the good in my hometown again. In showing her all the places I'd loved growing up, I'd relived them myself. I didn't want to forget it all. And I didn't want to leave. I couldn't imagine living somewhere else. Kirby Falls may have been my fallback plan, but it was also my home.

"All I want," Jordan said, drawing my attention away from my spiraling internal thoughts, "is for you to be happy, Will. You're my best friend. I've known you my whole life. You stood beside me on the hardest day of my life. You helped me bury my dad."

Jordan sniffed loudly, and I swallowed several times to keep my emotions in check. I'd remember that day, our sophomore year of high school, for the rest of my life. The unexpected death of a man I'd grown up with and respected and loved. And my best friend, who'd been lost and adrift in grief.

When Jordan could speak again, he managed with a tight voice, "You helped my mom. You helped me with Seth. When kids our age were out partying and having fun—being stupid kids—you were helping me change diapers and make bottles and rocking a baby to sleep. I know you won't say it, and that's fine. But I love you, Will. I love you."

"I do," I interrupted quickly. "You're my brother, Jordan. Of course I do."

My friend nodded, looking like he might tear up again, but finally said, "I want you to have something for yourself. That's why I pushed you to date and coach and live a little. And maybe I pushed too hard. I always thought baseball was the thing that made you happy, but I think it just made you determined. It gave you a goal, something to work toward. But it never loved you back."

I thought about how true that was. All the blood, sweat, and tears that I'd put into the sport. All the sacrifices. And it carried on without me. I had been driven. I'd pursued baseball relentlessly, but Jordan was right. I didn't know if that was really love.

It was easier to spot the differences now. Becca and her unexpected presence in my life was a big part of that awareness—as was her departure.

"As someone who knows you better than anyone," Jordan went on, "I'm telling you that girl makes you happy. I've never seen you how you were with Becca. I'm not saying rely on a woman as your only source of happiness. I just mean she's changed you. I was terrified before. Really worried about you. Working yourself to the bone, avoiding everyone in town in case they brought up that no-hitter you pitched in college. But something changed with Kernsy. She brought you back to life—this life, here in Kirby Falls."

I nearly smiled at the nickname, knowing how much it meant to her. Something so small but important. It meant she was included. It meant she belonged.

My eyes drifted closed as shame swelled within. All the things I'd said to her. The way I'd hurt her. Telling her it had all been a waste had been cruel—especially for someone like Becca who treasured and valued every relationship.

Jordan's voice was quiet. "But more than anything, you need to be happy with yourself. Baseball didn't do it. And I know you love your family, man, but the farm doesn't make you happy either. At least not with the way things are currently. You need to figure out how you can make yourself happy and then work your ass off achieving it, the way only Will Clark can, and then you can work on making Becca happy too."

I met my friend's gaze. It was full-on conviction, like he had complete faith in me. I didn't know that I deserved Jordan's confidence, but I could work to earn it.

"I think . . . " I began, the admission taking shape from all the times it had kept me up at night. "I think I need a change."

"Do you know what you want to do?" Jordan asked.

Slowly, I nodded. "Yeah. I think so."

"Well, good." He slapped a hand down on my good shoulder. "I want you to be happy. And maybe if you figure out how to ask for what you want, you will be."

To Jordan's obvious surprise, I pulled him in for a hug.

While my life hadn't turned out the way I'd envisioned, I could have ended up in worse places. I had a family who loved and supported me. I had friends and neighbors who braved my moods and attitudes. I had a home that meant something to me. And I still had time to course correct. I could change the things about my life I didn't like. Thirty wasn't dead.

Maybe my happiness looked different than it did a decade ago. Maybe now it was a house on a mountain, overlooking a farm and a legacy. It could be coaching baseball instead of playing it. It was definitely a dog who was just as grumpy as his owner. And hopefully it would be a tourist who belonged in Kirby Falls just as much as I did.

After a couple of manly slaps to the back, I pulled away from Jordan. He was grinning at me until he looked down at my shirt.

Then his gaze bounced back to his own shirt, frowning. "Did you just get white paint on me, you asshole?"

I took in the pale streak on his dark hoodie. "It's called Whisper White and it's very popular."

And then I laughed—for maybe the first time in nearly a month.

BECCA

"Am I doing the right thing? You guys would tell me if I was making a horrible mistake, right?"

I repositioned my open laptop so it was a little straighter on top on the cardboard box holding all my paperbacks. My friends' faces stared back at me with varying levels of enthusiasm. Pippa appeared cheerful as she flashed me two thumbs up. Cece frowned skeptically.

My eyes strayed to my own image in the bottom right corner of our friendship triangle video call. I looked somehow both tired and manic. Like I was giving a swamp hag a solid run for her money. Blond hair was piled on top of my head, and dark circles left helpful smudges beneath my eyes, telegraphing my lack of sleep lately. My leggings had seen better days, and my sweatshirt had a mystery stain above my left boob. Probably duck sauce. I peered closer at the screen. No, that was definitely chicken tikka masala. So I'd been wearing this shirt for far too long.

"Hold that thought!" I called to the screen. The sound echoed around the empty apartment. "I need to change my shirt."

I dodged stacks of boxes and slid into my bedroom on fuzzy-socked feet. The suitcase with my remaining clothes lay open on the floor next to my air mattress. I dug around until I found a different sweatshirt and swapped it out for the stained one. Then I figured it couldn't hurt and went into the bathroom to wash my face, brush my teeth, and put on deodorant and a dollop of lotion.

Sure, my friends couldn't actually smell my unwashed body or get a whiff of my sour breath as we spoke, but it would go a long way in showing them that I was okay if I appeared on screen a little more put together. I knew they were worried. And we'd been having video calls at least twice a week since I'd left North Carolina a month and a half ago.

If I could show my friends that I was alright, then I might start to believe it too.

I missed Will, and I missed Kirby Falls.

I'd heard from Chloe and Mac and Larry. I'd been texting with all of them. Guilt still nipped at me whenever I thought about my abrupt departure. I should have explained myself to Maggie and the others.

But hopefully, I'd be making up for it.

Settling cross-legged on the floor, I came back into camera view, and the low murmur of voices abruptly ceased. Cece and Pippa stopped the quiet conversation they'd been having in my absence.

"Sorry. I just needed to freshen up a little," I explained, trying for a smile.

"You look great!" Pippa offered.

"Sure," Cece added noncommittally.

"And," Pippa said, "back to your question. I think you're doing the right thing. Selling the apartment and moving is what's best for you. You're not happy in Detroit. And you need to put distance between you and your sister."

"Has Heather tried to bother you since the B and E thing," Cece interrupted, dark eyes narrowed.

I shook my head. "She hasn't been by and I changed my phone number already. Remember? You have the new number."

It had been weeks, and I hadn't heard from Heather. But that definitely wasn't unheard of. She often went long stretches without getting in touch. But when she needed money, she was very persistent.

I'd replaced the locks on the apartment when I'd gotten home and straightened the mess from the drawers Heather went through looking for cash. There'd been a struggle when the police officers had arrived, and I'd lost a lamp and a side table in the process. It had been strange to be in the apartment knowing that someone—even my sister—had entered without permission. It wasn't that I didn't feel safe, but there was a lingering sort of discomfort associated with the place.

But that wasn't why I'd sold it.

My friends were right. I *wasn't* happy in Detroit. I had never been, so leaving made sense. I'd meant what I said when I told Heather that she couldn't come around anymore because she wouldn't find me. At the time, I just hadn't worked out how to make that happen or where I'd end up.

But in the weeks since I'd confronted my sister outside the county building, I'd made a plan and found a buyer for Mrs. Walters's apartment. I hoped that my former friend and role model wouldn't be upset by my choices. I liked to think she'd want what was best for me. And her gift of a home had made it possible for me to find happiness elsewhere.

I just wasn't sure if following my heart meant I was ignoring my brain in this particular situation.

"So I'm guessing you haven't heard from Will?" Pippa asked. I shook my head. "Have you thought about calling him?"

I opened my mouth to respond that I'd thought about it plenty—usually multiple times an hour. But something held me back. Maybe embarrassment over what had gone down with my sister. I felt terrible for how I'd lashed out and brought up Will's own past. But part of me was still tender over how he'd hurt me with his words and his indifference. Maybe I thought if he wanted to apologize and work things out, he would have already.

But before I could say any of that, Cece piped up, "Why should she even waste her time on him? His whole life philosophy is out of sight, out of mind."

"Yeah, but Becca won't be out of sight for much—"

Pippa's words were interrupted by a sharp knock on my front door.

"Is it the cute delivery guy from the Thai place?" Cece asked, already fluffing her mane of beautiful, dark hair. "Turn us to face the door. This might be my meet cute and HEA all in one."

I rolled my eyes but spun the laptop around so the front-facing camera focused on the entryway. But it was too early for takeout, and the movers didn't come until the morning.

Hopping up, I hurried over and unlocked and opened the door. Shock had my fingers slipping off the knob, and the door banged loudly against the doorstop.

"Will," I breathed.

"Hey," he said softly. Will stood in the hallway, hands tucked down in the front pockets of his jeans. His hair was even longer than usual, the dark strands brushed back behind his ears, the ends curling up along his neck. He wore a green sweater. It looked like . . . my brain stuttered over what I was seeing. It looked like an ugly Christmas sweater with red apples and white snowflakes and, I squinted, were those black bears?

When my gaze made its way back to Will's face, I found him examining me. His gray eyes scanned me from head to toe, lingering on my face. While I was grateful I'd changed out of the stained sweatshirt and brushed my teeth, I sort of wished I'd traded the worn leggings for something else.

Amid the confused happiness at seeing him on my doorstep, I wondered what he was doing here.

Will cleared his throat. "How are you? How have you been?"

"Oh." I tried a smile on just to see how it fit. "I've been okay. How about you?"

He was already nodding. "Good. Yeah."

And then we sort of stared at each other for a minute or so—long enough that I registered frantic whispering from behind me.

Shoot. Pippa and Cece were watching this reunion.

But as I started turning to slam the lid of my laptop shut or to bicycle kick it across the room, Will snagged my hand. "No. Actually, no. I haven't been good, Becca. I've been fucking terrible. I came here—I wanted to tell you how sorry I am." The whispering from my computer speakers halted abruptly. "I never should have inserted myself in your relationship with your sister. And I regret the things I said. I had no right. I'm so sorry I hurt you."

I opened my mouth to shout *I'm sorry too*, but Will kept talking, "And I'm sorry to just show up here, like this, with no warning. I've been calling you for two weeks. I needed to apologize and hear your voice and see your face and beg you to come home. And I didn't know what to do, so I just—I just drove."

It was so good to see him, even this version who looked a little drained of his usual big crabstick energy.

And he'd come here to apologize. That meant something to me.

He wanted me to come home.

Home.

I smiled a little. "I changed my number. That's why you couldn't reach me. I needed to distance myself from Heather," I admitted. "But Mac and Larry have my new number. Chloe too."

Will made a face. "They, uh, failed to mention that."

I heard a cough from down the hallway. Frowning, I leaned out to investigate, but Will said abruptly, "What are all these boxes? Are you leaving?"

His focus was on all the moving boxes stacked around the apartment. Most of the furniture that hadn't been sold had been prepped with moving blankets and wrapped in plastic, but there wasn't a whole lot of it left.

Will stepped into the room a few feet, taking it all in.

"About that," I said.

But he stopped, his boots squeaking on the hardwood when he noticed my open laptop and the two women waving on the screen.

Tentatively, he held up a hand.

"It's so good to see you, Will!" Pippa's high-pitched voice emerged from the speakers.

"About damn time, Lumbersnack," Cece said, frowning. "Took you long enough to pull your head out of your admittedly nice—"

I lunged and closed the computer with a snap that seemed to reverberate in the air. "Sorry," I breathed, kneeling on the floor.

"Don't be," he said, holding out a hand to help me up. "She's right. I should have been here weeks ago. Hell, I never should have let you leave like that in the first place." He closed his eyes briefly, his warm calloused hand going tight around mine. "I am so damn sorry, Becca. I missed you. I just—I missed you."

That time, I did manage to say it. "I'm sorry too. I said some really terrible things that were none of my business."

"But you were right. And it is your business because I'm your business and you can say whatever you want to me. I don't want you to walk on eggshells just because I'm an ornery asshole. I'll do better. I swear to you. Can I just—" And with that, Will broke off and pulled me to him, wrapping me up in a hug that had my eyes welling with tears and my chin wobbling.

He felt so good—so right—and I'd missed him too, more than I thought possible. My arms went around his middle, and I squeezed him back hard.

I heard him breathe me in as I buried my face in the soft fabric covering his chest.

"What's going on, Becca? Where are you going?"

Swallowing around a hard lump of emotion, I admitted, "I'm coming home. Back to Kirby Falls."

Will leaned away, his expression warring between joy and confusion. "What?"

"I probably should have told you. But I was already coming back. I didn't want to stay away. And I realized I was never going to be happy here." I took a deep inhale, and then I admitted the really scary reality I'd been living since deciding to pack my things and go, "When I thought about all the places I could go, my heart only wanted Kirby Falls. Even if you didn't want me. Even if—"

"Honey, no," Will interrupted. "I want you. I couldn't *not* want you. I wanted you before I even knew you. I was aching for something in my life, and there you were, dropped down in my oak tree. Becca, I love you. I came here to bring you back home. Not to some rental or the tiny house. Home with me. To our house."

Emotion swelled inside me—so much love and happiness. Will's admission made me brave, so I confessed right back, "I love you too. The only place I want to be is with you. I missed the town and the farm and your family and our life together and Carl."

At my last word, there came a loud bark from out in the hallway.

My eyes widened, and Will grinned. "I'm shocked they were able to keep him away from you for this long."

"They?"

But just then, Carl bounded up, jumping and licking and so darn excited to see me. "Who's a good boy? That's right. It's you. Yes, you are. I missed you too, Carl."

When I straightened, I caught sight of several figures lingering in the hallway. "Oh my gosh."

Soon, I was enveloped in hugs from Mac and Larry and Will's mother and father. And they all had on the same green sweater. "I can't believe you're all here," I said, through my laughter and excitement. "And what are you all wearing?"

"Can't keep us out of things," Mac said with a wink. "And we'll let Will explain that."

"I have to say, Becca babe," Larry added, grinning, "I'm relieved that you finally have some drama, and I can ride to your rescue for a change."

I smiled at my friend.

"We wanted you to come home too, sweet pea," Maggie said, squeezing my hand. "It's not just Will who loves you. It's all of us. And so many others back in Kirby Falls."

William smiled, quiet and warm at his wife's words. "We missed you."

"I'm sorry about the way I left. So very—"

"Hush, now." Maggie smiled. "None of that. Now can we load up some of these boxes? We have a hotel for the night nearby. But we can be on our way in the morning."

I grinned at the prospect of being back in North Carolina by this time tomorrow. "The movers are coming in the morning."

Maggie cupped my cheeks. "Well, we'll take a load of stuff down now and give you two some time to catch up."

Will watched us with a soft look on his face and smiled when he caught his mother's gaze.

After another round of hugs and a moving box for everyone, Will's family made their way back down the hallway toward the elevator. Carl protested, but he went with them.

I led Will back inside and closed the door. "What's with the matching sweaters, Will?"

"Right," he replied, straightening and reaching toward his back pocket. Hanging halfway out was rolled-up green fabric. "This is for you."

I took the sweater he offered and held it up to get a better look. It was soft and definitely looked like an ugly Christmas sweater. It didn't light up or have ribbons or anything, but there were rows of alternating items—apples, snowflakes, ears of corn, black bears—all separated white lines in a Fair Isle background pattern. It looked like a Christmas sweater fit for Grandpappy's.

"I know it's not a B for Becca, but I thought it would make a nice new tradition for the holidays in a few weeks. And my family was on board."

Lowering the fabric, I met Will's earnest gaze. "You got me a matching sweater?"

"Well, yeah. I know we don't have gray hair and wrinkles yet, but we have to start somewhere."

I thought about that afternoon at the Orchard Festival, pointing at the old couple wearing the sweet potato and yam shirt. "Gray hair and wrinkles," I echoed softly, pretty sure my heart was going to explode and take me with it. The only thing I could love more than matching with Will would be matching with his whole family.

A hint of uncertainty crept into Will's features while I emoted inwardly nearby. "If you don't want it, that's okay."

I lunged forward, wrapping my arms around his shoulders and rising on tiptoe to kiss his lips. He helped me out, bending forward and then lifting me off my feet.

When our kisses softened and my fuzzy socks met the hardwood floor once more, Will said, "I'm so glad you're coming back to Kirby Falls."

I pressed one more kiss to his bottom lip before admitting, "Before this summer, I didn't realize I could ache for something I'd never known. Like a small town full of life and love and mountains and so many amazing people. Friends and family and unconditional love." And a man who was serious and reliable. "I was homesick for you, Will. And I didn't even know it."

Will's hands were gentle, stroking up and down my back. "Kirby Falls was always meant to be yours. And so am I. No matter where we go or where we end up, I'll be your home as long as you'll let me."

My hands strayed to his hair as he looked at me with so much love I could hardly believe it. "I want to be with you. Working on the house and playing softball and at the farm and going to festivals. All of it. And I'll run all the interference you need with Old Man Armstrong or whoever tries to bother you."

With a smile, Will said, "About that. I started working on the house. I can't wait for you to see it, but I want your help making decisions and figuring out what to keep and what to make our own."

"I can do that," I agreed eagerly.

"And I talked to my parents, and I'm going to be taking a big step back on the farm."

"Oh?"

His hand paused briefly on my back. "You were right, Becca. I wasn't happy with how things were. I was finally honest. We're going to hire a manager to oversee Grandpappy's. Someone to make the schedule and handle putting out the fires and filling in when it's needed. MacKenzie already threw her hat in the ring, and I'm supporting her. But she's going to interview along with a few other candidates. I'm going to be working strictly on the accounting. Mom said I'm only allowed to work remotely for the first six months to make sure I don't fall into old habits."

I grinned at that and so did Will.

"And I'm taking the coaching job at the high school next fall. I spoke to the principal and I've already started on the classes I'll need to be hired as head baseball coach."

I squeezed his shoulders in excitement. "I am so proud of you. That's amazing. I know you're going to be great."

Will looked down for a moment, bashful and completely adorable. "Thank you." He paused but I waited, knowing he was gathering his thoughts. "I was so worried for such a long time about being this former athlete cliché—coaching at my own high school. It seemed like my life was just stuck in reverse, spinning my tires. But I'm working on getting over my hang-ups and remembering the good parts of playing baseball. I have always loved being part of a team, and I'll get to do that again. Just in a different way."

Leaning forward, I hugged him again, so very proud of the decision he'd made.

"Becca?"

I pulled away to look at him. "Hmm?"

"What happened with your sister? Did you tell Heather you were leaving?"

It was instinctual to want to look away, avoid the topic, and enjoy our reunion. I didn't want to bring everything down by discussing what had happened. But despite that feeling, I knew I couldn't avoid the topic forever, and Will deserved to know.

Swallowing around a gigantic lump in my throat, I confessed, "I cleared things up with the prosecutor, and Heather was released a few weeks ago. It was a parting gift, really. I told her it would be the last time I lied or covered for her. I realized that you were right—"

"No." Will cut in. "I never should have said those things. It wasn't my place."

I shook my head. "Your words hurt, and maybe you didn't go about it the best way, but you were right. Heather was never going to change. She'd been using and hurting me for a long time. To know that she would have broken in my home to take what she wanted solidified the hurt a little more. She's never thanked me or appreciated anything I've ever done for her. And she's never once treated me like a sister. So I told her I was leaving, but I didn't tell her where I'd be. I put the apartment on the market and then I changed my number. I'd probably be pretty easy to find on social media, but it was another little jab to know that my sister would never even bother to look."

Will's rough hands—the ones I loved so much for their dependability and their strength—cupped my jaw, fingers sliding into my hair. "I am so sorry, honey. You deserve to be loved without stipulation. Without feeling like you need to earn it, over and over again."

I nodded, believing it for the first time in a long time. Over the years, I'd tried so hard to fit in that I'd forced it. All the favors I'd offered. All the ways I could earn my keep and earn my place. I wanted to be part of something, and for the first time, nothing about Kirby Falls felt like I needed to weasel my way in. I loved the sense of community among the people there. And I knew I'd be one more piece of the puzzle, snapping neatly into place with a whole host of friends and neighbors to help me should I ever need it.

I'd hung on to my grief and this apartment so that even without her here, I could still prove that all Mrs. Walters had done for me had been worth it. I couldn't keep trying to pay off the same debt for the rest of my life. And if she were here, Mrs. Walters would have shaken me and told me to stop trying to people-please her in the afterlife.

With Heather, I was only really losing the possibility of a sister. The fantasy I'd built up in my head.

It was time to live my life for myself, with the people I wanted to surround myself with, in a place where I actually felt at home.

I'd had several sessions with my therapist since I'd been back in Detroit. We were going to continue our meetings remotely, working through my issues with my family and the boundaries I now had in place. I felt like I was making progress.

"And, me and my family—we're not trying to replace anything you've lost," Will said gently. "Family doesn't always have to be the one you're born into. You know that already. You had your Mrs. Walters. And Cece and Pippa. And you can have all the crazy Clarks and a town full of people who love you." His thumb swiped beneath my eye. "And you can have me."

"I want that." I sniffed. "I really do."

TAKE IT OR LEAF IT

Will stayed with me on my final night in Mrs. Walters's apartment, wrapped in a colorful crocheted blanket. He didn't complain about the air mattress once, even when we woke up mostly on the floor at 6:00 a.m.

The movers packed up all my belongings not long after, and I set off on a road trip with the man I loved and the grumpy dog of my dreams.

Mac and Larry drove ahead of us in Mac's car. And Maggie and William brought up the rear. We stopped for lunch and snacks along the way, meeting up at rest areas and stretching our legs.

When we hit Tennessee, Mac made us all take a slight detour to East Knoxville to go to the Pizza Palace. But when we tasted the pie in the old-school place, no one complained.

Will drove while I sang Tom Petty, and Carl howled in the back seat.

It was the best trip I'd ever been on. Well, maybe the second best. Nothing compared to the first time I set foot in Kirby Falls. The peace I'd felt in the mountains had been perfect. Not to mention the man I'd seen scowling his way across the farm.

Glancing over at the driver's seat, I grinned. I couldn't help it.

Will laughed a quiet, happy thing that hit me right in the feels. "What's that smile for?"

It was for every incident that had brought us together. An oak tree that reached toward the rich blue Southern sky. A tiny house that gave me more than just shelter when I'd needed it. A farm that I ached to explore for the rest of my life. Mountains and forests that called to my soul. A book of four-leaf clovers pressed between pages that held memories right along with my heart.

"Nothing," I finally said, barely able to get the words out with my smile stretched so wide.

We hadn't even hit the North Carolina line, and I knew I was already home.

WILL

Five Months Later

The decorations in the gymnasium were a little over the top. And the pulsing, swirling colors from the light machines were not my thing, but the Kirby Falls High School 2024 prom wasn't the worst place I'd ever been. Plus, it was a big night, so I could suffer through the questionable dance moves of the gathered youth and whatever noises passed for music these days.

I took off my gray suit jacket and hung it on the back of a nearby chair. Rolling up the sleeves of my white dress shirt, I registered a bit of tightness in my right shoulder.

I'd probably overdone it at practice on Thursday. Maybe Becca would be interested in a massage later. Smiling, I thought about returning the favor and running my hands over every inch of her smooth skin.

The boys' baseball season was well underway. Practice started three months ago, back in February, with me as a new assistant coach. Coach Whitaker wouldn't be retiring until next month, so my head coaching duties wouldn't technically start until the fall. However, he was still sleeping in the dugout and content to let me run practices. I'd had very little pushback from the other assistants—mostly players' fathers volunteering their evenings and weekends. And the kids had been eager, for the most part, to have someone in charge who actually cared about their progress and development.

The boys were teenage jackasses, but they were *my* teenage jackasses. I was working on making them better players and humans. Not to mention, making sure they actually had fun playing baseball. No one should let a sport become their whole life.

But because they were self-absorbed adolescents, I didn't have to worry about that too much. Except for Mason Gentry, the principal's son. That kid would live in the infield if you let him.

I caught sight of the boy in question. He was blushing his way through a slow dance with a girl. Mason was all tall and lumbering in a black tux with a white bow tie, and I fought a smile.

Scanning the area as a designated chaperone, I made sure nobody was up to anything. Then I caught a nod and an eyebrow raise from Jordan across the way.

I bobbed my head in return and made for the deejay booth stationed on the stage at the front of the auditorium.

When that step was completed, I found Seth on the dance floor and gave him the signal. He wriggled his way out of the mass of dancing teen bodies as I skirted the edge of the room looking for Becca.

I spotted her standing near a round table in the back. It looked like she was deep in conversation with a group of her graphic design students from the library. She was the one doing all the talking while the kids—seven boys and two girls—stared adoringly at her.

Shaking my head and not bothering to fight the smile this time, I made my way over to interrupt. "Time for a dance, Country Girl."

Becca turned to me with a grin. "Hey, you." Her blond hair was parted in the middle and twisted into a complicated arrangement at the nape of her neck. Several wavy tendrils hung free and framed her gorgeous face. She wore what she called a "classy, grown-up prom dress."

It was black and silky against her skin. While it had a high neck and the gauzy hem brushed the floor, there wasn't much back of the dress to speak of. I liked being able to guide her to the dance floor with my hand on her bare back. I could feel the pattern of gooseflesh in my wake. And when the opening chords of "It's Your Love" came through the speakers, I put my hands on her waist and pressed a tender kiss to her bare shoulder.

"You having fun?" I asked, spotting Jordan and Chloe and guiding us in that direction.

"I am," Becca said happily. "When you asked me to help chaperone, I'd honestly been nervous. I didn't attend my own prom, and teenagers are pretty intimidating."

I frowned at that.

Becca saw my expression and rushed to add, "But don't worry! Everyone has been so nice and friendly. The girls in the bathroom were so sweet about my dress. And I'm having the best time."

"Good. You deserve it."

Her fingers worked their way to the hair at my nape, and she smiled.

Lowering her voice, Becca asked, "Did you see Grandpappy's social media today?"

"No. Why would I? Mac handles that as Manager of Farm Operations and Social Media Director." My cousin had given herself those titles when she'd taken over the majority of my tasks and my office back in January. She'd even had a plaque made up for the door. No one argued with her though, and I was just fine working from home and stopping by the farm every couple of weeks.

Becca made her "yikes" face, blues wide. "Well, then you probably don't want to look. She and the Judd's Orchard account got into it again."

I sighed.

"But people are loving it," Becca said with a shrug. "Probably good publicity. They're as funny as Wendy's and McDonald's roasting each other."

I wouldn't bother talking to Mac about her brand management and public conduct reflecting poorly on the farm. It wasn't my place. Besides, my cousin knew what she was doing. Well, unless Brady Judd was involved. And then all bets were off.

Just then, Jordan and Chloe swayed up next to us as the country song played.

"Hey, y'all," Jordan said.

"Are you two crashing prom?" I accused.

Jordan laughed. "No, man. They always need extra chaperones for this thing. And Chloe and I finally needed our turn at a Kirby Falls prom."

Chloe grinned at my friend, her blue eyes bright with happiness. After a moment, she tilted her head in Becca's direction and told her how much she loved her hair.

I eyed Jordan while the women talked. He looked like he could hardly contain himself. Joy radiated out of every pore. If Chloe didn't suspect something, then I'd eat my favorite ball cap.

Glancing behind me, I saw Seth, ready and waiting.

I nodded to Jordan as Tim McGraw and Faith Hill did their thing in the background.

Jordan took a deep breath and interrupted Chloe and Becca's conversation, "Hey, Chlo, can I ask you something real quick?"

Chloe narrowed her eyes suspiciously but faced my friend. Chloe's red hair was braided like a crown, and she looked happy in a way that said she'd done a lot of healing in the past year from her previous marriage.

I'd known these two since we were kids. We'd gone to elementary, middle, and high school together. Jordan had loved Chloe for a long time. And I knew he couldn't wait for the next stage of their lives.

Just then, Jordan slowly lowered to one knee. I heard Becca gasp and prepare to freak out, but I'd anticipated this. Hell, Jordan had made me practice this whole damn scenario while Chloe had been busy at Becca's book club last week. I didn't want to talk about who'd assumed the role of Chloe in the dry run.

With one arm around her waist and a hand covering her mouth, I lifted Becca off her feet and moved swiftly out of the way.

Seth smoothly took our place, phone out and recording, a huge grin on his face.

A few paces away, I set Becca down gently and removed my hand. She was too busy watching with tears in her eyes and her hands clasped to her chest to even notice.

Then I watched my best friend propose to the girl he'd loved all his life. He spoke soft words for Chloe's ears alone as a tear or two spilled down his cheeks. But Chloe cupped his jaw and pressed her mouth to his. I could see them both smiling into the kiss.

The whole place erupted in cheers, and I joined in with a loud whistle.

Seth and others crowded around to congratulate the happy couple, but we stayed back for a moment.

I looked at Becca who watched the whole thing with so much happiness, it was difficult to look away. And I knew . . . I knew it wouldn't be long before I'd be planning a proposal of my own, figuring out a way to make Becca my wife. But she deserved something perfect, something magical. Becca was the best person I knew, and after a lifetime of disappointment and making herself small, she'd never expect something for herself. But she was going to get it.

This woman was the love of my life. She made me happy in ways I never could have imagined. Through renovating the homestead and building a life together. Sharing an office on the days she didn't spend on the farm. We still went to Trivia Night and empanada evenings at Firefly. I read her book club picks, and we had our own heated discussions. We played rec softball together and had even added adult kickball to our weekly activities this spring. Then there was *The Walking Dead* marathons on the couch with Carl sandwiched between us. And four-leaf clovers every chance I got, just to make her smile.

Becca deserved the perfect proposal and the perfect life with as much happiness as I could fit into it.

We were finding our way together.

We had family and friends and a town that would always be home.

The fun in Kirby Falls continues with Leaf It to Me. *Now available in Kindle*

Unlimited! Scroll down for a sneak peek of Candace and Mark's swoony small-town romance.

If you missed Jordan and Chloe's story, it's a free second-chance novella available here.
Scan the QR code to download:

Want more of Will and Becca? Check out a bonus epilogue for Take It or Leaf It when you sign up for Laney's newsletter HERE! Scan the QR code to download:

Leaf It to Me sneak peek!
Chapter One
Candace

. . .

They said you can't go home again.

Well, Thomas Wolfe said it.

Which was kind of funny because the early twentieth-century novelist was born about twenty miles up the road from Kirby Falls.

But I completely understood the sentiment.

Perhaps better phrasing would be . . . you can't go home again and expect everything to be the same. Or maybe, you can't go home again and expect everyone to welcome you with open arms. And the lesser known proverb: you can't go home again because you'll fuck everything up, and why couldn't you just stay in New York City, Candace?

But the fact remained. I did go home again.

I flew into Asheville the second week of August when the humidity was thick enough to slather on my momma's award-winning buttermilk biscuits. I watched as hazy blue mountains grew bigger and sharper in my rounded airplane window until they parted on either side for the lone runway that would drop me within fifteen miles of my hometown.

Kirby Falls had been in my rearview for just over seven years.

I'd lit out of town on graduation day, my maroon cap and gown balled up in the back seat of my best friend's 1996 Toyota Camry. We'd had a plan and a little bit of money, and we'd decided to leave our hometown behind while we could.

I'd never had to explain it to Lo. She just got it. The overwhelming desire to break free, to do something completely different from the rest of my family. Lo knew what it was like to have an itch beneath your skin and a fire in your belly, driving you to grow up faster and prove yourself. She knew because she felt it too.

We'd bonded over being the youngest children among overachieving siblings. My big brother, Brady, had three years on me, but his personality beat me by miles. He was warm and funny and everyone's favorite Judd. And that wasn't just my warped perception. You could ask anyone in our hometown of Kirby Falls.

Then, there was my big sister, Joan, who was nine years my senior and basically my parents' dream child. She was responsible and dedicated and had known from a young age that she wanted to help run our family's apple orchard.

Lo had three older sisters, and they'd each been valedictorian on their respective graduation days. My friend figured *why bother?* She'd never loved school the way her sisters had, and her solid C-average throughout her high school career reflected that.

Community college the next town over had been Lo's destination at the end of that magical summer, but before that, we'd been determined to spend three whole months getting as far away from Kirby Falls and our responsibilities as possible.

I wondered what Lauren "Lo" Walker, my former best friend, would say when she heard I was back in town. Swallowing around the sudden golf ball that had formed in my throat, I lowered the shade on my window as the plane taxied briefly before depositing me—and the forty-eight other passengers—at our gate.

I watched as everyone hurried to grab their bags from the overhead compartments while a whole lot of nothing happened. The flight attendants hadn't even opened the cabin doors yet. Rolling my eyes at my overeager fellow passengers, I pulled out my cell phone and turned Airplane Mode off. My finger hovered over the text thread with my brother before tapping.

Brady: Text me when you land.

Me: Will do. Thanks for volunteering to pick me up.

Brady: Oh, I didn't volunteer. Mom's paying me.

Me: Shut up.

Brady: You shut up.

Brady: Have a safe flight. Can't wait to see your stupid face.

I rolled my eyes again—this time at my doofus brother as I reread our exchange from before I'd boarded at LaGuardia.

Now, I peeked toward the front of the plane to see the line's progress. Still not moving.

I typed: *Just landed. I'll let you know when I'm at baggage claim.*

Staring at the screen, I waited a few moments, but no dots appeared to indicate my brother was typing. I slid the phone back into my pocket and gathered my laptop bag and purse from beneath the seat in front of me.

The flight had been a short one, just a couple of hours. Long enough to get in the air, request my standard in-flight ginger ale, and then land between the rolling hills of the Blue Ridge Mountains.

When I finally made it off the plane, it was clear the airport was under construction. Equipment and employees were everywhere, and the plane wasn't connected to a covered walkway leading into the building. We deplaned directly outside into the humid August heat and onto a ramp that zigzagged a few times until we reached solid ground.

Stopping behind the elderly man in front of me as he readjusted his carry-on, I breathed in the late afternoon air. It felt like inhaling through a sweaty gym sock, but I couldn't help but smile.

My eyes landed on the tree-covered hills in the distance and the bright sunshine. My everyday landscape of glass-and-metal skyscrapers had been replaced by mountains and so much blue sky, I could hardly take it all in. The pace was slower here. I could feel it in the way the breeze picked up and my heartbeat evened out. The wind cut through the oppressive moisture for just a moment and then helpfully whipped some brown hair out of my ponytail. I grinned, tucking the strands behind my ear and scanning my surroundings once more. Some strange emotion worked its way up my tight throat, causing my nose to sting and pressure to build behind my eyes.

I was home.

Well, about twenty minutes from home, but I'd done the hard part. I'd gotten here. Even if I was dragging more heartache and baggage than the two checked bags I'd been allowed. That luggage was well over capacity as it held nearly everything I owned, plus a good helping of failure and regret.

I'd put my furniture and anything too big to pack in storage back in the city. It cost an arm and a leg for the unit for six months, but the idea of selling all my things felt like admitting I was never coming back.

This trip down south was just temporary. It had to be, or what was the point? Coming home for good would make everything I'd done in the past seven years

—everything I'd worked for and achieved and sacrificed—utterly pointless. I couldn't give it all up. Retreating to Kirby Falls was the best short-term solution to my problems, but if I stayed . . . I'd be doing more harm than good and undoing every bit of progress I'd made. I didn't want to let my parents down. They'd sacrificed so much for my education. And they'd be disappointed if they knew the truth. That was why they could never find out about the mess I'd left behind in Manhattan.

Leaf It to Me is available now!

acknowledgments

To Victoria: Thank you for your time, expertise, and thoughtful generosity with both. You are so appreciated.

To my wonderful beta readers (Jes, Meg, Jodie): Thank you for providing your feedback, and for being the first ones to love Becca and Will.

To my husband: Thank you for brainstorming the early days of this series with me, and for not complaining too much when I drag you to leafer-ridden apple farms every autumn.

author's note

Kirby Falls is loosely (and sometimes tightly) based on Hendersonville, North Carolina. *Leafer* is a term my husband and I made up. And we definitely grumble it good-naturedly when tourists clog up Main Street in October or occupy tables at our favorite spots. The Orchard Festival has been renamed, but it happens every Labor Day weekend and features all the charming small-town elements mentioned in the pages of this story. There is a private hiking trail for residents, made by reservation only. But I can't tell you any more about that, or I'll lose my local card. Some food trucks have been changed to protect the length of the queue line, but they exist and they are delicious. Trivia Night actually happens on Mondays at the Blue Ridge Beer Garden on Church Street. And the chime clock downtown is, in fact, ridiculously loud.

Like any good fictional location, Kirby Falls is a blend of nostalgia, reality, and fiction, but I just like to call it home.

This series is one I've been plotting and planning for years. When the time came to sit down and actually write it, I could hardly contain my excitement or pace my late nights in front of a computer screen. *Take It or Leaf It* has a big chunk of my heart—the part that was born and raised in a tiny town in the mountains.

I hope this story resonates with you. I hope you love the sweet tea and the lightning bugs and the pumpkin bread. And I hope you find Kirby Falls as warm and welcoming as Becca did.

also by laney hatcher

Kirby Falls Series
Take It or Leaf It: A Grumpy Sunshine Slow Burn Romance

Leaf It To Me: A Friends to Lovers Small-Town Romance

Leaf and Let Die: A Rivals to Lovers Small-Town Romance

Cozy Creek Collection
Fall Me Maybe

Bartholomew Series
First to Fall: A Friends to Lovers Historical Romance

Second Chance Dance: An Enemies to Lovers Historical Romance

Third Degree Yearn: A Second Chance Historical Romance

Last on the List: A Surprise Pregnancy Historical Romance

Smartypants Romance
London Ladies Embroidery Series
Neanderthal Seeks Duchess

Well Acquainted

Love Matched

Find bonus content, reading order, and other news at my website:
https://laneyhatcher.com/

about the author

Laney Hatcher is a firm believer that there is a spreadsheet for every occasion and pie is always the answer. She is an author of stories both old and new where the HEAs are always guaranteed. Often too practical for her own good, Laney enjoys her life in the southern United States with her husband, children, and incredibly entitled cat.

Find Laney Hatcher online:
Facebook: https://bit.ly/3s6KnuY
Newsletter: https://bit.ly/3SbXg2v
Amazon: https://amzn.to/3IaOwU7
Instagram: https://bit.ly/3s4IRcS
Website: https://laneyhatcher.com/
Goodreads: https://bit.ly/3BD0Gme
TikTok: https://www.tiktok.com/@laneyhatcherauthor
Threads: https://www.threads.net/@laney.hatcher

Newsletter sign up

Made in the USA
Monee, IL
19 April 2025